Up the Ladder

ANA D'ARCY

ISBN 978-2-9592344-0-8

Publisher: Ana D'Arcy

Cover & interior design: Ana D'Arcy

Editor: Katie Ducharme

Advance Review Edition: April, 2024

https://anadarcy.com

Trigger warning:

This work contains sexually explicit content and mature language, and is intended for an adult audience only (18+).

While the tone is mostly lighthearted, the book addresses sensitive topics that may be triggering for some readers. These include toxic/abusive family members (on-page), and the loss (off-page) and grief (on-page) of a close relative. There is also a brief approach on eating disorders and a short scene containing sexual harrassment.

Read at your own discretion.

Up the Ladder

When in Brooklyn—Book 1

ANA D'ARCY

TABLE OF CONTENT

PLAYLIST

Heartbeat — JJAMZ
Can't Get You Out Of My Head — Glimmer of Blooms
Crush — Tessa Violet
Fade Into You — Mazzy Star
Sweet Disposition — The Temper Trap
Sexy Boy — Air
Cherry Wine — Jasmine Thompson
Body Gold — Oh Wonder
Beneath Your Beautiful — Labrinth and Emeli Sandé
Never Be the Same — Camila Cabello
Adore You — Harry Styles
Lost and found — Isaac Delusion
I Found — Amber Run
I Belong In Your Arms — Chairlift
All I Want — Kodaline
I Will Follow You into the Dark — Death Cab for Cutie
Crazy In Love — Kadebostani
Love Will Tear Us Apart — Joy Division
Someone You Loved — Lewis Capaldi
Issues — Julia Michaels
Let It Go — James Bay
Never Let Me Go — Florence + The Machine
Teardrop — Massive Attack
Fix You - Live — Sam Smith
Ho Hey — The Lumineers
Shallows — Daughter
Home — Dotan
Mess Is Mine — Vance Joy
Only Love — Ben Howard
forever - acoustic version — Lewis Watson

For the book girlies stuck in their comfort zone,
Find your ladder and climb it.

CHAPTER One

Gen

"WE'RE REALLY DONE THIS TIME."

The words spear through my heart with vivid sharpness. Nothing comes out when I try to speak, as though five years of memories are jammed down my throat. Helpless and confused, I watch Edward shove handfuls of his things into a duffel bag. Two large suitcases are already filled with more of his stuff, waiting by the door.

I'm unsure what triggered this, but it's miles from how I expected our Saturday afternoon to unfold. Eddie has been in a frenzy for the past hour, scavenging through the apartment to gather his most prized belongings.

"Eddie, please. Let's talk about this."

"We already talked about it, Gen. A dozen times. I stayed because I hoped things would change, but they never do. Not with you."

"I'm sorry! You know work has been hectic lately, and—"

"It's been hectic since we started dating! You keep making excuses and promising you'll take a step back and have more time for me, but you never do."

"It's not that simple."

"And yet it is. All you need to do is to prioritize me rather than whatever big promotion comes next, for once."

"We made a deal, Edward. You agreed we'd wait until I became head of my department."

"I didn't think it would take that long! Everyone we know is getting married and having children. But for us ... It'll be what? Another decade before we get there?"

"We can get married if you want," I offer. "God knows our parents have been pushing us to."

"Will you make time for family life if we do?"

I press my lips together, seeing no point in lying. Marriage wouldn't change anything, at least on my side. I worked too long and too hard to let anything get in the way of my objective.

"See? This is why I can't do it any longer. You refuse to compromise, and that is not how a relationship works, Genevieve."

"And you? Are you compromising? You've been home even less than I have this week."

Before I can gloat over my excellent point, he says, "I've been finding excuses not to be home for months and you didn't even notice. What's the point of being here? We barely speak, ignore one another, don't have sex ..."

The last one stings, but I kind of deserve it. It's been a while since I initiated anything intimate between us, and the last few times he did, I rebuked him on account of being too tired or having work to deal with.

"I'm sorry," I say for the umpteenth time. "Maybe we can fix it. I promise I'll do better. We can set a clear schedule where I make time for you. And establish a weekly slot for sex. We can—"

"Do you hear yourself, Gen? A weekly slot? Is it a chore for you? Like some duty you'd go through to keep me happy?"

"No, it's not! I enjoy sex with you."

"Well, I don't," he states, his bitter tone sending icy shivers up my spine.

"What do you mean?"

"Sex with you is boring. You treat it with efficiency like everything else, and it's so dull."

Now, I'm confused. First, I didn't make enough time for him and sex, and now I'm bad at it? Somehow, that hurts me more than everything else he's said so far. Especially since I have to fake my climax most of the time when he *always* finishes.

I'm still processing his words when he returns to his drawers to pack more things. When he turns around this time, tears are veiling his eyes. That sends a twinge of pain to my heart.

It's really over, isn't it? The man I expected to spend the rest of my life with is leaving, and I can't stop him. Would I want to, anyway? Knowing what I do now, can I still go through with my life plan?

"I wish we could have made it work, Genevieve," he says, pulling on the zipper of his bag to close it. It's too full now, so I mindlessly walk up to him to help.

"Where will you stay?"

"I'll be with Frank until I can find a place."

"What should I do with the rest of your stuff?"

"I'll let you know when I have space to store it. Are you okay if I keep the keys in case I need to pick up some things and you're gone?"

"Yes, sure. It's still your home," I say. I own this place, but he's lived here for four years.

"Do you think you'll cry for me?" he asks, a lone tear rolling down his neatly shaven cheek.

My eyes drop to the first button of his shirt as I consider his question. He knows that I never cry. The last time I did was after losing my twin. Since those days, not a tear was shed for anyone.

When I can't find the answer within me, I truthfully reply, "I don't know."

He looks disappointed as he says, "I see …"

We grew used to one another, complacent in our arrangement, and our relationship hasn't felt like one in ages. It was practical and easy, something to hold on to rather than face the unknown with others. Have I slowly been falling out of love with him? When did this become our routine rather than the loving relationship it used to be?

"When will you tell your parents?" I ask.

"I'm not sure. Mom knows things have been complicated lately, so she won't be surprised."

While I dislike that he's been sharing our issues with his nosy mother, I suppose it's good to have her prepared for the shock. My father won't be an issue since he doesn't care much about my romantic life. But Mother will endlessly nag me about it.

As pathetic as it is, I say, "Let me know if you change your mind."

"I won't."

Standing in the middle of the bedroom, I watch as he hauls his bag over his shoulder. We hesitate on what to do next, and I settle on a brief and tight hug. Despite all that time with him, his body feels alien against mine, reminding me that things fell apart long ago.

"Take care of yourself, Gen," he says with a small, forced smile once we let go.

"See you around, Eddie," I tell him, returning a grin I'm not feeling.

I use his reluctance to leave to take one last look at him. His caramel eyes are weary, and his dirty blond hair is slightly askew, which is unusual. I grew accustomed to his face, so dashing when we first met. Then, I speechlessly stare as he makes his way out of our bedroom—*my* bedroom. Pain, betrayal, heartache … I wait for all those to wreck me, to crush my heart into a pulp in my chest. But they don't come, and that troubles me. Yes, I feel abandoned and lost, but the agony it should unleash on me is a mere squeeze.

The front door opens and closes, and I stay glued right where I stand. I can't do this whole thing again. I'm almost twenty-seven, which is too old to do it all over with another man.

It takes my phone dinging on the bed to rip me out of my thoughts. It's Hana, replying to a text I sent her earlier—when Eddie was packing his things and I panicked.

HANANANA
> WTH?? What's happening now? Is he still packing?

With a sigh, I type a reply.

ME
> He just left. I think it's really over this time.

HANANANA
> Holy fuck! What happened?!

ME
> I don't even know.

I send that because it's easier than listing everything that's been going on for the past year or so. She's well aware of my sex life anyway, or lack thereof. Because she knows me better than anyone else, she replies with just what I want to hear.

HANANANA
> Red or white?

ME

Both.

HANANANA

I'm coming to you as soon as I'm done pumping. Hang in there.

While I wait for my best friend to arrive, I assess what my life has suddenly become. My social circle got a lot smaller, because our mutual friends will pick a side and stick with it. And if I'm being honest, they were Eddie's friends first—meaning, I already know who'll get to keep them. At least we never got that dog I wanted, so we don't have to fight about who keeps it.

My biggest concern is our colleagues. While Eddie and I don't work in the same department, we work for the same company, and the ten floors that separate us might not be enough to prevent the spread of nasty gossip and rumors.

I still haven't fully come to terms with everything by the time Hana arrives. She enfolds me in her arms as soon as I open the door, and the relief is instantaneous. Maybe it's because she's a mom now, but there's something motherly in the hug she gives me, possibly the comforting plumpness of her figure.

Maternity really suits her, and the ease with which she's going through it almost makes me regret never giving it a try. But between Eddie's schedule and mine, there's no way we could have made it work.

The mere thought of the future that was pulled out from under my feet makes me hold her tighter.

"I'm so sorry this happened to you, honey," she says in my hair.

"You always hated him."

"No, I always thought you deserved better, which isn't the same."

Less than five minutes after we let go, we're sprawled on the couch with some random Girl Power playlist in the background and wine in our crystal glasses. She can sympathize with me because we've gone through the same strict upbringing, with too many expectations for what we're meant to become. Growing up in a Korean household, she was left with very little room for failure— which was how she got a full-ride scholarship to Harvard. Now, however, she managed to fight her way out of her strict parents' grip and lives her life without worrying about meeting their impossible standards.

It takes over an hour to recount everything that happened with Eddie, and we go through both bottles as well as a pizza we had delivered. I don't cry, so I have the answer to his question: no, despite five years together and the life I could see myself spending with him, I won't cry over him.

"You know what annoys me the most?" I ask Hana as I crack open the pricey vodka I found in a cupboard. The words drag on my tongue, which means we probably drank too much already. It doesn't matter though, so I pour some of the vodka into our empty wine glasses.

"That you don't have ginger beer for Moscow Mules?" she replies.

"No. That Eddie told me I was bad in bed. It's been *five* years! And he waited until he was breaking up with me to let me know? Who does that?!"

"A liar. I'm sure you're great in bed. You do everything with panache."

"Heck yeah, I do. I'm probably amazing. He was just making up excuses."

"Totally." There's a moment where I can see her intently thinking while I ruminate on Eddie's hurtful words. She picks up her phone from the low table before us and types something on it.

"If Tyrone tries to leave me, I might murder his ass."

I chortle at the mere notion. Tyrone, her fiancé, is too enamored to do anything like that. Their relationship is as flawless as it gets, their bond getting stronger with every day that passes. The baby they welcomed into their lives seven months ago, Lucas, brought them even closer.

And here I am, barely affected by my boyfriend of five years dumping me.

"Maybe I'm broken," I mumble.

"Nah, fuck that. You just slowly fell out of love with him."

"I walled up again, you know?"

She looks away from her phone to offer me a small, understanding smile, knowing all too well about my dissociative response to trauma. It's a fun, self-preserving method my brain developed over time—the unavoidable outcome of my parents' strict education.

"It's okay, honey. You and Edward were at the end of it, and you knew it in your heart."

"I still feel like I should have had a stronger reaction."

"It's like grief, Gen. There isn't one singular way to do it."

"Maybe it's because I knew it was my fault."

"Oh, hell no."

"I could have been a better girlfriend."

"And he could have been a better boyfriend. He always complained about your work hours, but his are just as bad. That man wanted you to step down and put your career aside for his own comfort. Why didn't he quit his job if he wanted kids so much? You're making more than he does—more than enough to maintain your lifestyle."

"He has his goals, and I have mine," I justify.

"Exactly." Her tone turns excited when she says, "Okay, I found a test!"

"For what?"

"To know if you're bad at sex or not. It's designed for heterosexual women and all."

I freeze, many questions running through my mind at once. What if I *am* bad at sex? What if Edward wasn't lying, and I'm boring in bed?

"First question," Hana says without waiting for my approval. "Have you ever had the nastiest, naughtiest sex in your childhood bed as an adult?"

I shake my head, horrified at the thought. Sex in my parents' house is something I would never do, for fear of whatever repercussions it might bring.

"Alright, so no on this one. Have you ever gone down on someone while pleasuring yourself?"

I shake my head again. Crap, it isn't starting well.

"Have you ever had sex in a public place?"

"Does being at home with an open window count?" I try.

She shakes her head disapprovingly. "Not when you live on the 28th floor, Gen."

The more questions she asks, the lower I sink on the couch. With every "no" I utter, I relive Edward saying that sex with me is boring. Hana doesn't give up though, convinced the test will come through and I'll get better questions later.

The good thing is that she fills our shot glasses every time I get sad, and we down more vodka. The bad thing is that I get sad a lot.

"What the hell is a Jacob's ladder?" she asks at some point. Intrigued, I stare at her screen while she googles it. "Holy shit," she breathes out, scrolling through the images.

I say nothing, too stunned to even speak. Penises. Heavily pierced penises. After a few pictures have passed, I realize that the "ladder" is a series of piercings arranged underneath the shaft. My knees come together on instinct, shuddering at the idea of *that* entering me. Why on earth would someone do this to themselves? It looks terribly painful—especially in such a sensitive body part.

"That must feel amazing," my friend murmurs with fascination.

As I watch the pictures of dicks parading under her ever-scrolling thumb, I find myself wondering if it would. It has to be an interesting sensation, for sure.

"So, have you ever had sex with that?" she asks.

"Absolutely not. I prefer my vagina not in shreds."

She mumbles something that sounds like "you wuss," and returns to the test to select yet another "no".

"How many questions are there?"

"Fifty. We have fourteen left."

"Maybe we should stop now so I can tell myself I might have answered yes to at least one."

"Come on, I'm sure you will. And who knows, maybe some of those questions were trick questions where you have to answer no to get it right."

I give her a doubtful pout, folding my arms across my chest. This is turning out to be humiliating, even more than Edward's words. Now, a curated test will confirm his claims.

When we complete the last question, she angles her phone away so I won't see the answer. "So?" I worriedly ask.

She remains silent, her eyes going left and right as she reads. "Never mind. This test is stupid," she concludes.

"Show me."

"No, it's dumb. They don't know what they're talking about."

Before she can react, especially given how much we drank, I snatch the phone away to see my pathetic results. "Please tell us you're joking," I read out loud. "There's no way you answered 'no' on every single question here unless you lied. If you didn't, you are the most excruciatingly bad-at-sex person anyone could ever come across. You lack imagination, boldness, and probably the will to live. Sex with you is, without a doubt, the greatest chore one might ever encounter. We hope for everyone's sake that they never enter your bed. Please, for the love of God, stop having sex."

For the first time in ten years, I feel like I might cry. Hana takes the phone away from me, her apologetic eyes not enough to shake me out of my thoughts.

I'm terrible at sex.

I'm beyond boring, and I now realize that Eddie was gentle with his choice of words.

"Oh God," I whimper with shame.

"It's just a stupid test, Gen. It's not true. Come on."

"It is. It's so true. I'm the most boring person in the world. No wonder Edward left."

"No, stop that right now! It's not true, and we can do another test to prove it."

"It will only confirm what this one said. Shit, Hana ... I'm awful at sex."

I fall back onto the couch, processing the terrible information. It's not like I ever believed that I was a sex goddess, but I didn't think it was *that* bad.

"Come on, you're young! You can improve!"

"No, the test said to stop having sex altogether. I think I'll do that."

"Fuck that test. It's just a stupid bucket list that one person decided on. It's their subjective opinion of what makes someone good in bed, not some globally agreed upon truth."

I lie there, staring at the high ceiling above us. Maybe it's the wine and the vodka—or perhaps desperation—but a ludicrous idea sprouts in my head. "It's a bucket list," I repeat.

"Yeah."

"Which anyone could go through."

"I guess."

"Even me."

Now she's catching my drift, and a glimmer of interest shines in her brown eyes when I look up at her. "Even you, yes," she confirms.

"Then I'll do every item on it and show that stupid test who's boss."

"Yes, you will!" She's beyond hyped up now, sitting straight up on the couch.

I push myself to the same position, slightly worried by how the earth spins too hard and too fast.

"There's one problem though," I say with a frown.

"What?"

"How am I going to find some guy with a Jared's ladder?"

"Jacob's. And I know exactly how."

"Really?"

"Yeah. Do you trust me?"

"With my life," I gravely reply.

"Good. First, we have to make you look hot. Then, we have to take a few pictures. Come on, get up."

Springing off the couch with an uncertain balance, she pulls on my arm to force me up. I let her, not because she's stronger than me, but because whatever she has in mind sounds like a great way to take my mind off Eddie. She drags me all the way to my bedroom and then into the walk-in closet. My chest tightens at the sight of the empty shelves and racks, and the few things that he left behind.

"He doesn't deserve you," Hana mutters, sensing my distress. "Come, honey, let's get you looking all sexy."

She pushes me to the back of the closet, where I keep the few party dresses I own. "The green one," Hana commands. "With the spaghetti straps. You look so hot in it."

Since she sounds so confident, I take out the Dior dress and examine it from top to bottom. It is a lovely garment, and the deep green satin molds my shape to perfection, leaving very little to the imagination. It reaches below my knees, but there's a slit that runs high on my thigh and makes it a little more daring than what I'm used to. The cleavage is also a little much, but I'm allowed to flaunt my breasts now and then. The color is ideal for my complexion, and it's a nice contrast with the auburn hues in my hair, which cascades in waves down my shoulders to the middle of my back.

"Go on," Hana bosses me. I comply, too tipsy to question anything that's happening. "Not gonna lie," she starts as I remove my clothes, "this comes at a perfect time. I've been wanting to go out clubbing, so I'll get to accompany you."

"How's clubbing related to any of this?"

"Well, you'll have to find Eddie's replacement."

I scoff, shaking my head disapprovingly. "I don't have time for that. My vibrator will have to do. At least it never misses, and orgasming in two minutes is so much better than wasting time with a man who can't figure out where my clitoris is."

"Only you could be so pragmatic," she laughs.

"I'm a busy woman."

"I'm well aware. This is nice, by the way. Shame you had to get dumped for us to have some quality time again."

An incredulous laugh bubbles in my chest. "I missed you too, Hana."

"Of course you did. I'm amazing."

She really is. My social life might be in shambles, but as long as I have this woman by my side, everything isn't entirely lost.

CHAPTER Two

Gen

THERE'S A POUNDING IN MY head that won't go away. Even in my sleep, I can feel it. What the hell is happening to me? Am I dying of some unknown disease?

Seeking some comfort, I wiggle closer to Edward with a mumble, wrapping an arm and a leg across his frame. I stay there for a few seconds until I realize something's wrong. This body is softer than Eddie's, and it's wearing sequins instead of the usual cotton and silk blend pajamas.

My heavy eyelids flutter open, and my gaze falls on a lush mass of black hair. Oh, right. Hana came over. And we drank way too much. Because Eddie dumped me after telling me I was boring in bed.

Which I am.

The reminder has my heart dropping low into my stomach, making me nauseous. Or maybe it's the alcohol painfully leaving my bloodstream.

I haven't been single in over five years, and I don't mind it as much as I should. My biggest issue is that it sets back my plans. Without Edward, I'll eventually have to start over and find someone else to build a future with. The prospect is unappealing, to say the least.

"Are you awake?" I whisper in Hana's ear. A vague grunt comes as a response. "How's that first postpartum hangover treating you?"

"My boobs hurt more than my head, so it's not that bad."

"Did you bring your pump?"

"Yeah, it's in my overnight bag by the door."

To thank her for rushing to me in my time of need, I slither out of the covers. That's when I remember that I'm not wearing a nightgown. At some point, Hana slipped on a blue sequin dress from my closet that fit her silhouette, and by the time we went to bed, we were both too drunk to change into something else. I broke one of the spaghetti straps in my sleep, a costly mistake.

Hana is sitting up when I return, and I hand her the pump before heading to the dressing room.

"As much as I regret it now," she says from the bedroom while I take the dress off and make a mental note to have it fixed soon, "I'm glad we caught up."

"Me too. You've been so busy lately with little Lucas."

"Yeah, who knew having a child would be so time consuming."

"Literally everybody, Hana."

"Hmm … And you? How's work going?"

I wince, slipping on a comfortable sweater while I think of my answer. "My boss is still a pain in the ass. But he's retiring in a few months, so I'm biting my tongue and waiting."

"You think you'll get his position?"

"No one else is as qualified as I am, so I should."

"That's exciting!"

Once I have flannel shorts on, I pick a similar outfit for my girl suffering out there. "I know. In three months, I could be the head of NexaCorp's legal department."

"Worldwide?"

"Just the US."

"Also impressive," she approves with a lopsided grin.

"Worldwide will be the step after that."

Her head is leaned back on the headboard when I return, her expression one of relief, while she holds the pump against her left breast. "Will you still remember me when you're head of the world?"

"Always," I promise with a chuckle.

"Good."

I sit on the bed, and we recuperate in silence for a moment. The only sound that fills the room is the rhythmic sucking of the pump, and I welcome it as it anchors us in time. "Did you get any matches?" she randomly asks.

"For what?"

"The dating app."

Oh.

Oh! Crap!

All the wine and vodka shots entirely wiped that part out of my memory. Full-on panicking, I seek my phone, fragments of what we did the night before resurfacing. Just how drunk was I to agree to this?! I find the iPhone lying face down by the foot of the bed and come back to sit next to Hana. I barely have any battery left, but enough to do a quick check. My teeth gnaw at my lower lip, anxiety wrenching and twisting my guts. Holy cow, I have over a hundred notifications, and they are all from that kinky dating app we drunkenly downloaded.

What a stupid thing to do.

I open the app, which leads me straight to my page. The profile picture I uploaded only shows my chin and the deep cleavage of my now-torn Dior dress. I vaguely remember telling Hana that I didn't want to be recognizable on an app like this, and I thank my drunk self for that.

There are two more pictures attached to my profile—one of my cleavage and one of my ass, which is only covered by the narrow V of my tanga. Alright, I take it back. My drunk self can go to hell. Before it's out there any longer, I head to the settings and remove the two extra pics, scolding myself internally. At least we used a fake name—Jessica.

Gathering my courage, I read the description Hana and I came up with. Oh, God … It's bad.

"Down to fuck with a man who has a Jacob's ladder. Please, only DM me if you have one. Otherwise, abstain," I read aloud, in case she forgot as well.

"Did it work?"

"Too well. I have 153 messages."

"I told you it would," she brags with a proud grin.

Mortified, I open the app's inbox, wondering what kind of desperate creatures my profile attracted. The first message is a very poorly executed dick pic.

"Ew," I let out with disgust.

"Damn, that is one ugly dong," Hana says with unmasked amusement.

"And it's not even pierced."

"Men will use every opportunity they get to show their dicks."

The other messages I open aren't any better. By the twentieth, I'm certain I won't go through with that stupid bucket list thing. This is providing terrifying insight into the dating pool out there, and if this is my alternative to being single, I'll get myself a couple of cats and call it a day. These men are pigs and the odds that I'll ever let another one inside me are getting slimmer with every dick pic.

The one that takes the cake is a picture with a spunk-covered hand with an attached message that brings back my nausea at once. "Look at what your ass did to me, you dirty, dirty slut," I read, scandalized. "Okay, I'm done."

"No, keep going!"

"This is turning me gay, Hana. I swear, I've never been as unattracted to men as I am right now."

"Do you want me to open them so you won't see how they defiled that beautiful bum of yours?"

Since there is no better alternative, I hand her the phone. While she scrolls through the many messages, I twist to collect the charger's cable to plug it in. "Okay, this one has potential," she says after a few minutes have passed.

She shoves the phone in my face and I read the message, reassured to see it isn't another inappropriate picture.

ELI

Hey, I don't have a Jacob's, but my best bud does. Let me know if you're interested and I'll set you two up!

"Well, that looks promising," I say.

"Right? He's the only one who wasn't downright sexual and trying to get into your panties."

"And he has good grammar."

I visit the man's profile to get a better idea of what he might be like. Eli, 31, apparently lives in Brooklyn. He looks like a decent guy and gets bonus points for not having a picture of himself with a fish. His light chestnut hair, a little too long in every picture, matches his eyes, which have something in them that beckons trust.

"Too bad it was all for nothing," I let out, throwing the phone on the covers.

"What?!"

"Oh, come on. It was a stupid, drunken idea. There's no way I'll go through with it."

"It's not like you're committing to anything," she carefully argues. "You can meet up with that guy and decide whether or not you want to go further."

Ugh, that sounds time consuming. "I don't like sex enough to go through all that."

"Then you've never had great sex, Gen, because it's *definitely* worth it."

It's my turn to purse my lips in a disapproving way. I always favored intimacy with long-term partners over one-night stands. Hana used to tell me I was doing it wrong, insistent that I'd never discover the true joys of sex that way. She's always been more adventurous than me, and I can't count how many times she encouraged me to put myself out there and experiment, try new men, or discover what I like. But this is going too far.

At the same time, I try to excel at everything I do, pushed by a deeply rooted need to gain my parents' approval—something my therapist and I are working on during our rare sessions.

I give my everything at work, doing better than all my colleagues. I made the dean's list at Harvard, finished high school as valedictorian, won championships for my extracurricular activities … Everything I undertake, I give my all and nail it. Somehow, my unhealthy need for perfection and nothing less is taking over my subpar sex life. While I don't have to become the best at it, I can't possibly remain the worst.

My drunken enterprise led me into a position I never thought I'd ever be in, and now I'm cornered, having to choose between my need for perfection and the comfort zone I so fiercely cherish.

"You have to try that ladder thing," Hana insists. "And then let me know if it's worth it. I'm sure I can convince Tyrone to get pierced."

My nose scrunches on its own at the idea of her poor fiancé going through that. It must take a certain kind of man to undergo such mutilations. And for what? Is it to receive more pleasure? Or is it to give more of it? Regardless, it seems entirely unnecessary.

When Hana grabs my phone, I'm still torn, unsure if I want to disturb my neatly organized life for this. Nearly every hour of my days is already claimed, and sacrificing my little leisure time doesn't sound appealing. But I say nothing and watch as she returns to the message Eli sent.

"Hi, thanks for reaching out," she says as she types the words. "I'd like to know more about your friend. Is he hot? Is he a serial killer? Or a weirdo?"

"Nice priorities," I scoff.

"You'll thank me later."

I'm genuinely surprised when Eli's answer comes five minutes later. Hana is now pumping on the other side, and I'm still trying to muster the energy to go get us some ibuprofen.

ELI

> It's my understanding that he's hot, yeah. And he was forced to put his serial killer career aside when he ran out of space to bury bodies in his basement. As for the weirdo part, I guess that one's subjective. But he isn't a creep, if that helps.

"A basement in New York? In this economy? He's a catch," Hana jokes.

I chuckle, rereading the response. It's odd how a man selling himself to get laid feels untrustworthy, but this doesn't. Not as much, at least. There's some amount of authenticity to it that I wouldn't trust otherwise.

We're not expecting another message, but it comes nevertheless.

ELI

> I realize this is weird, but you're looking for a Jacob's, and he's into redheads. I thought it might be a good match. Fair warning though, he isn't looking for anything serious. I hope you don't have expectations regarding that.

"See? The stars are aligning," Hana says with a grin.

"It's kind of perfect, yes."

"Then ask for the guy's number. You can make it safe if you're the one in charge."

As I type an answer to Eli, I wonder again how I ended up in this situation. My life was perfectly fine twenty-four hours ago, with my dream Upper East Side apartment, a successful man in my life, a coveted job … And now, I'm messaging a stranger on a dating app, already *way* down the rabbit hole. The only excuse I can think of is that I'm still a little drunk and definitely sleep deprived.

But like Hana said, I'm in charge, so what's the worst that can happen?

Eli is just as quick as before to send the number, and yet again, Hana spurs me on, encouraging me to send a text before my courage wavers. So, I save the number as "Ladder Guy" in my contact list and send a quick text.

ME

This is Jessica from the dating app. I think Eli told you about me? Would you like to meet?

There, that's it. Now, all I have to do is wait for Ladder Guy's answer. And if it never comes, then I'll focus on another item from that list and circle back to this one. I got 153 messages in one night, so I'm sure it won't be hard to find willing men.

When the phone vibrates in my hand, I almost drop it, surprised. My eyes widen when I see *he* is already texting me back. Oh, I'm not ready for this. I thought I'd have hours to prepare.

With a hand that slightly trembles from anticipation and worry, I unlock the screen to see his response.

LADDER GUY

Hello, Jessica from the dating app. He just sent me your profile's screenshots.

Then, there's nothing for a moment, and I wonder if he'll ignore my offer to meet. Which I understand if I'm being honest. Had Hana come to me with such an offer—setting me up with some random guy she came across on a dating app—I would have refused too.

Well, now that I've flipped the situation around and realized the absurdity of it, I'm beyond confident that he'll keep his distance. And if he doesn't, he might not be very sane.

Just as I think it's over, the phone vibrates again. He sent a second text.

LADDER GUY

Absolutely I'd like to meet.

My heart's in my throat, anxiety wrenching my gut. This is how women get killed, isn't it?

"If I end up murdered and found in a ditch, I hope you'll regret doing this to me for the rest of your life," I mumble to Hana.

"Oh, come on," she says with a roll of her eyes. "It's not like you have to meet him in Central Park in the dead of the night."

A quick look at my schedule informs me that the only time I'll have before a while is Friday. It's definitely short notice, but the sooner, the better. And it's the most scary and complicated item on that list, so I'm glad I get to cross it out first.

ME

> The only time I have this month is Friday evening. Is 6:30 alright for you?

As I wait for his reply, I fidget with my phone. "What the hell am I doing?" I mutter to myself.

"Living a little, for once," Hana replies, clearly excited about the whole situation.

My phone buzzes again, and my heart races. "Please, don't be free," I whisper as I unlock the screen.

LADDER GUY

> I can make that work. Do you have a place in mind?

The sensation under my ribs intensifies, and I can't tell if it's anxiety, excitement, or worry. Hana was right about making it safe, so I decide on somewhere with CCTV and a security detail where no one would attempt something. Even the elevators have cameras, so I'll feel safe enough to relax and let go of my worries.

ME

> The Plaza Hotel's bar on 5th Avenue.

I'm not entirely sure that we'll end up sleeping together, but it being a hotel would be convenient if we decide to.

LADDER GUY

> I'll be there.

ME

> Should I wear something specific so you'll recognize me?

He doesn't know what I look like, and I won't send him a picture of myself. I'm pretty wary of such things and maintain a low online presence.

LADDER GUY

> Cleavage.

My jaw drops, my cheeks burning from his audacity. Right, he doesn't know my face, but he has Eli's screenshots. Before I can get too offended by the rudeness of his suggestion, another message comes in.

LADDER GUY

I'll recognize the freckles.

Well, it's not as bad as him distinguishing me because of my breasts. But maybe he's being humorous or flirty and I'm not getting it.

ME

And how will I recognize you?

LADDER GUY

Oh, don't worry, love. You'll notice me.

That almost sounds like a threat. Or is it a promise?

CHAPTER Three

Gen

I OBSERVE THE BARTENDER, CONSIDERING calling him to order another drink. It would help soothe my nerves, but being tipsy by the time Ladder Guy arrives doesn't sound like a good idea.

I take a deep breath instead and gaze at the bar's entrance. He's nearly five minutes late. Already, this isn't starting well. I don't care what Hana will say about it—I'm not waiting more than ten minutes for someone I don't even know.

It's my first time doing something like this, and I don't like it. As soon as I sobered up after that drunken night, I deleted my profile from the app and removed it from my phone. The only reason I'm even here is because she forced my hand with blackmail, threatening to post Throwback Thursday photos of me that should never see the light of day.

Because I blame her entirely for the situation I'm currently in, I send her a text.

ME
This is the craziest thing I've ever done.

HANANANA
You haven't done it yet.

ME
Hana, it's too much.

HANANANA

Oh, come on. It's nothing millions of people haven't done before. Besides, he could arrive any minute now. Aren't you a little curious?

ME

The fact that he's late doesn't work in his favor. He has another five to arrive, and then I'm gone.

HANANANA

You're such a wuss, Gen. It's just a drink with some guy.

I set the phone down with a frustrated sigh. "This is ridiculous," I whisper to myself. I'm sure there are better and saner ways to hone my craft. It's been less than a week since Eddie broke things off, so being here now is way too early.

The thought of my ex makes my lips pinch with bitter discontentment. Although I haven't cried yet, nor am I feeling any deep emotions over it, the breakup is affecting my work. My mind isn't as focused as it used to be, and I've become paranoid, thinking every whisper I catch is about me.

Serves me right for dating someone who works for the same company.

We haven't spoken since he left. Not via messages, not on the phone, not in real life ... I'm unsure who should be the one reaching out first. I'm the dumpee, so it would be pathetic if I did. He said he'd keep me updated when he had a space for his things. Maybe I should wait for that. Or maybe he'll come to his senses and return home.

I grab my clutch from the bar top, deciding to put an end to this madness. I'll pay for my lemon drop martini and leave before Ladder Guy can arrive.

Just as I'm about to wave for the bartender, a movement to my right catches my attention. The tall, broad, and dark silhouette that just entered the lounge is hard to miss, so my gaze is drawn to it at once. And when my eyes land on him, my credit card nearly slips from my fingers.

I don't think anyone quite like this man ever stepped into The Plaza. The way the surrounding chatter slightly dims confirms my suspicions.

Despite everything going on with him, the first thing I notice is how strikingly attractive he is. His angular jaw can cut through granite, and his deep-set, hooded eyes have a laser-like sharpness to them as they scan the room's occupants. The man's bone structure is immaculate, his cheekbones high and mighty, with a strong brow that rests under a flat forehead. His nose is also of ideal proportion, narrow and balanced. The bump that sits high on it indicates it was broken at least once, but that, somehow, doesn't get in the way of his magnetism. His dark hair is neatly cut, short at the bottom, with a flawless fade that leads to longer hair, which is slicked back.

Once I'm done taking in the dazzling features of his face, my inspection lowers, which causes my eyebrows to shoot up. Below that remarkable jawline of his, reddish tattoos creep up from the collar of his black leather jacket. As much as I want to hate it, I can't deny that it not only heightens his gorgeous features, but also gives him a dangerous and daring aura like I've never seen before. I can't make out the intricate drawings inked on his skin from where I am, and my eyes dart lower on instinct. On his large hands, more inky drawings, all the way to his knuckles.

Who the hell is this man?

When his analysis of the bar's patrons ventures toward me, I tense on my stool. The tiny hairs on my arms and the back of my neck rise. Then, his intense gaze locks with mine, and my breath catches in my throat, my heart hammering in my chest. The flicker of recognition that sparks in his eyes nearly undoes me.

No.

No, no, no.

This isn't Ladder Guy.

But he doesn't continue his search, taking a confident step in my direction instead.

Oh, don't worry, love. You'll notice me. Well, his overly confident statement now makes sense. I could hardly *not* notice him. Jesus Christ, everyone in here noticed him. For some reason—probably naivety—I didn't expect him to have anything other than those piercings I need him for. But now that he's approaching me, I realize how stupid that was. If he isn't scared of a giant needle repeatedly stabbing his penis, he's definitely not worried about one running across his skin to draw tattoos all over it.

Panic slowly sets in, my breath returning in short and irregular pants. What the hell did I get myself into?

I should look away and pretend I have no idea who he is, so maybe he'll be on his way and ignore me. But my entire body has turned both tense and limp, refusing to bend to my brain's will.

The closer he gets, the more intimidated I am by his height and build. Even fully dressed, I can guess at the hard-earned muscles that ripple underneath his dark jeans and the black T-shirt under his leather jacket. He seems to be in his early thirties, which is when men peak, according to Hana. The stranger confirms that theory, clearly in his prime.

My mind goes entirely blank once he's two steps away, close enough to catch the jade green of his irises and the finer details of his stunning face—down to the grain of the stubble that dusts his carved cheeks.

"Hello, Jessica from the dating app," he says in a low voice that drips with sin. Australian. He has an Australian accent, which comes as an even greater surprise than the tattoos and the rest of him.

"I almost didn't recognize you without the ..." His eyes slowly descend to my chest, where purple satin covers me with modesty. April is too cold a month to wear something low cut, and I wouldn't have, anyway. "... freckles," he concludes.

Lie, a voice shouts in my head. *Lie and say he's got the wrong person.* My mouth opens, eager to put an end to all this madness, but not a sound comes out of it. Something's happening to me, and I hate it. His closeness is rendering me completely useless.

His head tilts slightly to the side, a devilish half grin pulling the corner of his lips. "Cat's got your tongue, love?"

Again, my vocal cords are unable to produce a sound. Not when my attention is on the tattoos that I can now see clearly on his stretched neck. Feathers. The incandescent tips of feathers are what's creeping out of his collar.

"Hmm ..." he continues, his face veiled with amusement. "Too bad. I had plans for that tongue of yours."

It's either the crudeness, the image, or the reminder of why he's here, but that shakes me out of the trance he put me in. This was a mistake, and I must end it before it derails any further.

"You must have me confused with someone else, sir," I boldly lie, my voice slightly trembling.

ANA D'ARCY 3 5

His assurance doesn't even waver at my statement, his eyes still determinedly staring at the details of my face. "Are you sure about that, love? I'd recognize that shade of red anywhere."

Everything inside me flutters when he sends a hand between us to catch a strand of my hair between his thumb and index.

"Again, sir, I'm not—I'm not Jessica."

"Let's make sure, yeah?"

The instant he pulls his phone out of his back pocket, I realize my mistake. I don't even need to look at his screen to know what his thumb is doing on it. When my phone rings and vibrates on the bar, I close my eyes to recompose myself and avoid his cocky smirk.

Alright, I was caught in a lie, but I can still wriggle out of this mess.

"You're a naughty liar, Jessica," he says with nothing but amusement after hanging up.

My eyes whip open. "And you're late."

For some reason, that earns me a dashing grin. And at that very moment, I'm glad my legs are tightly crossed as I sit on the stool because I feel it *inside* me.

Again, who the hell is this man?

"My apologies for the wait, but I was detained," he offers with a slight bow of his head. I can feel my cheeks warm up at the thought that the man is even more dangerous than he looks. He must catch my inner turmoil because he impishly adds, "At work."

My shoulders sink with relief, and he bites back a smile.

"Mister ..." I trail off, trying to remember a name I never even asked for. "Sir. I fear there's been—"

"Hold that thought. Excuse me, mate," he calls to the man behind the counter. The tattooed stranger points at my empty glass and says, "Another like this, and I'll have a draft beer."

The bartender nods and springs into action with quiet efficiency. Oh, no. We're not having drinks.

"Sir," I try again.

"Jake."

"Mr. Jake—"

He can't quite hold back the chuckle that rolls out of his throat. "Just Jake, love."

"Don't call me that."

"Would you prefer kitten? Baby? Sweetheart? Red?"

My cheeks, or rather my whole face, warm up at the flirty tone he uses for each endearment. I gather myself as swiftly as I can. "I would prefer Jessica," I reply dryly.

He laughs again, shaking his head. "Listen, I get that I'm not what you expected. But I came from too far to not at least have a drink," he nonchalantly explains. "So, I'll have a beer over there, and if you feel like not making this evening a waste of time, you're free to join me. We'll have a nice chat and part ways."

The bartender chooses that exact moment to return with the drinks the man—Jake—ordered and a bill. Once he's paid, this enigma of a man extends his tattooed hand to the tall glass of foamy beer, offers me a wink, and heads off to the table he gestured toward.

I sit there, dumbfounded, while he walks over to the empty booth. My eyes rake up and down his silhouette without my approval, and I marvel at the powerful legs I can perceive under his jeans and the roundness of his behind. This man is quite the specimen, and I don't recall ever meeting someone as effortlessly alluring as him.

Maybe one drink. That way, Hana won't be too hard on me when I tell her I chickened out and nothing happened. At least she'll think I gave this man a fair shot. Also, it would be rude of me to make him come all this way only to leave because of his unexpected appearance.

With a deep sigh, I slide down the stool, grab my phone, my clutch, and my lemon drop. He must hear the clicking of my heels on the polished marble of the floors, but he doesn't turn around. He's busy removing his jacket when I join him.

Adamant to make things clear before this goes any further, I say, "Sir, you—"

My interjection dies in my throat as the leather comes off, revealing more tattoos. His arms are covered in intricate designs of ink, and it only adds to his irresistible charm. The artworks are eclectic, but they somehow blend well together, showing a level of craftsmanship I never thought possible in tattoos. The incandescent feathers that creep up his neck are part of a much larger design, and more of them descend on his biceps. It looks like he has enormous wings spread across his back, which pour onto the rest of him.

A man from the hotel's staff is by us before I can remember how to speak, and he takes the jacket before disappearing back to the corner he came from.

With unwavering confidence, Jake lowers into a chair as I stand by the table's side, unsure what to do next. "Sit," he offers, gesturing at the cushioned seat opposite his. It's a suggestion more than an order, so I comply without a word.

For a moment, there's nothing but the chatter of the bar's patrons. My eyes dart to his inked forearms when he folds them across his broad chest and observes me. At this point, I have to admit it to myself, I'm beyond intrigued—I'm fascinated.

"Eli and I have been wondering," he starts, his green eyes commanding mine to meet them, "is it a dare?"

"Is what a dare?"

"The Jacob's ladder. Were you dared to try? Or is it a kink? Something you enjoy doing now and then?"

"No, I ..." My gaze shies away from his, and I fidget with the velvet of my tiny black clutch. "I've never tried, but I was curious about what it might feel like."

Another crooked smirk tugs at his lips. "Women usually come back for more. So, I'd imagine it feels good. You used the past tense. Are you not curious anymore?"

I can't hold back an embarrassed wince. "The drunk version of me was very keen on trying when she created that profile. But sober me is still debating it."

"Now you're testing my morals, red. I've never had to get a woman drunk so she'd want a ride," he says with humor. "And as tempting as you are, I won't stoop that low."

My face is in a state of constant heat, but he still manages to make me blush harder. "That's commendable of you, sir."

"Do I look like someone who goes by 'sir?'" He gestures at himself, compelling my gaze to examine him once more. "Call me Jake."

"And do I look like someone who calls people by their first name five minutes into meeting them?" I retort, echoing his gesture.

His eyes do the same as mine did, and I swear they linger on the fabric over my chest for a moment too long. "Clarke," he says.

"Excuse me?"

"My surname is Clarke."

"Oh … Alright, that works better for me, Mr. Clarke."

I can't put my finger on it, but there's something about this man's attitude that confuses me. When he arrived, everything about his demeanor told me he was a conqueror, a man who domineeringly took whatever he wanted. But since then, he's been nothing but respectful of my boundaries, despite the occasional flirting.

So, even though this won't lead to anything other than a drink and a conversation, I'm glad that I stuck around. This is a lesson in prejudice that I obviously needed.

CHAPTER *four*

Jake

ELI IS GETTING MORE THAN a pat on the back for this one. Jessica from the dating app is even more gorgeous than he reckoned. That means I lost our bet and owe him ten bucks. But I don't feel like a loser as I look at her freckled features.

My best mate knows me too well; the creature I found perched on a stool is exactly my type. Hair like flames licking down her perfect silhouette, and golden-brown specks that dust her face. If Eli's screenshots are unedited, they also scatter down her cleavage and her arse. But her beauty goes much beyond that.

Her doe eyes convey a natural innocence, the cornflower blue shade of her irises almost luminous. Above them, the perfectly drawn arches of her eyebrows match the auburn of her hair. Coral pink lips are pushed into a discontented pout just below her slightly upturned nose, and their fullness triggers fantasies I can't ignore. If I'm a lucky lad, I'll eventually know the feeling of that pretty little mouth wrapped around my cock.

There's something about her that calls to me. Maybe it's her uptight demeanor and how fun it would be to shake her out of it. I'm fine with her changing her mind and us not having sex, but part of me hopes she returns to her initial idea. Something tells me it wouldn't take much. She's trying to give the illusion of control and detachment, but I'm too well-versed in women to let it fool me. Is she aware I can see her knees pressing together whenever I'm flirting? Does she know her cheeks flush when I say dirty things? My only issue with the latter is that it makes her freckles fade away, and I'm torn between enjoying the sight of those or keeping up with the embarrassed arousal I can so effortlessly trigger.

But maybe she's feigning the innocence in her eyes to drive me mad. After all, she's the one who posted such a bold request on a famously debauched app. So maybe I'm the one unaware.

As my thoughts battle to discern if she's a naive little lamb or an expert puppeteer, I pick up my beer and take a long gulp. Good, it's European—none of that piss-poor American nonsense. She takes a sip from her glass, then a second, then a third, and puts it back. How many cocktails has she had? Is this her second or third? This one's going down fast, meaning we might get very little time together. Also, if there's a slim chance that we end up in a bed somewhere, I'll only indulge if she's sober. I meant what I said earlier.

"Did it hurt a lot?" she asks.

"The piercings?"

She nods. Will you look at that? Proper little Jessica is thinking about what's going on in my pants.

"Not as much as I thought it would," I reply.

Her frown tells me she doesn't believe my answer. "I'd expect getting four holes pierced *there* would be agonizing."

"Six."

"Pardon?"

"I've got six piercings there. Four looked too scattered."

Her eyes widen, her lips part, and I decide this is what I want to do all evening long: shock her with my brazen crudeness over and over again. She's madly alluring whenever I shake her conventional and proper manners.

I take another sip of beer to hide my proud grin and then decide she can take more. "The ladder hurt, but not as much as the apadravya." Her huge eyes become even rounder, and I can't hold back my grin anymore. "It's when you pierce the—"

"I know what it is," she cuts me off before she raises her glass, taking another sip.

When I cross my arms over my chest and lean back in my seat, I notice the way her eyes scan my tattoos again. I didn't miss the way she reacted when I removed the jacket, completely flabbergasted by the sight.

Posh women like her always go nuts for the ink. And the muscles, too. It tugs at their proper education and snobbish values, and they can't compute the thoughts they trigger. Their brains begin to wonder if maybe bland-and-boring-Bernard, or whatever the fuck their partner is called, is what they really need after all.

Given the place she picked for us to meet, I figured she was upper-class, so I knew my appearance would surprise her to some extent. But she had to know the kind of men her very specific request would bring, didn't she?

"Do you do this often?" I ask, already knowing the answer.

"Certainly not. This is the first and probably last time."

"Am I being so terribly disappointing, red?"

The nickname earns me a glare, but she still answers, "You're not what I expected."

"And what did you expect?"

She ponders for a moment, her pretty little head tilting to the side as she assesses me. "Not someone this intense."

Despite her earlier shock—which I was expecting—she seems to have a bit of spunk. That bold lie about her not being Jessica was greatly entertaining, and the way she owned it was admirable. It's a good thing. I like them fiery inside and out, or it quickly gets dull.

"You've seen nothing yet, red."

The freckles are gone again, and she squirms in her chair. Just like that, I know she's imagining my pierced cock in her pussy, and it compels me to do the same. Well, if this doesn't lead to sex, I'll be going home with the bluest balls I've ever sported.

As though reading my mind, she puts her glass down and faces me, her expression grave. "If we were to engage in coitus," she hesitantly starts.

"Don't call it coitus."

She disapprovingly frowns. "It's the proper terminology."

"Unless you want a man to go flaccid, don't call it that."

That's a lie, though. I'm hard as fuck in my jeans, somehow turned on by her rigid manners.

"I couldn't care less about the state of your … appendage."

I grin, unable to hold it back. Just thinking of my dick makes her cheeks pinker. "You were saying about us possibly fucking?"

"Yes, I need to clarify a few things."

"Clarify away."

"First, I'd need to see recent STI test results."

Well, she doesn't beat around the bush. "Sorry, love, but I always use condoms. Especially with strangers from random dating apps."

"It would be in addition to the use of a condom," she states firmly. Then, after a brief moment of silent thought, she asks, "Does the latex impede the sensation of the piercings?"

"No. If we fuck, you'll feel them. And me."

My crude words make her blush even redder, and the way she presses her crossed legs together isn't lost on me. She likes this, my attitude, the unknown territory she's venturing into, the way we couldn't be more mismatched ... It works for her as much as it works for me.

"I get tested every two months, and I'm currently waiting on the results from last Wednesday," I offer as a compromise. "Would that be recent enough?"

She thinks about it for a couple of beats and nods. "If we do this within the next ten days, that'll suffice, yes."

"Brilliant. Anything else you need? My social security number? Place and date of birth? My family's medical history?"

The playful banter doesn't land well this time, and her face falls into a vexed scowl. "If you'd rather not abide by my rules, we can put an end to this and call it a day."

"I have no issue with it, Jessica from the dating app. I'm just not used to this being so businesslike."

She winces, her blue gaze shying away from mine. Another long gulp of her drink gets swallowed, and I reckon she has two left before she's done with it. "I will be drafting a contract in the eventuality that I make up my mind and decide to indulge in this."

"A contract?"

"Yes."

Well, that's new. Kind of. I've never signed a contract for a one-night stand.

This isn't a date, so I won't ask personal questions, but if I had to guess, I'd say she either works in HR or she's a lawyer. This contract thing has to come from somewhere, and I can't think of another profession that would even come up with the idea.

I sense my mouth betray my amusement again. This woman is definitely a novelty. We're both experimenting tonight, aren't we?

"If we do fuck, I also have a condition," I say.

She looks slightly taken aback, as if I can't also have a say in this. "Go ahead."

"It's *just* sex. I'm not looking for anything serious, red, so this isn't the start of some great romance."

This time, she chortles. "Of course, it would only be sex. It's not like we're compatible anyway, Mr. Clarke."

Good. She gets it.

"I'm just making sure. I'm not the monogamous type, so you'd only hurt yourself if you expected more."

She rolls her eyes, unimpressed. "A man with commitment issues, how original."

My lips bend into a smile. "I reckon I'm doing a favor to your gender, red. My talents deserve to be shared around, spreading as many pairs of legs as I can."

"And you've spread many, is that it?" She can barely hold back from rolling her eyes again.

"They part for me, like the sea for Moses."

An unstoppable snicker pours out of her lush lips again. "You're so full of yourself."

"You'll get it once *you're* full of me."

Blood rushes to her cheeks while mine rushes to my cock as I trigger naughty images in both our minds. Goddammit, I feel like a hormonal teenager.

"Does this usually work?" she wonders, her blue eyes scanning mine intently.

"Does what work?"

"The arrogance. Does it get women going?"

I lean back into my seat, entertained by her spirit. "You call it arrogance; I call it confidence."

"It's overconfidence, at the very least."

"Maybe you should give me a try and judge for yourself."

She looks more comfortable now, but my offer takes us a couple steps back again. Women usually like my cocky attitude, but I'm realizing—maybe too late—that it might not work on someone like her.

"Well, rest assured, Mr. Clarke, I won't demand anything more from you than sex. Especially if you're God's gift to women. I'm a girl's girl, so I'd hate to rob my sisters of your talents."

"That's the spirit, red."

I'm not ready for this to end when she slips her phone into her clutch and downs the rest of her drink. "Well, it was interesting meeting you, Mr. Clarke. Let me know if you are still interested in furthering this encounter."

I'm a little ashamed at how fast I answer, "I very much am."

Her cheeks get rosy again, and just like that, I know she's imagining my cock once more—which, to my dismay, hasn't deflated through the whole encounter. I haven't prayed in two decades, but if that's what it takes not to head home with blue balls, I'm about ready to kneel and ask the Almighty to do me a solid. She intrigues me, and I'm dying to know what brought her here. Also, I'd love to see her under me, mewling my name as I fuck her hard and show her just how intense I can get.

"I might be in contact," she replies.

"And when would that be, red?"

"I'm not sure yet. All of this is still being debated."

I nod, take a long chug of my beer, and set the glass back down. "I don't normally do this, you know."

"You just said you only do hookups," she points out, confused.

"Exactly. Meet. Fuck. Move on. What I don't do are these little dates to get to know each other."

"That isn't what this was."

"Then what was it?"

She thinks about her answer for a moment. "See it as a job interview. A way to assess if we're compatible."

"I see ... And how did I do?"

The faintest smile makes the corner of her lush mouth twitch when she replies, "You did adequately, Mr. Clarke. I'll probably be in touch soon."

After a polite nod, she stands from the cushioned seat with her things and walks away. With what I can only describe as whiplash, I stare at the firm roundness of her bum, watching how the purple fabric of her dress clings to it. I almost regret seeing that third picture from Eli's screenshots. I wish I could have discovered what it looks like in person. But I've looked at that picture quite a bit, enchanted by the constellations that her freckles form there.

She's fucking stunning, and I'm a little offended that she never turns around to check me out one last time. Then, once she's done getting her coat back, it hits me.

"*Adequately*?" I mutter to myself.

No, that won't do.

I spring to my feet and hastily walk after her. She's already in the lobby when I catch up, and I call out, "Jessica!" She doesn't respond to it, which forces me to quicken my pace. "Red!" I call out again. This time, she stops and turns to me with a nonplussed frown.

There's a large potted palm right by where she stands, so I clasp her wrist and pull her toward it. "Adequately?" I ask as I release her, a little vexed.

"Adequately is good," she defends herself. "It could have gone a lot worse."

"It isn't good in my books. I can't let you leave finding me 'adequate.'"

"What's your plan?" Her big blue eyes squint at me, wary.

I hope I'm right about her being a lawyer when I say, "May I offer a closing argument?"

She hesitates for a couple of seconds, wondering if she should allow it or not. Fuck, I don't even know what I'll say if she agrees. She's close enough that I can smell the cherry scent etched on her skin and admire the specks on her face. But this means I can also see she's breathing a little too fast, and her pupils are bigger than they were moments ago. I'm not the only one affected by the closeness of our bodies.

"Alright," she eventually decides.

I'm not proud of what I do next, but I can't think past my need for her, especially not with the way her lips are slightly parted, as if inviting me to act on my ludicrous impulse.

Because I'm not one to force a woman to do anything without her consent, I *slowly* lower my face to level it with hers. She tenses all over but doesn't recoil, her gaze fixed on mine. When I'm sure she would have pulled away or pushed me if she didn't want this as much as I do, I close the small gap separating us and press my mouth to hers.

I have no fucking idea what's going on, but the softness of her lips feels damn right. Because I don't know what to do now, I stay frozen in place. As closing arguments go, this one's quite shit, isn't it? She'll give me a resounding slap, blush furiously, and leave me there like the moron that I am. *The fuck am I doing?*

The instant she rises a little higher to intensify it, all of my worries vanish. My hands reach out for her waist, and I pull her in as I tilt my head, aligning our lips and deepening the contact. I swear she melts against me, as affected as I am by this chaste kiss.

It's when her slender hand rises between us to rest on my chest that I lose it. I tentatively lick the seam of her lips, a rumbly groan rolling in my throat. She surprises me once more with how receptive she is when she unlocks her jaw to grant me access. The invitation couldn't be clearer, so I dip my tongue inside her warmth, licking with greed.

Things get out of hand in seconds, like a lit match thrown into gasoline. I'd blame it on the potted palm that isolates us, but she's the reason why I get lost in it, completely oblivious to the people surrounding us in the lobby. All the flirting from before led to this, and now that our minds have expressed themselves, it's our bodies' turn.

It seems she gets overwhelmed as well, shyly darting out her own tongue to sample me while she has a hand firmly clasped on my neck. She tastes like lemon and sin, and I don't think I could ever get tired of it. Not when her perfect body is pressed against mine, my cock hard and demanding between us.

My hands work faster than my brain as they lower down her back to grab her arse, eager to feel more of her. When I pull her closer to let her feel what she's doing to me, she lets out a helpless whimper that passes from her lips to mine. I know I'm in deep shit when it echoes all the way to my balls.

The wanton sound has a different effect on her though, and it seems to shake her out of the lustful exchange we're having. With a shocked gasp and a shove on my chest, she rips herself away from me.

Her glassy eyes look up at mine, filled with want, and her hand is over her mouth as if she can't believe what just happened. We stand there for a moment, our breathing slightly ragged as we try to recompose ourselves. I have to force myself not to grab her again, ignoring every cell in my body screaming for more.

With a trembling hand, she tucks a loose strand of hair behind her ear, and I notice that the tip of it is even redder than her cheeks. This. Her blushing ears are why she deserves to be called red.

She doesn't say a thing, adjusts her bag over her shoulder, and turns away from me. Before I know it, she's back to her walk out of this place. I watch, feeling like an imbecile, until she disappears through the revolving doors.

Fuck, I messed it all up, didn't I? She was a wild deer, and I scared her by acting like a tactless brute. "Fucking idiot," I mutter to myself.

I'm so mad about the way I handled things that I don't finish my beer when I return to the bar. I fetch my jacket and the helmet I left with the valet service by the hotel's entrance. During the entire ride back to Brooklyn, I scold myself for my abrasive manners. I'm usually a lot better with the ladies, but it seems this one isn't like anything I've known before. She stressed me out somehow, and I panicked.

When I arrive at The Devil's Court, there's barely any space left for my bike. I still make do and enter the crowded bar. The familiar atmosphere helps with the frustration, and the rock band on stage does a great job shushing the thoughts of failure. Ever since we bought it, this place has become a second home to me and my mates. It doesn't matter if the floor is always sticky, regardless of how much we mop it, or if the smell of cigarettes is etched into the old wallpaper. This poorly lit bar with loud rock, good booze, and questionable company is ours, and we love it exactly the way it is.

After a quick scan of the crowd, I spot Eli by the bar, talking to Killian behind it. We're a tight trio, and I know that two minutes with them will be enough to get my mind off the stunning redhead I just botched it with.

"Already back?" Eli asks when I arrive next to him. "I see your stamina hasn't improved."

"You're one to talk. When was the last time you got your dick wet, you twat?" The reminder makes him scowl, but he deserved it.

"What happened?" Kill wonders, pouring a beer for me.

"Nothing, we just had a drink."

"Oh, so it was a date?" Eli interjects.

"No. It was a ... job interview of sorts."

Kill sets the pint before me as Eli continues the interrogation with, "Did you pass?"

"I don't know yet. Probably not."

"Why aren't you asking him the important question?" Kill asks Eli.

"I'm savoring it because I already know the answer. See how defeated he looks?"

Fuck, right. I forgot about that. With a discontented mumble, I take my wallet out and find a ten-dollar bill that I smack in front of Eli.

"So, she was hot?"

"Yeah." I don't say that she was stunning, with the body of a goddess, the face of an angel, and the bearing of a queen. They'd never let it die otherwise.

"Told you. Some women don't put their faces on those apps because they're so pretty they'd get stalked and all kinds of creepy shit."

"Well, in my experience, it's usually because they don't have much to offer. Now, can we move on to another topic, or should I go find someone more amenable to spend the evening with?" I ask, mindlessly eyeing the packed room.

I have a pair of balls that need emptying, and I can spot a few women I've already shagged and who'd probably be more than willing to help me out. While I wish the night ended with proper little Jessica, I'm not opposed to finding some relief with a woman less complicated than her.

A woman who doesn't need a contract to fuck. One who won't think I'm only *adequate*. And one who won't make my cock ache every time her face turns red with arousal.

Shit, I really messed this one up, didn't I?

CHAPTER *five*

Gen

I'VE BEEN RANDOMLY STARING AT the number since what happened at The Plaza, wondering if I'll ever find the courage to text it again. I haven't renamed him—his caller ID is still Ladder Guy.

It would be completely insane to go through with my original plan. I want to get better at sex and prove that Edward's wrong about me, but I'm not *that* desperate to do it. This isn't me, which means I'll probably end up deleting Mr. Clarke's number without ever contacting him again.

I don't know why I didn't do that as soon as I exited The Plaza. Maybe because that kiss has been haunting me ever since. I'm not used to men being so domineeringly in charge, so his boldness frightened me. But the sensations it unleashed are even more worrying than that. How can a kiss be the most sexually loaded experience of my life? How is it possible that I felt more aroused by his expert lips devouring mine than I ever was during intercourse?

After all, maybe Hana was right, and saving intimacy for long-term partners is nothing like doing it with perfect strangers. That's probably why I reacted so strongly to the ruggedly handsome Mr. Clarke. The forbidden aspect of our encounter had my body in a frenzy.

For the third time this Tuesday morning, I look away from my work and grab my phone. Rather than face the vast space of my corner office, I spin my desk chair toward the floor-to-ceiling windows that offer a stunning view over Manhattan's skyscrapers. Once my screen is unlocked, I open my messages with Edward.

Still nothing, even though today marks the tenth day of our separation. I'll give it two weeks, and then I'll reach out to ask if he's settled at Frank's and doing alright. I'm not sure yet if I want to salvage things with Eddie or move on. And if I decide on the latter course of action, is this the way? Sex with a stranger?

Before I know it, my thumb takes me to my exchanges with Ladder Guy. At this point, I know the few texts by heart.

Three knocks on my door shake me out of my thoughts. "Yes?" I call, turning my chair back in place. The door opens and Daisy, my assistant, enters my office holding a tall pile of carefully arranged folders.

"I'm done with it," she says, setting the papers on the corner of my desk. Before I can straighten them myself, she does it, used to my orderly ways. "They said to contact them if you want to implement more changes."

"Thank you, Daisy."

"Oh, and your lunch meeting just called to see if you'd be alright with moving it back by an hour."

I check my watch, do some calculations, and nod. "Call the restaurant to let them know."

"Alright." She then exits my office, her heels clicking on the polished floor.

My hand reaches out to the first folder on the pile, but I reconsider. I slept too little for this, and even though Daisy used sticky tabs to mark the edited paragraphs, it'll take me hours to review it all. I need coffee.

As I make my way to the breakroom, it feels like everyone's eyes are on me, but I blame it on fatigue-induced paranoia. Ever since the breakup, I've been perceiving every whisper as gossip about me, which is ridiculous. Nothing has changed regarding my professional life, so it's all in my head. I'm still hard-working, still in designer clothes, and still running my department with a hand of steel.

It's hard to keep believing it's all a fabrication when I enter the spacious breakroom, and silence falls at once. Some people skedaddle back to the open floor as if I caught them slacking off, and the few that remain look away.

Eager to escape this oppressive space, I quickly pour myself a tall cup of coffee, grab stevia and creamer, and head back toward the door. Upon seeing Isabel though, I'm reminded of a matter I've meant to talk to her about.

"Isabel, are you done laying out the protocol for the new instruction manual's format?"

Her eyes go round, betraying the fact that she forgot despite my reminding her several times. "I'm still working on that, sorry."

"It's a one-week task, Isabel. Which I gave to you three weeks ago. A lot of peoples' work depends on it. Please, have it on my desk by tomorrow evening."

"I'll see what I can do."

"Thank you."

Glad to have sorted this out, I resume my journey back to my office. I'm only a few steps from the breakroom when I decide on a chocolate muffin. My lunch is delayed, and I skipped breakfast.

"One week for her, maybe," Isabel is muttering when I reach the door. "Frigid bitch."

"Can you believe Eddie stayed with her for *five* years?"

The room suddenly spins around me as if the world decided to invert its rotational axis and flip everything, including my guts.

"I don't know how he did it," a feminine voice continues.

"For real. Even her parents' money isn't enough to make up for it."

What must be bile gathers in the back of my throat, its acrid taste coating my tongue. So, it wasn't paranoia after all. They *are* talking about me behind my back, insulting me, covering me in shame.

"Must feel like a block of ice with a hole in it," Larry says.

The others laugh, and each passing second feels like a stab in my chest. I always knew I wasn't very popular, but I had no idea it was so bad.

I need to move. I want to, but my feet are glued to the blue carpet below my red soles, uncooperative. I don't need that muffin anymore. Hell, I don't even think I can drink the coffee currently burning my palm. I want to leave, go home, and never see the people in there again. But it's not just them, is it? It's everyone on this floor, and maybe a few on the other ones. They despise me, and my recent breakup has given them ammunition to humiliate me.

But I'm the only one who can give them that satisfaction. I'm the one who can break and bend at their offenses. And there's no way I'll let them win. For the first time in a decade, I'm thankful for my lack of tears because it allows me to straighten up and act as if I'm not deeply hurt by their baseless insults.

"Can you imagine the—" Isabel stops whatever she was about to sneer as soon as I enter the room.

Holding myself straight and staring ahead, I walk up to the pastry stand to pick up a muffin I already know I won't eat. They all remain silent now that I am in their presence.

On my way out again, I halt my steps. "Don't you have work to do, Isabel?"

With her cup of tea in hand, she swiftly makes her way out of the break room.

"And Larry?" I call out next.

"Yes, Miss Kensington?"

"I'm nothing like a block of ice, but you'll never be lucky enough to find out for yourself."

The words feel like razor blades coming out of my throat because I know they are a lie. I'm terrible in bed, and I hope to God Larry never finds out. The way their jaws drop makes it all worth it, and I offer them a faked, amiable smile before continuing on my way back to my office.

Once I'm safely behind closed doors, I curse the glass walls that separate me from the open floor, wishing I could crumble into a pile of mashed Gen. But I maintain my composure, settle the snack and searing cup on my desk, and return to the glass wall to pull the privacy curtain closed. Only when I'm finally isolated do I take deep and long breaths, struggling to soothe myself.

My life is on a rapid descent to hell, and I have no idea how to stop it from happening.

Frigid bitch …

As much as I want to deny it, I can't help but wonder. Is it just my leading style that compelled the insult, or are people aware of my lack of bedroom skills? Did Edward say something? The idea that anyone else might know is chilling, and I shudder at the thought. Especially since I'm supposed to have authority over them. How are they meant to respect me now?

When my breathing has returned to a semblance of normalcy, I straighten my blouse, skirt, and hair before walking up to my door. As I go to the elevator lobby, I avoid everyone's gaze, worried I might crumble if I catch even one nasty side glare. Since only a few floors are above mine, I'm alone when I enter the elevator. On my way down though, a couple of people join the ride, and we stand in utter silence. Then, I'm out again, walking through the familiar hallways leading to Eddie's office. It's been months since my last visit there, an unpleasant reminder of how poorly our relationship evolved.

I knock on his door, staring at the golden letters of his nameplate, and wait for his "Come in!"

The office is familiar since we used to have lunch together here. It's smaller than mine, but I have faith that he'll one day become the company's chief accountant, given his skills.

He's crunching numbers on his calculator, his thin-rimmed glasses low on his straight nose. When he looks up, surprise strikes him. He stops what he's doing, hastily taking off his glasses.

"Gen! Hi."

"Hello, Edward."

The awkward tension prevents us from saying anything else, both uncertain about how to proceed. "How have you been doing?" I ask first.

"Uh, alright. Frank's apartment is big, so we're not in each other's faces too much."

"Good. Good, good," I say with a nod, fidgeting with the seam of my blazer.

"And you?"

"I've been fine, thank you." Weirdly enough, I *have* been fine. A little lonely, which I didn't expect, but definitely fine for someone who was just dumped after five years.

"Good."

Just like that, silence fills the space again. For heaven's sake, we've dated for half a decade. We should have more to say to one another. He tries to act relaxed, leaning back in his chair and crossing his arms, but I know him too well to be fooled. This is as awkward for him as it is for me.

This time, he's the one breaking the tense stillness. "You need something?"

"Yes, I have … a question."

"Shoot."

"Did you tell anyone about what happened?"

"My parents know. And a few friends."

"I meant here. At work."

"Oh … Well, we went out for drinks after work last week, and I think I mentioned it, yes."

"What did you mention exactly?"

"That we're not together anymore. Why, what's going on?"

"Nothing, I just—I heard *things*."

He leans forward, resting his forearms on his desk, his expression one of concern. "What kind of things?"

For several seconds, I hesitate to tell him, reluctant to discuss my lack of sex skills. It would be an admission, and I'm not ready for that. "Actually, forget it," I say, waving a dismissive hand. "It's probably all in my head."

I take a couple of steps toward the door, but he gets up and joins me before I can open it. "Gen, are you sure you're alright?" he insists, his coppery eyes fixed on mine.

"Yes, I am. Sorry, I'm just a little tired today, and it got the best of me."

"You know you can talk to me, right? We're not together anymore, but I'll always care for you."

This should feel comforting, but it doesn't. If only he could care slightly more, we wouldn't be in this situation. "Likewise, Eddie."

Something passes between us, some kind of agreement that we're really over and we'll never be more than this. Friendly.

"I have a lunch meeting I need to prepare for," I say, only partially lying.

"Yeah, of course. I'll see you around, Gen."

I smile as a reply and leave his office without another word. For some reason, I expected seeing him again to hurt more, but I can't deny the indisputable truth as I walk back to the elevators. Our relationship died a long time ago, not on that Saturday. And I fear there's nothing salvageable.

My steps toward my office lack their usual determination because doubts occupy my mind. As Hana put it, I will need to start over and find myself a replacement for Eddie. While I don't necessarily need a man in my life for it to be complete, I have goals and aspirations for a family, and I need a man for that. As a very last resort, I'll do it all alone. But I would rather have someone to share it with.

All these thoughts are running through my head for the next few hours, making it impossible to focus on my business lunch. Thankfully, or maybe not, my boss has decided to tag along for the meeting, which means he handles most of it while I distractedly sit there.

That stupid list won't leave my mind, and the phone in my pocket weighs a ton.

The issue is that entering into another relationship right now would probably end as badly as the last. Men like sex, and my mediocre skills aren't enough, so my next partner is bound to cheat or leave.

When the luncheon ends, my boss hops in a luxurious hired car, not offering to share it even though I'm also returning to NexaCorp's headquarters. But it's fine, because it gives me some time alone as I ride in my own taxi. I have fifteen to twenty minutes to myself.

The solution to my problem is relatively simple, isn't it? First, get better at sex, try all those things I never did, and become a sex goddess. Then, find myself a nice, decent man to spend the rest of my life with.

Clear, concise, and straightforward. I can't mess this up, can I? And I'm sure I can have some fun crossing out those fifty questions, too. But that's all it must be—fun. I'm definitely not ready for anything serious again, not so soon after Eddie. But I also must ensure I don't get attached to anyone. And the most basic way to do so is by not seeing too much of whomever I'll experiment with.

One man per item on my list. Unless I can do more things in a single encounter, which would be rather efficient, wouldn't it? This is my one rule, then. No seeing anyone twice. That's easy. And I have the perfect candidate to start my quest—a certain pierced man.

One who manages to rob me of my attention despite barely knowing him.

Invigorated by what must be adrenaline, I pull out my phone from my pocket and make my way to Ladder Guy's number. Before I can give myself time to change my mind, I type a quick message and hit send in the same go.

ME

Are you still interested?

By the time his answer arrives, I've returned to my office and am already hard at work.

LADDER GUY

I am. But just as a reminder, I don't do dates.

I should give myself more time to think about this, but all it will do is make me change my mind. Staying in my comfort zone clearly didn't serve me well. This is something I need to do if I want the life I've been working so hard for.

So, after a deep breath, I ignore my trembling thumbs and send another text.

ME

> This won't be a date. You got the job, Mr. Clarke.

My heart is racing in my chest, and I can't help but wonder if I'm making a terrible mistake. But what's the worst that can happen? Ladder Guy turns out to be awful in bed? That would be a waste of my precious time, but nothing critical.

Just to ensure that nothing bad can actually happen, I send another text to remind him of my ground rules.

ME

> I'll need a copy of your STI test results. We'll meet at The Plaza again on Friday, same time. Don't be late.

Missing after-work drinks with my colleagues again should be alright, and I'd much rather cross out this item. At this pace, it would take me two years to go over all fifty questions, so I need to swallow back my worries and woman up.

LADDER GUY

> I can't wait to fuck this bossy attitude out of you, red. Though, I must admit it turns me on.

His reply is so bold that I feel my face heat up. I'm pretty sure this doesn't qualify as sexting, but I've never sexted before, so it feels very close to it. Something tells me he isn't even aiming for that effect.

I'm practically squirming on my chair as I type a reply.

ME

> You can definitely try, but I'm afraid it's a default setting.

LADDER GUY

> I'll try and succeed, even if it takes me the whole night. Can't boss anyone around if you've been fucked so good you can barely remember your name, can you?

Something pulses low inside me, and I cross my knees under my desk. Alright, I'll be sorely disappointed if he turns out to be all talk. But then, he wouldn't be the first man to over-promise and under-deliver. If there's some justice in this world, Ladder Guy will be good enough for me to enjoy some of it, if not most of it.

But ultimately, that doesn't matter. I'm in this to make that bucket list my bitch, and prove to Edward and Larry they are wrong about me.

I'm not a block of ice with a hole in it.

CHAPTER
Six

Jake

I'M TEN MINUTES EARLY THIS time. No way I'll fuck this up again.

I could barely believe it when Jessica texted me on Tuesday. The silence that followed our encounter left me quite certain the kiss ruined my chances with her. But here I am, sitting in the fancy bar of The Plaza, waiting for her to arrive. I still don't look the part and attract some curious side glances, but just like last time, I don't give a shit.

The beer is as good as it was then, but the knowledge that I might get lucky with the sexy redhead tonight makes it taste even better.

When the large wall-mounted clock strikes seven, a grin tugs at the corner of my lips. Look who's late now …

I'm sipping my drink when she appears in the doorway, just as stunning as I remember.

The anthracite dress she's wearing is a mix of business and night out, hugging her hourglass figure to perfection. Her feet are adorned by shiny black stilettos, and the ease with which she walks in them implies she has experience. This time, she has her hair up, gathered loosely in a high bun by a stick that I can see poking out on the sides of her gorgeous head.

Her eyes, so blue that I can see their shade from where I sit, anxiously scan the bar for me. I don't make a move, absorbed by her. The moment her gaze reaches me, I swear she stops breathing for a brief moment, her face turning slightly pink. She looks a little surprised, as if she expected me to be late again. Maybe she hoped I wouldn't realize *she* is.

We do nothing but stare at one another for a moment, then she takes a step my way. I watch as she approaches, her strides graceful yet determined.

"Evening, red," I greet her when she reaches me. "You're late."

"I know, sorry. The contract took longer than I thought to finalize."

The reminder of that damn contract makes me smile as she sits down in front of me. When she scoots her chair forward, my attention lowers to the mounds that bounce under her modest cleavage. While I know what her arse looks like, I have yet to discover her tits.

She signals to a waitress nearby, who's quick to come and take her order. "I'll have a lemon drop martini and a glass of water, please," she asks.

The blonde nods and leaves.

"If it's fine with you, Mr. Clarke, we'll review the contract together and get on with it," she pragmatically offers.

"We're here to fuck, red, so I think you can start calling me Jake."

That's all it takes for her face to redden, and I bite back a grin. I can't fucking wait to give her a real reason to blush like that.

Intrigued, I watch as she withdraws two sheets of paper from a folder and hands me one with practiced elegance.

"Are you a lawyer?" I ask, curious to finally know. From how she's acting, I know my suspicions are probably right.

"That's none of your concern."

I decide that she is, and for some reason, it makes me want her even more. Jessica, the proper little lawyer dying to try a pierced dick. *My* pierced dick.

With her hair up like this, I can admire the symmetry of her collarbones and the delicate column of her throat. It takes a conscious effort to tear my eyes from her enticing face and focus on the contract instead. "Consensual engagement in coitus," I read. "That has to be the worst way to describe sex I've ever seen."

"Keep reading."

There's a bit about the dates of effect of the contract, which she already dated from today to a month from now. Then there's a standard statement that we're both of legal age and of healthy mind and body at the moment of this contract's signature.

The first clause is about the sexual acts we'll engage in. Of the four dotted lines she's put there, only one is filled in. "Vaginal penetration by penis?" I ask, holding back my laughter.

"Something unclear about that?"

It should probably deflate my dick, but every time I look at her and see how adorably embarrassed she is, I'm compelled to show her what proper sex is. There's no way this woman ever got a good fuck in her life, or she wouldn't handle this matter in such a formal manner. It's supposed to be fun, not whatever this is. But maybe she sees it as foreplay, in which case, I can help with that.

"No, it's a remarkably clinical way to put it. The second slot should be oral."

The pink tint on her cheeks is slowly but surely becoming my favorite color.

"Which way?" she asks.

"Either way is fine by me. More than fine, actually. Strongly encouraged."

She writhes on her seat in a vain attempt to relieve whatever discomfort I triggered in her core. Her hairstyle allows me to appreciate the way her ears get bright red, betraying the naughty thoughts her mind conjures.

The intensity with which I want to fuck this woman is uncanny. Eli is getting nothing less than a medal for putting us in contact.

While she produces a fancy ballpoint pen from her clutch, the waitress returns with a tray and her two drinks. Once the glasses are settled on the table, she vanishes, and Jessica downs half of her water in one go. Then, in slot B, she adds: *Oral sex performed on genitals.*

"You can add fingering too," I suggest. "In slot C."

I swear I can hear her breath growing a little ragged as her eyes shift to my tattooed hands. She stares at them for several seconds, then shakes her head a little, stretches her neck, and writes: *Genital penetration or stimulation by use of fingers and hands.*

"What a fancy way to put it," I tease. "Ah, and kissing."

Her heated gaze lifts to me, and I suspect she'll tell me that's not allowed due to some weird idea that kissing would be more intimate than me being balls deep in her pussy. She proves me wrong, though. "It's such a mundane thing that I considered it a given."

"Kissing isn't mundane. Not when I do it."

Something flickers in her pupils, and I bite the inside of my cheek. "I noticed," she admits with a small voice. "There's a mention of it in the third clause."

Since I'm heading there, I quickly skim over clause two, which is about contract revisions. Clause three, titled "Health Requirements", stipulates that we both have to produce an STI result that isn't more than two weeks old at the time of the contract's signature. I take the test results out of my jacket pocket and hand them to her. After a quick scan of it, she slips it into her folder.

Then, the bit about kissing she spoke of. "If one of the parties suffers from oral herpes, kissing on the herpes-receptive parts of the body shall be excluded from the proceedings," I read aloud, not minding whoever can hear us. She does though, her eyes darting left and right. "I don't have herpes," I explain, setting the sheet down again to drink from my beer.

"Perfect."

"Since kissing is already included, that leaves us with an empty slot, doesn't it?"

"We don't *have* to fill it. I can just cross it out," she says, picking up her cocktail.

"But what would be the fun in that? Is anal off the table?"

How she nearly chokes on her drink tells me I might have gone too far. She coughs away the discomfort and shakes her head vigorously. "We're absolutely not engaging in that."

"Hmm ..."

Before I can come up with something else to put in there, she draws a straight line to cross out the empty slot. *Killjoy.*

"Clause four," she spurs on. "Contraception method. The participants are required to produce contraception to the best of their abilities."

I read on when she stops, and a smile tugs at the corner of my lips. She's on the pill, and I am tasked with providing one or more condoms that "must be the right fit, unexpired, and unaltered". I'm free to pick whichever brand I favor as long as "their products are reputedly qualitative".

Is it weird that this is working for me? It's giving me insight into her clever mind, and I kind of like it. I've never done this before, even though it's just sex.

The following clause is in case the condom rips. It demands that we both get tested again and stipulates that she'll take Plan B. I have nothing to add, actually reassured to read this. I'm not about to have a kid with a perfect stranger, and it looks like she's just as opposed to it.

Clause six though, poses a problem for me. "While consent to engage in coitus is given at the moment of this contract's signature, consent can be retracted at any point, even during intercourse," I read out loud. "Well, that's a given," I say with a shrug before I continue reading. "If consent is retracted, the participants must stop whichever activity they are engaged in at the moment of the retraction. The words 'no' and 'stop' shall serve as indicators of consent withdrawal." I wince, again sensing her inexperience with all this. "Those aren't good words."

I might as well have grown a third head with how she looks at me. Even though I know I'm right, her eyes make me feel stupider than I ever have.

"I disagree," she says. "They leave no room for doubt and couldn't be clearer."

I cross my arms and lean back in my seat. I guess she'll just have to learn it the hard way. "So, I am to stop everything I'm doing the moment you say 'no' or 'stop?'"

"That's how consent works, yes."

"Alright. I'll comply."

"See? That wasn't so hard, was it?"

What's hard is my dick. I'm already imagining ways to make her realize her mistake. Little Miss Know-It-All will learn a lesson whenever I get to fuck her.

We review the few clauses left, one of which is a basic NDA, and then she requests, "Your full legal name, please."

"Jacob Daniel Clarke."

She quirks an inquisitive, perfectly arched brow at me, aware of the fun twist. An amused grin tugs at the corner of my lips. "Yes, I got the ladder because of it. Might have just done a magic cross otherwise."

The way she squirms on her chair has me holding back a smirk. God, I can't wait to fuck her.

She writes my name down, slides both sheets as well as her pen, and instructs, "Sign here." I comply, still greatly entertained by how formal this whole thing is. When I hand everything back, she scribbles whatever's left to write on one of the pages and hands it to me. "This one will be yours."

I skim over it while she fills the second one, and I quickly spot an unexpected detail. "Genevieve Charlotte Kensington," I read, trying out her actual name on my tongue. "How sneaky of you, Genevieve."

"Don't call me that. Genevieve is for when I get scolded."

"Hmm … I'll try to remember that whenever you're being a bad girl."

She crosses her legs under the table, which brings a wolfish grin to my face. This is too fucking easy. I wonder if she can ever get used to my teasing. I hope the fuck not. "What should I call you then, red?"

"Call me Gen."

"Does everyone call you that?"

"Most people, yes. Some call me Miss Kensington."

"Oh, I like that better. I need to find you a flogger and a latex catsuit."

She drops her pen with a sigh and meets my eyes with a ferocious glare. "Will you stop?"

"Stop what?"

"Trying to turn me on."

"But am I only trying, red? If we're being *very* honest with ourselves, am I not succeeding?"

She thinks about it for the longest time, and I'm nearly positive she'll deny it. She's too prideful and proper to admit she's sitting in her juices, dripping for me and my dirty tongue.

For the God-knows-how-manyeth time since I met her, she surprises me again when she replies.

"What if you are?"

My cock twitches, my mind flooding with images of us fucking until there's nothing left but cum, sweat, and sore limbs. I'll wreck that pussy of hers like no other man has before. I'll dick her down so thoroughly that her world will never be the same.

This poor woman has no idea what she's getting herself into, does she?

"If I am," I say, "we need to get ourselves a fucking room."

Her eyes flutter while she takes in my bold statement. When she nods with her lips parted, I swear my cock gets even harder than it already was. Without a word, we both finish our drinks in one go and get out of our chairs. I fold my copy of the contract and tuck it in the back pocket of my jeans before I slip on my jacket. We make our way to the bar, where she pays for her drink, and we walk together to the front desk.

She looks tense as she books a room for us, so while the clerk processes everything, I bend forward to whisper in her ear, "You know you can change your mind anytime, right?"

"Yes, the contract stipulates that—"

"Forget about the contract, red," I interrupt her. I can smell the cherry scent of her skin, and as much as I want to head upstairs with her, I need her to understand she's in charge of what does or doesn't happen. "There is no obligation of any kind, no engagement, no commitment, and no expectations. We're only going up there, taking it slow, and seeing where it goes."

"This is light speed compared to what I'm used to."

"Look at me, love." She does, and when her blue eyes meet mine, I swear a wave of calm confidence rushes through her. I might be crude and terribly straightforward, but I'm not a bad person, and I hope she knows that. My intimidating physique and the rebellious attitude that sticks to me like a second skin aren't an accurate projection of the man within.

"You said you didn't do dates," she says.

"Fuck that. Because we met tonight doesn't mean you *have* to give me something in return."

There's a moment of silence, interrupted by the clerk who slides a keycard on the counter beside us. "There you go, miss."

But Gen doesn't look at him—only me. "What if I want to?" she whispers.

"If you want to, that's another thing, red."

I pick up the card, offer the clerk a nod, and we walk further into the lobby toward the elevator.

"You've done this plenty of times before, right?" she asks, controlling the faint trembling of her voice.

"Not this exact way, no. And not in a palace," I answer with a sardonic grin, looking around at the luxurious surroundings. "But I've had one-night stands, yes. It's actually my specialty."

"I'm lucky to have stumbled upon a professional, then."

My low chuckle is interrupted by the elevator doors opening.

"Do you want to do this, red?" The fabric of her dress is thin, and it serves as a mediocre barrier to my touch when I set a hand on her lower back. I can feel her warmth and want to rip the silk away until there's nothing between us.

She takes a bold step forward, following my invitation. "Yes, I want to."

We enter the confined space together, soon followed by more guests. They all look forward as we end up in the back and my hand returns to her waist. Once the doors close, I look down at her, mesmerized by her unique appeal.

"And you?" she almost whispers. "Do you want to do this?"

I can't hide the crooked smirk this compels. My palm slides from her back to her hip, and I clutch the curve of it to pull her closer to me. She complies with the command as I relocate her before me, and it's only when my hand slips to her front to press her against me that she understands my intentions. I'm hard as steel between us, my cock straining against my jeans and pressing against her arse.

I sense the shiver that shakes her from head to toe, her entire body tensing at the touch of my hard-on. My hand and fingers are still spread right under her navel, and I tug her even closer. Given how red her ear is, I bet she's as wet as I am hard.

"I think I've been hard since you strolled in wearing that sexy little dress," I whisper.

I'm bent over enough to see her eyelids flutter, her mind probably overpowered by adrenaline and lust. My hold is light, and she can step forward to put some space between us whenever she wants. It would be the right thing to do for a proper woman like her, especially since we're not alone on the ride up. Instead, she presses harder into me, the firmness of her bum squeezing my cock between us.

"And you, red? Are you wet for me?" I can't help but ask.

She gulps and says nothing, her cheeks flushed. "Cat got your tongue again, Miss Kensington?"

She shakes her head, worriedly eyeing the oblivious guests. Soft music is playing, and I'm speaking low enough so no one can hear aside from her. There's only us in this moment—us and the need we have for one another.

"Maybe you want me to find out for myself, then?" I suggest, the warmth of my breath fanning across the tendrils on the back of her neck.

When my fingers slowly descend down the fabric of her dress, her hand instinctively wraps around my wrist, adamantly stopping me.

"Then tell me, Gen. Are you wet?"

She tremblingly confesses, "Yes," and I feel precum seep out of me.

Jesus fucking Christ, I haven't even entered this woman yet, and she's already testing my stamina. She can probably hear the low groan that rumbles in my throat, given how she shivers against me. We reach our floor before anything else can happen, and I escort her out of there, people parting for my imposing frame.

We're drowning in silence as we walk through the hallways, the thick carpet absorbing our steps. Because I miss the soft waves of her red hair, I tug at the stick holding it together, sending it cascading down. When she glances at me, I'm twirling the stick around my tattooed knuckles.

Tonight, she'll learn what proper sex is. And I'll finally get my fill of this woman after obsessing over her for an entire week.

CHAPTER
Seven

Gen

I'VE STOPPED QUESTIONING WHAT I'M DOING because nothing makes sense anymore. Mr. Clarke—Jake—keeps surprising me, and I can't comprehend why I want him as much as I do. Is it narcissistic pride? Am I reveling in the knowledge that the most unique man I've ever met is interested in me? Or at least in my body.

His tattoos and cavalier attitude might as well be a giant billboard warning me not to approach. Everything about him should push me away, but I'm drawn to him instead. Why am I by his side, walking toward the room we just secured for ourselves? It's as though I'm on autopilot, and I'm not sure I want to take back control of my body and mind. I can't explain what's happening, but I'll have a lot to unload the next time I see my therapist.

Once we get to our door, it opens in one try, despite my trembling hands. Before I can step inside, Jake presses his hand to my back again, spurring me on.

The room is comfortably large, but not enough to ignore how oppressive the massive bed feels. Especially when Jake closes the door behind us. In an attempt to earn myself some time to relax, I come up with a simple idea.

"We'll take turns in the shower," I say, twisting around to face him. He's much closer to me than I expected, so I take a surprised step back.

"I showered right before coming." *Oh* ... Since he continues coming closer, his face inches from mine, I keep stepping back until I'm stopped by the bed. "And I can't let you get rid of the evidence, red. I want to see it."

"See what?"

"How much you want me."

This only causes more "evidence" to coat the lace of my underwear, and I press my knees together, desperate to muffle how my core aches. A lot. I want him a lot. Which is disconcerting, to say the least.

He grabs my coat and throws it on an armchair to the side. Then, his fingers brush against my shoulder, and he rids me of my clutch bag. He dips a hand in his pocket, and when he takes out two condoms from there and throws them on the bed behind me, I sense my face warm up. I'm as mesmerized as the first time when he removes his leather jacket, revealing muscular arms covered in intricate drawings. This is another reason why we're here. I want to discover it all.

When he bends toward my face with his to the side, I'm struck by a surge of cowardice.

"You-you said we'd take it slow," I remind him, flustered.

"Oh, but this is slow, red."

"Then what is fast?"

"Fast is me pouncing on you as soon as we passed through that door. Fast is me ramming into you within seconds, like I've been eager to do since I found you perched on that stool last week. Fast is you already moaning my name because I'm balls deep into your tight little cunt."

These crude, almost vile words shouldn't do the things they do to me. I should find them revolting and walk out because who is he to treat me so crassly? But in that very moment, as my body contends with desires I've never experienced before, I realize no one's ever wanted me with the intensity he does. And I've never needed someone so much in my life.

This is what Hana spoke of. This is pure, unadulterated lust. This is sex in its truest and most potent form. And it's about time I experienced it.

"Ah, then if this is slow," I say, pushing myself up on the tips of my Louboutins.

I see how my boldness surprises him, but he doesn't recoil when my lips meet his. It takes him a couple of seconds to gather himself, then all hell breaks loose.

His powerful hands slither on the silk of my dress as he wraps his arms around me, and then I'm caged in his tight embrace, my entire front plastered onto his. His head tilts to the side when he deepens our kiss, and the warm and wet brush of his tongue drags across my lips.

Damned be everything I know and who I am. For now, I'm whatever he wants me to be. Time to finally let loose and prove to everyone that I'm not a block of ice or a frigid bitch.

I part my lips, responding to his lewd request. A split second later, his deft tongue slips into my mouth, famished and daring. While he explores this part of me with adamant passion, his hands course over my body, tugging and pulling, igniting intense shivers wherever he touches.

This brings me back to a week ago when I panicked and abandoned him in the lobby downstairs. This kiss feels just as good as then, but the promise of what's to come makes it even better—if that's possible. It isn't just him trying to sway my mind in his favor. It's a preamble for the sex we're about to have.

My fingers climb up his broad torso, exploring the tight muscles over his T-shirt, and my hand slips around his nape while the other one grabs onto his shoulder. When his devious hands dig into my behind and shove me into his erection, a wanton moan escapes me. He's so hard against my core, the bulge alarmingly imposing.

Once more, his version of slow gives me a rush of adrenaline, like I just jumped off a plane and am free-falling. But I don't even have a parachute to slow my descent.

Heaven's sake, this is the most erotic thing I've ever experienced, and neither of us is even naked yet.

"You want this, red?" he groans into our kiss. Another moan from me, another shiver that spreads from my core to my extremities. When I don't answer, too overwhelmed for it, he pulls me harder against him. "You want my cock? My pierced cock?"

"Yes …"

"Will you take it all? Every last inch of it?"

"I'll try."

My answer, although genuine, triggers his laughter. It comes in the way of our embrace, but he finds something else to focus on. I stand still before him as he pulls down the zipper on the back of my dress. I let him, discarding my modesty, and when he takes a step back, I use the distance to admire his gorgeous features once more. He really is a magnificent specimen.

I barely notice when he pushes the straps of my dress to the side, but the garment falls into a murmur of silk. His pupils double in size when he takes me in, and I fight the urge to shield myself from his penetrative stare.

Because sex was the determined outcome of our encounter, I'm wearing the prettiest lingerie set I own—a cream lace duo that almost matches my skin tone. He says nothing for the longest time, his eyes ravenously devouring me. When he unconsciously reaches down for his crotch and gives his hard-on a pinch and a tug through his jeans, I urgently squeeze my thighs together. That part of him will be in me soon, and everything in me longs to fast forward.

"Fucking hell, red ..." he mutters.

"Your turn," I order, desperate to discover the rest of his tattoos.

His eyes never stop raking up and down my body while he reaches for the collar on the back of his neck. Then he slips off his top in one smooth gesture, and it's my turn to be in awe. Arranged feathers do indeed cover his shoulders, but his chest has a different design, something too complex for me to properly make out, given my advanced state of lust. I do notice the small bar in his nipple though, an eighth piercing I didn't know existed. Most of the ribbed plane of his abs is devoid of ink, as if he decided that the lean muscles there were enough art. They are like a Renaissance sculpture, a masterpiece made of flesh and skin.

"They said checkout at noon, right?" he asks, meeting my eyes again.

"Yes."

"We better get on with it, then. Otherwise, we won't have enough time for all the things I plan on doing to you."

My eyes widen at his statement. We have nearly fifteen hours before then. Surely, we'll have more than enough for whatever he has in mind.

Jake doesn't allow me time to respond, back against me in a blink, retaking my lips with fervor. This time, when his tongue comes to meet mine, I feel bolder and return his enthusiasm. As we kiss like we're possessed, his hands expertly unclasp my bra before discarding it.

As soon as they are freed, my breasts disappear under his palms. When he pinches both my nipples, deep and powerful jolts bolt to my core, making my knees buckle.

"Jake," I moan into his mouth.

He pulls away, and we look down at what he's doing to me. His big, rough, and tanned hands starkly contrast with the delicate cream color of my mounds and the soft pink of my tips, especially with the inky drawings tattooed on the back of them. It feels like we were never supposed to meet, but here we are, about to engage in the most intimate act two people can share.

"You're so fucking perfect, red. I was half-convinced I was getting catfished, but Jesus fucking Christ ... I'm beyond glad I gave you a try."

I never thought I'd say this, but, "I'm glad I made that profile."

When his lips return to me, they latch on my neck. He kisses his way down, licking and nibbling as he does, and when he lowers enough to engulf a rosy nipple in the warmth of his mouth, I finally get a glimpse at the intricate design on his muscular back. He has an enormous phoenix in orange and red hues that take up most of it, and its spread wings pour onto his arms and neck.

The sheer size of it is a reminder that we couldn't be more mismatched. But somehow, I cannot imagine him differently than how he appears before me now. Rebellious, unique, and brimming with sex appeal.

It takes some focus to think past the pleasure of his teeth, lips, and tongue on my nipple, but I reach for his belt, eager to see all of him.

"These stay on for now," he grunts, pushing my hands away.

"Why?"

He lets go of my tip and straightens to meet my gaze. "I don't want to scare you away."

The idea has me smiling. "I'm here for the piercings. I know what you're working with."

"Oh, sweet red. You really don't."

I'm still trying to process his answer when he lifts me off my feet by the back of my thighs and pulls me onto him. With just my thong to shield me, the hard bulge of his erection feels more real than ever despite the thick fabric of his jeans.

We're lost in our kiss when he lowers me onto the bed. The mattress is soft underneath me, but all I can think of is the hardness of his body over mine. And his voice … I swear I could get drunk on it. I've never been with a man like him. Not even close. This enterprise of mine is a novelty in many ways.

"May I initiate—No, don't do that, love," he grunts when I writhe my aching center onto his hard length. He stills me with a solid hand and resumes his request. "May I initiate 'oral sex performed on genitals?'"

God, yes! I don't even care that he's teasing me, obsessed by the idea of his mouth on that part of me. I nod, noticing the way his eyes darken.

Leisurely, he lays kisses down my body, torturing my nipples on his way to my core. I've forgotten who I am. My morals and principles are completely gone. He set them ablaze, and they went up in flames before I could even try to contain the arson.

When his fingers slip into the sides of my thong, his tatted knuckles brushing on my pale skin, I tense, my hands fisting the sheets so I don't try to stop him. He's about to see. As soon as the lace is gone, he'll see exactly how much I want him and how his dirty words worked on me. As if he's aware of this, he makes it last, slowly pulling on it. When the triangle of curls that I keep there is unveiled, he gives me a wolfish grin.

Yes. I'm red everywhere. I get irrationally mad whenever a man asks me if I'm a natural redhead. But Jake wondering doesn't hit the same.

He finishes tugging at my underwear, getting a second big reveal. To add to my embarrassment, I feel the fabric stick to me, completely soaked.

"Fuck, red," he curses.

My instinct is to hide myself, so I attempt to press my thighs together. But he stops me swiftly, hooking his hands behind my knees and bringing them higher, spreading me. His eyes are on my intimacy, unyielding, and I close mine to preserve my sanity.

"No, look at me," he orders. I comply, powered by a force deep within me. He's so big and mighty, so domineering as he looms over me like a threat, that I question again what led me to this. "You will look at me while I eat your drenched pussy."

He slowly lowers, never breaking the link of our gazes, and a realization hits me. His perfect physique, his striking face, the tattoos, the searing intensity of his light green eyes … He's the devil, isn't he?

And I just signed a contract with him.

The first lick he gives me is a revelation. It sends prickling shivers through my entire body, making my back arch. And he doesn't even touch that sweet spot but merely laps at my slit, where wetness has gathered.

The low "hmm" that rumbles in his throat, like I'm some delicious treat, nearly undoes me.

Then he licks me again. And again. And again. And my head quickly falls back onto the mattress with a long sigh.

Once I'm free of excess wetness, his tongue lazily explores the rest of me, and I brace for the sparks. They do come, but every time the pointed tip misses that one critical spot, I grow increasingly impatient. It drags slightly to the right of it. Then to the left. Then, he draws an arch that manages to miss it entirely. After what must be an entire minute of torture, I realize he might not be as good at this as I expected.

"Do you not know where it is?!" I frustratedly ask, pushing myself up on my elbows.

He barely lifts his head, his gaze now on mine. "Oh, I know exactly where it is."

"Then why do you keep missing it?"

His deep chuckle fans across my folds, making me shiver. "Because it would be too easy. If I start licking your clit, you'll come in twenty seconds."

I snort. Twenty seconds? That's unlikely.

His eyebrow cocks up as if I just issued a challenge. It seems I did because his face lowers again, and his mouth falls right on my clitoris, confirming his words. Then, he endeavors to show me just how wrong I was.

Oh, he does know where it is. And he also knows exactly what to do with it.

His lips maintain a suction that heightens everything, and the rapid pace at which he flicks my clit has me recoiling, struck by too much pleasure to endure. But his hands are on my hips, holding me firmly in place. Sparks ignite from my core to spread through my limbs and end in my fingers and toes.

With a whimper, my hand leaves the duvet to tangle into his hair, the thick strands soft under my fingers. "Oh God," I moan, sensing myself ascending faster than I can handle.

Twenty seconds wasn't that far off. Actually, I think his devious tongue gets me to the finish line with two to spare.

I explode, hips bucking, back lifting off the bed, legs pressing together and imprisoning his head. His name is on my lips as I orgasm, my entire body taut, my nipples hard, my core spasming. Wave after wave of bliss wreck me, tearing loud moans out of my throat. I've never orgasmed like this. Not with such magnitude, not to such heights. No man or toy ever brought me this amount of pleasure. In fact, I never suspected it was possible.

Jake never halts his ministrations, maintaining a quick and expert pace that drags and drags my pleasure for many seconds. This, too, I didn't know. That an orgasm could last more than three fleeting beats.

When it becomes too much and lasts for too long, I force my legs to part and try to push against his head to make him stop. This is too much pleasure. Too much stimulation. It scares me, almost.

He clasps his hand around one of my wrists to shove it away, and with his other hand, he—

"Oh, God," I cry out, my insides pulsing around the two thick fingers he harshly thrusts into me.

When he begins pumping them in and out, it makes it all so much better and so much worse. I'm pretty sure a second orgasm has seamlessly melted into the first one because I'm shaking and arching all over again, flooded once more by ripples of pleasure.

When his gestures slow, I thank whatever compelled him to. I need a break after all this. An hour-long break.

"Do you have any more complaints regarding my technique?" he cockily asks, moving up enough for me to see his wet and pink lips. I shake my head, distrustful of my tongue. "Good. Then let me proceed without interrupting. I need to focus on this 'genital penetration by use of fingers' thing. It's very technical."

This further teasing almost makes me miss the most essential part of his sentence. "Proceed?"

"That was just to get you relaxed. Now I'll show you what I can really do."

This time, he isn't as forward, leisurely exploring me. I quickly understand that his goal isn't to make me come anymore, but instead climb, and climb, and climb, until I'm a pleading and begging mess.

He gives and withdraws with perfect accuracy, pushing me to beg a few times. But as soon as I'm about to shatter under his deft tongue and around his clever fingers, he changes something that delays the impending climax.

While he fingers me with his right hand, grazing his fingertips onto that spot that feels so good, the other one twists and pulls on my nipples, inflicting another kind of torture. His tongue is the perfect mix of soft and rough, knowing precisely what to do with my swollen and pulsing bud.

After God knows how many minutes of this, I decide I can't take more of his edging. He'll drive me mad if he denies me again.

When he makes me climb once more, my fingers tighten into his hair, my hips lifting to press my core harder into his mouth.

"Oh, God ... Don't stop! Don't st—"

But then everything stops. His tongue is gone, his hands have freed me, and I'm alone on the verge of a devastating orgasm.

There's a glimmer in his eyes that I don't quite understand. "What are you doing?" I whimper.

"You used one of the consent-withdrawing words."

It takes me a second to understand what he's implying. "I said *don't* stop."

"Still said stop."

I let out a frustrated groan. "You know exactly what I meant."

"I warned you those weren't good words, red. You didn't believe me."

I press my lips together, refusing to admit he was right. But he made his point, and I now understand what he meant earlier, even though it made no sense then.

"Just admit you were wrong, and I'll continue," he demands.

Everything in me wants to deny him, but the precipice I was about to fall over is slowly fading away. I need him to finish what he started. "I was wrong," I mutter lowly.

"What was that?"

Asshole. "I was wrong."

He smirks, all cocky and satisfied, before resuming like he promised. Three fingers enter me this time, stretching my walls with their thickness, and his tongue comes down on my aching spot with precision.

"Yes!" I moan, shamelessly grinding onto him. "Right there—Don't stop!"

As soon as I feel his retreat, I lock my thighs around his head. "Continue!" I say instead, on the brink of orgasm. I can feel his smile on my core, but I don't care. I'm so, *so* close.

When I finally tilt, it feels like my entire being shatters into a thousand pieces. All the teasing, the edging, the delay ... It makes my release even more intense than the first two he brought.

I'm lost in a sea of pleasure, an abandoned ship at the mercy of the tumultuous waves of a tempest. And he's the one who conjured this mighty hurricane.

My mind is still foggy when he lets go of me, so I barely realize it when he releases my legs. But as he stands by the bed to open his jeans, the sound of the zipper pulls me out of the misty haze of lust. My movements are heavy and shaky as I lift myself to my elbows. I have to see his shaft and his piercings. I need to, for my own sake.

When he pulls his pants down, along with his black underwear, his erection springs out. And I forget how to breathe.

Holy ...

His penis is so hard that it's angled up, allowing me to see the ladder that led us to this moment. Six piercings are perfectly arranged on the underside of him, and then there's a bigger one that goes through his glans, from the sensitive crest below to the upper part.

It looks like a weapon, meant to hurt more than give pleasure—not only because of his sheer size, but also because of the jewels embedded in the flesh. His tip is wet, glistening with desire, but I barely notice it, too absorbed by the bars of surgical steel.

"So? Do you think that'll do?" he asks with a brazen grin.

Do what? Wreck me? Shred my vagina to pieces? Surely. But do I care? Not anymore.

I don't reply, but my expression doesn't seem to leave room for doubt. I watch, mesmerized by his nudity, as he finishes getting undressed, and then I observe with fascination when he unrolls a condom that he picked up next to me. It's not an easy feat, but his practiced gestures tell me he's done it more than enough times to master it. Once he's fully sheathed, he comes back on top of me and helps me slide higher on the bed.

I spread my legs to welcome his broad frame, and his gaze leisurely strolls between us, starting with the red curls at my mound, lifting to the pink tips of my breasts, and landing on my face.

"Time for my favorite thing in the world: vaginal penetration by penis," he teases yet again. He can't let it go, can he?

I don't even try to resist the temptation and slip a hand between us, wrapping it around his imposing girth. Blindly, my fingers and palm explore him. He remains patient as I do, his breath hitching when I squeeze him a little harder. The piercings of the ladder are quite spaced out already, and I see why four would be too few. With his length, he needed more than that.

"Do they bring you pleasure?" I ask, teasing the metallic balls I can feel under the latex.

"The apadravya, yes. Some."

"And the others?"

"The others aren't for me, red."

My walls pulse at the thought. I shouldn't be so ready to have him, not with the way I just orgasmed. But I lost touch with reality long ago, which is probably why I use my hold on him to align his head with my awaiting opening.

"Should we count them together?" he suggests, his hand replacing mine. My throat swells with a stuck breath when he teases my folds, dragging his round head up and down, the ends of the largest piercing adding to the sensation. Then, before I can beg him to get on with it, he presses into my slit.

The first bar of steel—the largest one—enters, and I can already understand its appeal. Then, a full inch sinks into me, and while he's thicker than anything I've ever welcomed, I'm too wet and aroused to find it uncomfortable.

"One," he grunts, pausing. Displaying an unexpected amount of restraint, he pushes further, enough to pass another piercing. "Two."

My hips jolt forward, compelled by an unstoppable spasm, and more of him disappears into me.

"Fuck," he swears, as surprised as I am. "Well, three and four, then."

He leans on a single elbow so his hand can still me. Seconds stretch, and I'm going half-mad by the time two more piercings enter me. There's one left, but I'm not sure it'll fit. I feel fuller than I ever have, my walls distended to their limits by his thickness.

Unhurriedly, he pulls out, the piercings rippling against my walls as he does. I don't expect it when he punches back into me, but before I can even gasp in surprise, he mutters, "Seven," right into my ear.

There. The reason why I'm here is officially accomplished. I'm trying a Jacob's ladder. I'm experimenting, being audacious and bold. I'm not so boring now, am I?

"Fuck, red ... I've been wondering if you were as tight as you're uptight. You so fucking are."

That makes my cheeks burn while I quiver around him. He draws out for a tentative thrust, and I feel his large jewel drag against my front wall. It feels amazing. Those mutilations I couldn't fathom now make sense. This is an upgrade, and the pain it must have caused him is worth it—on my end, at least.

When I stretch my neck up, he gets my silent demand and kisses me. His tongue enters me, mimicking what's going on between us. He's slow, but I can feel the tension of his muscles under my coursing hands. He's holding back, mindful of my lack of practice.

"Harder," I beg into our kiss, bringing my knees higher onto his sides to be more open. "And faster."

I swallow his crude curse, welcoming the increased pace and intensity of his thrusts.

It's clear that he knows precisely how female anatomy works. The rolls of his hips are sinuous, deep, and firm. Every time he rams into me, not only do the metal balls drag on my walls, but his base also slams onto my overworked clit, adding to the sensations. With his earlier ministrations, I'm way too receptive to these thrusts, and my oversensitive flesh feels raw, its nerve endings on fire.

This feels like nothing I've ever known before. It's like sex is a hundred times better than it ever was, like I've experienced it from behind a veil until now. But it's not just the piercings, even though they make this extraordinarily unique. It's him, Ladder Guy, the cocky, overconfident, rebellious man currently plowing into me. It's the tattoos between us every time I look down. It's his stupidly attractive face, his whole aura. He's what makes it so terribly amazing.

In fact, it's all so shockingly incredible that I end up exploding again, way too soon after my last climax.

"Aah, Jake! Yes!" I shout, ravaged by my orgasm. My walls clench and spasm, squeezing him and the jewels, shivers making my body jolt beneath his.

"Shit, red, I—Fuck!" he mutters. His thrusts lose their pointed precision, and the roar he can't quite contain tells me why. My climax took him by surprise and triggered his. My arms and legs hold onto him tightly as he punches into me with intensity. He's as lost in bliss as I am.

His grunts in my ear while his body tremors propel my orgasm to even greater heights.

Hana was right. Oh, God. She was so right. Great sex is worth everything.

CHAPTER
Eight

Jake

IT'S LIKE THE CUM SURGING out of me is bone marrow. Every rope of it that spurts into the condom feels like lava, searing, thick, and coming from my very core.

What is it with this woman? I can't get enough of her moans, cries, and sighs. And when she begs, whimpering my name, I feel like a conqueror. I suspect it's because she's so stuck up and formal outside of this bed. There's something about knowing that I turned her into this needy and desperate mess that flatters my ego.

That's why the foreplay lasted so fucking long. I couldn't get enough of her supplications, of her sweet moans and cries, of the way she arched and writhed. In those moments, I owned the proper little Miss Kensington. But by the time I was balls deep into her, I was already too far gone.

Three minutes. Three fucking minutes. That has to be a new record for me, but not the good kind. With one last grunt, I pull out of her pulsing cunt and roll to the side.

Jesus fucking Christ. I knew it would be good, but this is something else.

Just as stunned as I am, she makes no move to cover herself, merely bringing her thighs together. She might be clueless and inexperienced, but she isn't shy, I'll give her that. That tells me she's been having sex, but not the fun kind like we just did. For three minutes.

Fuck. I have a reputation to uphold.

When I look to the side to gaze at her pretty profile, I find myself wondering again what makes her unique. I've never fucked anyone like her, that's for certain. Who comes to a one-night stand with a contract?

She's also authoritative and demanding, which I find oddly appealing. In other words, she's *spicy*. But I think it's her lack of experience that gets to me the most. It makes me want to reach out and show her everything she's been missing, show her how fucking fantastic sex can be when it's done right.

But also, I long to fucking ruin her for all other men. From this day forward, proper little Miss Kensington will think of me when she's lying alone in the dark. She'll remember how good I fucked her, and take out whatever toy she uses and fucks herself with me in her mind. Whenever another man's inside her, she'll wish he were me, so he can make her touch the sky and see stars like I did.

For that though, I'll need to last more than three pathetic minutes. I guess the good thing is that my boner isn't going anywhere. Or barely.

"So? How was that?" I ask, my voice a throaty mess. Fuck, I hope her answer won't completely crush my ego.

"I—I don't have the words. I couldn't understand why you'd do such a thing to yourself, but now, I don't get why more men don't have it done."

So, I wasn't so bad despite the premature ending. "A lot of them do. You just have to know where to look. I think half the patrons at The Devil's Court have some kind of genital piercing going on."

"What's that?"

"It's a bar in Brooklyn."

"It doesn't sound like a place I would frequent," she says, sounding a lot more conceited than she probably means to.

"It seems you like fucking men that do, though. And if you give me a second, I'll fuck you again," I say.

"I don't think I can."

I chuckle, amused by how spent she sounds. "We haven't even started, red. You'll be leaving this hotel with a severe limp once I'm done with you."

She tilts her face so her big blue eyes are on me, slightly widened with incredulity. "It was just supposed to be the one time. I wanted to know what it felt like."

"I haven't even fucked you the proper way."

"This *wasn't* the proper way?"

Oh, sweet, clueless red. "Not yet, no."

I can see that my words trigger some curiosity in her. She's in for a surprise. Not only will I last longer, but I'll also show her how the piercings were meant to be used. Because that wasn't it.

Eager to get on with it and change her world forever, I rid myself of the condom, tie a knot to contain the fuck load of cum in there, and reach out for another one. Shit, I only grabbed two condoms before leaving my place earlier. But I remember reloading my wallet after I emptied my emergency reserve with that blonde from The Devil's Court, meaning there are two more in there.

While I'm wrapping my cock in latex again, I decide I'll make it last this time. Four condoms don't quite seem like enough with her, but we'll make do.

Genevieve's a little surprised when I settle myself on top of her again, but she allows it without protest, spreading her perfect legs for me.

The fact that she's never had decent sex before is madness. It's as though her body was built for this. Her breasts are generous enough to fill my palms, her body is flexible, and she's incredibly receptive to my touch. Maybe she's been waiting her whole life for me to finally step in and give it all meaning.

Time to uphold my duties.

"Get on your hands and knees," I order, rising up so she has enough room to move. She doesn't comply for a few seconds, and I notice the reluctance in the look she gives me. "Please, tell me you've gotten your back blown out before, red."

"I don't like that one. It's degrading and humiliating."

All of a sudden, her lack of knowledge isn't as charming. Instead, I'm mad at whoever the fuck gave her the impression that doggy style is either of those things. I mean, it can be, but it most certainly doesn't *have* to.

"Not when I do it, love," I say. That isn't enough to sell it, so I move over her again and grab her hand to bring it to my cock. Her slim fingers instinctively wrap around me, and I make them glide up and down my length. "You liked having these inside you, didn't you?" A blush creeps on her cheekbones before she nods. "Then you'll love it that way, red. Trust me, I know what I'm doing."

This time, she overcomes whatever bias she has and spins into action. My hands assist her as she arranges herself on her hands and knees on the mattress, and I take a moment to admire that side of her. Her arse is glorious, and the narrow dip of her waist gives it a heart-like shape. She has more freckles there, and like the rest of her, dark beauty marks are scattered in random places. If time allows, I'll explore them all with my lips and tongue later.

She's tense when I position myself behind her, so I decide something must be done before we proceed. Bending forward, I rasp into her ear, "You're fucking stunning." Then, my hand comes around her, dips between her legs, and I roll two fingertips over her swollen clit. When she shudders below me, I kiss the curve of her shoulder. "And so fucking receptive."

At the next roll, she instinctively presses back into me, into my cock that's settled between the creamy mounds of her bum. "We'll have to do this again someday, love," I say.

"We can't."

"Why?"

"This is just a one-time thing. We can't—Aah! We can't meet again."

I adjust myself so the tip of my cock is what's dragging onto her clit, and she lets out a raspy moan. "Are you not from New York?"

"Upper East Side, but that's not the point. I'm not interested in more."

Well, that stings a bit. But maybe because I'm not used to being the one on this end of things. I'm definitely interested in more of her, so I can thoroughly defile her in every way I can think of. I guess there's only one way to go about this: fuck her so good she'll change her mind.

I enter her without warning this time, ramming into her tight and wet pussy. We don't count. We don't go slow. But it's okay because she's more than ready for me. Her surprised cry goes straight to my balls, the pleasure in it impossible to miss.

"That's a shame," I say, straightening up behind her. "I was looking forward to fucking your arse one day."

She makes a reproachful sound, but I can feel the way her walls pulse around me. The Genevieve I met downstairs at the bar dislikes the idea, but the one in this bed is intrigued, curious to try. Those two sides of her are fun to explore and navigate. I've never met a woman quite like her before.

My theory is that she's been so brainwashed by her formal education that she's oblivious to her needs and desires. And despite what she might think, she has a lot of those. Maybe even more than average, if all this is any indication.

Adamant to educate her, I begin at a slow but implacable pace, showing her why we had to do it this way. The ribbed underside of my cock drags along her front wall with each thrust and retreat, causing a vibrating sensation that ripples all the way to her clit. If I had any doubt that this is the best way to fuck with my piercings, her reaction would dismiss it. She already forgot about not liking doggy style, pushing back into me, clutching the sheets as she makes the lewdest sounds. Her creamy, freckled bum slaps onto my hips in rhythm, and I grit my teeth, struggling to keep a lead on my own enjoyment.

She arches her back, giving me a splendid view of her puckered little arsehole, and I worry I might nut too soon again. Two condoms. That's all we have left. And then I'm done enjoying that sweet cunt of hers and her amazing body.

When I slow down for my own sake, she takes over and maintains the pace. My hands clutch her hips, but she's determined. "Slow down, red. You don't want to come again so soon, do you?"

"Yes, I do," she breathes out.

"What a demanding little thing you are. You want to come around my cock again?" She nods, and I regret not seeing her flushed, pleasure-distorted expression. I lower again, my thrusts sinuous as my front meets her back. "What would they say, down at the bar, if they could see you now?" I rasp into her ear. "You're not looking so proper now, are you?"

The question earns me a trembling whine, her walls spasmodically squeezing me. When my fingers wrap around her neck to force her to meet my eyes, I feel how much the gesture affects her. I won't apply any pressure because we didn't discuss this, but I love the sight of my rough hand on her delicate throat.

Her state of abandon is absolute, and I can hardly equate the woman below me with the one at the bar. I doubt she would recognize herself if she saw us right now, fucking like wild beasts. Her blue eyes are glassy, her face reddened, her lips swollen ... She's the embodiment of lust, the most outrageously sexual thing I've ever seen. She looks like she's about to pass out, overwhelmed by too much pleasure.

"Do you want me to stop?" I pour into her ear, my words as harsh as my thrusts into her swollen pussy.

"No," she begs, the word vibrating against my palm.

"*No?* That's a consent-withdrawing word, Miss Kensington. I must stop at once."

"Aah! Fuck you."

"Fuck me? No, red, I'm fucking you. Fucking your tight cunt. You're so wet, love. Can you hear it?"

For a few seconds, we both focus on the noises. Past the slapping of our flesh and heavy breaths and moans, we can hear the moist sounds my dick makes every time it moves in and out of her. With my free hand, I reach around once more and give her clit a soft pinch.

That's all it takes. She comes, trembling, moaning, and clutching at the sheets, squeezing me so hard that I almost follow her again. But I ride through it with gritted teeth, shielding myself from the sensations of her, from her sounds, and from the fruity scent that emanates from her heated skin.

Her climax lasts for endless seconds, and it takes everything in me not to give in. Which is insane because I already came like a madman minutes ago. But she's so warm, and soft, and tight ... Best pussy I've had in a while.

After one last moan, one last spasm, and one last squeeze, she turns limp in my hold, her eyelids heavy and her plump lips parted as she pants. My cock twitches, and I know the amount of precum gathered into the condom is embarrassing.

With a hand under her breasts, I gather her onto my chest and pull her in an upward position, half kneeling and half sitting on me, keeping her impaled on my dick. She's covered in a thin veil of sweat now, like me, and under my palm, I can feel her heart beating erratically.

"So, how was that, love?" Her head falls back onto my shoulder with a sigh, but she doesn't answer. "Was that good?" I insist.

"Yes."

"Was it degrading or humiliating?" This time, she shakes her head. "Good. Now, I'll make you come again, and I'll come with you. Do you think you can do that?"

She twists her neck to meet my eyes, the blue pearls of her irises filled with doubt and curiosity. I'm already wearing her out, but we've barely started. She'll learn a lot tonight. How high pleasure can go, how much I can give, and how much she can take. I'll push back her limits the whole night, one orgasm at a time.

"I want your cunt clenching around my cock, love. I want you to milk every last drop of my cum," I say. As if compelled, her pussy does exactly that, triggered by my naughty words. "Will you do that for me, red?"

"Yes," she breathes out.

"Good girl."

Unable to resist their tempting call any longer, I claim her lips again, dipping my tongue between her parted teeth. This makes her regain some autonomy, and her hand latches around my neck while we heavily make out. In unison, our hips begin moving again, and she rolls sinuously on top of me while I slowly thrust into her.

Already, I can feel the familiar tightening of my balls and know I'll have to fight with my life not to come before her. Fucking hell.

Who knew sex with an uptight lawyer from the Upper East Side would be so much fun?

CHAPTER *Nine*

Gen

I WAKE UP WITH A startle, pushing against the unfamiliar mattress to sit up. Everything is so foggy and disorienting that I might as well be waking up from a coma. As my gaze falls on a room that isn't mine, everything comes back to me at once, flooding me with carnal images of the most intensely sexual night of my life.

Ladder Guy.

Jake, the tattooed devil, proved much more accomplished than I expected. Heaven's sake … *Four.* We went at it four impossibly intense rounds. And I practically begged for it every single time.

I look around at the brightly lit room, searching for him. The side of the bed he slept on is cold when I reach out, and the sun is shining outside, meaning it's much later than my usual waking hour. Crap, I missed my Saturday morning yoga session. But given how sore I feel everywhere, it's for the best.

I can see that the bathroom door is open, but no sounds come from it.

"Jake?" I softly call out. Nothing. Not even when I call a second time, louder.

With a sigh, I fall back onto the pillow. He left, and I don't know if I'm glad about it or annoyed. I didn't plan on spending the night here, but after he granted me a break following our second shattering round, he took me twice again, and I pretty much passed out. The man's stamina was out of this world.

Now, as my core feels raw and overused, the magnitude of what I did hits me. I had sex with a perfect stranger. Well, I know his full legal name, but that's about it. And it wasn't just sex, but a cataclysmic experience that will leave me changed for life.

A coy smile slowly claims my lips as I stare at the white ceiling. I did it. I crossed out one item on my list. Well, actually, two. *Have you ever been edged until you begged to come?*

Now I have. And I get the hype. It was uniquely erotic to be at his mercy like that, a mere puppet in his dexterous hands. He denied and gave with precision, and I shattered more times than I can count.

To think I just had the best night of my life, and it was just two out of fifty on my list. Going through all the questions from that quiz might not be as terrible as I thought. All I need is a way to meet men for it. But that stupid profile attracted 153 of them overnight, so I'm sure that won't be too much of an issue.

Nested in the warm comfort of the luxurious bedding, I slowly drift back into slumber, exhausted from the intense night. With my eyes closed like this, I can vividly see Jake ramming into me with all his might, his tattoos glistening with sweat, his raspy voice uttering the most salacious words with that cursed accent, his piercings rippling against my walls ... Although it shouldn't be possible, warmth spreads into my core. I can't possibly want more sex. Not after last night.

Forcing my eyes to open, I rip myself out of my naughty thoughts.

"Siri," I call out into the vastness of the room. "What time is it?"

"It's eleven thirty-five a.m."

Crap. I need to be in the lobby by noon.

With a grunt, I force myself out of the bed. The lingering ache between my legs gets worse when I stand, and I notice how sticky I am everywhere. I'll need three showers to feel clean again, but a quick one will suffice for now. On my way to the bathroom, I retrieve my phone from my clutch.

Since Hana knew what I was doing yesterday before going MIA, she sent me twenty-three messages asking if everything was fine. I quickly type a reply, telling her I'm okay and will call her in a bit.

Then, I see a text from Ladder Guy, which he sent over three hours ago. My heart skips a beat when I open it and then speeds up as I read it.

LADDER GUY

You know where to find me if you change your mind.

I read it three times, standing naked and still feeling his influence all over my body. And inside, too. I'm definitely flattered that he wants more of me. I thought he would have had his fill after all that. The offer is tempting, but it feels like a complication waiting to happen. I take him up on his offer, and then what? We meet up once more? And again?

No, that won't do. I'm in this to explore and experiment, not meet new people, learn about them, and grow attached. The rule I gave myself, one man, one item—or as many as can fit in a single encounter—is the way to go.

Twenty minutes later, I'm making my way out of The Plaza, wearing my gray dress from yesterday and doing my best not to appear as sore as I feel. I removed my ruined makeup, so my face is bare, which I'm not used to in public. Next time I do this, I'll have to bring an overnight bag because this is embarrassing.

As soon as I'm into a taxi on my way home, I dial Hana. She picks up before the first tone is over.

"Gen, oh my God! I've been worried sick all night!"

"I'm okay, *Mom*," I humor.

"Where have you been? You were supposed to meet that guy again and tell me about it, but then, nothing!"

"I was busy."

"Doing what?"

"Doing him," I whisper into the phone so the driver can't hear. "Or rather letting him do me."

There's a long pause on the other side of the line, where I can practically hear the gears in her mind running. "All night?"

"Most of it."

She lets out a long, excited shriek, which forces me to push the phone away to preserve my eardrum. "I can't believe you did it!" she screams. "How was it? Should I beg Tyrone to get those piercings?"

"It was good."

"Could you sound any less enthusiastic? Was it meh, or was it mind-blowing?"

I sigh, rolling my eyes before looking out the taxi's window. "It was devastatingly amazing. I'm forever ruined."

Another shriek, another enthusiastic question. "Will you see him again?"

I hate how my throat clutches when I answer, "No."

"Why?"

"It was just a one-time thing, Hana. It's simpler if I move on to someone else."

During the entire ride, which thankfully doesn't last very long, she asks me more questions about Jake and my night with him. All she gets from me are vague replies though, because I don't feel like disclosing too much, fearing she'll read into it. But it's also in the contract. I'm not allowed to speak of what happened between us. Nor can I give Hana his identity to check him out herself. That, again, wouldn't be a good idea because she'd probably beg me to see him again.

As soon as I get home, I hop in the shower for a second time, feeling like Jake is still all over me. While I scrub every inch with a soapy loofah, leaving my skin pink and cherry scented, I can't stop myself from reliving parts of our night. Especially when I pass my hand between my legs, where I can still feel the ghost of his shaft.

His text, the offer to meet again, lingers in the back of my mind. Of course I want to. I'm not stupid enough to think that any other guy I'll meet will be as impressive as he was. But work and life are too intense for anything other than no-strings-attached, and given how strongly I reacted to Jake, I'm worried things might not stay so simple if we keep seeing each other.

Not that we could ever evolve into something serious. He couldn't be more different from me. And he's the opposite of my type, really.

So, once I'm out of the shower, I'll create a profile on a less unhinged dating app and find whoever comes next. I don't need sex gods to go through my list, just men willing to engage in sex.

That shouldn't be too hard to find.

ALMOST TWO WEEKS LATER, I have to accept that this isn't working as well as I'd hoped. The faceless profile I created isn't the problem—it's attracting plenty of potential partners. The issue is that as soon as they message me with those cheesy and reheated pickup lines, I lose all interest in them.

With a long sigh, I scroll through the conversations I've been entertaining so far. Three days of that were enough to make me wonder if I genuinely like men. The more I speak to them, the less I want them. That doesn't feel very heterosexual of me. Or maybe I just have standards that are way too high, and I need to lower my expectations to near zero. But I'm not asking for the moon, just for a guy that doesn't make my vagina dry the second he messages me.

I guess I could try harder, though. It's just for sex, after all. I'm not trying to build a life with these guys—just spend an hour in bed. Or, if they prove as exceptional as Jake, an entire night.

The fact that he pops up into my mind irritates me, and I look away from my screen with a groan. He's the real reason why none of this is working out. That's why I'm still at work on a Friday evening despite having connected with over thirty acceptable candidates. Each of them should be enough, but they all seem so boring compared to Jake.

I tried envisioning items from my list with those guys, but it only brings shudders and winces. In fact, every time I go over the list, I can't stop fantasies of Jake from filling my mind. *Ever had sex tied up?* I can see Jake expertly securing my hands and feet to bedposts. *Ever gave anal a try?* As scary as it sounds, given his size and piercings, he put the idea in my head, and I can't shake it off. *Ever tried breath play?* I imagine his hand around my neck like he did that night, but this time, he squeezes to rob me of oxygen.

It's actually worrying how often that last thought popped into my mind. I've become obsessed with the idea of his large, inked hands wrapping around my neck and choking me. Maybe because the gesture is so domineering, or maybe because I've heard about how good it can feel ... But this isn't normal. None of this is normal.

Several times in the past two weeks, I fantasized about him while lying in bed, trying to dismiss my needs before giving up and fishing out my vibrator from my nightstand. Out of pride, I stopped counting how often I masturbated thinking about Jake and his tattoos, piercings, and devious tongue.

He ruined me when he showed me what was out there and how amazing intercourse can be. I honestly would rather stay home with a bottle of chardonnay and a documentary than have the kind of sex I've had for the past five years.

Aware that Jake might not be the only man with something to offer, I open my private messages and tap on the most promising candidate. Owen, twenty-three, is a little too young for my taste, but like I said, I'm not trying to build a life here. He's a med student who doesn't have time for anything more than what I need him for. He's also easy on the eyes, and his humor is alright. But again, those are extras, not actual requirements.

This is just a leap I must take, and then everything will be fine. Like with Jake, this is the hardest part, and the rest will flow. After a deep breath to gather my courage, I send him a message.

ME
Hey, would you still like to meet up?

Now, I wait and see. Not too long though, because Owen is always quick to respond—another thing to appreciate.

OWEN
It's like you read my mind. I need a break from revisions.

ME
Do you want to meet up tonight?

OWEN
Yeah, if you're free!

I didn't expect it to be so soon. Then again, I like the idea of getting it out of the way. If I don't want to spend a whole year going over the list, I need to speed it up. A quick check of my phone tells me it's already late, so the evening will be well-advanced by the time I get home and change. I look down, gauging my outfit. I'm wearing a black dress with just enough cleavage—I had a meeting that required feminine diplomacy. It's enough for what I have in mind.

ME
I'm free. How soon can you be at The Plaza on 5th?

OWEN
Wow, that is way out of my budget.

ME
Don't worry about it. I'm paying.

OWEN

Sugar mama vibes, I like it. Well, I'm all the way in Brooklyn, and I have something I need to finish before I go. Maybe an hour or so? Or if you can't wait to get your hands on all this, I guess you can come over ;)

I pinch the bridge of my nose, taking a moment before I reply. This is my best option? Really? Before I can reconsider everything and put an end to it, I come up with a new strategy.

ME

I'll come to you. Do you know a good place to meet?

OWEN

Yeah, for sure. I'll send you the address.

"It's just for a drink," I tell myself as I gather my things. If I don't like him, we don't *have* to have sex.

I need to lower my standards, not dismiss them entirely.

THE NAME OF THE BAR is eerily familiar, but I can't quite place it. I rarely ever come to Brooklyn, and this is definitely not the kind of establishment I would frequent. It looks popular, so maybe an article mentioned it.

Ultimately, it's a good thing that I didn't go home to change because I'm already overdressed as it is. Everyone's in jeans, T-shirts, or plaid shirts, and most also wear leather jackets. This is what happens when I don't take charge and decide where to go—I end up in weird places. Next time, I'll stick to The Plaza.

While I wait for Owen to arrive, standing by the side of the entrance, I watch the patrons come in and out. It sounds like there's live music in there, some rock band playing. I haven't listened to rock since high school, so this feels like a step back in time.

"Jessica?" someone calls to my right.

It takes me a second to remember that's me, and I twist to meet Owen's warm brown eyes. "Hi," I say with a polite smile. He looks even younger in real life, but the scarce stubble on his jaw helps. He's certainly not 6'2" like he said in his profile, because I'm 5'7" in

102 УП ТНЕ LADDER

four-inch heels, and he's exactly my height. While I dislike the deception, it doesn't matter.

"Wow, you're gorgeous," he says, looking me up and down.

"Uh, thank you."

"You definitely don't look your age."

My eyebrows come together, unsure if the comment is warranted. I'm four years older than him, not an entire decade.

"Shall we?" he offers, gesturing at the door.

I nod, and we head inside. A hallway leads further in, and the music grows louder with each step we take. "Do you come here often?" I ask.

"Never, but I pass it all the time and wanted to check it out."

"Oh." I definitely should have been in charge then. We don't even know if it's a good place.

When we reach the crowded room, I worriedly glance at the people. It's not a bikers' bar, but it also isn't *not* a bikers' bar.

One drink, and then I'm on my way home.

Owen puts his hand in the middle of my back, pushing me slightly, and when I follow his gaze, I see a free booth. It's close to the bar and far from the stage, where four musicians are skillfully interpreting "Welcome to the Jungle" by Guns and Roses—a rather apt choice of song. A couple of coasters are on the table, and I frown at the slogan printed on them—*Good whisky, good rock, bad company*. That isn't a good sign.

"I'll go get us drinks," Owen offers while I remove my blazer. "Is a beer okay?"

"I would rather have a lemon drop martini. And if they don't have it, just a vodka martini with lime."

"On it!"

I sit in the booth, watching him elbow his way through the crowd. Strategically, this place wasn't the right choice for him. He looks terribly uninteresting compared to the eclectic patrons.

The numerous tattoos and other body modifications inevitably make me think of *him*.

Annoyed that Jake yet again bursts into my mind, I pull my phone out of my Dolce & Gabbana purse to distract myself. In the search bar, I write the name of this place, curious to see its ratings. Oh, it's a solid 4.6 stars, with over five thousand reviews. Maybe I misjudged it after all. I'm going through the pictures when someone smoothly sits on the bench opposite mine.

Before I can even look up from my screen, a deep voice says, "Look what the cat dragged in."

If it wasn't terribly familiar, the accent would be enough to recognize its bearer. My whole body tenses, the hairs on the back of my neck rising. Slowly, I force my gaze up, only to meet two light green irises.

This is why the name sounds so familiar. *The Devil's Court.* Jake mentioned it during our night together, but I was too sexed up to remember.

He says nothing, merely stares, and my skin prickles with a mix of excitement and embarrassment, warmth spreading from the inside out. He's right there. Out of some lousy karmic luck, Ladder Guy is sitting right in front of me, right as I'm giving another man a shot.

"I don't think I've ever met a lawyer who gets as tongue-tied as you do, red," he amusedly says after several seconds.

"What are you doing here?"

He cocks his eyebrow up, leans back, and crosses his muscular arms over his broad chest. The sleeves of his Iron Maiden hoodie are bunched up, revealing his tattooed forearms. "Me? I'm here every Friday evening, love. But you, why are you here? Were you missing me terribly?"

"I've barely given you a thought, actually," I boldly lie. I might get tongue-tied, but lying is something I've been perfecting since childhood.

His intense gaze darkens, his jaw ticking. "Really? You haven't been thinking about me fucking you? About me ravaging your tight and drenched little—"

"I'm here on a date," I interrupt before he can finish his question. Somehow, his cocky assurance pushes me to fight and show him he isn't all that. "He picked the place, so I had no idea we'd end up here."

Jake switches positions, leaning forward and resting his forearms on the side of the table, interlacing his inked fingers together. I can't stop my eyes from dropping to them, vividly remembering how they were inside me, deftly pleasuring me.

"You expect me to believe that, Genevieve?" he asks.

"Believe whatever you want, *Jacob*. The fact of the matter is that I'm here with someone, and I'd appreciate it if you were gone when he comes back."

"Why? Are you worried I'll scare him away?"

I open my mouth to reply, but Owen picks that exact moment to return with a pint of beer and my martini. I look away from Jake's cavernous gaze to witness his confused expression. "Uh, Jessica, do you know this guy?"

"Yes," Jake replies right when I say, "No."

I glare at him, far from being as amused as he is. "He was leaving," I say, offering a fake smile to the invader.

"Was I?"

"You were."

To my surprise, he chuckles, raises his hands in surrender, and steps out of the booth.

"Have a nice date, *Jessica*," he offers, clearly entertained. Then he pats Owen's shoulder harder than needed, which shakes him enough to make beer spill on the wooden floor. "Good luck with that one, mate."

The entire time Jake walks to the bar, my eyes throw daggers at his back. Something about his impunity stirs at my core, making me want to prove him wrong, to show him he isn't the demigod he clearly thinks he is.

"Small world, eh?" Owen says, tearing me from my thoughts. He's sitting in front of me now, and the first thing that comes to mind is how frail he looks compared to the man who was just there.

"*Too* small, if you ask me," I reply sardonically.

"It's nice that we got to do this. I seriously needed a break after the awful week I had."

"Oh?"

That's all it takes for Owen to launch himself into a lengthy monologue, telling me how his courses are too complicated and how he can barely keep up with his assignments. He picked the wrong person because while med school is challenging, I had it harder—a JD/MBA joint degree with a triple specialization in corporate law, international law, and labor and employment law. *That* was inhumane, but I managed.

As much as I want to pretend that any of this interests me, my attention keeps drifting to Jake, who stands by the bar five paces away from us. He's leaning back on the counter, his tall frame dressed in black, jeans molding his powerful legs to perfection, while his hoodie barely hides the broadness of his chest and shoulders.

To make matters worse, it seems he's decided to stare at me all night, his razor-sharp focus fixed on me every time I dare to meet his eyes. Under their influence, I sense myself growing embarrassingly hot, that space between my legs slowly awakening. Of all the bars in Brooklyn, we had to end up in this one?

When ten minutes have passed and Jake hasn't stopped staring, I decide I must do something about it. My martini is already half gone, and I empty the rest in three gulps. "Excuse me," I cut Owen off. "I need to get myself another one."

Without waiting for his reply, I slide off the cushioned bench and make my way to the bar, pulling out a twenty-dollar bill from my purse. Jake's impudent smile as I approach is hard to miss, and when I squeeze into the space by his side, he turns to face away from the room, too.

"How's your date going, red?" he asks while I try to get a bartender's attention. The woman is pouring a row of shots, and the man, a broad and dangerous-looking guy, is busy serving draft beers.

"Great. He's very interesting."

"Could have fooled me with how you keep looking in my direction."

"That's because you stare too much. You need to stop."

"Why?"

"It's distracting."

"How so?" he asks with feigned innocence. I glare at him but don't answer. He knows exactly what he's doing, and there's no way I'll inflate his ego by spelling it out. "Will you make him sign a contract, too?"

"It's none of your business."

The woman finally notices me and comes to take my order. Once it's placed, I watch as she prepares it.

"Did you really not think of me?" Jake asks, his voice like warm honey pouring down my ear.

The tips of his fingers graze up my spine, where the zipper of my dress is, and lustful shivers run across my entire body. When something pulses between my legs, I press my knees together, adamantly shushing it. I shake my head, aware that my body just gave the opposite answer.

"I see," he whispers. "I, for one, have been thinking of you a lot, red. Every time I'm fucking another woman, I find myself regretting she isn't covered in freckles, with fire for hair and legs for days. That taste of yours haunts me, and when I close my eyes, I can still hear your sweet moans, those whimpers when you begged, how you screamed my name …"

This time, I can do nothing to muffle the way my clitoris palpitates. Wetness nearly gushes out of me, my core begging to give in and accept the invitation he's so brazenly issuing.

His hand is on my hip now, pressing me closer to him, and I can't think past the lust to pry it away. "Ditch the boy toy and spend the night with me, red. I promise you won't regret it."

But I will regret it. One night with him and he's been in my head ever since. A second night would be a stupid decision because how am I supposed to move on then? It would be like tempting the devil, and I know better than to do that.

The bartender sets the drink on the counter before me. "Fourteen dollars."

"It's on me," Jake tries.

"No." I set the bill on the counter and grab my glass, eager to escape him. "Keep the change."

My knees are unstable as I make my way back to Owen. Crap, my enterprise couldn't have gone worse. I'm even more likely to get distracted by Jake's looming presence now, and my mind is filled with the lustful desires he ignited.

I still haven't recuperated by the time I sit back down, but two long sips of my drink are gone. Soon, the alcohol will help me relax, and I'll be free of Jake's invisible hold.

Owen looks tense, and I realize he could see everything from here, including Jake's hand slithering up and down my back. When he speaks, my worries are confirmed.

"You and the guy at the bar have history, right?"

My eyes instantly dart to Jake, who's looking at us again. "No. I mean—it's complicated."

"I told you I can't do complicated."

"He won't be an issue."

Owen discreetly glances at Jake, who gives him a dark, dangerous glare. "He looks like someone who owns a shovel and knows ten good spots to bury a body." I want to deny, but yes, Jake does look like that. "I think I should head home," Owen decides.

"Wait, really?"

"Yeah, it's better. You told me it would be a simple, no-strings-attached thing, but it looks like more than that."

"We can go to another place if you want. Another bar."

"No, I think—I think it's safer to leave it at that."

Baffled, I watch as he gets up from the bench and picks up his jacket. Is it cowardice, or is Jake much more intimidating than I give him credit for? Or maybe I'm not tempting enough to make up for the potential complications.

"Whatever's up between you and this guy, I hope you sort it out."

And then he's gone. *Gone.* I came all the way here, and he leaves like it's nothing.

I'm still trying to process what happened when a broad, familiar silhouette sits on the bench. Jake looks very smug as he sets his full pint on the table, pushing Owen's half-empty one away.

"Are you proud of yourself?" I ask, irritated.

"For what?"

"You scared my date away."

"I didn't do anything, red."

I snort, unimpressed by his failed attempt at appearing innocent. "You knew exactly what you were doing, with the whole ..." I'm unsure how to explain it, so I gesture toward his general demeanor.

"It's not my fault if he was a wuss, love."

"But it's your fault for acting like a territorial caveman."

He pinches his lips, aware there's nothing to reply to that. Because it annoys me that he thinks he can decide who I hang out with, I ignore him and look around instead. Out of spite, I want to find a guy and flirt with him all evening while Jake can do nothing but watch.

That sounds insane, but I can't help the crazy thoughts this man triggers in me. It's like he accesses the deep confines of my mind that I so fiercely try to keep locked. In his wake, I'm careless, impulsive, and uncontrollable. And I hate that. I hate not having a hold of myself and not being in charge of my mind and body.

I'm not that person anymore.

"If you're looking for a replacement date, you should know that half of the people here are convicted felons."

It works like a charm on me, and I swiftly halt my search, focusing back on him instead. "Well, since you're the reason I'm dateless, the least you can do is point me in the right direction."

He tilts his head to the side and gives me a look that clearly says, "And why would I do that?" Instead, he offers, "Spend an hour with me, red, and if you don't want more when we're done, I'll tell you which blokes here are worth a shot."

His suggestion is tempting, even just to move on after that hour and show him he doesn't have nearly as much dominion over me as he thinks. But in all truth, an hour might get the best of my resolve, so it's a risky bet.

"Half an hour," I counter.

"Forty-five minutes."

"Half an hour."

He smiles one of his lopsided smirks, and I feel it echo within me. "A hard bargain you drive, Miss Kensington. Half an hour it is."

And just like that, I made another deal with the devil. Whenever will I learn?

CHAPTER *Ten*

Jake

IF GEN WAS TRUTHFUL AND had no idea she was coming to the one place I mentioned, then I'm confident there's someone up there looking out for me.

I wasn't lying when I told her she's been on my mind since that night. For two weeks now, I've been trying to find that high again, to relive a fraction of the fun I had with her. But nothing's been as thrilling as fucking the uptight lawyer turned sex-crazed siren.

And now she's here, handling something on her phone, and I have half an hour to convince her she wants to give it another go. She probably does since her body language is all over the place, but she's too proud—or stubborn—to admit it. I have to get past those thick and tall walls of hers again. I did it once before, so I'm sure I'll manage.

"Alright, let's get on with it," I say, picking up our glasses and getting up from our booth.

Ah, I almost forgot how her doe eyes widen whenever she's surprised or shocked. "Where are we going?"

"The back room. This is too loud." When she hesitates, I give her an encouraging wink. "Come on, love. Where's your sense of adventure?"

She pouts as she shimmies her way out of the booth. She looks fucking gorgeous in that dress, her appealing curves heightened by the perfect fit. Because she can't help herself, she takes the lead and walks over to the back room, easily noticeable thanks to the sign. I don't mind, as it allows me to admire her perky bum.

The music there isn't as loud, and the ambiance is more intimate. There's a pool table in a corner, where two blokes are having a game, and low couches are arranged in private sections. I planned on us sitting in one of those, but the way she eyes the table changes my mind.

"Do you play?" I ask.

"I haven't in a while."

That's all I need. I head over to the guys. "Sorry mates, I'm gonna need the pool table."

They comply without issue, and I settle our glasses on a table nearby to retrieve the balls and start a new game. Gen is by my side when I look up, gazing at me with curiosity. "So, it's not just The Plaza. You walk around like you own the place *everywhere*."

I chuckle, amused by her perception of me. "Well, in this case, I own a third of the place."

"Really?"

"Yeah, I bought it from the owners with two mates a few years back. Eli and I stay in the background, but Kill handles it."

"Kill?"

"Killian. The tough-looking bloke behind the bar."

"Are you here a lot, then?"

"You're full of queries tonight, red. How about this: We play a game, and for every ball you sink, I'll allow you a question."

She considers it for several seconds. "Will I have to answer a question for every ball you sink?"

"That would only be fair."

"Not really, since you own this place and probably play pool often."

"Alright. I get one question for every two balls, so you have twice as many."

"Better. And I have one veto, where I don't have to answer."

"Let's do this then. Do you want to break?" I offer, pointing at the balls I just finished setting.

"No, go ahead."

I walk over to the wall to pick a cue, and she does the same, setting her blazer on a tall stool by our table. With her hip leaning onto the pool table, she watches as I bend over to break. My firm and precise hit sends the white ball rolling into the foot spot. Colorful balls scatter over the green felt, and two stripes sink.

First question, then. "What kind of lawyer are you?"

She raises a perfect eyebrow at me. "Why are you so certain I'm a lawyer?"

"Because I hardly see any other profession draft a sex contract for a one-night stand."

Her plump lips pinch into a straight line, and I hide my smile by going around the table for my next shot. "I'm a corporate lawyer," she eventually reveals.

"You work for a big corporation, then?"

"That's a second question—which you haven't earned yet."

Cheeky little ... I take my shot, expertly sinking another ball. One hit later, I have the right to another answer. I straighten up, give it a good pondering, and meet her ocean eyes again.

"What's up with the random hookups?"

"Excuse me?"

"No judging here. You're free to do whatever you want. But you don't strike me as someone who does that."

"Why?"

"Because you don't seem comfortable doing it."

The longer she takes to think about it, the more I believe she'll use her veto. Maybe I was a little too forward here, but I've been dying to know since our first encounter.

"I have a ... list," she reluctantly confesses.

"A list?"

"Of things I want to explore, of stuff I want to try."

"Sex stuff?"

She nods, and my dick nods in return. So, she's working her way through the ABCs of sex? And I was unknowingly part of it?

"How many have you done so far?"

I know she's a little overwhelmed because instead of telling me it's another question, she answers, "Two."

So, I was one, and there was someone else. Earlier, when I saw her with that guy, I realized she has an uncanny ability to trigger jealousy in me. But the way my body reacts to this is ridiculous. My hand fists the cue I'm holding, enough for my knuckles to turn white.

"Which ones?" I ask.

She looks up almost timidly. "Try a Jacob's ladder, and being edged so much I begged for it."

Granite. My cock's turned to granite. So I was *both* those things. Good.

Now, I need to get another two balls in there because I'm not done asking questions. It's getting tricky with hers taking up most of the space, but I manage one. To sink the second one though, I have to hit a solid first, which makes it a foul.

"My turn," she says with enthusiasm.

"Wait a second, I got two."

"With a foul."

"Still two, love."

She squints her eyes at me, unimpressed by my logic. In the end, she surprises me by giving in. "This counts as cheating in my books, but I'll allow it."

"How magnanimous of you." I lean back onto the table, its edge leveled with my bum, and fold my arms over my chest as I study her freckled face. "Did you really not think of me during those two weeks?"

Redness spreads across her cheeks, eating away the golden specks, and I know this gives me a better answer than anything she could say. She did think about me. Just like I thought about her.

"I'm using my veto for this one," she says, eyes fluttering to the pool table to assess the game's situation.

This is a strategic error from her; I now get to have two answers. To give her some space to breathe after my invasive questions, I decide to be lenient. "Tell me a random fact about yourself, then."

She's on the other end of the table now, and I watch her precise motions as she lowers to align her cue. When she looks up to meet my eyes, I read the mischievousness in them but also evident pride. "I grew up in a house with a billiard room," she answers.

With remarkable accuracy, she sends the white ball rolling—right into an awaiting stripe that falls into a nearby hole.

Never trust a lawyer. Especially when that lawyer has the ability to relocate all of the blood in my body to my cock, rather than my brain.

She looks at me from head to toe, trying to come up with her first question.

"Why the tattoos and piercings?"

"It's my idea of aesthetics. Why? Do you not like them?"

She scans my forearms, tilting her head to the side as she does. There's nothing but want on her face. "I don't hate them."

Then she returns to the game and easily scores another ball. "Do you have a favorite one?"

"Of course."

When I don't make a move, she sighs with impatience. "Can I see it?"

"It's not in a showable place, love. Not right now, at least."

Her cheeks turn pink again, and I don't hide the grin it brings to my lips. For the next ball she decides to sink, she has to lean far forward, which raises the skirt of her dress and gives me a delightful view of her long legs and perky arse. When she turns back to me, my eyes are high enough not to betray my crassness.

The next question she decides on is, "Since you own the place and are quite the manwhore, have you ever had sex on this pool table?"

It's so unexpected that I can't stop the genuine laughter that pours out of me. "Why? Do you want me to throw everyone out and show you what it's like?"

"No, I was wondering if I'll need an anti-bacterial shower after this. So?"

"I have, yeah. A few times. Kill and Eli, too. The women ask for it, and we're nothing if not gentlemen, so we indulge."

She grimaces and comes toward me for her next hit. This time, she bends over right in front of me, and while she probably expects me to move, I don't. So when she backs up to adjust herself, she ends up pressed right onto my cock.

"Do you mind?" she asks, half-irritated, half-flustered.

"Not at all, love. Go for it."

She sighs but stays right there, focusing on her game. Just as she's about to hit the cue ball, I lay a hand on her hip. It destabilizes her, but not enough to make her fail. "Why did you leave Australia?" she asks, turning around.

"I needed a fresh start and a clean slate."

"When was that?"

"That's another question, Miss Kensington."

That doesn't buy me much time, as she swiftly scores once more. Fuck, she's too good at this. I might not get to ask something else.

"Since you mentioned a clean slate, do you have a criminal record there?"

She's a little too perspicacious for my liking. "I did six months of juvie when I was fifteen. And they gave me a year in prison when I was seventeen."

"For what?"

"I fell into the wrong circles and became involved in drugs."

"Selling or using?"

"Moving it."

She thinks about it for a moment, and I hate that some dumb mistakes I made as a kid will affect the way she sees me from now on. I'm not that person anymore.

"And now?" she asks.

"I haven't been involved in all that since I came to America thirteen years ago. In fact, this place has a zero-tolerance policy."

The entire time she processes my words, her eyes remain on mine. I hope she'll see that I was a stupid child who was given a shit hand—not an addict, not a criminal, and not a bad guy. Just some dumb teenager who tried to crawl his way out of the gutter the only way he could think of.

"Good," she concludes, moving to the other side of the table.

A long, deep sigh flows out of me, reassured to see she doesn't seem too affected by my past.

"What's written on your knuckles?" she decides next.

Well, that's the perfect follow-up. I align my hands, one above the other, thumbs facing up, to show her. The letters there are blurry because it's old and on a part that doesn't heal well, but close like she is, she can read *EVER* and *GAIN*—an incentive to keep moving forward and bettering myself. Then, once she has read them, I show her my thumbs along with them, which transforms the meaning into *NEVER AGAIN.*

There's something genuine, an understanding in the smile she offers me when she looks up. "Is the phoenix also a symbol of this?" she cleverly wonders.

"It is. It might be a bit tacky, but I was young and wanted something big to remind me that I was on a better path."

We get lost in one another's eyes, and for a second, there, we're having a moment. I've made a small breach in her walls and am a step closer to getting past them.

Until someone barges in, displaying his usual lack of tact and sense of timing. "There you are!" Eli says. "Kill wants to know if—"

he notices Gen, and whatever he was about to say dies then and there. "Oh, hello."

Given Gen's expression, I reckon she remembers who he is—from his profile on the dating app. He, however, can't place her since he's never seen her face. "Why are you somehow familiar?" he asks after a few seconds, intently focused on her features.

"This is Jessica," I explain.

His expression lightens up as if struck by an epiphany. "Oh my God, of course!" He then turns to me and slaps my shoulder. "Did you finally grow some balls and text her?"

"Go away," I order.

He ignores me, turning to Gen instead. "He's been a bit of a mess since you two—"

"Elijah, I will smother you in your sleep. Go. Away."

"Alright, alright." He turns around but remembers he needs something, doing a full spin instead. "Killian sent you the program for next month, and he wanted to know if you'll have enough time to make us a poster."

"I will. Now, sod off."

He does, slowly backing up while his eyes travel between Gen and me, a stupid grin plastered on his face. Once he's gone, she looks up at me with an expression I can't quite read.

"Were you really a mess?" she asks. *Fucking Eli ...*

"You're out of questions, love."

Again, that doesn't buy me much time, as she promptly scores another ball. "Were you really a mess?" she repeats.

"A mess might be a big word for it. But I was agitated."

"Why?"

"Because I had a great time with you, and it was hard to accept there wouldn't be any more of it."

She's wholly unimpressed by my explanation, her auburn eyebrow lifting high. "So, the sex was nice, and you wanted more of it?"

I chuckle, entertained by the fire within her, like always. "*Great* sex is a motivator, for sure. But you were uniquely intriguing. You were as much a part of my agitation as the fantastic sex."

For a moment, there's only the sound of the rock band in the other room. Then, another melody rises. She reacts to it, walking up to her purse to retrieve her phone. Her screen is lit up, and the music stops when she slides a finger on it.

"It's been half an hour," she tells me.

"You set a timer?"

"It felt necessary."

As much as I hope she'll want to stay, I'm not convinced I did such a great job selling myself. "So, what do you want to do, red?"

When she looks around, I'm convinced I failed. Her blue irises scan the room, appraising her options. Since a deal is a deal, I look along with her. "Alan, right here, is a nice bloke. He does charity work around here, and I've never seen him bother a lady. Jared, over there, is pretty decent, too. Dylan though, that one with the red cap, you don't want to go near him."

"Maybe we should finish first," she suggests.

Right. She has the eight ball to sink, and then we're done. I'm still not over how good she is at this. She fucking wiped the floor with me. But that doesn't strike my ego as much as it does my interest. Something tells me she's full of surprises like this, and I long to uncover them one by one.

She looks mighty focused when she bends over to align herself with the cue and eight balls. It's a straightforward shot, so I doubt she'll miss it, but I hope for it. I'd still have two balls to get in there and earn myself one last question.

Her hit is precise, and as soon as the white ball is sent rolling, I know she nailed it. It knocks into the eight ball, sending it right into a corner where it sinks. When she turns around this time, she's uncharacteristically uncertain, lacking her usual assurance.

"What if—" she starts before meeting my eyes, her hands fidgeting around the cue. "What if I've been agitated too?"

I already knew it, but the admission feels grand. Slowly, I take a step toward her. "You have?"

"I have, yes. Restless, even."

"What do you want to do about it, red?" Now, I'm right in front of her, holding back everything within me not to rush her, not to take what I so fiercely want—what I *need*. She settles her cue down on the table, and her hands come to the strings of my hoodie.

She's torn, debating what she should do about me, about this insane chemistry that sizzles between us. Everything else disappears—the music, the patrons, the smell of spilled drinks ... All I can see are those beautiful eyes so full of questions and desires.

"Do you think we can do this and stay casual? No-strings-attached?"

"That's all I can do, love. I don't have time for anything else." My skin is on fire, burning everywhere we touch, and when I bend a knee, she spreads her legs just a little to allow my thigh between them.

"Me neither. So maybe you could help me with my list?"

"It would be my greatest pleasure, Gen."

"Really?"

I nod, touched by her lack of self-confidence. She's one of the most beautiful women I've ever seen, and she must feel how hard I am right now.

Time seems to have stalled, and I don't dare move for fear that I'll break whatever spell has fallen upon us. This tension, this suspense, drives me mad, but my soul feeds on it, reveling in the knowledge that I might be inside her again.

When she pulls up the hood of my hoodie, I think she's fidgeting again. But then, once it's secured on my head, she grabs onto the sides and tugs me down, lowering my lips onto her awaiting mouth. My hand instantly reaches around her slim figure, holding her close as I deepen the shy kiss she initiated.

Safely hidden in the small alcove of my hood that she firmly keeps down, we lose ourselves in the moment, getting reacquainted with one another. She isn't shy anymore when I unlock my jaw, her warm tongue coming to meet mine in its territory.

I've been wondering if the memory of what happened between us wasn't altered for some reason, questioning if I could really have reacted so strongly to the proper little Miss Kensington. But as we kiss and devour each other in the middle of the back room of The Devil's Court, I realize that no, I didn't imagine this intense attraction or the magnitude of the sparks she ignites. In fact, those memories might have been dulled because I don't remember ever feeling this entranced by anyone before.

When my thigh presses harder on that heated space between her legs, she lets out a delicious moan that goes straight to my balls. It seems I'm not the only one who forgot we're not alone, an easy feat, given how isolated we feel under my hood.

"Red, slow down."

"I want you," she breathes out.

"I want you too. Do you—How do you want tonight to go?"

"Maybe we could start working on my list," she suggests, her pupils three times their size, her arousal unmistakable.

"Order, and I shall obey, love."

"How about sex in a public place?"

I chuckle, appreciative of her enthusiasm. "Should I throw everyone out and fuck you on that pool table, after all?"

She shakes her head, her lush hair dancing with the gesture. "Don't you have a more isolated place in mind?"

I do. In fact, I have the perfect place for this. But before that, I need more of her. She's feeling the same way because she pulls me down at the exact moment I lower to reclaim her lips.

CHAPTER *Eleven*

Gen

JAKE IS QUICK TO LEAD me down a short hallway where the restrooms are located. But instead of picking one of those, he pushes open a door with a baby on it.

As soon as we're in the room, he locks the door and plasters me to it, his lips falling on mine again. I barely have time to notice the large mirror on a wall and a counter that must serve as a baby changing station.

I can't believe I'm doing this. His influence on me goes beyond anything I've ever known, and with every minute I spend with him, it only grows stronger. Before we started that game of pool, I was certain I'd rebuke him and leave him high and dry. But as we caress and grope each other in the isolated space he picked, I realize how stupid of me that was. I'm not equipped to refuse him. He's too intense, too irresistible.

His hands fist the skirt of my dress and I feel him pull it up, the fabric resisting around my hips before bending to his will and rising to my waist.

Never breaking our kiss, he grabs me by the back of my thighs and lifts me. When he pushes me against the door with my legs wrapped around his waist, I let out a wanton moan, overwhelmed by the sensation of his shaft pressing onto my sensitive core. He is hard against me, as eager as I am to get it started.

"Aah, Jake," I whimper when he starts grinding into me.

"You want this? You want me inside you? You want me to make you come around my cock again?"

"You know I do."

"Then say it, sweet red. Say you want me to fuck you."

I'm torn between glaring at him and complying so we can move on. He knows exactly how to push my buttons, and it annoys me that I have no idea how to push his. But I'm here to experiment after all, so I might as well do just that.

I run my manicured nails through the short hair at the back of his head, bringing my lips closer to his ear. "You have no idea how much I've thought about this, Jake. About you filling my tight little pussy, about you ravaging me with your huge cock, about you leaving me spent, and used, and sore for days." I take a break, shocked by my own crassness. I never use such words, but this is all a game, isn't it? We're only having fun. And it's working, given the way he grunts and gives me a hard shove, his hips bucking of their own will.

Hiding my smile, I nip the lobe of his ear, sucking on it, gently nibbling. "You did, you know?" I whisper.

"What?"

"Leave me sore. I could feel you inside me every time I sat. I could feel the pumping, the stretching, the orgasms … You ruined me, Jake. And I think it's about time you do it again."

That conquers him, and he rips me away from the door and spins me around. When he sits me on the counter, my hands fly to his belt, desperate to get it undone.

I don't have time to do that though, because he easily slides me closer to the edge and kneels before me, lifting my thighs over his shoulders so he can bring his head between my parted legs. I'm still wearing my underwear, but it doesn't get in the way of his enthusiasm. His tongue runs over the drenched La Perla thong and goes straight to my clit, which he immediately finds despite the thin barrier.

"Ah, yes!" I moan, arching against the mirror.

He does everything right, sucking, licking, and teasing, but the fabric alters his touch, muffling the sensations. Since he isn't making an effort to remove it, I'm the one who does, shoving the lace to the side, baring my folds to him. His tongue ignites sparks that make me bite my lower lip, worried someone might hear if I'm too loud. We can distinguish the faint music of the band on the other side of the bar, which means this room isn't soundproof.

"No, let me hear it," he commands, pulling away just enough to utter the order.

"What if someone—"

"Let them. Let them hear how much you like when I lick your cunt, and then how much you love when my cock's crammed into you. But most of all, let them hear how hard I make you come."

He returns to his sweet torture before I can reply, and I internally debate his lewd request. Those people out there are nothing to me. Why should I care so much about what they hear? I'll never see them again, anyway.

I don't exactly have a choice in the matter because when Jake shoves his tongue inside me, I lose the ability to hold anything back. A girl could sell her soul for a tongue like his. While he pumps it in and out, his hand reaches around so he can roll the flesh of his thumb onto my clit with precise circles.

With my hand gripping his thick, dark strands, I let out a loud, trembling cry. When I look down, the green of his eyes is on me, looking up with mischievousness as if he knows exactly what he's doing to me. He's too good at this.

He's my only option, isn't he? No other man will be as competent for that stupid list. It's him or no one. Ladder Guy.

Just when I think it couldn't get any better, he switches things around, licking my clit and shoving two thick and long fingers inside me, curling them to graze that part that feels so fucking good.

"Ah, yes! Right there," I cry out, oblivious to the people outside, to the music, to everything that isn't him.

With uncanny precision, he makes me climb and climb. My core tightens, the pressure rises, my legs tremble over his broad shoulders … I'm going to come hard, to shatter under his tongue and around his fingers. How is he so good at this?

Just as I'm about to tip over, he pulls away. Distraught and confused, frustrated by the receding climax he was about to grant me, I stare as he rises from his kneeling position, a smirk tugging at the corner of his lips. *Bastard.*

"You have to stop doing this," I mutter, glaring at him while he fumbles with his belt.

"I want to be balls deep inside you when you come, red. I want to feel you squeezing me."

Within seconds, he's freed himself, and my mouth waters at the sight of his magnificent erection. Since when are penises beautiful? I never saw them as more than a somewhat sentient appendage, but Jake's is perfect—straight, long, and thick. For the first time, I look past the piercings and admire *him*. The plump head is pink and swollen, glistening with precum, and below it, the sinuous veins that lead to it are bulging, dancing under thin skin. I watch as he rolls a condom down his bejeweled length, almost regretting that there needs to be latex between us.

The thought is quickly dismissed when I welcome him into the cradle of my thighs as he steps forward, and I shiver when his fingers slip close to my folds to push the thong further out of the way.

"Do I need to sign something before I enter you?" he asks, pressing the head of his latex-sheathed shaft onto me.

"No, the contract is still valid."

"Brilliant."

He goes slowly but unstoppably, his girthy length sinking into me. I can feel the piercings as he does, remembering how good they felt when he rammed in and out of me with intensity. We don't kiss, staring into each other's eyes as he enters me, which makes the moment strangely intimate. It's like I feel him in my body and in my soul.

When his advance is restricted by my recalcitrant flesh, he slowly pulls out and then dips back inside further. Unable to stop myself, I look down, proud to see I'm almost taking him whole despite his impressive size. The way my thong is bunched to the side is a novelty for me, as I never had sex entirely dressed before. His gaze drops to where we join too, and when he retreats to the tip, we both see just how drenched I am, the latex coated with my arousal. It takes three more careful thrusts, and then he's fully buried in me, the trimmed dark hair at his base meeting my dampened red curls.

"Fuck, you feel fucking amazing," he groans.

"And I don't even need piercings for that."

I'm the one who initiates the following kiss, swallowing his chuckle, and while I'm absorbed by the way our tongues tangle and mingle, he slowly starts pumping in and out of me. *God, it feels incredible.*

The stretch comes with a slight amount of discomfort, but I don't mind. It makes it all feel more real, and it makes the round ends of his numerous piercings drag on my walls deliciously. I'm full of him, and I miss the feeling every time he retreats, only to be satisfied again.

"You're so fucking warm," he rasps into my ear. "And so fucking tight."

His pace changes, as well as his angle and amplitude. A mewl flies out of my lips as the head of him drags onto my front wall. Once more, I'm amazed by how well he knows female anatomy. That truth becomes even more glaring when one of his hands leaves my hip to dip between us and tease my sensitive crest.

"Jake," I whimper, my nails digging into his shoulders through his thick hoodie.

Desperate to get more of him, I pull on the fabric, silently asking him to take it off. He quickly understands and removes it, along with what's underneath, before discarding it on the counter next to us. His momentum never wavers, and my eyes glide down the perfection of his torso, the muscles, the tattoos, and land on the piercing in his nipple.

When his thumb returns to my clitoris, it all becomes too much. Sparks shoot up my spine, spawning from my core. My legs begin to tremble again, hooked around his narrow hips. "I'm gonna come," I moan.

"I know, I can feel your pussy throb. Come, red. Come for me."

And I do. I'm not sure if it's because he ordered it or because of the baritone pitch, but I explode around him, my hands gripping his solid shoulders, nails clawing at the tattooed skin.

Jake shows no mercy, plowing into me as I come, his strong hands keeping me in place despite the bucking of my hips. And when I press my mouth onto his shoulder to muffle my moans, he grabs a handful of my hair and harshly tugs on it, forcing my soft cries to echo in the small room. The jolt of pain it triggers in my scalp travels down my spine to end in my core, making my walls clamp harder.

"Let them hear," he demands, ravishing me with deeper thrusts. "Let them hear how much you enjoy my cock."

His crude words propel me to even greater heights, and I can't hold back the strangled cry that escapes me as my walls pulse tightly around him. This is why sex in a public place is on the list. The possibility of being caught or heard makes everything that much more thrilling. I'm lost in Jake's embrace, and anyone outside might hear us.

I should hate it and be embarrassed, but I'm neither of those things. I'm invigorated, shaken by an unrelenting orgasm.

But it eventually relents, and Jake slows down just enough to let me catch my breath. My head falls back with a long sigh when he comes to a full stop, and my hooded eyes meet his green ones.

"You didn't come," I breathe out, realizing it just now.

"Not yet."

"You're like a machine."

He chuckles, which makes his length shift inside my spent center. "You're the one who comes too easily, love."

"That was never an issue before."

His cocky smile reminds me that I shouldn't stroke his ego. It's potent enough as is.

"Are you really complaining about my abilities, Miss Kensington?"

I don't answer, pushing against his torso instead, my pale hand a stark contrast with the dark design inked there—a flaming heart with two hands that seem to cup it among an intricate nest of thorns and roses spread across the width of his pecs. He follows my silent order and slips out of me to take a couple of steps back. Before he can worry that I consider this done, I slide down the counter on wobbly legs and spin around.

Our eyes meet in the mirror I'm now facing, and when I bend over, I notice how his pupils dilate. "Not finding it so degrading now, are we?" he asks with unmasked cockiness.

Never breaking the link of our gazes, I pull my dress higher on my waist, arching my back in a manner I hope is seductive. It seems to be because he comes back against me, his index and middle finger fishing out my thong from my behind to stretch it all the way to the side.

When he fists himself and drags the round head of his erection on my dampened folds, my eyelids flutter. "How many items are on your list?" he asks.

"Fifty. But I'm not doing some of them because they are too much."

My eyes widen when his shaft slides right over the taut hole too far back. This is an item, but if Jake's the one I'm doing everything with, it will likely go in the "nope" pile. I'm not letting his enormous penis ruin that part of me.

All my doubts fall into nothingness when he aligns himself with my drenched opening and slides in with ease. In this position, the sensation of the ladder is incredible.

"Aah, yes," I moan, bracing myself with a hand on the mirror.

He wastes no time mounting me, and I watch him doing it, reveling in the sight. He looks mighty and dangerous, especially with that rough expression. It seems I'm as enjoyable as he is, and it's a great compliment.

He rams into me with maddening intensity, his hips slapping against my ass and the back of my thighs every time he does, the metallic sound of his belt echoing in rhythm.

When his heavy breaths slowly turn into groans, I know he's nearing his climax. But he doesn't want to come alone because he straightens me up, one of his inked hands wrapping around my throat while the other palms my heaving breasts.

"Can you come for me again, red?"

"I don't know," I whimper.

"Do you need help?"

His shaft is still hammering into me with precision, my insides aching for one more release. I look at us in the mirror, barely recognizing myself. My face is flushed, my eyes glassy, and my lips parted with never-ending moans and pants. His big bad hand on my throat is like a looming threat, like a glorious promise. I've thought of this these past two weeks, of him choking me, of trying out that item from the quiz with him. But it's such a taboo act that I don't know if I'll ever have the courage to ask for it.

"Choke me," I impulsively beg. I don't give my brain time to think about this. I don't question whether I should allow a near-stranger to perform such a violent act on me in the back room of a shady bar. I just ask for it, hoping he'll comply because I might never have the absence of mind to do it again.

"Fuck, Gen," he curses, his hips bucking hard. "We didn't sign on this."

"I don't care. Please, Jake ..."

Maybe it's something in the look I give him, maybe my plea works, but he releases another curse and adjusts his hand around my neck. "I will go slow. If you need me to stop, tap on my arm," he instructs. Just like that, I understand he's the right man for this.

Despite being lost in the throes of passion, he knows what he's doing and makes it safe.

The slapping of his hips on my ass never stops as the pressure of his palm and fingers increases on that delicate part of me. He doesn't push against the front of my throat but on the sides, which I guess is to restrict the arteries' oxygen flow.

There's something about the gesture that hits some kink deeply hidden within me. The dominating aspect of it is overwhelming, even more than the sense of helplessness that slowly seeps into me as survival instinct kicks in. I'm at his mercy, my entire life literally in his hand. He could kill me or leave me unconscious. I'm in more danger than I've ever been, but I somehow feel safe.

I've also never felt so alive. It's exhilarating.

The hand teasing my nipple, pinching and twisting it over my dress and bra, travels south. I watch in the mirror as his tattooed fingers reach between my legs, past the triangle of red curls, and begin to roll around my clit in tight circles. I can't believe how greedy he makes me, but I press harder onto him with each thrust to take everything and more. My hand covers his between my legs, so pale and delicate against his tattoos.

I mewl his name, the sound coming out as a strangled mess, and his eyes darken in the reflection. His grip tightens until I can't breathe anymore, not even shallow gasps. Adrenaline bursts through me, triggered by the heightened sense of danger, and that sets off my orgasm. The instant I tilt, the moment my insides clench around him, he releases my throat and wraps a solid arm around my middle instead.

Suddenly, I can breathe. And it all becomes overwhelming. Between the orgasm that ravages me and the oxygen that returns to my brain, I'm feeling everything at once. My mind goes blank, consumed by pleasure, and shivers, and jolts of pure, untamable bliss. As far gone as I am, I still hear the groan that rumbles out of his throat as his hammering shaft stops to pull out of me, leaving nothing but pulsing and empty soreness behind.

I hear the snap of the latex when he tugs at the condom, and then I see his reflection grab himself to jack off. In seconds, he roars as the first splash of his orgasm lands on my bare behind. More of it comes, hot and thick against my skin, and it somehow triggers more quivers and jolts within me.

When Jake lets out one last whimper and drags the head of his shaft on me as if to wipe off the last drop of his cum, I know he's done. His forehead comes to rest against my shoulder, and I feel the warmth of his breath fanning on the flimsy fabric of my dress. The moment stretches until I'm done shivering, satiated beyond words, with nothing but our hectic breaths to fill the void. *Jesus.* That was amazing.

"That's one more off your list," he says, his voice low and raspy.

"There was more than one."

"Oh?"

"Give my brain a second."

He's close enough for me to feel his penis gradually soften against my lower back. While I try to regain my senses, he pushes away my messy hair and drops a series of soft kisses along the slope of my neck. When he licks the soft spot right behind my ear, I let out one last trembling whimper and feel myself clench an ultimate time.

He approvingly hums in my ear, gives my throat one last kiss, and retreats.

I watch his reflection as he throws the condom in the trash can under the counter. There's a bag of wet wipes by the mirror, but when he reaches for one, it's empty. After a mumbled curse, he looks around to find an alternative. I'm too dickmatized to help him out, so I watch, still dazed by my orgasm, as he pulls his T-shirt out of his hoodie and uses it to clean me up. He's thorough, wiping every last drop of his cum off my skin, and I silently enjoy the softness of the moment. Eddie was never into aftercare, and I appreciate that Jake doesn't mind cleaning up his own mess. Once he's done with me, he dries himself before staring down at the soiled garment for a second, wondering what to do with it.

"Fuck it," he mumbles, throwing it in the trash. While he shoves himself back into his pants, I realign my underwear before pulling down my dress.

"Why do you guys have a baby changing station in your bar?" I ask, only realizing now that it's an odd perk in such an establishment.

"Well, it's officially a changing station, but unofficially, it's the baby-making room," he says with amusement.

"Really?"

"Yeah. The counter can withstand up to three hundred pounds, and the mirror is for added fun," he explains with a wink.

I look around the small room with a new eye. Knowing I'm just one more woman he dragged in here for sex makes me feel dirty somehow. He's so good at making me feel unique during those moments of passion that I forget that for him, I'm just one more face in a sea of conquests. A twinge of resentment starts building up inside me, but I quickly squash it. It doesn't matter how many women have been in here before me and how many he'll pleasure on this counter after me. Jake is helping me with my list and doing it splendidly.

"Six," I breathe out, stunned. "We did six things from my list. Sex in a public place, sex in front of a mirror, sex entirely dressed, choking, music in the background ... Also, there was hair-pulling at some point."

Jake raises an eyebrow, sending me a disapproving look through our reflections. "I removed my hoodie, so not entirely dressed. And there was barely any hair-pulling, so it didn't count. The music doesn't either because that isn't sex music."

"And what would sex music be?" I ask.

His hands come to my hips, and he spins me around to face him. Watching him through the mirror and like this are two very different things, and the desire I can read in his eyes makes me weak in the knees. Especially when he pins me against the counter. "Let's go to my place, and I'll show you."

How can he want more right now? I'm already over-sexed, and I worry that things might be even more intense if I accept his offer.

Anyhow, it feels too intimate. A hotel room and this was easy, impartial, neutral. But his place?

"Maybe another time," I say, hoping he'll take my rebuttal gracefully.

When he tilts his head down to claim my lips, I don't fight it, even though I suspect he'll try to sway my mind with it. The way he kisses me is deeply sexual, lascivious, and hungry. My core aches from it, desire respawning from its ashes. Maybe it wouldn't be the worst thing in the world if I went to his place.

My hand is firmly clasped around the back of his neck when he pulls away.

"You have my number. Let me know when you want to cross another item off your list," he says with something devilish in his eyes.

I'm still trying to understand what's happening when he grabs his discarded Iron Maiden hoodie from the counter and exits the small room, putting it on as he does. Did he just leave me wanting more? And why do I even want more right now? What we did should be plenty enough. I came twice in under ten minutes, and impossibly hard each time.

I stay there for a moment, struggling to collect my wits. His offer is tempting, and when I get back out there, I know he'll be waiting for me to take him up on it. Clearly, he wants more of me, and I can't help but want more of him.

We nearly checked off six items tonight, which means going through everything might be faster than I anticipated. If I go to his place right now, I could be done with ten of them before tomorrow starts. But as much as I want to go through that stupid list, I have things to do this weekend. I can't spend it recovering from Jake's ridiculous stamina.

Finding this a good enough excuse not to cave in, I face the mirror to adjust my dress, wipe off my smudged mascara, and quickly brush my hair with my fingers.

As soon as I exit the "baby-making room," I'm thrown back into reality, and my eyes widen at the few women waiting in line to enter the ladies' restroom. Heaven's sake … Were there people here the whole time? Did they hear everything?

The two women closest to the front inspect me thoroughly, their eyes knowing. I sense my face heat up. Gosh, they most certainly heard something, or at least saw Jake leave before me.

Steadfastly, I return to the back room, where we carelessly left everything, too absorbed by lust and desire to be rational. Jake's back at the high table where my bag and our drinks are, and the two men from earlier have returned to their pool game. The whole time I approach, I sense Jake's jade gaze on me, and with each step I take, my resolve to go home alone wavers.

I'm parched after all that intense activity, but I can't drink from my unsupervised glass. So, I pick up Jake's glass instead, hoping no one would be mad enough to try to roofie him, and down what's left of his tepid beer.

"Thirsty, are we?" Jake teases.

"And tired." Once the glass is back on the table, I grab my blazer and step closer to him to get my bag. My chest is pressed onto his side, his warmth seeping through our clothes, and when I look up at his dashing face, I'm tempted once more to spend the night with him. "I'll text you," I say, my voice just as conflicted as my mind.

He knows I'm torn. And I know that he knows because my torment seems entertaining for him, amusement veiling his handsome features. But he doesn't insist or give me the slight push I need to stay. Instead, he presses a soft kiss right on the corner of my lips.

"I'll see you around, red."

I swallow, failing to chase away the lump in my throat, and then rip myself from his bewitching proximity. As I walk out of the room, it takes everything in me not to turn around and glance at him one last time. Especially since I can still feel his presence between my legs—a pleasurable ache accentuated by every step.

There was a reason why I wasn't supposed to see the same person twice. I don't want to *want* someone.

But it's too late for that, isn't it?

CHAPTER *Twelve*

Jake

BOOKKEEPING ISN'T OFFERING ANY DISTRACTION. My mind would rather drift to anything but the numbers displayed before my eyes. With a deep sigh, I move away from my laptop, leaning back into the chair.

My gaze falls on Mulligrubs, peacefully sleeping on her cushioned bed in the corner. Oh, to be a lazy Rottweiler without care in the world for anything other than scratches and food. As if she knows I'm silently judging her, she lets out a huff in her sleep before licking her drooly chops.

Yes, I'd like to be as unbothered by things as she is. But my brain is scattered, my focus entirely gone. Five days. I haven't shagged anyone in five days. And not because I am overwhelmed with work like when this usually happens. No, it's all because I have a certain redhead stuck in my brain, and I can't imagine banging anyone else. But I should go to The Devil's Court tonight, pick up a consenting woman, and bring her home to take the edge off.

That's not working, though. Every evening since I met Gen there, I've tried to get her scent out of my nose, her moans out of my ears, and her taste out of my mouth by fucking other women. I even went as far as to bring a pretty brunette to the baby room, but as soon as we entered it, my desire for the chick faded away. Even when she kneeled to suck me off. And despite her enthusiastic efforts, I barely got half hard before pulling her onto her feet, away from my limp dick. The brunette's shrill noises as I finger fucked her to make up for it were dull compared to the sweet, desperate, and raspy moans Gen lets out when I make her come.

My eyes land on the hair stick in the pen cup. It's a souvenir I accidentally brought back from our first night. The small accessory has been sitting there ever since, a taunting reminder of the sexy redhead.

I'm not usually this single-minded, especially not when it comes to women, but *fuck*, I can't get the proper little Miss Kensington out of my head. And what drives me even crazier is, why *her*? I get it to some extent, but it still shouldn't be happening.

Instead of being respectful and chivalrous, I should have made her stay the night. She wanted to go to my place as much as she wanted to set some boundaries and leave. Winning her over would have required barely any effort. But how I felt at that moment worried me a little. After I nut, I usually want to distance myself from whoever I was fucking, not spend more time with them.

At least this time, I know I'll see her again. That list of hers is my insurance. We have fifty items to go through together, minus a handful. I'll have to be careful, because doing them six at a time would be a waste.

With a frustrated grunt, I return my attention to the bookkeeping software on my screen. What am I doing? Oh, right. The quarterly report.

I'm barely getting back into it when my phone buzzes on the desk. I jump on it like an idiotic teenager, only to see it's Killian in the group chat.

KILL

The whisky lads are coming on Friday at six.

Eli replies before I can.

ELI

In the morning?

KILL

In the evening, eejit.

ELI

Ok, no need to be a dickhead about it.

KILL

No need to be as thick as shite.

Kill isn't a morning person, and noon hasn't passed yet. Since those two love to bicker like an old couple, I exit the conversation and mute it for an hour. I'll let them kiss and make up in private.

Before I know what I'm doing, my thumb leads me to the few messages I exchanged with Gen. They date back three weeks now, and I still remember the detached curiosity I felt while I sent those texts. She was nothing more than an afterthought, someone I planned on meeting just to prove to Eli that when a woman doesn't put her face in those apps, it means she has nothing worth showing. I was bloody wrong, wasn't I?

I'm a fool for thinking I'd be alright fucking her whenever she has some time she can grace me with. I'm in my prime, and I've always had a solid sex drive. I'll need more than a quickie every fortnight.

On impulse, I send her a text.

ME
Any plans tonight?

Well, that sounds desperate. I don't want to come off as desperate. But I kind of am. I can't seem to fuck anyone else right now, and wanking is already getting old—even if the fantasies I conjure of her are delightfully naughty. Those screenshots from her dating profile are proving handy, but they're nothing like the real thing. I'll need to dip my cock in some pussy before I go mad.

Because I'm not pathetic enough to stare at my phone until she answers, I return my focus to the bloody numbers I've been staring at all morning. I should be elated about our record revenue this quarter, but it's become the norm. We do better every time, on a solid climb since The Parlour opened five years ago. This time is quite the jump, though.

When the phone buzzes again about ten minutes after I sent the text, I force myself not to check it immediately. This woman does things to me that I'm not comfortable with. Instead, I finish going through the page I'm on and use the text as motivation.

It's not exactly rewarding, though.

SEXY REDHEAD
I have a work dinner.

ME
Can't get out of it?

SEXY REDHEAD

> Afraid not.

ME

> Not even for great dick?

There's a pause there, where I imagine her squirming on her chair, thinking of all the things she could be doing with me tonight rather than sit with her boring colleagues or whatever.

SEXY REDHEAD

> It would have to be the greatest dick of my life.

That needy little woman ... Is she issuing a challenge we both know I've already won?

ME

> I already am, am I not?

SEXY REDHEAD

> Now you're getting cocky again.

ME

> Cockiness is a big part of me. You've seen the size. You've had it in you.

Another pause, and I smile at the screen like an idiot, waiting for her answer.

SEXY REDHEAD

> I really can't tonight. It's my boss and a few colleagues who are all gunning to take over when he leaves.

ME

> You too, I reckon?

SEXY REDHEAD

> Yeah. I haven't gone through two years of misogynistic jokes just to let the position slip away from me months before his retirement.

ME

> Ah, so he's a twat. Well, if you need any cheering up, let me know.

SEXY REDHEAD

> I'll probably have to work afterward to compensate for the lost time. Thanks for the offer, though.

Why do I feel used? Actually, do I feel used, or am I disappointed that she isn't as eager to meet again as I am? I think it's both. And frustrated too, because I'm usually the one in control—or I have *some* control, at the very least. But in this situation, she holds all the cards. All I can do is wait for whenever she wants me to help with something from her list, ready and willing.

And I don't even know what those things are, which adds to my feeling of powerlessness.

ME

> Would you mind sending me your list so I can mentally prepare for what's to come?

SEXY REDHEAD

> Sure. I'll type it out and send it to you whenever I have time. See you around, Jake.

I officially feel used *and* discarded. For the first time since my teenage years, I question my sexual abilities. With a frustrated groan, I drop the phone on the desk and lean into my chair. Genevieve fucking Kensington.

The chemistry between us is undeniable, raw, electric … But as soon as there's some distance, she acts uninterested. I'm not used to this. Women always come back for more. They often beg for it even, and I have to set boundaries to ensure they don't start getting ideas.

This time, I'm the one about to beg, and I fucking hate it.

The door to the office opens without a knock first, and Eli takes a step in. "Did you mute us again?" he asks. Mulli springs up as soon as she recognizes the voice and stumbles out of her bed to welcome him.

"Yes, you two need space for your little foreplay," I reply while he bends down to enthusiastically pet my dog.

"Ha-ha. Kill wants us to be there on Friday so we can help pick the best bottles. I think he just wants to spend some quality time with us. He's been working like a maniac for weeks."

"The ransom of glory, I reckon. I'm up for drinks, yeah."

"When are you not?" he says with a chuckle. When I don't respond to his fit of humor, his eyebrows twist and come together. "What's up with you? You've been moody."

"Just the bloody quarterly reports."

He examines me for several seconds and then shakes his head. "Nah, it usually doesn't frustrate you this much. Is it because of a certain red-haired beauty?"

My first instinct is to deny, but I can sense the way my jaw ticks, betraying my thoughts before I can fabricate a lie. Eli doesn't miss it, a smile splitting his face in two as he comes in and closes the door behind him, Mulli bouncing for more of his attention.

"Okay, tell Uncle Elijah everything. What did the little redhead riding your hood do to you?"

"You know I'm circumcised."

"And I'm paraphrasing. Don't try to change the subject. What's going on?" He comes to sit on the sofa opposite me and looks at me over the desk. The Rottie comes between his knees, still in the mood for more head scratches.

"What is this? Therapy? I'm not telling you shit, Eli."

"Don't be shy, now. We're above this toxic masculinity crap—we communicate our feelings in this house."

"I've seen her *three times*, mate. There are no feelings to communicate." Eli raises a doubtful eyebrow, not fooled by my attempt to get him off my back. "She isn't on my mind, Elijah. Let it go."

"I mean … she should be. I've seen the pictures. She's one sexy—" Whatever look I give him makes him stop the joke he's about to utter. His following smirk tells me it was a trap, and I fell headfirst into it. "There you go. I knew it was about her. So, what? She's special?"

Knowing he won't let it go until I give him something, I sigh and stare at the phone. "I don't know. I thought I knew women. But this one … I can't figure her out."

"Of course you can't. You never fuck around with sophisticated career-driven women."

Maybe that's it. She's just a new flavor in a world where I already know them all. Once I get my fill of her, she'll become like any other woman—a taste I know all too well that blends with the rest. Then, I'll be able to move on, and things will return to normal.

"Will you see her again?" Eli asks.

"We have an arrangement."

"What kind?"

"I'm not sure exactly how it'll work, but we'll keep fucking."

There's a moment where he doesn't ask anything more, studying me with interest instead. I've known him and Killian for thirteen years now, and we all know one another too well for our own good.

"Not gonna lie," Eli starts, not masking how entertaining he finds my predicament, "it's fun to see you like this. When I found Jessica, I knew she would drive you mad, but I didn't think it would be that way. This is much better."

Fucker.

"Her name's Genevieve—Gen," I finally correct him. Since I'll supposedly see more of her in the future, I might as well set this right.

"Ah! I knew she wasn't a Jessica. She's not a Genevieve either though," he adds pensively.

"I think she's old money, so it suits her."

"Hmm. I feel like she should be an Ariel, or a Lola, or a Roxane."

"I truly fear the day you'll have to name a newborn. Now, get the fuck out so I can finish these fucking reports."

"I think I'll hang out here with you two. My office is boring."

"Don't you have work to do?" I ask, raising an eyebrow at him.

"Got everything I need right here," he replies, pulling his phone out of his pocket.

"Wanker."

"I prefer marketeer extraordinaire, thank you very much."

I shake my head with a smile, watching as he focuses on his phone to work his magic. The dynamics of our little trio turned fraternal a while ago. Elijah and Killian might as well be blood to me, and we give each other shit like any brothers would. Eli is a genius at what he does, and we have him to thank for the popularity of The Devil's Court and The Parlour. But since a lot of his work happens sprawled on a couch while he's on his phone, the joke that he's a lazy twat sticks around.

Eventually, I manage to return to my accounting problems, and Eli being there somewhat helps. Even though we don't speak, I'm aware of his presence, and it's as though my brain refuses to think of Gen with him in the room.

This goes on for maybe half an hour until my phone vibrates. I'm too eager when I check it, so Elijah sits up to look at me. "Is that her?"

It is. She sent me her list. "Mind your own shit," I tell my friend, impatiently reading the first items. He lies back on the couch with a mumble.

Reading this is a terrible idea because I'm rock-hard under my desk before I even reach the twentieth line. With every item I read, images of Gen and I flash into my mind. I envision myself doing these things to her, seeing the potential in each and every entry. I'm feeling hot, my dick aching by the time I read it all. *Fucking hell.*

When my boner recedes just enough to leave some blood for my brain, I text her back.

> **ME**
> I only see 39 things.

> **SEXY REDHEAD**
> I removed the ones we already did and the ones I don't feel comfortable doing.

> **ME**
> Like what?

Her next answer takes a moment to arrive as if she's debating whether she should be candid. Probably not. I want to do it all with her, so I might try—and manage—to sway her mind. Not in a pushy way, but encouragingly. Sex is fucking amazing, and she deserves to experience all its aspects.

> **SEXY REDHEAD**
> I'm still debating everything anal. A threesome is also not my style. And I'm not ever doing a sex tape. Also, nipple clamps sound scary.

Well, that's alright. The sex tape thing makes sense because we're not comfortable or familiar enough with each other to do it. As for the clamps, my fingers will do just fine. The threesome is trickier. I've done that in the past, with two women or sharing one with Elijah or Kill. I understand, however, that it can be a scary step, and I respect that it might not be her thing. Also, it's her exploration, and I'm not particularly into sharing—I merely do it when the occasion calls for it.

It's good that she's debating the anal part because it's an entire side of sex that she'd be dismissing. From rimming to having an anal orgasm, she'd be missing a lot of pleasurable fun.

> **ME**
> We'll do anything you're comfortable with, red. And if you come up with more stuff, I'm at your disposal for that too.

SEXY REDHEAD
What a gentleman.

> **ME**
> I aim to serve, love. Now, I don't know about you, but I reckon this is an excellent time for number 23.

SEXY REDHEAD
I'm not sending you a nude.

> **ME**
> What am I supposed to do with my stiffy, then? How do I get rid of it?

SEXY REDHEAD
You really need me to spell it out for you?

> **ME**
> What I need is new material. I've been wanking to your dating app pics so much, I think I could place every freckle you have on your arse with perfect accuracy.

"You do realize that you have the stupidest grin on your face, right?" Eli asks from the couch.

"Fuck off."

"No, this is too good. I've never seen you like this."

I flip him the bird, my eyes glued to the screen as I wait for Gen's response. It takes forever to come, and I wonder if she'll leave me on read.

SEXY REDHEAD
If this gets passed around in any way, I will sue you for everything you own.

I'm trying to figure out what she means by that when a pic comes in. Her face isn't in the frame, and she's seated on a big leather desk chair, the camera looking down at her. The blazer of her business suit is opened, and so is the white shirt underneath it. She's pushed it to the side, along with the cup of her lacey black bra, exposing a rosy nipple, all taut and pebbled.

It's far from being the most scandalous nude I've ever received, but I don't remember a single one making my cock jolt the way this one does.

Fuck.

"Now your face is getting red," Eli points out. "Did she just—"

"Get out. I'm not joking, Elijah. Get the fuck out."

He doesn't take my harshness poorly, chuckling low as he stands from the couch. "I'm taking Mulls because she deserves better than your bad energy. Come, Grubsy. Come!" Mulli jumps out of her bed like a traitor and excitedly goes to him.

"Do you want me to put a sock on the handle for you?" Eli asks, half outside. I glare at him, ripping my eyes from the picture for barely a second. That only makes him laugh more. "You need to get laid, bro. Celibacy isn't good for you."

"Five days isn't celibacy."

"It is for you. Anyhow, enjoy your alone time," he says with a wink, closing the door behind them.

As soon as I'm alone, I tug at my cock through my pants, trying to alleviate some of the discomfort. This woman drives me insane.

ME
Fuck, Gen.

SEXY REDHEAD
What?

ME
I didn't think you'd do it.

SEXY REDHEAD
I surprised myself. But one more down, 38 to go.

Damn, those items are going down like lead balloons. If I'm not careful, she'll be out of things to need me for by the end of the month. Thank fuck I negotiated the baby room was only three.

I need to make this last because when it's over, the freckled beauty will move on. And then what? I'm left with a dick that only rises for her and a mind that refuses to focus?

Can't afford that.

Whatever has got her racing through that list, whatever motivation drives her, I'll have to navigate around it. I need to get my fill of the proper little Miss Kensington, and when I'm bored with the novelty of her, everything will return to normal, and I'll get my perfect life back.

That sounds like a solid plan. One I'll undoubtedly enjoy enacting.

CHAPTER
Thirteen

Gen

IT'S THE FOURTH TIME RECENTLY that I've skipped Friday evening drinks with my coworkers. My boss insists the ritual isn't mandatory, but strongly encouraged for "team building purposes". I don't miss attending. I've seen too many male colleagues intoxicated to the point where they start groping or flirting with their female counterparts.

If I'm going to be flirted with or inappropriately touched, I'd rather it be by someone I want to have sex with. That's why I'm deep in Brooklyn while most of NexaCorp's legal department is in downtown Manhattan, where I impulsively left them.

When I enter the dark hallway of The Devil's Court, I still don't belong, but at least it feels a little more familiar. As I step further in, my heart drums against my ribs, my breath shallow and quick. I'm about to see Jake again, and my entire body has come alive at the thought.

I still can't believe I sent him that raunchy photo. I've never done anything like that in the past, and I'm not sure what came over me, but I stood from my chair, closed the privacy curtains of my office, locked the door, and undressed enough to snap the photo. But as mortifying as it was, I'm one item closer to fulfilling my list. I'm amazed at how fast I'm going through it. If Jake is as eager as I am, we might be done in mere *weeks*.

The dark and packed atmosphere is the same as when I was here last, with all types of people mingling together. The band performing on the stage isn't the same as last week, and the alternative rock vibes are softer.

As I look around in search of Jake, I question my decision to come here unannounced. In my defense, I didn't know I'd end up here until thirty minutes ago when I snuck away from my colleagues. Jake told me he was here every Friday evening, so I assumed he would be today. What if he's already busy with another woman? Something twinges in my chest at the thought. I hate wasting time and coming all the way here for nothing would be precisely that.

Since I can't spot his tall silhouette in the main room, I make my way to the back, where it's calmer. Maybe he's indulging in a game of pool.

My eyes instantly fall on his familiar face when I get there. He's sitting on a low leather couch with his friend Eli by his side, and on the opposite side is another man—the one from behind the bar. A dozen bottles of whiskey are on the table between them, with glasses scattered around. Crap, he's already in the middle of something. It was stupid to come and think he'd be available.

Since I don't want to interrupt whatever is going on, I decide to discreetly retreat, send him a text asking if he wants to meet up, and then pretend I'm on my way if he says yes.

Just as I'm about to back away, his green gaze lifts to me. Something lights up in his eyes, and I discern satisfaction despite his surprise. Feeling like an idiot, I stand there while he says something to his friends and gets up to come to me.

"We have to stop meeting like this, red," he says once he's close enough, his smirk devilish and charming. His hand snakes around my waist, and he bends toward me. "Here to work on that list of yours?"

I nod, entranced by his aura, which fills the air surrounding us. He gives me a small, lopsided smile and lowers the rest of the way to press his lips on mine. The kiss is soft, almost chaste, and then he straightens up.

"But I can—I can go if you prefer," I offer, my eyes fluttering to his friends. "I didn't realize you'd be busy."

"Nonsense. We're just trying some whiskies to add to the bar's selection. Do you want to join?"

"And meet your friends?" That sounds intimate and personal. I'm not entirely sure how sex arrangements work, but this might be off-limits.

"Gen!" someone calls from behind him. When I look, Eli is waving for me to join them, and the other guy—Killian, I think it was—is twisted around to watch me.

"They know about me?"

"Well, Eli knew about you before I did. And because he's a little twat, Kill also knows."

"And what do they know exactly?"

"That you're the woman I'm currently fucking," he nonchalantly explains. That's crude but accurate, I suppose. "Come, love. We'll have a few drinks and head out."

His hand is still around my waist, and he uses it to pull me toward the couches. I'm not shy, nor do I mind meeting new people, but the circumstances are awkward, making me uncomfortable. Jake doesn't seem to be though, and when we reach his business associates, he proceeds to introduce me.

"This is Gen. Love, this is Elijah and Killian." The former smiles and gives me a wave, and the latter offers me a small nod. "Move over, mate."

Eli immediately follows the command, joining Killian on the other couch while Jake and I sit side by side. I set my bag down, remove my short trench coat, and adjust the hem of my dress over my thighs. Maybe I subconsciously knew how the day would end when I dressed this morning because my outfit isn't too out of place. I'm wearing a teal wrap dress with sleeves that reach just above my elbows.

My eyes fall on the man I don't know, the other member of their trio, and I quickly study him. He also has tattoos slithering out of his black T-shirt, but not as many as Jake. His shoulder-length hair is a dark shade of auburn, its upper half tied into a bun at the back of his skull. He has a beard, darker than his hair, and it gives him a rough-around-the-edges look. Maybe it's his stoic expression or the dark brown of his eyes, but he doesn't seem as open or social as his two friends.

"It's nice to officially meet you," Eli says genuinely. "Jake's told us so much about you."

My attention switches to the man by my side, who's throwing metaphorical daggers at his friend. Jake's not supposed to disclose anything intimate about me to anyone, and I hope to God he didn't. When he turns to me, I give him a disapproving look.

"Ignore him. Being a cunt is his favorite pastime."

"He can't help himself," Killian adds caustically. It's the first time I hear him talk, and I realize he's undoubtedly Irish.

"Alright, alright. Jake didn't say much," Eli concedes. "But he said enough."

Probably to make his friend stop talking, Jake grabs a bottle of whiskey and pours a finger into four glasses.

"Do you like whiskey?" he asks as he hands me one. "We're trying new ones for the bar."

"It's not my favorite alcohol, but I indulge occasionally."

"I can get you something else if you want."

He's about to stand up, so I mindlessly rest my hand on his muscular thigh to stop him. "No, it's good. I'm a bit of a connoisseur, so I can help decide which one's worth investing in."

"Really?"

There's a hint of amusement in his eyes, so I decide to satiate his curiosity. "My parents have these trays of alcohol all over the house, and whenever I wanted to get drunk as a teenager, I used to take the smallest sips from each bottle so they wouldn't notice. I still do it whenever I visit. Needless to say, I became acquainted with many vodkas, whiskies, gins ..."

The glimmer in his gaze is even more apparent, and he chuckles with a head shake. "I never imagined you were a rebellious teenager."

The lightness of the moment fades as soon as I think back to my problematic high school years. I open my mouth to try to reply with something humorous, but nothing comes, so I bring the glass to my lips and take a small sip. The liquor clings to my tongue, raspy and heady, and a smoky aftertaste is etched in my mouth when I swallow. The men try it as well, and they debate for a moment. Since it's the first one I've tried, I can't compare it to the others, but I share my thoughts—it's good, not too rough on the tongue, and the smokiness adds an interesting nuance to the flavor.

"Scotts really make the best whiskies, don't they?" Eli says, making the amber liquid twirl in his glass.

"Not this again," Jake groans, falling back onto the couch.

"You little shite," Killian snarls at Eli. "They make more of it, but it's not the best. When will that big thick head on you get it?"

Elijah watches with contained hilarity as he continues into a tirade that I can't focus on because Jake bends over. "He always does this," he discreetly explains. "And Kill is way too proud to let it slide."

"How did you guys meet?"

"We were flatmates. Eli had a place in the Bronx, and his mates bailed on him. So he was looking for new ones. I wanted out of the roach motel I'd been in since arriving in the US, Kill was thrown out by his ex, and we ended up shacking together."

"So you've known them for thirteen years?" I ask, hoping I remember it right.

"Good memory, red. Yes, I have."

I look at the two men before us, wondering what these three have been through together. A lot, it seems, given how close they are. My glass isn't empty yet, but Jake leans over, pours another one, and extends it toward me. Its color is lighter than the other, but I've learned that it doesn't always mean something.

"Try that one. It's my favorite so far."

We switch glasses, and our fingers brush together a little longer than necessary.

Curious to see what good whiskey is to him, I take a small mouthful and let it linger on my tongue before swallowing. It's raspier than the other one, but I discern more flavors when the pungent taste of alcohol fades away. This one is older and more sophisticated.

Jake's waiting for my verdict. "It's good," I say with a smile. "I prefer it to the other one."

"Right?" He looks very satisfied that I agree with him, and I find it amusing that my opinion has any weight in his eyes. His friends are still arguing when he interrupts their banter. "We're getting this one," he decides, pointing at the bottle I just tried.

"This one's expensive," Killian objects.

"We'll sell it at top shelf price, then."

Jake tops up his empty glass with it and leans back until his side is against mine. When his hand comes to rest on my leg, just under the hem of my dress, sparks fly up to my center.

I almost forgot what I came here for, enjoying the moment. But as his fingers trace mindless circles on the soft skin of my inner thigh, I'm reminded of why I escaped my colleagues to join him here. I consider swatting his hand away, unused to such displays of intimacy, but it feels too good to deprive myself of it. Also, his friends already know what we've been doing and don't bat an eye at the gesture.

All I can manage is ten minutes. Ten long and insufferable minutes where he caresses me like it's the most normal thing in the world, conversing with his friends and making me try more amber liquors, his hand barely ever leaving my skin. He makes sure to include me in the conversation, but the brief responses I give are pathetic. I'm on fire by minute one, overwhelmed by shivers and desires, my core growing wetter with every faint graze. Is he even aware of what he's doing to me?

When Killian and Eli launch themselves into another heated debate about whether there should be ice in whiskey, I lean closer to Jake, bringing my lips to his ear. "Let's go to your place," I whisper.

His hand freezes on my leg, his focus shifting to me. It seems he forgot about what I'm here for too, because arousal suddenly strikes him, his pupils dilating until only a thin ring of green is left. I don't need to say anything more as he rips himself from my side to stand up. When he offers me assistance to do the same, I gladly take his hand.

"You guys are leaving?" Eli asks once I'm up, clearly disappointed.

"We've got better ways to spend our evening than entertaining you two bellends," Jake replies, picking up my jacket. He helps me slip it on and then bends to take his.

"I need to return behind the bar, anyway," Killian says, standing as well.

Eli looks positively discontent when his eyes dart to all three of us. "So what? I am to spend my Friday evening alone?"

"Your inability to pick up women isn't our problem," Jake muses with a stifled smirk.

"You know what I mean."

"If it can reassure you, I'll drop Mulli at your place so you won't be entirely alone."

With that, he gives Eli a wink, slips a hand to the middle of my back, and leads me out of The Devil's Court.

Once we're out in the quiet streets, where the air is fresh and the night dark, I look up at him with curiosity. "Mulli?"

"Mulligrubs, my dog."

That unexpected piece of information makes me smile broadly. "Oh, you have a dog?"

"Yeah. Had her since she was a pup. She's mean-looking, but really, she's a softie inside."

The evident fondness in his voice has me grinning even harder. "That reminds me of someone."

"Do you mean me?"

I nod. "You look like a bloodthirsty gang member, yet you've been nothing but kind and patient with me."

"Hmm ... I suppose I could be considered a softie. Although, soft isn't the adjective I'd use whenever you're around."

The salacious joke makes me laugh, and I fight the urge to look down and confirm what he's implying. I'm still chuckling when he urgently lowers to claim my lips. The intoxicating graze of his tongue in my mouth sends my heart racing, and I clasp a hand on his neck to save my balance, my knees buckling.

Only a week has passed since we last saw each other, and I missed this terribly. So much so that I considered dropping everything on Wednesday and taking him up on his offer to meet.

There's something empowering about the way he holds me, about how he craves me. His towering height and muscular broadness should make me feel small and delicate, but it's the opposite. I feel mighty and strong in his hold, like I could take on the world and conquer it. When his large hands pull me in closer, plastering me to him, I'm convinced of it.

"Do you-do you live far?" I breathe out, ripping myself away from the kiss.

"Too fucking far," he mumbles, tracing a burning line down my neck with his soft lips.

"Really?"

"Yeah." He gives the base of my throat a long and hungry kiss, making everything in me palpitate. Then he gestures to his left with his chin. "Two blocks that way."

I quench the laughter that tries to climb up my throat. "Terribly far indeed. Maybe we should get on with it right here, in the middle of the street."

His chuckle ripples across my collarbone in a gentle caress. "Don't tempt me, red." After one last kiss on my heated skin, he straightens up with a groan. "Let's go."

My heart expands when he intertwines his tattooed fingers with mine before pulling me alongside him. "Oh, before I forget. I have a late brunch tomorrow morning," I explain as we make our way to his place.

"We should be done by then," he says with a cocky smirk, squeezing my hand gently. "I'm glad you came."

"I didn't plan on it, but I'm glad I did too."

"The temptation was hard to resist, was it?"

I give him a side glance, struggling to contain a shy smile. "You have to stop fishing for compliments, Jake. It's very insecure of you."

"Well, that's what you do to me."

"Me?"

"Yes, you, Miss Kensington. You intimidate me."

I reflect on his words for a few silent seconds, wondering how that's even possible. He's the most intimidating man I've ever met, and I'm ... Well, I'm great at my job, and I know people fear me in that field. But on an intimacy level, I'm not much, am I? It's a fact that I'm boring, even.

We pass by the wide entrance of what seems to be a tattoo parlor set in an old warehouse. A few paces later, Jake stops us before a large door. "This is it," he states, releasing my hand and robbing my palm of his warmth.

"Very far indeed," I muse, watching as he pulls a set of keys out of his pocket.

Moments later, he holds the door open and invites me in. My body wakes as soon as we enter the dark hallway, and the lights flickering on aren't enough to tame the wild desires growing within me. We're minutes from having sex again, and I'm absurdly excited about it. I can't wait to revel in his magnificent body once more, to drown in pleasure, to bask in the rawness of passion ...

If things had been this incredible with Edward, I most likely would have made more time for intimacy rather than forget about it altogether.

Jake leads me to the end of the hallway, pulls up the railing of an industrial elevator, and parts a second gate in the middle. His hand on my back gently encourages me in, and he then does the opposite process. The ride up is filled with silence but heavy with anticipation.

There's only one door when we reach the fifth level, so I understand he has the whole floor to himself. Still, when I step inside and he turns the lights on, I'm not ready for how big and beautifully decorated his place is.

The entire apartment is one ample space, compartmented in various areas with bits of walls that never form a fully closed room—aside from what must be a toilet, in the far corner from where we stand, near a massive bed. I'm more of a sleek Scandinavian or minimalist kind of person, but the industrial decor fits the place to perfection, and it also suits Jake. Exposed red bricks adorn the walls, and tall, wide windows open to a view of the night outside. The space must be remarkably luminous during the daytime. That explains why so many green plants are scattered all over, including a few dangling from the high ceiling. Wherever there is space on the walls, art hangs against the brick—colorful, abstract, and often oversized.

I'm still taking all that in when an enormous, excited Rottweiler rushes to us. "Mulli, be nice," Jake warns, to no avail. The dog welcomes him with cheerfulness and then turns her attention to me, coming to sniff me while wagging her tail.

"Hey, Mulligrubs," I greet her, extending a hand to let her get familiar with my smell. When she seems to approve of me, I pet her imposing head, scratching her between the ears.

"You like dogs?" Jake asks when I lower to give her more pets.

"I've always wanted one, but my parents refused. Then I was in college, and after that … Let's just say my ex kept delaying getting one, so that never happened either."

"I got her three years ago, and my life has felt fuller ever since."

I give him a contrite smile, shrugging my shoulders. "Maybe it's better that I never got one. I probably wouldn't have time to care for a dog like it deserves."

"Yeah, I get that. I'm glad I can take Mulligrubs with me to work most days."

It looks like the dog got enough scratches because she leaves us to return to the huge round pillow set on the floor for her. "What field do you work in?" I ask, pushing my jacket off my shoulders.

He gallantly helps me with it. "I'm an artist."

"Really? What medium?"

"Skin."

It instantly clicks into my mind. "You're a tattoo artist."

"I am."

That explains a lot, actually. "Are you a good one?" I feel compelled to ask, even though his fantastic apartment is all the information I need to get my answer.

"Some think I am, yes. Forever growing though, as any good artist."

"You never showed me your favorite tattoo, by the way."

"Let me take Mulli to Eli's, and we'll correct the oversight," Jake says in a flirty manner. "Grubs, come here," he calls, picking up a leash from the coat hanger by the door. Although reluctantly, the Rottweiler comes when he encouragingly pats his solid thigh.

"I'll be right back," he promises. Then, he seems to remember something. "Fuck, I also have to walk her. Give me five minutes. There are beers in the fridge and liquor in that console right there. Glasses are on the shelves in the kitchen. Oh, and there's a cat somewhere—Beelzebub. Unless he's out exploring again. He's ... well, you'll see. But maybe don't pet him if you find him."

I nod, watching as he exits the apartment with a very docile Mulli.

Although I didn't expect to end up alone at his place, I welcome the opportunity to snoop around unsupervised. Leisurely, I stroll around the vast space, admiring the art, decorations, plants, and little details. There is no cat in sight, so I guess I won't have to see why Beelzebub shouldn't be touched. There's a sketchbook open on a low table, and I bend over to admire the intricate details of the beetle on the white page. If he's as skilled with a tattoo gun as with graphite, he must be quite good indeed. When I pass a bookshelf filled with hundreds of works, I tilt my head to the side and read the titles on a few spines. He seems to have versatile tastes, with an interest in contemporary fiction, art, history, and autobiographies.

My little promenade through his personal space leads me to a vintage stereo cabinet. A vinyl record is already set, and a sleeve lies next to it—*Moon Safari* by Air. Curious, I examine the sound system to figure out how to play the record. It takes me a minute, but the tonearm eventually moves into place and the needle gently lands on the vinyl. The sound of rain rises from the silence before a melody emerges from it, and I adjust the volume to fill the entire space.

I'm just returning to my exploration when the main door opens again, startling me. Those five minutes flew by.

He removes his jacket, hangs it next to mine, and after he locks the door and throws his keys on a console, he comes further in, joining me in the living room area. "You didn't get yourself a drink," he notes. "Do you want something?"

I shake my head. "I'm not here for drinks."

"What are you here for, then?" The challenge in his eyes sets a small fire within me.

Instead of answering, I step closer to him until I can feel the warmth radiating off his skin. Even in my stilettos, I have to tilt my head back to meet his ravenous gaze. Slowly, seductively, I drag my hands up his stomach, enjoying the rigid musculature under his T-shirt. I feel the piercing in his nipple when I pass it, and it makes me want to undress him even more.

"About that tattoo," I start. He doesn't expect it when I give him a sudden shove, but I'm not foolish enough to think it makes him fall back onto the couch behind him. He made that happen as much as I did.

I lift my dress higher on my thighs, which he observes with interest, and then straddle him. His hands instantly come to rest over my hips, his smirk carnivorous.

"By the way, that's sex music," he explains.

"Is it?" Frowning slightly, I focus on the music instead. The rhythm is slow, knowing, and I guess I can see how it can be sensuous, too. That's not music for rough sex though. It's a song for lascivious sex. Which I'm very fine with. "I suppose it is. Another item we'll tick tonight."

He eagerly welcomes my lips, his hands grasping me tightly as I ravish him. I swerve and grind on top of him while my tongue samples his, subconsciously following the song's tempo. Time slows, nothing exists but him for several moments, and I don't register it right away when he speaks into our kiss.

"Love, wait," he groans, gently pushing me away. "I was wondering. Why are you doing this?"

Still seated on him and very aware of his erection below me, I stare at him confusingly. "I told you. I have a list."

"Yes, I know. But why are you going through it now? What compelled you to?"

"Why does it matter?"

His hand rises to my face, and he tucks a loose red strand behind my ear. "I just want to understand you a little better, what pushed you to meet me, and what keeps you coming back."

My chest tightens at the thought of telling him. He's been doing all the work, so he hasn't realized how unimaginative I am in bed. But he will eventually notice because that can only go undetected for so long.

Which is why I have to tell him. It's better if I'm honest and it doesn't suddenly become clear to him. And while it's a nerve-racking thing to admit, knowing we're not anything serious helps. I'm not trying to bag him and keep him close for the rest of my life. We're just having casual sex, and we'll part ways as soon as we're bored with one another.

Something that might happen for him much sooner than it will for me. But that's alright.

I always knew what I signed up for.

CHAPTER
fourteen

Jake

GEN LOOKS TORN AND UNCERTAIN. The passionate and eager woman writhing on my lap moments ago is gone. And I'm a fucking idiot for ruining the mood.

My hands are still planted on her hips, and I consider making them roll on top of me again so we can return to what we were doing and dismiss my stupid question. When she meets my eyes again with her magnificent blue ones, I read all the insecurities and doubts she harbors.

"My boyfriend dumped me the day I made that dating app profile," she carefully starts. "We were together for five years, and he left like it meant nothing."

Well, the man was a fucking moron for letting her go. How blind can someone be to leave such a woman? "So, what? You're trying to get over him? Doing all the things he never tried with you?"

She shakes her head, and I see her throat bob as she swallows hard. To offer her some comfort and distraction, I slip my hands up her thighs—under the smooth fabric of her pretty dress. When she shivers on top of me, I'm glad to see the mood isn't completely gone.

"I—When he left, he told me I sucked in bed, that I was boring," she confesses, looking away before she can finish.

Now I'm getting pissed at the arsehole. Her? Boring? I don't remember having this much fun in my life. Fucking her has been brilliant, way better than a lot of my past experiences. Carefully, I take her chin, which slightly wobbles, between my thumb and index, forcing her to look up.

"Sweetheart, I wouldn't have brought you home if you were boring."

Her eyes widen, but doubt doesn't leave them entirely. "That's because you've been doing all the work. All I do is lie there, or stand, or get on all fours. And you make it all happen."

"Okay, I see the point you're trying to make, red, but I reckon you're still pretty spectacular. You're responsive, vocal, passionate, uninhibited ... You give back as much as you can, even if I'm a domineering prick who doesn't leave you much room to do it. You're not bad or boring in bed. Quite the opposite."

Her eyes are glassy, but not a tear spills over, which I take as an encouragement to keep going. "Tell you what, love. Tonight, I'm not doing anything. Tonight, you're the one in charge, the one who does the fucking."

My suggestion does the opposite of what I intended, and she looks even more uncertain, almost panicked. "What if I *am* boring, and you never want to see me again?"

The notion is so absurd that I can't hold back my laughter. "Red, where do you get these ideas? Can't you see that there's no way I won't thoroughly enjoy whatever you do to me?" I ask, thrusting up so she can feel without a doubt how much I want her.

Her eyelids flutter, her cheeks flushing bright pink. Because it's the most adorable thing I've ever seen, I push her hair back to admire the tips of her ears turning red. Fuck, everything about her is so endearing.

"If-if I'm not doing well, can you ... take over? Rather than stay bored, can you take the lead and keep things going?"

Just because I can see how much she needs that safety net, I nod and say, "I promise. But I doubt I'll need to, love."

She doesn't entirely believe me, but it must be enough because she bends over to lay a shy, uncertain kiss on my lips. My hands rise higher under her dress, to the sides of her lacy underwear, and my head tilts to give her better access to me.

The music changes around us, shifting into the album's second track—"Sexy Boy", one of my all-time favorites. When she resumes her grinding against my crotch, I understand she quite likes it too. I'm a little confused when she pulls away to stand before me while I stay slouched on the sofa. Before I can ask what's going on, her hips slowly begin to sway in rhythm with the beats.

Is she going to dance for me? God, I love seeing her in charge even more than I expected.

Her gaze is planted on me as she dances languorously, and when she sends a hand to her waist, where a knot keeps her dress closed, I quirk an inquisitive eyebrow. "Giving me a little show, are we?"

"Number nineteen," she answers, tugging at the blue strap.

Give someone a strip tease. Fuck, that is indeed on the list.

With soft hands and maddening leisure, she unveils more of her body, still undulating in rhythm with Air's song. I'll never be able to hear that record and not get painfully hard. Which is a shame because I listen to it a lot.

When I get a glimpse of the black bra that cradles her beautiful breasts, I fight the urge to impatiently pull her in and ravish her. Especially when she hides it again, like a fucking tease. Finally, she lets the dress hang loosely on her shoulders, revealing her toned stomach, the curve of her hips, the auburn curls visible through her underwear … I'm forced to send a hand to my cock and give my knob a pinch through my jeans. She's way too fucking sexy for this. I'll go bloody mad before the song is over.

She notices the motion, and I see confidence in her freckled features for the first time since she made her confession. Determined to send me to an asylum before the night is over, she lifts her arms above her head and weaves them in the air with sensual gestures, her hips never halting their hypnotizing dance.

Someone recently dumped her. The man must have been as daft as a bag of dicks to let such a goddess go. Were she mine, I'd worship her day and night, relentlessly guarding her like a ferocious dragon and its priceless treasure.

As she turns around, robbing me of the sight of her pebbled nipples under the lingerie, I'm tempted once more to grab her and never let her go. But then she slides the dress off her shoulders, and slowly—*frustratingly* slowly—she lowers it down, revealing the freckles and beauty spots on her back. Then, God almighty, the perfect shape of her swaying bum.

That's it. Her ex is the dumbest piece of shit that ever roamed this planet.

My hand is over my cock, stroking it through the fabric. When she swings around to face me again, her doubts and uncertainty are entirely gone, replaced by arousal and want. I'm mesmerized when she reaches behind her back to unhook her bra.

Unable to resist any longer, I unfasten my belt. My dick's harder than a rock, painfully aching, and I need some release before I go insane.

"No," she stops me, holding her bra so it doesn't fall off yet.

"Gen, I'm fucking dying here."

"And I'm the one in charge of the teasing for once."

With a grunt, I let go of my zipper and force my hands to rest on the couch instead. It delights her, a massive smile stretching her plump lips. "Payback's a bitch, isn't it?" she asks, letting the strap of her bra fall to the side.

I don't get how she can be this good at it and yet think she's anywhere near boring. Not when she's the most mesmerizing creature I've ever seen.

As if confirming my thoughts, she reveals one breast, then the other, and flings the damned thing at me, right on my gawking face. I grab it, enjoying its warmth, and bunch the fabric together before inhaling her scent, my gaze never veering from her perfect tits. They swing gently with her undulations, their rosy tips erect and small, begging for my lips to wrap around them.

"Enough with this, red."

"Oh, so you can dish it, but you can't take it?"

My restraint finally breaks when she grabs them and pushes them together. I lunge forward before she can see it coming and clasp her behind the thighs. Her squeal turns into a helpless laugh when I haul her onto me, back into her original straddling position.

Like a starving man, I swallow her giggles, sending a bold tongue into her. Her amusement fades in seconds, subjugated by my wandering hands. When I palm the roundness of her breasts and pinch their tips, she lets out a loud, greedy moan.

"Take me to your bed," she begs, arms wrapping around my neck.

I oblige, lifting myself and her from the couch. We never halt our kiss, entranced by one another as I make my way through the loft to reach my bed. So I'm not tempted to take over, I let myself fall back rather than topple onto her. That leaves her on top of me, almost naked while I only have my belt undone.

It seems she wants to even the field too, because she grabs the hem of my T-shirt to pull it up. In seconds and while barely interrupting our kiss, she undresses me down to my boxer briefs, her sweet little cunt pressed onto me with only our underwear shielding the contact.

"You're so fucking hot," I groan, filling my hands with her arse and tugging her closer.

"Aren't you bored yet?"

I didn't think I could laugh in such an abandoned state of arousal, so the genuine laughter that rips out of me surprises me as much as it does her. "Red, I could do this and only this for the rest of my life, and I'd never get bored."

Her delighted smile goes straight to my balls, taking a detour past my chest first, making it tighten.

"I think you inspire me," she says, kissing my chest. Helpless, I lie there, panting, while she explores my tattoos, her clever little tongue slick against my skin. "Which one's your favorite, Jake?"

"It's the—Fuck!" My answer is lost when she nips at the piercing in my nipple, pulling on it enough to make it ache deliciously. "It's the one on my hip."

Like she's about to uncover one of humanity's biggest secrets, she excitedly wriggles down to slip her hands under the elastic band of my boxers and tugs on it. I lift myself just enough to help her, and my cock springs free, wet with precum and so hard that my tip is a worrying shade of red. *Fucking hell.*

Her eyes linger on my erection first, but then she seeks which tattoo I meant. I can't hold back the way my frame trembles when her delicate fingers graze over the geisha on my side, which spans from the middle of my thigh to under the V dip at my hip.

"She's beautiful," Gen says with appreciation. "The details are amazing. Did you do it?"

I shake my head. "My body is a limited canvas, and I'd rather leave as much room as possible for other artists to leave their mark on it."

"So all of these were done by different people?"

"Yes. Friends, colleagues, and important figures of the craft. The geisha is from Haruki Tanaka, the first person who believed in me."

She nods distractedly, the tortuous tips of her fingers exploring more of the inky drawings on me. A pearly laugh bubbles out of her when she finds the terrible one I have on the inside of my bicep. "What's this one?"

I look down at it, holding back a grimace. "This one is the reason why Eli isn't allowed within three feet of a tattoo gun."

Her amusement doesn't fade as she examines the terribly drawn dick Elijah inked there with a trembling hand. The wanker even added strings of jizz at the tip and hairs on the balls. "Did you ever get revenge for it?"

"No. The coward is scared of needles, so he refuses to let anyone tattoo him."

"Hmm …"

When she resumes her exploration, I decide I've had enough of this. "Gen, I'm going to need you to put a pin in this and get on with the fucking. I'm in actual pain right now."

Her attention shifts from my arm to my third leg, which is hard and throbbing against my lower abdomen, reaching all the way to my navel. "It does look painful," she notes, not looking sorry at all for my suffering.

"Are you going to do something about it?"

She sends a tentative hand to my cock and wraps her fingers around it, lifting it off my stomach. Way too softly, she runs her fist up and down the length a couple of times and then settles her thumb over the wet tip, spreading the translucent drop that seeps out of it. "Do you find the piercings worth it?" she wonders, toying with the big one in the head.

"Well, I'd go through it again a hundred times just to hear the way you scream my name when you come, so I suppose I do."

Her cheekbones turn pink again, and my cock twitches in her soft hold. Fuck, I need to be inside her right now. "Condoms are in the nightstand," I tell her, gesturing toward it.

She releases me, and I don't know if it's mindless or if she intended it, but I stare as she slips the glistening tip of her thumb in her mouth, sampling me as she makes her way to the drawer.

Then, she lets out an appreciative "hmm" and my cock twitches so hard it does a little jump off my stomach.

Fuck, fuck, fuck.

When she returns with a silvery packet, I help her out of her lacy knickers and assist her when she comes back to straddle me. She's confident enough in how she handles the condom, but she pauses when the time comes to roll it down on me. The piercings are a bit tricky, so I understand her hesitation.

"Do you want me to show you?" I offer.

"I've seen you do it before, so I think I can manage. Can I try first, and we get another one if I fail?"

It's like she was made to unearth some protective and devoted parts of me I buried deep down ages ago. "Anything you want, red."

She looks very focused as she handles the condom, and just to give her a hand, I grab my cock at the base to hold it up for her. She thanks me with a quick grin and slips four fingertips inside the condom to stretch it as she pulls it down—exactly like I do. In no time, I'm sheathed and ready to go, and she looks way too proud to resist the urgent kiss she gives me.

Her small hand slips between us, and when she aligns herself with me, I stop her with my grip on her hips. "Wait, you're not quite ready for me, red."

"But I want you," she whimpers.

"You'll have me. Just—do this for a moment," I encourage, making her slide her hips back and forth so her damp folds glide along the underside of me.

"Oh …"

Her surprised breath doesn't help with my restraint, so I clench my teeth and hope for the best. I can't fucking ejaculate prematurely again, or she'll start believing I'm a two-pump chump. With her hands resting flat over my chest, she sways her body in rhythm with the music still running, her lips parted with soft pants, her eyes sparkling with lust.

"That's it, love. Get wet and ready for me."

"Jake, you feel so good," she moans.

So does she. But I bet the ribbed underside of me and the piercings feel fantastic on her. Her tempo slowly increases, disassociating with the music, as do the moans and sighs that she lets out. And I can hear the moist sounds we make where we rub together. I'm tempted to let her come like this first, but then I'll be at a great disadvantage, nearing my release while she'd have to climb to another climax.

"Now, red. Put me inside you *now*."

She doesn't need to be told twice, rising from me and angling my cock with her slick entrance. My hands are holding on to her tightly as she lowers, so fucking slowly that I nearly lose it. I'm not in control of anything when my hips jolt up, making my dick disappear entirely into her tight pussy.

Her scream, half pleasure and half surprise, and the way her walls clamp down on me have me cursing and instantly releasing her. "Fuck, I'm sorry. You're in charge; you're in control," I promise, entwining my fingers and laying my hands under my head so I'm not tempted to do anything more.

"It's fine, you're just ... *big*," she says, gently rocking her hips.

The soft touch of her palms returns to my chest as she leans onto me, and I admire how her tits dangle with her movements. It's like a spectacle, an exclusive performance—one I'd give my left ball to see every fucking night.

A show that's at risk of ending way too early.

It takes her a few attempts, but she eventually figures out how to make my entire cock disappear inside her. Now, every time she sinks onto me, she gives a little sway with her hips to make the seventh piercing slip inside.

"You like this, red?" I ask, hoping I can make her topple fast. "You like fucking me?"

Her strangled "Yes," is like ambrosia.

"You're doing it so well. Look at how much of me you take." We both gaze between us, where my cock goes in and out of her, sopping wet with her juices. "Do you know how good you feel, love? Has anyone ever told you how wet, tight, and warm you are?"

"Aah, Jake!"

The measured pace of her hips increases, her body jolting involuntarily. I feel a spasm around me, the promise of her looming orgasm. All I have to do is ride through it, and then I should last until the next one. In the meantime, I must do my best to ignore how incredible she feels and discard her breasts swinging right above me, the lustful expression on her face, the sounds she makes ...

"A man could sell his soul for such a perfect cunt. You know that, right?"

That rips another moan out of her, and she quivers inside and out. When she closes her eyes to experience it all better, I feel robbed. Sensing she's close, I remove a hand from under my head and send it between us, rolling the tip of my thumb over her swollen clit. "Look at me," I order. She obeys, wanton and heated. "That prick was so fucking wrong, Gen. You couldn't be boring even if you tried."

Just like that, she shatters, moaning my name with an abandoned whimper that makes it hard not to follow her. Her pussy contracts around me, her hands clenching over my chest, the rolls of her hips desperate and uncoordinated. I hold her through it in a bruising grasp, forcing her down on me so I'm not too overwhelmed.

"Fuck," I mutter through clenched teeth, trying to think of anything that isn't her.

She writhes and grinds, lost in her own version of heaven while I'm fighting like a devil not to join her. Eventually, when her pleasure slowly recedes, I feel prouder than if I'd won a gold medal in the Olympics. That shit was more challenging than running a bloody marathon.

With my cock still deep inside her, she leans back, her chest heaving as she tries to recuperate. Her entire body is flushed, covered in a thin veil of perspiration, and I want to scold myself for not letting her be on top sooner. She's the most beautiful thing I've ever laid my eyes on. And as an artist, I've seen a lot of beauty in this world.

"Jesus fucking Christ, red," I whimper, thankful for the intermission.

"Was that okay?"

"Okay? Genevieve, it was far beyond *okay*."

A small smile spreads on her lips, which contradicts the way her brows frown. When she rolls her hips, testing me inside her, I understand why. "Then why didn't you come?"

"Because I want to make it last, red. I can't orgasm the entire night like you do, so I have to pace myself."

She pouts, tempting me with the fullness of her lips. "You know, you don't have to make me orgasm all night. We could be more reasonable."

I chuckle, and her eyes flutter—probably because that feels great inside her. "With you, reason goes out the window. All I want is to feel your cunt come over and over around my cock."

"It's a good thing you're great at making it happen, then."

She bends over, answering my earlier thought, and steals my breath with a longing kiss. We're still in the middle of it when she resumes her writhing, and I move in unison with her, thrusting upward.

My hands explore her body with greed, filling up with every part of her I can reach. I wish I had more so I could appreciate it all at once, playing with her nipples, fondling her arse, and guiding her hips simultaneously.

"Do you trust me, love?" I rasp into her ear, giving her a rougher shove and groping the roundness of her behind.

"Yes."

With the tip of my index, I graze the plumpness of her lower lip, following its outline before I push my finger in. Although the gesture surprises her at first, she quickly adjusts and sucks it in, her cheeks hollowed while her tongue swirls and licks. Because I can't help myself, I thrust it in and out, mirroring what's going on between us. She almost looks disappointed when I pull my spit-coated finger out of her mouth, so, I distract her by cupping her breast. When my glistening index presses against her tight hole, she lets out a strangled protest.

"It won't hurt, sweetheart," I promise.

With her hands on each side of me, she pushes herself up enough to meet my eyes. I'd never force her to do something she doesn't want, but I know she's curious about this, desirous to know what it feels like. The wet fingertip is drawing small circles around that part of her, nudging but never taking the leap. Not without her explicit consent. When I run it across the hole, I notice how her pupils expand.

"Do it," she whispers, eyes locked on mine.

"You're sure?"

"Yes. Do it, Jake."

"Use more words. Express formal consent, Miss Kensington."

Her glare tells me what she thinks of my teasing, but I don't flinch. "Put your finger inside me, Jacob," she demands.

"Where?"

"In my—Jake, seriously. You know where."

"Ask properly, and I'll do it, Genevieve."

I might believe she's displeased, but I can feel how much this makes her spasm around me. She likes it when I defy her by pushing her buttons and limits.

"I, Genevieve Charlotte Kensington, formerly consent and demand that you, Jacob Daniel Clarke, insert your finger in my rectum."

I chuckle, not expecting this formal approach. "You know exactly how to talk dirty to me, red."

"You're at fault here. Now, get on with it."

She's perfectly still, but I have enough room to initiate a small momentum between us. So I do that, fucking her gently, and then settle my finger right where she wants me.

The moment my knuckle sinks in, she releases a heavy, trembling breath. "Relax, red. It won't hurt if you let it in."

As soon as the tight muscle loosens around my finger, I push it further in, making another knuckle disappear into her, my cock never halting the soft momentum from underneath. "You like that?" I ask, pumping it in and out of her.

She reflects on the question for a moment, but the way her body reacts by lowering to take my whole finger inside her is response enough. "I do," she admits, nevertheless. "It feels unique and—Aah! It feels good."

Her arsehole is still tight around the digit, so I don't attempt to add another one. Not even when she resumes the fucking, rolling her hips in a manner that drives me mad, taking my finger and my cock all the way in each time.

"That's it, baby. You're such a good girl. So responsive, so naughty."

We fuck like this for several minutes, and I think I'm doing good, holding back while she climbs to her next climax until she moans, "I want more," right into my ear.

Fuck.

"You want another one?"

She nods. "Please, don't make me beg for it."

I pull my index out of her and run it across her inner thigh where she's slick with wetness, along with my middle finger. Once they are lubricated enough, I press their tips back onto her arsehole. "Push," I instruct, doing the same on my side.

Both fingers carefully sink into her, into the hot and willing channel, and she cries out my name, shaking over me. Her face is red, her hair is a mess, her eyes are glassy, her lips are swollen ... Everything about her is the sexiest thing I've ever seen. I barely have time to fuck her with them when the first spasm of her pussy starts. Her other hole clenches so tightly that I struggle to keep pumping my fingers into her. She holds onto me, moaning and crying, her mouth filled with my name and other supplications. I'm so unprepared for her orgasm that I fall victim to it, cum jetting out of me while she buckles and grinds, fucking my cock and hand with desperate intensity.

We're so tightly wound together as we come that I can't tell where I end and where she starts. At this point, we're nothing more than a mass of shaking limbs, lost in complete abandon as the skies open to welcome us. Or I reckon they open because I swear I can see fucking stars lined up behind my tightly shut eyelids.

I have no idea how long this lasts, but by the time I regain my senses, the record is over, and our hectic breathing is the only thing filling the silence. She's sprawled over me, and I wish this could become the rest of our lives. Tightly woven together, basking in post-nut bliss, swimming in immaculate euphoria.

This woman is something else. She's … I don't even know. A revelation? God-sent? The best lay of my fucking life?

And she thought she was boring? How the hell did she get it so wrong?

"Wow," she breathes out, clearly as spent as I am. "That was—"

"Fucking incredible. I know."

Still sticking to me like a second skin, she twists her head to look at me, and I gaze down to meet her glassy eyes. "You enjoyed it?" she asks.

"Are you kidding? I think that was the best sex of my life."

Something in the way I say it finally breaks through her insecurities. Her face lights up, her mouth stretching into the brightest smile, and I feel her elation echo under my ribs.

After she gives me a small but intense kiss, she lies down, flush against me while my dick softens inside her.

"Oh, I almost forgot," she starts with a small voice. "The contract we signed is coming to an end. So, I drafted a new one with all the other things. I'll need to make edits to add anal play and penetration."

"Really?"

"Yes. We'll go slow, though."

"Of course."

A few beats pass, and I feel like she's got more to say, so I wait for it. "Also, I created an addendum."

"For what?"

When she looks up at me, I meet her eyes again. "You're not obligated to sign it at all, it's just a thought I had."

"About?"

"Well, I—You're going to be the only one helping me with the list, and I thought that maybe …"

Since I have no idea what she's getting at, I can't even help her spill it out. "Go on, red."

"It demands a little more commitment, but I promise it's not like we'd be something serious. It's just that one item on that list requires … well, it requires that we don't use a condom."

Just like that, my dick begins to swell again, still planted into her warmth. For fuck's sake, it hasn't even gone entirely soft yet. "You want me to fuck you raw?"

"Uh, yes. I want to know what you feel like without protection. And I'm not sure how else we'd do the cum play thing otherwise. It means we'd get tested again. And ideally, we'd only sleep with one another during the length of our arrangement. Which is why you're not obligated to sign. You told me you weren't the monogamous type, so we can keep doing things this way."

She stays silent while I come to terms with the idea, my fingers drawing random spirals and curves on her sweaty back. Right now, I can't imagine fucking another woman. Not after the fantastic sex we just had. And the few times I've tried lately, I wasn't able to get it started, much less bring it to completion. So it's not like the exclusivity thing would be a problem. And really, the pleasure of getting to fuck her without a condom would overpower my usual reticence. I haven't been in a monogamous relationship for nearly a decade now, so I haven't fucked without a rubber for almost that long.

"I'm game if you are," I decide.

"For real?"

"Yeah. I'll get tested soon. But I'll need to see you more. It'll have to be twice a week, at the very least."

"I suppose I can skip Pilates on Tuesday evenings. Would that work?"

"Yeah. But don't worry, we'll find fun ways to exercise and make up for it."

I can feel the smile on her lips when she kisses my torso before wriggling even closer until there isn't a lick of space left between us.

Shit, I'm almost ready to go again. The things this woman does to me are uncanny.

"When's your brunch tomorrow?" I ask.

She sighs, "Eleven-thirty."

"Hmm …" With a mighty shove of my hips, I make us roll over, pulling out of her once she's lying on her back to change the condom. "We better get on with it, then."

"I guess we should."

Before I can do anything, she pulls me in for a long, deep, and thorough kiss. Seconds into it, I'm already high on her taste, feeling like I'll never get enough of it.

Yes, fucking only her for the next few weeks or months won't be an issue.

What comes after that might become a problem.

CHAPTER
fifteen

Gen

I'M VERY AWARE OF MY surroundings before I even open an eye. This isn't my mattress, these aren't my sheets, and I've been sleeping alone for over a month now, but there's a warm and solid body against me.

Also, I feel deliciously sore, a lingering ache etched at the junction of my thighs.

Jake ...

We came to his place and had sex. The entire night. With breaks and naps of course, but I remember us still going at it by the time the night sky was slowly turning into dawn. When I flutter my eyes open, I notice that the sun is completely out now, its warm light bathing the loft.

My interest then shifts to the broad torso under my cheek and the tattoos drawn on it. With a contented sigh, I inch closer to him, tightening the hold of my arm thrown over his waist.

Ah, this feels great.

I hadn't realized how much I missed sleeping with someone. There's something comforting about having a warm body to wake up to—a comfortable coziness to it. And when that body provided that much delight through the night, there's even some pride.

We got a little carried away, and the list became the last thing on my mind. I was too busy enjoying everything he did to me, lost in the moment. We still worked through two items: the striptease and the music.

Hmm ... Maybe we could have sex one more time before I leave for my—

Crap!

We were so lost in it that I completely forgot to set an alarm. Moving urgently while ensuring I won't wake up Jake, I rip myself away from him and look around for a clock.

Before I can find one, my eyes land on a surprising witness. A black cat is sitting on the nightstand on my side, staring at me with yellow eyes. So, that's Beelzebub?

Because I don't have time to figure out what Jake's cryptic warning meant, I continue my search for time. When I find a large clock set on a wall, I hold back a curse. It's almost ten. This means I have an hour and a half to leave, get home, shower, change, and head to the restaurant. And I can't, under any circumstances, be late. Not for *that*.

Scolding myself internally, I untangle my limbs from the sheets, ensuring again that I don't stir Jake too much. He deserves the rest after the night we had. As soon as I find my phone, I order a hired car. Once I'm fully dressed, I gaze at his sleeping shape, the sheets resting low on his muscular stomach. As tempting as it is to wake him up and say goodbye, I worry he'll lure me into more sex. Because I'm late and sore enough as it is, I walk up to the door.

The cat is now on the high console right next to it, by the set of keys I need to get out. *Shoot.*

"Hey, kitty," I say with a soft voice, bringing my hand closer to him. He takes an interest in it, and I hold back from pulling away. Hana has a cat, so I'm relatively familiar with them.

Beelzebub smells my hand, and to my surprise, he doesn't react poorly. Instead, he rubs his face on it, seeking affection. "You're not a bad cat at all," I whisper, adding my second hand to the mix.

When he starts purring, I have to physically force myself to let go. I grab the keys and unlock the door. I'm as quiet as a church mouse when I exit Jake's apartment, promising myself I'll text him to apologize for sneaking out like this.

The freight elevator isn't too complex to navigate, but I might have made a mistake because it stops just one level below. Two familiar faces appear on the other side of the gates.

"Hey there," Eli greets me as he gets in, accompanied by Mulligrubs.

I pet her when she enthusiastically comes to me. "Hi, you two."

Elijah closes the gates, and we're going down again in no time. "I didn't know you lived in the same building," I say, my hand still grazing Mulli's soft fur.

"Yeah, Jake lets me have one of the apartments for a symbolic dollar per month."

My exhausted brain takes a little too long to process that piece of information. "He owns another apartment here?"

"Oh, he owns the whole building. As well as the art gallery on the ground floor and the tattoo and piercing parlor on the second one. The third floor has four small apartments, and the fourth has two—including mine. And then there's his loft. And the roof."

Heaven's sake. That is quite the real estate investment. Which means Jake is even more successful than I imagined.

We arrive at the ground floor, and my phone buzzes in my hand the moment Eli opens the gates. My car is here.

When we reach the door, Eli kneels to hook Mulli's leash on her collar. "I have to go, I'm late for brunch," I explain with a wince. "It was nice seeing you again, Eli."

"You too. Take care, Gen!"

"Ditto."

A black sedan is waiting for me right in front of the exit, so I slip into it within seconds. I want to believe there won't be too much traffic, but who am I kidding?

The next hour and some will be stressful and tense, which is a shame because Jake worked hard all night to relax me. A small smile appears on my lips as I recall all the things we did. I spend the entire way home reminiscing, hoping we'll get an encore soon. *Very* soon.

We did things I had never tried before, including some that weren't even on my list. Jake is proving to be a very prolific and imaginative lover. Before him, I generally enjoyed sex—when done well—but I could never sympathize with people who put it on a pedestal and dedicate so much time to it.

Now, however, I'd be willing to spend every single one of my evenings exploring pleasure with Jake, finding new challenges, and pushing my limits over and over. I still can't believe how good it felt to have his fingers in that other part of me. It shouldn't have been this pleasurable, but I exploded into the best orgasm of my life thanks to it. Thanks to *him*.

Following an intense moment in my apartment rushing to be ready on time, I hail a cab at the foot of my building. I'm clean, have fresh makeup on, and wear a proper outfit—rosewood palazzo pants with a loose white silk shirt tucked in. I wasted most of my time giving myself a blowout—an unavoidable necessity given who I'm meeting with.

The yellow car stops before me, and I enter it while minding my pants so I don't arrive all rumpled and messy. "Columbus Circle, please," I tell the driver. The woman nods and drives right away.

I did everything I could to be on time, and if the roads are clear enough, I should succeed.

When my phone buzzes in my purse, I anxiously expect it to be a message from *her*, telling me she's already there and waiting. So, when I see it's a text from Ladder Guy, my heart lightens at once.

LADDER GUY

> I can't believe you snuck out on me like that. I must have been in a proper coma.

ME

> You were. And you knew I had plans.

LADDER GUY

> Still, I wanted to make breakfast and eat it off you. With whipped cream and all.

ME

> What an unhealthy way to start the day. But food play is on the list, after all.

There's a moment where he doesn't answer, and it gives me enough time to fantasize about him spreading all sorts of things on me and licking them clean. And then doing the same to him. That is something I will enjoy a lot.

LADDER GUY

> Woman, what the hell did you do to me? My dick is fucking sore.

ME

> My EVERYTHING is sore, Jake. I can barely walk straight.

LADDER GUY

> I have no regrets.

> **ME**
> Of course you don't. It's good that I won't see you until Tuesday because I need serious time to recuperate.

> **LADDER GUY**
> I have all the regrets.

> **ME**
> There, there. Your penis will appreciate the rest.

> **LADDER GUY**
> Maybe you can come by tonight and kiss it better? I'm sure it would help. I'll kiss your everything better too.

I laugh, hiding my gleeful smile behind my fingers, like I'm not supposed to enjoy this so much. As tempting as it is to take him up on his offer, I'm already seeing Hana tonight. A friend of ours from Harvard has a big unveiling at her art gallery, and we agreed we'd be there ages ago.

> **ME**
> I'm busy tonight.

> **LADDER GUY**
> What about tomorrow?

> **ME**
> No, Sunday is the one day I get to myself. I need it to recharge so I can get back to work without killing any of my colleagues.

> **LADDER GUY**
> :(

> **ME**
> Tuesday it is. By the way, I saw your cat. He was perfectly fine.

> **LADDER GUY**
> I have scars all over my hands and forearms that say otherwise.

> **ME**
> You poor thing. Maybe your cat knows your penchant for self-mutilation.

> **LADDER GUY**
> Stop acting like you don't like my self-mutilations. You enjoyed the shit out of them all night long.

Christ, I did. I really, really did.

ME
And now I'm in convalescence.

LADDER GUY
Again. No regrets.

"We've arrived, miss," the taxi driver says.

Startled, I look around, seeing that we have indeed arrived. I shuffle through my bag to take my credit card out, and once the ride is paid for, I exit the vehicle.

Before I'm forced away from my phone for God knows how long, I quickly send one last text to Jake.

ME
Me neither. I arrived at my brunch, so I'll be off for a bit. Take good care of that poor, mutilated, and sore penis of yours ;)

Containing my smile, I walk toward the overpriced restaurant I'm meant to be at. God probably reached down to help me because I enter it five minutes before eleven thirty. But while it might be considered on time for most, it'll still be late for the person I'm meeting.

Which reminds me to put my phone on Do Not Disturb. She always found it disrespectful and demanded that if we shared time, we ought to give each other our undivided attention.

Stress is making my heart race and my throat tighten. Ugh, I should have devised an excuse and spent the morning with Jake instead. It would have been a lot more fun than whatever this will turn into.

I easily spot her, with her platinum blonde hair styled into a chic bob with a perfect blowout. Before I even come closer, I know she's wearing one of her timeless Chanel ensembles. Its color will help me determine what sort of mood she's in. The tweed is pink, to my relief, which means she's in a good one.

"Hi! I'm so sorry I'm late," I say as I reach her.

She doesn't contradict me, even though I'm not late, pursing her lips instead. But I expected that, so I don't take it poorly. I bend to give her a feigned kiss on her cheek, my lips never touching her skin. One mustn't ruin Vivienne Kensington's makeup.

When I reach my chair, a waiter is already there, pulling it out for me and pushing it in when I sit. "Darling, you look terrible," is the first thing Mother tells me.

"I slept scarcely, sorry for that."

She rolls her eyes disapprovingly. "I already told you to always keep a gel mask in your freezer. It will help with those horrendous dark circles under your eyes."

It serves no purpose to tell her I didn't have time for that, so I abstain.

She sighs, signaling the waiter to come and fill her glass. "Being a career woman has consequences, Genevieve, which you don't seem capable of handling."

For once, work wasn't the reason for my lack of rest. But she doesn't need to know that. She'd have an aneurysm if she knew I spent the night with a man covered in tattoos and piercings.

I realize just how tired I am when she veers the conversation into a topic I didn't foresee. "Edward called me, you know."

Crap, not this.

I've had her on the phone a few times since the breakup, but it's the first time seeing her in person. It was naive to hope I'd be spared from this.

"He told me what happened and why he left," she continues. "I don't understand why you insist on following the wrong path."

"Why is it the wrong path?"

Her eye roll isn't a good sign. Right now, she wouldn't pick that powder pink skirt suit, but probably something green. Or worse: *red.*

"You know what I mean, Genevieve. Your father offered to give you whatever position you want in one of his companies. You wouldn't have to work as hard as you do now and for better pay."

"Nepotism isn't a good look," I counter. This tired debate is one we go over a few times a year, and no matter what I say, neither of them realize they won't change my mind about it.

"It's not nepotism, it's your birthright. You wouldn't question the legitimacy of a prince for being born into royalty, would you?"

I frown, wondering if she can hear herself. "Actually, I would. A lot of people are condemning monarchies around the world."

She huffs deeply, clearly bothered by my impertinence, and I decide to hold back. We haven't even placed our orders yet, so I'm in for a very long and tiresome brunch if I anger her this early.

I examine the menu while she does the same. It gives us enough time to recompose ourselves so we can start over. She finds what she wants before I do, so I feel pressured to pick. I settle on the salmon, judging it reasonable enough.

"It's not too late, you know," she tells me once I set my menu down.

"For what?"

"Edward. He told me he would take you back if you promised to dedicate more time to your relationship."

That one feels like a swift punch to the gut. Knowing the two of them spoke behind my back feels like an invasion of privacy. But the fact that my own mother blames me for the failed relationship hurts even more. All the work I've been doing on myself, the reassurance Hana gave me, the confidence I've been building back up … they go down the drain in an instant.

The five years I spent with Eddie, our plans for a future, the family we wanted to have … It rushes back to me like a bullet train, and I can't stop the thoughts that make their way into my mind.

What if this is just a break? Eddie and I can spend some time apart, I hone my sexual abilities, he works on himself, and then we meet in the middle, ready to start over, to get back to our perfect plans. God knows I've gotten better at sex already, and I surely wouldn't be as boring as before. My parents approve of him, and I enjoy his conciliatory temperament. He was the person I meant to spend the rest of my life with, after all, and this whole mess doesn't have to be anything more than a bump on our way there.

We've had breaks in the past, where one of us usually went to spend a few days away for some space. This doesn't have to be the end, but rather a longer, more significant pause in our relationship.

Unexpectedly, Jake jumps into my mind. I'm having a lot of fun with him, but it was never meant to be anything more than that. Good old fun that leaves me weak in the legs and sore between them. He isn't the kind of person one builds a life with. Especially not someone like me. So that means I can keep seeing him for the time being, learn everything he has to teach me where sex is concerned, and then jump back into a stable and durable relationship.

Possibly with Edward.

"How have you been?" Mother asks, ignoring the havoc she just wreaked on me.

"Uh, fine. Working a lot."

"Yes, we've already established that it shows. Weren't you after a promotion or something?"

"Head of the legal department."

She lets out a mocking sound I'm too familiar with, halfway between a sneer and a chuckle. "Your father could give you a position three promotions above this if you allowed him. Look at your brother. Gerry's second in command and he's thriving. You could be by their side if you allowed it."

"I'm happy making my own way up the professional ladder, Mother. Once I've earned it the fair way, I might take Father up on his offer. But I refuse to have preferential treatment."

"I do not understand your insistence on doing things like everyone else. You are a Kensington, not some commoner without any other choice."

The waiter comes, and I silently thank the distraction. Mother orders a salad with the dressing on the side, and when I ask for the salmon, she frowns disapprovingly.

"What is the salmon served with?" she asks the server.

"Roasted asparagus and the chef's rice, ma'am."

"And the sauce?"

"A *beurre blanc*."

She pinches her lips, shaking her head as if to say that wouldn't do. "She'll have it without rice. And only a drizzle of lemon over the salmon."

"No sauce at all?"

She shakes her head, and the man looks at me for confirmation. Holding back an angered huff, I nod, and he leaves with our menus.

"You have to watch your figure, Genevieve."

"I am, Mother. I exercise four times a week and haven't had candy in years."

"Well, I suppose your body has a proclivity to store fat, then."

The worst part about her hurtful words is that they don't even shock me. Not anymore. Vivienne Kensington always demanded excellence, and I've tried to rise to her standards for most of my life. But with people like her, there is simply no winning.

I can't help but quickly observe her slim figure. She was a model until Father swept her off her feet with the promise of a luxurious life. She still looks the part despite the traces of time adorning her skin. I think that was their agreement before they got married. As long as she stays fit and put together, Father will give her a monstrous allowance.

That would explain why their marriage has been failing for as long as I can remember. Yes, she has more money than she could ever spend, but that's it. Her artificial life is devoid of everything that truly matters, like a loving family.

"How is Father?" I ask.

"Still doing his thing, working, traveling, seeing his whore …"

Oh, so now we openly acknowledge my father's affair? Noted.

"And his health?"

"The doctor tried to set restrictions, but you know your father. Nothing can keep him away from his bourbon and cigars."

And mistress.

When the waiter returns with a basket of fresh bread, my mother dismisses it with a hand gesture before it even reaches the table.

Crap, I should have expected this and eaten something before coming. After all that nocturnal activity, I'm starving. I cannot possibly stuff my face with my mother right in front of me, though. Unless I want her to call me fat again.

"It will be ten years in three weeks," she says gravely.

That instantly replaces my hunger with nausea. My stomach is suddenly in knots, tugging and aching, and I stare at the white tablecloth, unsure what to say.

"I know. In nineteen days, to be exact."

"She would have turned twenty-seven," Mother continues. I also know that because *I'm* turning twenty-seven. "Will you be coming home?"

"Of course."

We always do this together. Every single year. Father makes sure to be present, even if he has to fly in from halfway around the world. In fact, I put in my request for a day off months ago to make sure I'd be able to spend the day on the family estate.

It's *her* day, after all. Victoria's birth and death wrapped up in one gruesome date.

"I thought we could do something special this year since it's such a significant number," Mother suggests.

"Did you have anything in mind?"

"Maybe have a few friends and family members over. People who knew and loved her."

"Don't you think it might be a bit much?"

Although my question is innocent, she glares at me with discontentment. "Ten years, Genevieve. I'm allowed to commemorate my daughter's death in whatever way I want."

"Right, of course."

I hate that. I hate that she's so good at making me feel like a child again. I hate that she can crush my adult spirit until I'm left confused and ashamed. But it's something I'm used to, especially when we approach that cursed anniversary. So I clench my teeth and take it like I always have.

"The invitations have already gone out, anyway. Over fifty people have RSVP'd so far."

Leave it to Vivienne to turn such a commemoration into a social event.

"I was thinking about her the other day," Mother says pensively. "And I'm convinced she would have become a mother by now. She would have found a nice, respectable man in college—like Edward—and they would have given me a beautiful grandchild with blue eyes and blond hair."

I knew my sister more than she ever did or will, so I know that the fantasy she has of her isn't right. For one, Victoria was always adamant about building a career, determined to make her own mark in the world. So, I'm not so sure she would have put it all aside so early in favor of a family.

More importantly, my twin was never into boys, but that is a secret I will take to my grave because it isn't mine to share. Our parents weren't open enough to accept it, so Vicky spent her brief existence deeply hidden in a closet—one I couldn't pull her out of, regardless of how much support and encouragement I offered. She was so scared of how they might react that she never allowed herself to kiss another girl. Not even Penelope, the senior she had a reciprocated crush on.

"She would have been an amazing mom," I say, forcing a smile onto my lips. That isn't a lie, and it entertains my mother's delusions.

Whatever she wants to believe, I'll let her. She lost a child, so she's allowed any and every indulgence. That is a truth I have lived with for nearly ten years.

Because I can't handle this in my sober state, I raise a hand to catch the waiter's attention. "Could I have a lemon drop martini, please?" I ask when he comes.

"Of course, miss. Anything for you, ma'am?"

Mother hesitates, and when she asks for an old-fashioned, I know the meal will be rough. Whatever good mood she was in when I arrived is long gone.

So now, I just have to toughen up and endure the next hour.

I really should have found an excuse and stayed with Jake. That would have been a much better use of my time.

CHAPTER *Sixteen*

Gen

"YOU HAVE NO IDEA HOW much I needed this," I tell Hana as we walk toward the gallery.

"I take it your brunch with 'Mother' didn't go well?"

"Oh, it went exactly as it always does."

"Ew," she says with a grimace. "Well, I'm glad we get to do this too. I love my son, but good God, he has quite the pair of lungs on him."

"Which he got from you because Tyrone *never* raises his voice."

"Yes, my man is a perfectly mild-mannered introvert," she says with unmistakable pride.

When we arrive before the massive, glassed front of the gallery, a few people are already waiting to enter. The exclusive event is invitation only, and Hana and I have our names on the list. Two people enter, three are sent on their way, and then it's our turn.

"Genevieve Kensington and Hana Yun," I tell the man behind the stand.

He finds us quickly and invites us to enter with a sweep of his arm. "Have an enlightening evening, ladies."

We thank him with a smile and a nod and then enter the gallery. The place is magnificent, with high ceilings, expensive materials, designer furniture ... Soft music is playing, present enough to fill the air but discreet enough to allow conversations. And the art exposed is brought forward by perfect and clever dispositions. A woman comes to help us out of our coats, and another one approaches with a tray filled with champagne flutes. We both take one and then venture into the artful space. It's so massive that one might call it a museum rather than a gallery. Our old friend is doing very well for herself.

"Do you think there'll be other people here from Harvard?" Hana asks before taking a sip.

"God, I hope not. I don't want to spend the evening catching up with people I couldn't even bear back then."

Hana giggles into her champagne. "They were such pretentious assholes."

"Constance was fine though," I feel compelled to say. Hana nods.

"She was. Which is why we're here to support her tonight. Not that she needs us."

We look around the room, and I admit that I'm impressed by the turnout. Constance must have quite the social network to pull such a successful opening. In the five years since she took over, this gallery has become a landmark in the New York art scene. And it's my understanding that tonight is her consecration, exposing some of the hottest artists in the world. No wonder so many people are present, some even trying to get in without an invitation.

Among the many guests, I recognize a few faces, including friends of my parents. We all frequent the same circles after all, so it makes sense that such an event would bring us together.

When someone from the waitstaff passes with a tray of canapés, Hana picks up a napkin and takes two. I, however, shake my head, still not over my mother's words. I do have a tendency to gain weight, and I haven't been very good at controlling myself in the past few weeks. Stress will do that to a person, and having to reassess my entire life after the breakup hasn't been exactly restful.

"Ugh, this is so good," Hana moans after taking a bite of what looks like foie gras on toasted brioche.

My stomach protests with gurgles, reminding me that all I had today was a slice of salmon and four asparagus. I pass a hand over my front, soothing my dress. That attracts my friend's gaze.

"Still can't believe how amazing that dress is on you," Hana compliments.

I look down at the green satin. The Dior dress was returned to me yesterday, its spaghetti strap fixed like nothing happened. It's a bold choice for an evening like this, but after the night I had, I was feeling sexy and wanted, so I impulsively picked it. It's the dress that started everything after all, with those dating app pictures.

"Don't you think it's too much?" I ask Hana. She's wearing a midnight-blue cocktail dress with long chiffon sleeves and a skirt that reaches mid-calf. She looks stunning with her hair up and gold accessories.

"No, you look perfect. And I love the shoes. Are they new?"

I bring a foot forward to show her the pearl-encrusted Jimmy Choo. "Yes, I deserved a reward for not killing my mother."

"Fair. Should we start looking around?" she asks after another sip of her champagne.

I agree, so we make our way toward the closest canvas. It's a mess of drops, splashes, and smears of paint, the colors dark and gloomy. The composition of it is oppressive, like a dark forest that harbors even darker secrets. If the goal of art is to trigger feelings, then it's accomplished. It's not my type, but it works.

"That's depressing," Hana mumbles next to me before we move on to the next one.

A few canvases later, we come across Constance. She greets us with warmth, thanking us for coming. We congratulate her on such a successful soiree, and before we can catch up on the last couple of years, her attention is called elsewhere.

Another waiter comes to us with a tray of food, Hana picks a couple of things, and we look around again. I'm distractedly looking at the buffet from afar when Hana gently shoves her elbow into my ribs.

"Isn't that the guy from the dating app?" she asks.

"What?"

"There, the man with the burgundy jacket," she insists. I look in the direction of her stare. "Isn't it that Eli guy?"

Holy crap. It is.

Elijah is right there, talking to a couple of people in the back of the gallery. The same Elijah I shared an elevator ride with this morning. What is he doing here?

Before I can even register his presence, a low, raspy, and devilish voice I know all too well says from behind me, "I think I know this dress."

Thinking my mind is playing tricks on me, I swiftly spin around. A pair of green eyes is staring down at me with amusement. Eyes that I was lost in for hours last night. Eyes that witnessed me in the most abandoned state I've ever been in.

Why is Jake here? How?!

"Is this the ladder guy?" Hana whispers, putting two and two together despite being as shocked as I am.

And there are many reasons to be shocked. I have always found Jake stunning, but seeing him in a suit requires a whole new set of adjectives. The charcoal jacket and pants fit him perfectly, accentuating his solid build and powerful muscles. And the dark red dress shirt he has underneath is reminiscent of the reddish feathers that creep up his neck out of the unbuttoned collar.

This man is so ridiculously attractive, it's not even funny.

"The ladder guy?" he asks, intrigued. Then he smirks—a half one that awakens the parts of me he overused. "I don't know. Am I *the* ladder guy, red?"

What the hell can I answer to that? I've been fantastic at not sharing too much information with Hana because she'd push me to give Jake a lot more than I should. But she's seen him now. She'll know precisely just how deeply screwed I am.

"Don't tell me Beelzebub took your tongue on your way out this morning," he teases.

"You were at his place?" Hana asks. *Shoot!* "You told me you fell asleep early yesterday, and that's why you didn't answer my messages," Hana says, squinting her eyes at me. To my relief, she doesn't seem annoyed but rather amused.

"She definitely didn't fall asleep early," Jake says, also quite entertained by this. "Am I your naughty little secret, red?"

I'm speechless, completely blindsided by the turn of events. This cannot be happening.

"Red for the hair?" Hana wonders, as if it isn't obvious.

"No," he replies, surprising me.

I'm still trying to find something to say, fighting through the embarrassment, when he slips a delicate fingertip across my temple and tucks my hair behind my ear.

"Ooh," Hana lets out before smiling broadly.

The gesture is so intimate that it fills me with warmth, as well as the awareness that anyone might notice the sparks flying between us. Finally, I fight through my shock and step away from him. "You two stop conniving," I protest. There's no way I'll let them form an alliance at my expense. "Jake, what are you doing here?"

"The network in the art industry runs tight in this city, so I'm familiar with the gallery owner."

"Oh, you're an artist?" Hana wonders.

"I also own a gallery."

Before they get engrossed in the conversation, I grab Jake by the arm, dismissing how thick and solid it is in my hand, and drag him off to the side.

"Jake, I know people here. They can't see us together."

"We're only talking, love—nothing incriminating in that. It's the way you look at me that might give us away."

Whatever look I have on my face turns into a glare. It doesn't stop him from inching closer to me, though.

"Are you still sore?" he murmurs in my ear.

I step back, determined not to let anyone guess our shared intimacy. "Are you?"

His wolfish grin reminds me exactly why my core is tender. He's irresistible, and he knows it. "I am, yes."

"Well, I'll let you recuperate then." With that, I leave him and return to Hana, who's observing us from afar. I already know what we'll talk about as I make my way back across the room.

"Hot damn. Gen, you didn't tell me he was so hot."

"I told you he was attractive," I counter with an unsteady voice.

"No, that isn't just attractive. That is a black hole that attracts everything that comes near it. He is … I don't have the words. And he has piercings on his schlong? God*damn*."

She fans her face as if the thought itself is too much. Jake's attention is on us, and I can guess how much he enjoys this.

"Stop looking at him like that," I tell Hana. "His ego doesn't need it, trust me."

"Staring is a God-given right, and I'll keep doing it until the day I die."

Thankfully, Eli arrives by Jake's side, and that pulls his attention away from us. After they've exchanged a few words, the newcomer turns toward us with surprise. When he spots me, Eli grins and waves but doesn't approach. Good. It's better that way.

As Hana and I continue our journey through the pieces, I'm hyper-aware of Jake's presence nearby. Wherever I go, I sense his eyes on me, lurking from a retreated corner like a predator waiting for the right moment to strike.

We stumble on a couple Hana is acquainted with, but since I'm unfamiliar with them, I struggle to participate. "I'll get myself another drink," I tell Hana, grazing her arm before leaving her to her friends.

A buffet is set up along the wall on the side of the gallery, so I walk there to get another flute of champagne. I take a few sips of it as soon as it's in my hands.

Today has been exhausting, and I can't wait to get home and sleep until noon tomorrow. Good thing it's Sunday, and I have no engagements, as I always make sure of.

"How was your brunch?" Jake asks behind me.

I hold back a sigh, spinning around. "Is it so hard to stay ten feet away from me?"

"Come on, love. No one cares about us, they're too busy staring at their own arseholes. How's yours doing, by the way?" I worriedly glance around, mortified at the idea someone might have heard him. But he's right, no one cares about us, lost in their own conversations. Still, I would rather we avoid one another altogether.

"You're a piece of work, you know that?"

Just as I'm about to storm off, my head spins, and my balance wavers, possibly from the hunger, lack of sleep, and champagne. Jake is quick to grab my arm and help me straighten up. "Are you alright, red?"

"Yes, I—" My stomach picks this precise moment to release a rumble so loud that we both hear it.

"Have you eaten since your brunch?" The concern in his tone is touching, but I can't fully appreciate it, given the situation. I shake my head. "That was hours ago," he scolds disapprovingly. "You need sustenance after a sexathon."

He takes a porcelain plate from the buffet and fills it with whatever he can find.

"Is that what it was?" I ask. "A sexathon?"

He lets out a surprised chuckle, sending me a side glance. "Going after my ego now, red?"

"You'll survive. But I didn't realize we also took care of number eight yesterday. I thought a sexathon had to last twenty-six hours and twenty-one minutes or something. Like how many miles it takes to run a marathon."

"We'll do it your way, then. It sounds challenging, but I do love a challenge." He gives me an impish wink as he places the overflowing plate in my hands. "Eat, sweetheart."

"I'm not hungry."

"Your stomach says otherwise. Eat before you faint and people think you swooned because of how sexy I am."

I scoff to mask my grin. "See? Your ego is doing very well."

"How could it not when you're looking at me like this?"

"Like what?"

"Like you wish you could rip my clothes off."

This time, I roll my eyes. It's not entirely false, but he doesn't have to know that. Because I don't want him to cause a scene, I pick up a canapé from the plate and eat it. Ugh, that's good. Another one goes down before I know it, and then I'm bringing a third to my lips.

"Right, you weren't hungry," he laughs.

I glare at him. "I'm trying to watch my figure."

"Well, watching your figure is quickly becoming my favorite pastime, so I can relate."

He looks way too proud of himself while I chew on the mini quiche. "How do you know Constance?" he asks once I swallow.

"We went to Harvard together."

"Are you close?"

"Not anymore. You?"

He winces, looking at the crowd. "No, but we might have fucked once or twice."

My jaw drops, and I hate the way my heart does, too. Why do I care who he's slept with? Constance is a beautiful woman with wheat-blonde hair and the body of a model. Of course, he'd get in bed with her if given the opportunity.

"It's been a while, though. She got married, and I avoid vengeful husbands."

"Shame you won't get to finish the night with her, then," I say with bitterness.

My fit of jealousy, which I know I should have held back, seems to delight him. He gives me one of his bone-melting smiles, making me forget everything else. "I wouldn't have anyway," he says, coming closer. "I'm saving myself so I get to creampie the sexy as fuck redhead who drives me mad."

Heat flashes across my face, so incandescent that I know I'm bright pink. He really is so crass, which is something I wish I could say I hate, but the wetness gathering between my legs says otherwise.

"I got tested this afternoon, by the way. Even paid extra to get the results quickly," he explains.

"Eager, are we?"

"Oh, you have no idea."

As I chew on another canapé to hide my smile, I observe the room's occupants. My eyes fall on Constance, and a pinch of resentment hits me. Jake catches what's going on.

"Would it help to know I didn't have the ladder back then? Your friend from Harvard doesn't know just how good my cock feels now."

It does help a little. Constance might have gotten lucky, but I got even luckier.

"Gen!" Hana whisper-shouts, rushing toward us. It breaks the spell Jake weaved around me, and I take a few steps back from his intoxicating presence. "Gen, we have a problem! A 9-1-1 emergency."

Hana isn't one to exaggerate in such circumstances, so when she tugs at my arm, I distractedly hand my plate to Jake and follow her. "What's going on?"

"I don't know why we didn't realize this could happen. But we should have because Constance invited both of you," she explains, making little sense as she pulls me toward the middle of the gallery.

"What are you saying?"

She stops, scanning the room for something. *Someone.* "I'm saying that while you were busy flirting with that tall glass of water over there, a small glass of vinegar came in."

I'm still confused until my eyes land on the person she is seeking. I haven't seen him in weeks, but those caramel eyes will forever be familiar.

Edward …

Eddie is here. And if I ever wish to have another chance with my ex, I can't let this get messy. If Edward hears or guesses about Jake, he'll have the wrong impression, thinking I came with some guy I already replaced him with.

I can't let that happen.

My brain is going a mile a second as panic seeps through me. Eddie notices me, and I barely manage to wave back at him.

"Fuck," Hana curses when he walks up to us.

"Act normal," I mutter between my teeth. "And as soon as you can, go tell Jake to keep his distance."

"Wait, are you seri—"

"Hey, Gen!" Eddie greets me. "Good God, you look beautiful."

"Having regrets yet?" my protective friend insolently replies.

"Hello, Hana. It's been a while."

"It has."

Ignoring her acerbic tone, he turns to me again. "Gen, I saw the Waltons over there. Maybe we should greet them?"

"Uh, yes, sure." Harry and Liz Walton are close friends of my parents, and if I don't take a moment to talk to them, I'll never hear the end of it. Eddie slips an arm under mine and pulls me with him as he walks away. "Hana, I'll be right back," I tell my friend, discreetly gesturing toward where Jake is.

She rolls her eyes, clearly annoyed to be left alone, but I'm already too far to say anything more.

"How have you been?" Edward asks on our way to the old couple.

"Good. A bit tired."

"Work has been a lot, eh?"

"Like always. How about you?"

"Well, I've missed you, for one."

"You have?"

"Yes. I thought I'd be happier alone, but it's the opposite. I preferred having you around—even if it wasn't very often."

"Oh, I see."

"And you? Do you miss me?"

My hands are clammy, and my heart is beating too fast. I haven't felt the absence of Eddie as a person. I'm actually amazed at how little I think of him. But I miss being in a relationship, having someone to count on, to come home to, to support and be supported by ... I miss the comfort of knowing the rest of my life is set and headed in the right direction. All I can think of is how simple things were with him, how we barely ever argued, how we had the same wishes for our future—down to the number of children we wanted.

Edward can help me become the person I'm meant to be. Mother made it beyond clear during our brunch that I messed up and might never find someone as ideally suited for me. I even know that Victoria would have liked him, with his conciliatory temperament and classic good looks. Edward Hoffman is the perfect catch, the man every woman wants—something that was very clear at Harvard before we got together.

He's everything I've ever wanted, and I am lucky that this page of my life isn't entirely turned yet.

So, why do I feel like such a fraud when I say, "I've missed you too, Eddie."

How can doing the right thing feel so wrong?

CHAPTER
Seventeen

Jake

I DON'T THINK I HAVE ever seen someone who screams "trust fund knobhead" as much as the man Gen is standing with. One second she was with me, we were flirting and having fun, and the next, she was rushing to that arsehole.

Since I have no idea what the fuck is happening, I stay in the background and eat the stuff on the plate I made for her. Why does he have his hand around her waist like that, and why isn't she whacking it away as she would for me?

I'm taken out of my thoughts when her friend appears next to me. Her eyes are on them too, on Gen and the twat, talking to an old couple.

When I extend the plate before her, she picks up something and eats it.

"Who is he?" I ask.

"Her ex." The animosity she puts in those two short words lets me know exactly what she thinks of the golden douchebag.

"The one who told her she sucked in bed?"

Gen's friend turns to me with wide eyes, surprised. "She told you about that?"

"Yeah. She was so upset that I could have punched him in the face."

When she speaks again, she's hesitant. "And is she?"

"Is she what?"

"Bad in bed."

"Fuck no. I've actually never had this much fun in my life."

"Okay, good. I suspected it wasn't true, but Edward put this idea in her head, and she became convinced he was right."

"No, your friend is fucking dynamite in the sack. I told her he was a twat for saying that. And I didn't even know he looked the part."

The brunette giggles. "He does, doesn't he?"

"Look at his shoes. Who the fuck under fifty wears those?"

"A trust fund baby."

Then and there, I know I like this woman. "What's your name, love?" I ask her.

"Hana. And you're Jake, right?"

"Yeah, Jacob."

We shake hands and then return to our silent observation. The dickhead says something supposedly funny, and the old couple chuckles. Gen does too, but it's delayed, forced. She's uncomfortable, and it's obvious even from where I stand.

I don't get it. She deserves so much better than a prick who can't even appreciate her splendor. The idiot was never invested enough to uncover the sensuality within her, judging her as boring rather than questioning himself. And he had five years to do it.

I unlocked it in under an hour.

But what bothers me the most is that he's nothing like me. We couldn't be more different physically, and it's clear that we're nothing alike where lifestyle is concerned. He's what Gen picked, what she wanted to spend the rest of her life with. A proper little posh like her, who comes from money and went to an Ivy League school. But me … I'm an anomaly, someone she stumbled upon because she was looking for a Jacob's ladder.

I couldn't be further from her type.

"What are we staring at?" Eli looks in their direction, having just joined us. "Who's with Gen?"

"Her ex," Hana and I answer in unison.

"Oh, shit." Eli thinks about it for a moment, then carefully goes on to say, "And how are we feeling about it?"

"Not great," I answer.

"I have it on good authority that Eddie never made her orgasm as hard as you do," Hana says with a shrug, taking a sip of champagne and picking a mini club sandwich from the plate.

It helps a little. "Here, hold this," I order Eli, shoving the plate into his hands.

"Oh, wait," Gen's friend stops me. "I'm supposed to tell you to keep your distance. But you're old enough to make your own decisions."

I *definitely* like her.

As I leave them behind, Eli says, "That's gonna be interesting."

"I wish I had popcorn," Hana replies.

On my way toward the couple, I adjust the collar of my red shirt and tug on my jacket to straighten it. She doesn't want what we're doing in the darkest hours of the night to be exposed, and I respect that. But I'm not about to watch her spend the evening with her ex and do nothing about it.

She still isn't aware of me when I reach them, and I hear the ongoing conversation. "Vivienne told me you two had split," the old woman says. "Are you getting back together, then?"

The ex rests a hand on the small of Gen's back, and I fight the urge to tear it away. "You know how volatile love can be … We're just figuring things out at the moment," he says.

"Excuse me, miss?" I call, gently tapping Gen's shoulder. She tenses, and I see the hairs on her arm rise. Everyone turns to me, so I put on my best poker face. Which isn't easy when the beautiful redhead glares at me, warning me not to mess this up for her. "Sorry for interrupting you, but I have the uncanny feeling we've met before. Are you, by any chance, a friend of Hana?"

"I am," she hesitantly replies.

"Then that's it. We probably met at her …" Fuck, I should have planned this better.

"Engagement party?" Gen finishes for me.

"That's it, yeah."

"Right."

This is such a fucked up situation. Twenty-four hours ago, we were getting started with our not-a-sexathon sexathon, and now we can't even be acquaintances. For fuck's sake, I licked this woman's clit, fingered her arse, choked her … And she really expects me to sit back while she enjoys a pleasant evening with her ex?

"I was there, and I don't recall seeing you," her ex interjects. *Stay out of this, prick.*

"I don't remember you either, which makes sense. But come on, mate. A six-foot-two handsome devil with tattoos? I'm hard to forget."

"Sorry, but I don't recall meeting you either," Gen adds. I won't lie, that one stings.

That's when the old couple decides to leave, probably sensing that the situation is slowly getting out of control.

"Well, *I* remember you very well because I'm into redheads," I say in return.

My words get her ex to show some spine, finally. He wraps a hand around her waist to pull her closer, and I see just how uncomfortable that makes her.

"Excuse me, but who are you?" he asks.

"We already established that I'm a friend of Hana's and her fiancé."

"Your name?"

"So you really forgot about me, mate? I'm Jake. And you are?"

"Edward Hoffman the Third."

"The Third?" I whistle, feigning being impressed. "So, there are two more like you out there?" *A catastrophe, really.*

The imbecile squares his shoulders, which makes him look ridiculous because I'm five inches taller and probably outweigh him by fifty pounds of muscle mass.

Before he can dig himself into a deeper hole, Gen comes to his aid. "What do you want, sir?"

"Nothing, love. I was just wondering if you were taken. Is that your boyfriend?" I point at the dickhead, who tugs her even closer.

"That is none of your concern," Gen says, her tone icy.

The fire behind the blue of her eyes makes me question if this little pissing contest of mine is worth angering her. Maybe I went a little too far. Time to retreat. "Sorry, you two are busy. I'll leave you be."

Before she can react, I take her hand and gallantly bend to press a kiss on the back of it. I witness the duality of her reaction as her pupils dilate at the discreet touch of my tongue, but her scowl clearly disapproves of my methods. My fingers graze the softness of her palm before I release her, and I give Edward a rough pat on the shoulder. "See you around, mate."

"Let's hope not," Gen mutters.

"Oh, I think you will," I counter. I give her a wink, and then I'm off.

As much as I try to keep a contained facade, I'm seething. Why would she even bother giving him the time of day? He's a joke turned loafer-wearing bratty little shit. Edward Hoffman the fucking Third. What a clown.

When I return to Elijah and Hana, they seem riveted. "How did that go?"

"Not well. I think she's pissed."

"Oh, she is," Hana confirms. "But so is Edward, so I see it as a win."

"You're not a very good friend, are you?" Eli pensively asks.

"I've been telling her for years that she can do better than Eddie. Honestly, she deserved the reminder."

"I think I'll go home," I decide.

"Really? We just arrived," Eli protests.

When I look back at Gen and her ex, he still has an arm around her, and they are now talking to another couple. This is bullshit. "You can stay and take a cab home—don't forget your helmet. I just don't think I can witness this for much longer."

"Alright, I get it."

"I'll take a leak first, then I'm off. Hana, it was a pleasure meeting you. Keep fighting the good death-to-Eddie fight, love."

She laughs, shaking her head with amusement. "I'll die on that hill."

I give them a nod and head toward the back of the gallery, where I spotted the restrooms earlier. You know the place is fancy when each booth is a proper build, rather than shitty stalls.

Once I'm done pissing, I wash my hands and give myself a little pep talk in the mirror, remembering that I'm better than that prick, even though I'm not the third of some empire.

When I open the door, ready to leave this place entirely, a fury of red hair, green satin, and creamy freckled skin shoves me back inside. She locks the door and then meets my eyes with rage plastered all over her pretty face.

"What the hell was that!" Gen explodes, barely managing to contain her voice. She is ridiculously hot when angry, but I do my best to dismiss it and handle this seriously.

"What?"

"This is my life, Jacob! My *real* life. You can't sabotage it because you feel offended."

"I was appalled, not offended."

"What did you think you would accomplish with that caveman display of ownership?"

"Nothing, really. I was just curious to meet the man who spent five years with you and never even learned to fuck you properly. And now that I have, I can confirm that I don't fucking get it, Genevieve."

"Get what?"

"Why are you wasting your time with that cunt?"

"Excuse me?"

"Why would you even entertain the possibility of him?"

"I—Eddie is a friend, Jake. We dated for five years, and I've known him for even longer than that. He knows me more than anybody else, and there will *always* be something between us."

"He didn't know you, or he wouldn't have left you. He's a fucking loser."

That one might be a low blow, but she needs to hear it. Those five years she spent with him mean nothing if he couldn't love her enough to fight for her.

"So what?" she snarls. "You think you know me better than he does?"

"Honestly? I think you don't even know yourself, Genevieve. You have this idea of who you want to be, this proper little Upper East Side lawyer, but then you come to *me* to feel alive. I'm the opposite of what you want, red, yet it looks like I'm what you need."

That one hits her like a slap. She never noticed her duality, did she? There are two sides to her. The one that demands that I stay away so we won't be discovered, and the one that can't help but flirt back. The one that drafts an exhaustive sex contract and the one that begs me to choke her in the dark back room of a shady bar. It's like there's the person she should be and the person who craves to get out of the rigid frame she built for herself.

"We're just having sex, Jake. You're helping me with my list, and then I'll be with whoever I want."

Now, it's my turn to endure the blow. Shit, we're as good at hurting as we are at pleasuring.

"I know that, and I'm fine with it. I don't need anything more. But please, not him. He doesn't deserve you."

"You don't know him, Jake."

"I know enough."

She rolls her eyes, unconvinced. "He's a good man. He respects me, and our energies match perfectly. Also, you can think whatever you want of Edward, but at least *he* told me I look beautiful tonight."

Now she's making stupid excuses for him, which pisses me off. I move closer to her, and it has her backing away until she's pressed against the slick marble wall by the sink.

"Is that it? Is the bar so fucking low that that's enough? You want me to call you pretty? To tell you that dress was made for you? That this color exists solely to compliment your skin? Or would you maybe prefer the crude truth?"

She blinks several times, struggling to process the ardent words I can't stop from pouring out.

"The truth, red, is that you look so fucking stunning that I've been sporting a semi since I noticed you. But then, you're always so fuckable it's ridiculous. I don't care if my cock needs to rest and your pussy can't take more of me—I would've pinned you down and fucked you if there weren't a hundred witnesses around us."

Nothing comes when she tries to speak, so she licks her lips, her pink tongue dragging over their plumpness, and tries again.

"You really think I'm stunning?"

How can she even doubt it? Because I don't know how else to make her believe me, I grab her hand that's clutching the marble counter by her hip and bring it between us, flattening it over my hardened cock.

"What do you think?" I ask.

She bats her lashes, contending with desires and needs that can't be contained. When she makes a small move forward, as if to kiss me, I fucking lose it.

My mouth is on hers before she can see it coming, but she quickly reacts, wrapping her arms around my neck and bringing me closer. Our tongues meet, our embrace is brutally passionate, and everything outside this room becomes irrelevant. Fuck her ex, fuck whoever she ends up with when we're done with her list. She's mine for now, and I'll make sure she doesn't forget it.

I eagerly pull up her dress—the same fucking dress she wore in those screenshots Eli sent me—with impatient hands, swallowing her sighs.

"Jake, wait. We already—we already did sex in a public place."

"And we're doing it again."

The next protest dies when I press a hand over the space between her legs, and I feel just how wet she is. Did the arguing work on her, too? What does that say about us?

"Who are you dripping for, red?" I groan, pressing harder on her pussy. "Me or him?"

She doesn't even hesitate before saying, "You. This is all for you."

Fucking right it is.

With my thumbs shoved into the sides, I tug her underwear down, making it slip to her ankles. When I kneel, she lifts a foot so I can pass it and then the other. Once the pearl-white lace is off, I ball it and slip it into my pocket.

As much as I want to fuck her right now, I won't indulge. Some part of me worries that if I do, it will make for an acceptable parting quickie. And I'm not ready to part yet. So, I might as well leave her wanting more.

Still kneeling, I bunch her dress at her waist and press my mouth onto her awaiting cunt.

"Aah—Jake!" she moans, weaving her fingers into my hair.

Her hips buck, pressing herself harder into me, offering me a better angle to work with. I reach behind her thigh to set her leg on my shoulder, and she allows me, releasing the sweetest whimpers and sighs. My tongue rasps against her clit with precision while I handle her other leg, and soon, she's hoisted on me, her thighs on either side of my head as I eat her out.

The small nub of her clit is slick and warm against my tongue, and when I pause my movements, I can feel it pulse. But she never lets me stop for too long, letting out a trembling protest and tightening her grip on my hair. When I suck on her hard, she lets out a small cry, her thighs clamping on my skull. But I also feel how that makes her tremble all over, so I reach around her legs, grab onto her knees, and pry her open.

I'm already looking up when she glimpses down, her ocean eyes veiled with pleasure and lust, her face already flushed. With our gazes locked together, I give her a series of fast, coordinated licks right where she fucking needs me.

"Oh, God—" she moans, arching against the wall. "Oh God, yes!"

"Stop calling out His name," I say, pulling away enough for my words to make sense. "Unless you want God to pay attention to us right now."

Her jaw snaps closed, her eyes going wide. *That's what I thought.*

I return to my ministrations, reveling in her moans, taste, and scent. She's like a heavenly delicacy, a nectar that was never meant for us mortals. And yet, here I am, feasting on her like she's my own slice of heaven.

Because I want her to have only me in her mind for the next few hours, I release one of her knees, keeping her open on the other side, and align three fingers with her entrance. Before she can see it coming, I slip them inside her, stretching her tightness around my thick knuckles. She's so wet though, that they enter her with no resistance, her greedy little cunt swallowing them entirely.

"Aah! Yes!" She writhes like a possessed woman, and I don't need more than this to start fucking her with my hand while my tongue keeps taking care of her clit. This only lasts a few seconds before I sense the first spasms of her walls, squeezing my fingers together.

"Jake—" she softly cries out. "Jake, I'm gonna come."

"Good. Come for me, red. Come all over my fingers and tongue."

The pace of my hand increases, and so does the one of my tongue. Then it happens—the explosion, the peak. Her insides clench so hard that I can barely keep up with my thrusts, and her hips jolt and arch, her body tense under the ravaging orgasm I just gave her. And I keep going, bringing her more pleasure until it finally recedes.

When the tight fists holding my hair loosen and her entire body has turned lax, I pull my fingers out of her. Then, making sure she's stable enough, I let down her legs one after the other. She leans heavily on the wall behind her, completely dazed by the intensity of her climax.

With the sleeve of my jacket, I wipe my lower face. As soon as I'm upright, she pulls me into her and kisses me. We share her taste

for a moment, and when she reaches for the belt at my hips, I stop
her with a firm hand.

"No, not tonight."

"What? Why?"

I take a few steps away from her, closer to the door. "It's better
that way."

"What is?"

I'm not even sure, so I don't answer. Instead, I let my earlier
rancor take over again. "When you're out there, spending the
evening with your ex, remember who's the reason for that tingling
sensation between your legs."

She looks properly appalled, her jaw dropping with indignation.
"Are you serious right now? Is that what this was about?"

"I don't know what it was about, Gen. But don't act like you
didn't enjoy it." When I put my hand over the knob and unlock the
door, she protests again.

"Wait, Jake!" she calls. But it isn't to hold me back this time. "My
underwear."

I shove my hand in my pocket, grazing at the humid lace.
"Number thirteen," I say.

Drive your partner crazy by giving them a special present during an outing.

"I'm only here to help with that list after all, am I not?" I remind
her. "I'll see you on Tuesday, Gen." She still hasn't answered by the
time I exit the restroom.

As I walk back to the gallery, I can still sense her everywhere. In
my ears, my mouth, my nose … Even on my hand, my fingers are
still wet with the remnants of her climax.

When I spot her fucking ex, irrational jealousy strikes me again.
What I do next, I blame on the insanity caused by blue balls.

"Edward, mate," I call out when I approach him. With my left
hand on his shoulder, I offer the right one to shake his. Because he's
with people, he doesn't leave me hanging and returns the gesture. I
squeeze it harder than I need to, doing the same to his shoulder. "It
was great seeing you again," I continue. "Take care, yeah?"

He nods, wholly disoriented by my friendliness, and I let go of
him. The clueless cunt will probably think I had clammy hands,
never realizing that this, the moistness I left on him, it's his fucking
ex-girlfriend—the woman he'll spend the evening with—coming all
over my hand minutes prior.

And he's such a daft prick that he probably won't even recognize the smell despite spending five fucking years with its origin. He didn't deserve her, and I hope she'll see that.

I don't look for Eli or Hana because I'm not lingering here for another minute. Instead, I ask for my helmet from the woman in charge of coats and shit. I walk out into the night as soon as I have it.

Five times. I've seen this woman five times, and she's already fucked me up more than anyone ever has. Keeping up with this, seeing her again and again, might not be the smartest thing to do.

The problem is that I'm not sure I can stop.

CHAPTER
Eighteen

Gen

WHAT HAPPENED AT THE GALLERY remains etched in the back of my mind for the following days. I can't get over it or figure out what I should do about it.

After what happened in the restroom, I returned to Eddie, only to let him know I had to leave, pretending I had a headache. Hana was over it too, so we headed back to our respective homes, sharing a cab. As suspected, she's now a fervent Jake defender. Which I can't blame her for because he's the most charismatic person I've ever met. But as handsome, humorous, and charming as he is, he's only a fun time, the kind of person to fool around with for a bit and move on.

He himself made it very clear that he wasn't into relationships. Jake is in this for the sex, just like me, and I don't understand why everything suddenly got so complicated. It's supposed to be a mindless, no-strings-attached pastime, and I don't get why it derailed.

But now, Jake isn't texting me, I'm too scared to reach out, and I have no idea if our arrangement still stands. He did say we'd meet on Tuesday, but what if he digested everything and decided I wasn't worth the hassle?

And as if things weren't complicated enough, Eddie is slowly trying to creep back into my life. Thankfully, it's just good morning messages for now and the occasional, "Hey, what's up?" He hasn't suggested that we meet somewhere, and I dread the day he might. It's too early for that. I'm not finished with my list and haven't had my fill of Jacob Clarke. Far from it.

In the meantime, my heart races with every text notification I get, only to squeeze with disappointment when it's either Hana or Edward.

Ugh, why is this so messy?

I'm still in my NexaCorp office late on Tuesday, fixing mistakes my colleagues left behind or picking up their slack. I'm *so* done with this position, and I cannot wait to get my boss's job.

When my phone vibrates on my desk, I know it'll be Edward asking what I'm eating or whatever excuse he found to text me again. I distractedly check the screen, knowing I won't answer right away. In an attempt to slow down his advances, I've been giving myself a couple of hours to reply to him every time.

But it isn't Eddie. Nor Hana.

My hands fly to the phone to pick it up eagerly.

Jake finally texted!

LADDER GUY

> Are you still skipping Pilates?

I check on the time. I'm already late for that, so there's my answer. The evening is even more advanced than I'd realized. Although I try not to let it hurt me, it's hard to ignore how his text feels like an afterthought, like he completely forgot we were supposed to meet and only sent it because he's bored and trying to occupy the rest of his evening. But I can't let it affect me because we're supposed to be detached and distant outside of sex. We're not friends or a couple. Just two adults with needs and pieces that fit well together.

So, swallowing back my pride, I rise above my conflicted feelings and send him an answer.

ME

> Yes, but I'm still at work. I have to finish something before I leave, so it'll be about an hour before I'm at your place.

LADDER GUY

> What if I come to you?

ME

> I can be at my place in 20-25 minutes.

LADDER GUY

> Send me your address.

My thumbs are unsteady as I type the reply. He's being very clinical and cold, which I'm not used to from him. No nicknames or flirting. He's doing the bare minimum, so I suppose he's still pissed about Saturday.

I try to finish what I was doing, but it's useless. I could hardly focus before, and now it's even worse. So, with a long and trembling sigh, I give up and grab my things, turning my computer off.

The old security guard is at his desk when I pass it in the ground floor lobby. "Another late night, Miss Kensington?"

"You know me, Farrell. Always girl-bossing."

He laughs, his pearly white teeth contrasting with the dark brown of his skin. "You have a good evening, miss."

"You too! And say hi to your wife for me."

"Will do."

A sedan is already waiting for me by NexaCorp's entrance, and ten minutes later, I'm entering my building. Mickey—the night concierge—started his shift, and just like Farrell, he's used to seeing me finish my day so late.

As soon as I'm in my apartment, I make the rounds, ensuring everything is alright. The maid came this morning while I was at work, so it's squeaky clean, and aside from some messy folders in my office, there isn't anything out of place. Then I inspect the fridge, looking for what we could drink. There isn't much aside from beer, but I have ice cubes and liquors, so that'll have to do. I already ate a small salad at the office, and given the time, I suppose Jake will have eaten as well.

When the intercom rings, I'm in the bathroom, adjusting my makeup and fluffing my hair. I also changed into a dress more comfortable than my work clothes. My legs are a little unstable as I go to answer the call. I'm impatient to see Jake, but also apprehensive. How will he behave after what happened at the gallery? Those texts he sent aren't a good sign, are they?

Once I tell Mickey to let Jake up, I stand by the entrance, taking long and deep breaths. My heart is in my throat, and I wish I weren't so damn affected by all this. It's supposed to be a mindless sex thing, not whatever this is.

Every few seconds, I peek into the peephole because things might be a little easier if I see him coming. My anxiety peaks anyway when he appears, wearing all black and holding a brown paper bag on one side and what looks like a helmet on the other. I didn't even know he had a bike, and the mere idea of it makes me weak in the knees.

Why does he have to be so hot all the time?

So I don't look too pathetic, I wait for him to ring the bell, count to ten, and then unlock the door to open it.

The lump in my throat swells enough to cut off my breath as I take him in. He's wearing a black sweater, its long sleeves rolled up his artfully tattooed forearms, and he has thick black leather gloves on his hands. As always, his jeans are the perfect fit, tucked into his military boots.

Once I'm done drooling over his wardrobe choices, I meet his green gaze. His face is closed off, but his eyes hold an intensity that I can't miss.

"Uh, come in," I say, shaking myself out of this. He does, and I let him in the foyer.

"I didn't know if you already ate," he explains, setting the paper bag on a console table. "I had some things to deal with at The Parlour, so I didn't have time to."

"Were you tattooing someone?"

"No, I barely ever get time to do that now," he explains, pulling off his gloves and revealing his inked knuckles. "I was handling the accommodations for our next guest artist."

"Oh, I see …"

We stay silent for a moment, sitting in awkward tension. The delicious smell of whatever he brought gives me the presence of mind to do something about it.

"Let's go to the kitchen," I offer, picking up the bag.

"Should I remove my shoes?"

"As you prefer. I usually remove mine because they are uncomfortable," I explain, which makes him look at my elegant slippers.

When he kneels to undo his laces, I offer, "I think there's a pair of—" No. Suggesting that he uses the slippers Eddie left behind is probably not a good idea. "Never mind," I say instead.

Even though I make my way to the kitchen alone, I'm tense all over. Things will get better. As soon as we're naked, everything will flow like it always does. By the time he joins me, I've taken out plates and cutlery and am emptying the bag to discover what he brought. Lebanese food. Yum!

Now that he's with me, the tension builds up again. This silence between us is so uncharacteristic that it's all I can hear. We're never like this, we always have things to say, even just to provoke or tease one another.

We both try to put an end to it at the same time.

"Jake, I—"

"Gen, I wanted to—"

We stop, stare at each other, and amusement cracks through his unreadable expression. "You first," I insist.

He passes a nervous hand through his hair, averting his eyes. "I wanted to apologize for the way I behaved at the gallery. I shouldn't have done or said those things. It was weird."

"It was, wasn't it? Maybe Constance put something in the champagne," I say pensively, trying to lighten the mood.

He chuckles, scratching his angular jawline in an embarrassed manner. "I'm sorry for acting like a prick."

I appreciate that he acknowledges it, and I hope the incident was only a fluke, not the worrisome preview of more problematic behavior to come.

"I'm sorry too," I say in return, hoping for a clean slate.

"For what?"

"I didn't know Eddie would be there, and I'm sorry you had to … I don't know, see me with him? I'm not familiar with sex arrangements, but they often get messy, don't they?" I ask.

He thinks about his answer for way too long, so it doesn't feel genuine when he settles on, "They do, yes."

But I dismiss my doubts, deciding to believe the gallery was indeed a fluke. "So, we're good?" I insist.

"Yeah, of course. I told you I was fantastic at one-night stands. I just need to get used to having several of them with the same person," he humors.

I grin, amused by how he puts it. "Let's eat."

Before I can pick up the plates, I feel his looming presence right beside me. When I questioningly glance up, he frames my face with his big hands and holds me in place while his lips softly land on mine. He doesn't devour me like he usually does but gives me a series of brief and intense pecks instead. My heart flutters with every single one. Then, he pulls away, enough for me to get lost in the lush green of his eyes.

"I missed you, red."

"I missed you too."

And I mean it this time. I'm not embellishing like I did with Eddie—not just saying it because I should. This is the undeniable and unaltered truth. I missed his texts, his touch, his humor, his face ...

"Alright, food first, then you," he declares, releasing me. Before he moves on with it though, he gives me one last adamant peck.

We fill our plates with food and then move on to the dinner table between the kitchen and lounge space. "Do you want something to drink?" I offer.

"Whatever you'll have."

"I'm having water. If you prefer, I also have a couple of fancy Belgian beers in the fridge."

"Water's perfect, love."

As I return with a bottle and glasses, I sense how different the atmosphere is now. We're not quite there yet, but it's not as tense and awkward. Especially not when we start eating and the conversation flows.

"I never asked where you work," Jake realizes.

"NexaCorp's headquarters, on 7th Avenue."

"Is that the glass one shaped like an obelisk?"

"Yep. There's an amazing view from the 63rd floor."

"Which is where you are, I reckon?"

I nod. We talk about my work a little longer, and he listens, even though it must bore him to death. By the time I'm done explaining my situation, we're done eating, with nothing left on our plates but falafel crumbs and humus smears.

"Your boss sounds like a proper cunt."

I chuckle. "I painted an accurate portrait, then."

"What happens once you get his job? Will it make your life easier?"

"Probably not. If I do things the way he does, I would have fewer hours than I do now. But I'm too much of a perfectionist to half-ass the job like him. So I'd probably end up with more hours overall, and I can kiss goodbye most of my Saturdays."

"Then why are you gunning for it?" I can tell he's intrigued and curious to understand my reasoning.

"Well, the work will be more satisfactory, and I'll make a bigger difference. It's also one step closer to the top, which is my goal."

"And once you get to that?"

"I probably won't have Sundays either," I humor. But the joke doesn't land, leaving him even more perplexed. "Anyhow, what about you?"

"I'm making my way through the world one day at a time."

"Really? No big goals, no ten-year plan?"

"Not exactly, no. I've been working my arse off for fourteen years. But I'm doing the things I love, so I'm enjoying it. It's been working well for me so far."

"More than well, I'd say."

"Yeah, I'm good at what I do, and that paid off. I have gotten to a point where I get to tattoo whatever I want, and people will accept it as an honor. I can do all sorts of personalized projects, but those come at a high price."

"So, you're reserved for the elite?"

"I also take on smaller clients as long as I like the project. But yes, more than one celebrity out there has my work on their skin."

"Maybe I've already seen one, then. Do you have a particular style?"

"Insects."

"Insects?" I echo, surprised. I do remember seeing a beautiful beetle drawing at his place.

"Hyper-realistic ones. I get people from all around the world coming to get one done."

"That is such a peculiar choice."

He dismissively shrugs his broad shoulders. "I grew up with too many of those fuckers in Australia, so I was familiar with the topic. And when I was a kid, we had this neighbor in Brisbane who collected insects. He was a retired researcher who wasn't quite done with his passion. His home office was filled with hundreds of preserved bugs in cabinets, drawers, or even framed on the walls."

"Did you develop a fondness for them, then?"

"Not really. It's more of an appreciation. The varieties in shapes, sizes, colors … When you observe them well enough, some actually look like they come from another world."

I ponder on that for a moment. Yes, there are some beautiful insects out there. "My sister had a thing for ladybugs," I disclose fondly.

"You have a sister?"

Ah, shoot. I shouldn't have brought up Victoria. That'll ruin the mood. "I had a twin. She died almost ten years ago."

"I'm sorry to hear that."

"It's alright, it-it was a long time ago."

He reaches out, resting a hand over mine. "Still. It couldn't have been easy."

"No, it really wasn't."

"Can I ask what happened to her?" he wonders.

"Car accident. She was driving at night, hit a deer, and ..." I shake my head, the pinch in my heart preventing me from saying more. Almost a decade, and it hasn't stopped hurting.

Jake arranges my hand into his and gently squeezes it as if to let me know I'm not alone. Desperate to change the topic, I ask, "What about you? Do you have siblings?"

"Not that I know of. My father was quick to disappear though, so who knows?"

I wince, too familiar with broken families, even though my parents remained together. "Was it just you and your mom, then?"

"Yeah. She was a nurse, earning a shit salary and working long hours. But she always provided me with everything a child needs."

"Is she still in Australia?"

"Technically, yes. She died when I was thirteen."

Oof. Now, I properly managed to ruin the mood. I try to find something to say other than the usual condolences—which are too generic to sound sincere. Before I have something, Jake chuckles.

"We're a depressing duo, aren't we?" he asks humorously. "Thank God we're better at fucking than small talk."

I giggle, impressed by how easily he diffused the situation. "We should venture into a more fun territory and leave our chaotic pasts behind us," he suggests in a flirty way.

"Oh, I know! I finalized the new contract!" I spring to my feet to go get the copies in my office.

"I said *fun* territory, red!" he protests.

"It will be!" I promise. The first time we did this was very entertaining, so this time will be too.

When I return with everything, he has brought the dinner stuff back into the kitchen and is on the couch. I giddily join him there, hand him a copy, and sit.

"You know we don't need a contract, right?" he carefully asks. "I'm a decent bloke, and I don't have to sign something to treat you right."

"I realize that, but I like the idea of it. It gives me a sense of security—like I'm in control. I know you would be the same with or without it, but having it is like a safety blanket."

He says nothing for a while, and I expect him to tell me it's ridiculous. The contract isn't because I don't trust him, but because it reassures me that we are legally obligated to behave well. And I also like the idea that we're bound together by it.

To my surprise, he focuses on the sheet he holds and says, "So, what's new?"

"Well, most of it is the same as before," I start. "I have changed the consent part to include a clear word. It's a dotted line, so we can decide on it together, but I was thinking of 'Jessica' as a safe word."

He chuckles, his eyes skimming over the contract. "It works."

"Then, I also added more sexual practices so we can go through the entire list."

"I see that, yes."

"Now, I already told you about the no-condom addendum. I know you got tested and are waiting on the results, but we can get over the—"

"I got the results this afternoon," he interrupts.

"Really? That fast?"

"With the small fortune I paid to get them quickly, yes."

His impatience is evident, and I wish I'd done my part with that much zeal. "Hmm, I'm still waiting for mine."

A dark expression passes over his face. "Have you had sex with anyone but me since the test from last time?" My cheeks warm up, and I shake my head. "Then you don't need one."

"It was for the fairness of it."

"Love, I couldn't care less about fairness if it means I get to fuck you raw tonight."

Well, when he puts it like that.

"I take it everything came back negative?" I venture.

"I'm as clean as it gets, red."

He picks up the pen I came with, and when he sets the papers on the table to sign them, I suggest, "Do you want us to review the contract and the addendum, like last time?"

"No, I trust you."

Less than a minute later, everything's signed, and I added our safe word. I'm going over everything again when he moves close enough for his warmth to envelop me and his lips to drop on my neck. Tingles ignite everywhere he kisses, soft and patient, and I close my eyes and tilt my head to the side so he has better access. The caress of his tongue on the tender spot below my ear has me sighing.

I feel the papers being pulled from my hands, and I let him. When I open my eyes, I see how he sends them flying on the coffee table. And when I turn to face him, his hands cradle my cheeks, pulling me in for a famished kiss. Before I know it, I'm wrapped in his embrace, the dizzying graze of his tongue demanding entrance. The instant I indulge, he invades me like a conqueror. His enthusiasm makes me laugh, which comes in the way of our kiss.

"Are you by any chance impatient, Jake?" I giggle.

"I've been thinking about it non-stop since you suggested it."

Then he's kissing me again, one of his large hands slithering up my side to cup my breast. He pinches the hard tip of it, and I moan into his mouth. As always with us, we get caught in a loop of wanting more, and more, and more. Before long, I end up straddling him, grinding onto the hardness of his crotch.

"Bedroom," I breathe out, relinquishing the kiss for an instant.

His big hands squeeze my behind intently, which is bared, thanks to my bunched-up dress. I'm airborne in a split second, clinging to him while he carries me away from the couch.

"Where?"

Between heated kisses and the entwining of tongues, I guide him through the apartment all the way to my bedroom. Once we reach it, he drops me on the bed and looks down at me with hunger.

"Undress," I order, rising to my elbows to watch him do it. The command brings out a cursed smirk that has me pressing my knees together. He swiftly sends a hand behind his head to remove his form-fitting sweater, but that won't do. "Slowly," I add.

Now, it's arousal more than amusement that has his eyes sparkling.

"How bossy you are, Miss Kensington."

"You've seen nothing yet, Mr. Clarke. Now, undress for me—slowly."

This time, his gestures are deliberate and seductive. Wholly delighted, I gnaw at my bottom lip, preparing for a spectacular show just for me.

Lucky Gen …

CHAPTER
Nineteen

Jake

I CAN'T DANCE LIKE GEN did and be all sexy, but I can sure as hell make it work for her. Or I think I can, given how she's eyeing me like she could eat me up.

She's as alluring as ever, wearing an emerald-green dress that I reckon is her own version of comfortable. It brings out the red in her hair and the freckles scattered on her creamy skin. I can't wait to get her out of it. But first …

Taking my time, I lift my sweater, gradually revealing more and more of my stomach and tattoos. Her eyes follow the nonchalant display, her teeth planted in the plumpness of her bottom lip. Maybe I'm flexing a little to appear even more muscular than I am, but she's the one who asked for a show.

Once it's off, I throw the sweater next to her on the bed, and she reaches out for it, fisting the soft fabric with her delicate hand while her eyes never leave me. I'm just as slow when I unbuckle my belt and pull it out of the loops of my jeans. It falls on the floor, and she presses her knees together. And when I unbutton my jeans and unhurriedly slide the zipper down, her eyes darken.

Turns out I don't need to do anything to turn her on. The anticipation is doing the trick on its own.

I bend over to remove my socks and then slide the denim down my legs. Once I'm left with nothing but my underwear—a pair of black boxer briefs—I cross my arms and wait, holding back a smile as I look down at her. I'm hard as steel in there, my cock stretching the fabric. I'm sure she can see the outline of the piercings and all.

"Everything," she demands.

"Tits for tats, love. Remove your dress."

She considers arguing, but the dress will have to come off at some point, so she undoes the zipper on her side. She doesn't remove it seductively, but damn, I don't care. Not when she reveals the ivory lingerie she's wearing underneath it. And beneath that, her taut pink nipples and auburn curls. Fuck, this woman is sin incarnate.

Because I'm a man of my word, I tug down my underwear until it falls at my feet and kick it away.

"What now?" I ask, raising an eyebrow.

Her eyes remain glued on my hard and thick cock for a moment, arrogantly angled up. Then she rises from the mattress, standing beside me, and presses a hand on my chest.

"Now, you lie on the bed."

She gives me a gentle push, and I comply with an amused grin, lying in the middle of it. Maybe I should relinquish control during sex more often because I genuinely love this. Especially when she joins me, crawling on her hands and knees until she's straddling me. When the drenched lace of her thong comes to rest on the underside of my cock, I don't fight the urge to bring her even closer, fingers digging into her hips.

Holding back a growl, I ask again, "And now?"

"Now, Jacob Clarke, I finally get to taste you." She seals her declaration with a deep and ardent kiss.

I'm not ready to let go when she pulls away, but I don't have time to reclaim her lips before they drop to my jaw. With fervent intensity, she lays pecks everywhere she can reach, teasing me with her tongue's wet and warm touch. Like the little minx she is, she takes her time, languidly exploring my neck and chest. When she reaches my nipple, she nips at the piercing there, tugging it with her teeth until the pain makes me groan. Satisfied with herself, she lets go and returns to her exploration of my torso.

When, finally, she reaches my cock, I'm throbbing and aching, dying to bury myself in her warmth for some comfort. But because she's decided to drive me mad, she purposefully ignores it.

"Red, what are you doing?"

"Having fun."

"This isn't fun. Stop torturing me, Genevieve."

"Not so nice being on the other side, is it?"

"If you think I was tormenting you before, you're not ready for the next time I'm in charge."

The sweet threat seems to work because her soft lips come to press a lingering kiss right on the head of my cock. Then, she uses the tip of her tongue to play with the end of the piercing, rolling it around the small steel ball. An intense and pleasurable jolt travels down my length, making it twitch. A few drops of precum seep from the tip to land on my stomach, and she greedily licks them.

"Fucking hell, red."

She looks up, her beautiful face framed by wavy red hair, her blue eyes sparkling with promises of more agony to come. The day she realizes how much power she has over me, she'll become my doom. Right now, I'd give anything just to feel her mouth around me.

Her small hand grabs the base of my cock to set it perpendicular to my stomach, and she gives it a wet kiss right on the tip. When she takes it into her mouth, I clench my jaw, struggling to control myself.

"Careful with your teeth," I warn.

"I know the basic rules of giving blowjobs, Jacob."

"I meant with the piercings. Don't hurt yourself."

She looks down again, assessing this new information. Her fingers hold each side of the apadravya, and she slightly tugs, triggering more jolts. "I can remove them if you prefer," I suggest.

She shakes her head. "No, I want to try it this way."

Then, like the greedy little woman she is, she engulfs more of my cock in her mouth. I'm still trying to recover from that when she pulls away, her plump lips dragging against the skin and piercings, and then she dives in again, taking more. I endure it, whimpering when she sucks in her cheeks, grunting when she runs her tongue on the underside, and when she takes my balls to cradle them, I curse.

Fuck, she really knows the basics of giving head.

My fingers knead through her hair as I gather it to clear the view. The sight of my dick pumping into her mouth is otherworldly, and when she looks up to stare at me while she does it, my cock jolts.

Despite my desire to let her go at her own pace, I can't help but press a little on her head in earnest. She tries to comply, but the piercing reaching the back of her throat and tongue stops her. She's determined though, and before I can even say something, she adjusts to a better angle. That seems to do the trick because now she can take over half of me. And every time she lowers, her hungry little tongue sticks out to reach even further.

When she pulls away to breathe, a string of spit stretches between her and me. She catches it with her hand and spreads everything on my length, coating my cock with wetness. Then she returns to the sucking, fucking the base with her soft palm and fingers while her hot mouth handles the rest. Fucking hell, how does she feel so right?

Her technique is good but not stellar—I've been given head in the past by women who took the entirety of me, women who sucked harder, women who apparently didn't value breathing as much as making me come. But Gen's efforts are testing my limits, forcing me to hold back so I don't fill her throat with cum. Maybe it's her flushed face, the redness of her abused lips, the soft moans that vibrate against my cock ...

As always, there's something about her that goes beyond my understanding.

The hand fondling my balls leaves, and when I look down, I see that she's using it to touch herself, rolling her fingertips over her clit. My body tenses, pleasure building dangerously fast inside me, and I decide I can't indulge more.

"Alright, enough of this," I groan, pulling her away from my cock.

Her eyes are round with surprise when I handle her to lay her down on the bed. "Did I-did I do something wrong?" she worriedly asks.

"Are you kidding? You were about to make me come, red. I can't let that happen."

Her reassured smile goes straight into my chest. "Why?"

"Because tonight, I want every drop of my cum to be in your pussy."

That brings even more pinkness to her cheeks, and her ears are red like they get when she's overly flustered. "What if I want to swallow it?"

It's my turn to be dazed, tempted to take her up on her offer. After a few seconds, I reply, "Another time."

In three seconds, I have her out of her sexy lingerie. Her limbs wrap themselves around me when I cover her with my body, and we end up grinding and writhing onto one another. Under my cock, her folds are sopping wet as I rub onto them.

"You liked that a little too much, didn't you?" I groan into our kiss.

"Yes."

"I can feel it. You're such a naughty girl, red. You were getting off on it. On sucking my thick cock." My words make her whimper, shivering under me. "And now you want it inside you. You want me to fuck you raw and fill you up."

"Jake, please."

"Please, what? Please, fuck me? Please, make me come? Please, fill my pussy with cum?"

"All of them! I want all of them."

There's something in her voice, the desperation, the impatience, that makes me lose my restraint. Without using my hands, I align myself with her greedy slit and ram into her with one merciless thrust.

She cries out my name and arches below me, her nails clawing at my back. Fuck, she feels fantastic. So warm, tight, and drenched. In theory, I could fuck her for hours because this feels like heaven. In practice, I'll nut before things can even start.

"This is what you wanted?" I grunt in her ear, already pumping in and out of her. She nods, her mouth too busy with sweet moans. "You feel so fucking good, red. You feel like paradise wrapped in soaked silk.

"Y-you were wrong," she lets out between two hiccups of pleasure.

"How so?"

"You said condoms didn't get in the way of the piercings, but— Oh God!"

"You feel them better now?" I ask. She nods, pulling me closer with her hands gripping my bum. "You feel them dragging against your walls?" Another confirmation, muffled by a helpless cry.

Only God fucking knows how I manage to hold back, but I make her come in a few minutes while containing myself. She becomes even creamier, and the sensation of her walls pulsing and squeezing triggers some urgency in me. Because a position switch is always a good idea to help with stamina, I pull out, flip her around, and slam into her from behind.

Time becomes irrelevant, and I lose the notion of it entirely. The only things that matter are her moans and cries, the slaps of my hips on her arse, the soft pleas she whimpers ... I fuck her like a madman, like my life depends on it. And when I feel that she's close again, when I sense the spasms and the tension in her, I pull her up from her elbows and press her onto my torso. Her head rolls back on my shoulder, her face a mask of pure lust.

"I'll come with you this time, red," I warn.

"Aah, yes."

"I'll give you everything I have. Will you take it?"

"Yes! All of it."

"And will you keep it, love? Will you keep it all inside you, like the greedy woman you are?"

"Jake, please."

"Say you'll keep my cum inside you, Gen."

"I will! I'll keep it!"

That's all I need to hear, so I send a hand between her legs, where my cock is still ramming inside her with intensity. I can feel how wet she is, the inside of her upper thighs glistening with it. Under my fingertips, her clit is swollen and pulsing, so sensitive that she cries out at the first graze. Within seconds, she's coming undone, moaning my name and shaking with bliss. This time, I'm too far gone to resist her spasmodic tightening.

I climax with a roar, white-hot jets shooting inside her, coating her walls, filling her up with all the desire and passion I hold. Every time I think I'm done, another rope of cum spurts out, and I don't think I've ever emptied my balls this much before. This is, without a doubt, the most satisfying nut I've ever experienced.

We're both panting and sweaty by the time it all ends, our limbs heavy, our bodies limp. My cock's still encased in her, her hips seated on me as I'm sat back on my heels.

"Fucking hell," I mutter.

"I think you mean heaven."

I chuckle, which rips an ultimate moan out of her.

We stay like that for a moment, my hands coursing over the flat surface of her stomach, cupping her breasts, or running along her thighs. Her skin is the softest thing I've ever been graced to touch, and I don't think I'll ever get my fill of it. When I've recovered enough to move, I press a kiss on her temple.

"I'm going to pull out," I warn. "Remember your promise, Gen."

I grab her arse and lift her up, my semi-limp dick slipping out of her. Almost immediately, the mess we made drips back onto me. But I'm quick to reach between her legs and fix it. Dragging my fingers over her inner thighs, I scoop what's seeping out of her and shove it right back inside, entering her with two thick knuckles.

"You said you'd keep me inside you," I remind her when she moans.

"But you came too much."

"Still, you promised." I gather more cum, stuffing it back into her messy cunt. However, as soon as my fingers come out, more of it leaks out. So I do it again and again.

This little game is more entertaining than it should be, especially since I can feel how much she enjoys it. "What am I going to do with you, Genevieve?" I ask while pushing more of it in, feigning a graveness I'm not feeling. "Do you know what bad girls who don't keep their promises get?"

Her walls clench around my finger, which only pushes more of it out. "I'm trying," she whimpers.

"Not hard enough."

I don't really know what I expected out of this other than teasing her, but I'm definitely not ready when she grabs my hand and brings it to her mouth. I watch, mesmerized, as she takes my cum-coated fingers between her lips and sucks them clean.

"That counts as inside me, right?" she asks, meeting my eyes with her hooded ones.

It really fucking does. Kudos to her for thinking outside the box.

When I return my hand between her thighs and gather more of it, she avidly repeats the gesture, feasting on the taste of our climaxes mixed together.

"See?" I taunt her. "You did get to swallow it."

I grow envious after a few back and forths of this, so I ram two fingers inside her, scoop as much of our mess as I can, and instead of her mouth, I bring it to mine.

Fuck, we taste good. I'm familiar with her sweet saltiness, her sleek texture, and the flavor that's uniquely hers. I'm also aware of the taste of my own cum, although I haven't experienced it in a minute. But the two of us together is the taste of perfect sin.

How the fuck am I supposed to give that up once the time comes?

GEN'S APARTMENT IS EXACTLY WHAT I'd expect of an Upper East Side lawyer who comes from generational wealth. It's tastefully decorated, vast, sleek, and has a fantastic view over the city and Central Park. It looks like the perfect home one might see in magazines. But it doesn't *feel* like a home. I'm not seeing her, no personal touches, no pictures …

There's something sterile to it, which doesn't match her intrepid personality.

I have nothing to say about the kitchen, though. It's very well-equipped, and preparing breakfast before heading out has been a delight. I'm done with the omelet when Gen arrives in the living space, adjusting her blouse into her skirt.

"I can't believe I'm going to be late," she anxiously mutters.

She's busy pinning pearl earrings on when she reaches the kitchen. Her eyes widen when she sees everything I cooked. "Jake, you didn't have to do all this. I don't even have time for breakfast."

"You can't start your day on an empty stomach, love. Not after *that*."

Her cheeks flush to a mild pink. "It was a lot, wasn't it?"

"Waking up to someone eating you out was on your list."

"The rest wasn't, though."

True, but what can I say? I fucking love watching my cum seep out of her overworked pussy. It's like a work of art, really, with her folds glistening from her own orgasm while mine runs down, white against pink, all the way to her puckered little arsehole.

Shit, just thinking about it makes me swell in my jeans.

I give her a proud grin. "No, I improvised the rest. But stop acting like I'm the one at fault here. I vividly remember you begging for it."

After a brief silence, she eyes the gargantuan breakfast I cooked for us. I can tell she's tempted, but the prospect of being late holds her back.

"I can drop you off if you want," I offer. "You can have my helmet and gloves."

"Isn't it dangerous?"

"It can be. But I'm a careful driver—especially with a precious package on board."

Her lips purse in a failed attempt to hide how much she enjoys the compliment. "If we crash and I die, I'll come back and haunt you forever," she warns.

I slip a hand around her waist and pull her closer. "You promise?"

"I'll poltergeist the crap out of you."

A chuckle pours out of me as I bend to claim her lips and seal the deal. She better return and haunt me because I'm not done with her yet.

"Come on, love. Let's eat."

With a resigned sigh, she gives in and sits on a high stool. I set a plate with an avocado toast before her and one where I'll sit. Then, I cut the omelet in two and give us a slice each. I've already poured orange juice into two glasses, which I add to the counter. The coffee seems to be done brewing, so I take the pot off the state-of-the-art machine and settle it between us.

"You're really good at this," she appreciatively says.

"I started cooking for myself at an early age, so my mum had less work to do at home. Turns out I enjoy eating well, so I got good at it."

"It looks delicious." She doesn't wait any longer to dig in, bringing the avocado toast to her lips. The raspy little moan she lets out brings a crooked smile to my lips. "It *is* delicious."

"It's just avocado on bread, love." Although, I did come through with the seasoning, cherry tomatoes, smoked salmon, and all.

The omelet gets the same reaction, and only then do I allow myself to eat. "Do you have any big plans for the rest of the week?" I ask.

"Yeah, I have this thing on Friday evening."

My brows come together at her answer. I thought we were seeing each other on Friday. "What thing?"

"I'm heading down to Brooklyn for my bi-weekly dicking appointment," she says with an impish smirk.

That cheeky little ...

"Well then, I'll be sure to keep my evening free."

"Perfect. I'm actually busy on Saturday, though. Just so you know."

"Really?"

"Yes, it's Hana's birthday. Since she was pregnant last time, she wants us to go overboard this year."

"I take it you mean getting hammered?"

"Mhm. It's also her last birthday in her twenties, and she's terrified of entering the next decade."

"Thirties are great," I say.

"It's not the same for a woman." She chews on her piece of omelet, takes a sip of orange juice, and meets my eyes inquisitively. "How old are you, by the way?"

"Thirty-two. You?"

"Almost twenty-seven."

"Your birthday is coming up?"

"On the ninth."

"Any plans?"

"I will be out of town for it, visiting my parents."

"I didn't realize you were a close-knit family."

"We're not," she mumbles, taking another bite of toast.

I can tell there's more to it, but I don't push her. Family matters can be delicate, and her mood doesn't deserve to be ruined to satisfy my curiosity.

It seems I don't need to ask, because she voluntarily continues with, "My sister died on the day we turned seventeen. So we don't celebrate it as a birthday anymore. We commemorate her instead."

Fuck, that is heavy. I reach for her hand, wrapping mine over it. "I'm sorry to hear that, love. It must have been tough."

"It was. And this year marks a decade, so it's a lot."

"So you haven't celebrated your birthday in ten years?"

She shrugs, removing her hand from under mine to grab her mug of coffee. "It's fine. I'm used to it."

It's the saddest part, really. She shouldn't be discarded on a day that also belongs to her, but I don't point it out. When her hand is free again, I grab it once more and bring it to my lips to lay a kiss on its back. "If you feel like celebrating it this year, give me a call, yeah? I'll worship you all day like you deserve."

The somber expression on her face fades slightly. "Don't I deserve to be worshiped every day of the year?"

I chuckle. "You do. Let's say I'll worship you even more on your birthday, then. Does that sound alright to you, Miss Kensington?"

She bends closer, bringing her lips near mine. "It sounds very alright to me, Mr. Clarke."

Our kiss tastes like coffee, avocado, and her. Just for that latter flavor, I'd linger there and keep doing it until we can't physically continue. But she's late for work as it is, so I force myself to pull away after granting her one last peck.

Following our breakfast together, she returns to her room to rearrange her hair for the helmet. In the meantime, I load the dishwasher and take care of the utensils in the sink. When she comes back with a low bun, I consider suggesting she changes her shoes as well. But I've seen women manage with stilettos, so I hold back. The same goes for her skirt. I like the idea of her bare legs wrapped around me too much to have her put on a pair of pants.

I'll be extra careful.

Minutes later, she's got her handbag, I have my stuff, and we're outside on the street. The morning concierge looked at me sideways when we passed, like the one from yesterday. Clearly, her world isn't used to people like me. I'm sure they never side-eyed her prissy ex like that.

My bike isn't far from the entrance, and I guide us to it. Gen scans it with uncertainty, a pout pursing her lips together. "It looks fast."

"It can be. But I promise we'll go slow."

"So far, your slow has been anyone else's light speed, Jake. Yamaha is a good brand, right?"

"Yeah, 'their products are reputedly qualitative,'" I tease, remembering the contract.

When I approach with the helmet, she still seems distressed. "Come on, love. I won't let anything happen to you," I promise, leaning in to give her lips a reassuring peck.

I slip the helmet on her, and she allows me, gulping hard. "Have you ever had an accident?"

"Not in a while. And it was nothing major." I clip the strap below her chin and adjust it. "Nothing will happen to you, sweetheart."

Although I can't see her face anymore, her gestures are more assertive when I hand her the gloves. While she puts them on, I slip the key in the ignition.

"Shoot," she mutters behind the visor.

"What?"

"I should have worn pants."

Thank fuck she looks down and doesn't see my grin. "Probably, yeah. Too late for that though."

I hop onto the bike, kick the stand back, balance it, and hit the red start button. The engine roars below me, and Gen takes a step back, intimidated.

"Come on, love. I'll help you up."

I offer her a solid hand and do my best to assist her as she climbs behind me. Once she's on, I help her put her feet in the rests. Her slim hands come around me, and I feel her front plaster itself against my back as she holds on tightly to me. I stifle a small laugh, amused by her apprehension. Does she not trust me?

"Is there anything special I should do?" she asks, adjusting herself.

"All you have to do is hang on to me and follow my gestures. You weigh nothing compared to me or the bike, so you won't pose a balance problem."

She nods. "Good, okay."

"Are you ready, red?" I ask, twisting to the side. Her helmet-covered head tilts up and down. "Alright, then."

Before we're off, I give her forearms a gentle caress, a last attempt to appease her. Seconds later, we're making our way through the streets of the Upper East Side.

The traffic is heavy, given the hour, but I carefully drive through it, earning precious minutes that'll make her arrive earlier than if she took a cab. Her legs are pressed against my sides, and every time we take a turn, they squeeze me into their embrace, just like her arms. But I can feel her relax after a few minutes, which is good.

Halfway through it, I give in to the temptation at a red light and reach down to graze at her delicate ankle, appreciating the smoothness of her skin. My fingertips dance around it for a moment, and I swear I can feel her shiver. I'm just starting to trail my hand up when the traffic light turns green, and we're off again.

From then on, I use every opportunity to touch her, caressing her all the way to the hem of her skirt, which is bunched high on her thigh. This is a lot more enjoyable than when I'm with Eli. The fact that I'm half hard confirms that.

Much too soon for my tastes, we arrive at the NexaCorp building, its paved front swarming with people. They all look as serious and professional as Gen, their suits an array of grays and blacks. I turn the engine off, set the side stand, and help her slip off the seat. Once she's safely planted on solid ground again, I get off.

"So, how was that, love? Did I scare you?"

"No, it was fine," she approves, embarrassingly pulling her skirt down. "You were very good at distracting me away from my fears."

"Happy to serve."

I unclasp the helmet while she removes the gloves. When it comes off, revealing her beautiful face, I realize I might have a problem. In the few minutes it took us to get here, I missed those cornflower eyes and caramel freckles.

I slip on the helmet while she rearranges her skirt and blazer, and then she looks up at me. With a push on the button by my chin, I lift the modular front so she can see me rather than the visor.

"Thank you for the ride. And the breakfast. And the night."

"And the wake-up sex?" I tease.

As I expected, a blush spreads on her nose and cheekbones. "Yes, that too. I'll see you on Friday?"

"You know where to find me," I say with a wink.

She gives me a small smile, nods, and squares her shoulders before spinning around and walking off to her building's entrance. I lean onto the bike, ready to look at her until she disappears, but she surprises me by swiftly turning around. With short but quick steps, she hurriedly returns to me. Still confused about what's happening, my body reacts before my brain can, and when she comes right against me, I wrap an arm around her waist and lower to grant her the kiss she demands.

It's not exactly easy with the helmet, but she still manages to slip a bold tongue past my parted lips, her hands clutching my sweater to pull me closer. I'm good to do this all fucking day long, but she eventually shoves herself away from me with a sigh. Her cheeks are now red, her lips wet, and her eyes glimmery.

"See you on Friday," she asserts, right before giving me one last firm and intense peck.

Just like that, she's off again, and I watch her sway her perky little bum all the way to the massive revolving door of the building. It's only when she disappears behind it that I regain my senses.

A chuckle pours out of me, and my head shakes, amazed at how she constantly manages to surprise me. I'll take her to work every single day if I get paid in kisses like these.

I feel like a fucking idiot on my way back to Brooklyn, grinning like a twat. Thankfully, people can't see it, so to them, I'm still some imposing bloke with tattoos on a monster of a bike. Not a smiling moron.

Once I arrive at The Parlour, I park the bike on the underground level and head straight to my office. I'm late as hell, and I have things to handle. I pass the door to it and jump slightly, startled by the familiar voice that comes from the couch.

"You didn't come home last night, you little slut," Eli says with amusement.

"Fuck off."

"Were you with Gen again?"

"Yes."

"How's she doing? Did she say hi to me? Does she miss me?"

"Eli, it's ten in the morning. How the fuck do you have so much energy already?"

"Some of us didn't spend the night having sex."

"Because some of us can't," I retort.

"Ouch, *touché*. Anyhow, how's Gen? It's the fourth time you're seeing her now, right?"

"Sixth."

"Are things getting serious, then?" he wonders, closely studying my face.

"No, we're just fucking."

His eyes squint dubiously. "Yeah, right. When was the last time you were 'just fucking' with the same woman more than twice?"

"Why are you all up my arse this morning?"

"No reason in particular. Grubsy and I talked about it last night, and we're happy to see you evolve."

"I'm not evolving, Elijah. We're fucking. That's it."

"Sure, sure. By the way, remember that hot model from the Court a couple of months ago? I think she came from Slovenia?"

"What about her?"

"I saw her yesterday. She's back in town for a photoshoot, and you made an impression because she asked about you."

I clench my teeth, aware that I have to tread carefully. "What did you do about it?"

"She's coming in five minutes. Told her you could probably squeeze in a quickie in your busy schedule—before her shoot."

"Are you fucking serious right now?"

We wage a silent battle there for a moment, our eyes locked into one another's, waiting to see who'll break first. Eli is a goofball, and he's terrible at lying. Right now though, I legitimately can't tell if he's pulling my leg. Part of me knows where he's going with this, and as much as I want that information to remain private, I know he'll eventually find out.

Resigned, I let out a grunt. "I'm not fucking anyone other than Gen."

"Why?"

"We're exclusive."

He explodes with satisfaction, smacking his hands together and pointing at me. "Ah-ha! I knew it! 'We're just fucking,' my ass! You two are getting serious!"

"We're not. This is just so we don't have to use protection."

"Right, how eco-friendly of you. Saving the sea turtles one condom at a time. Is there a Nobel Prize for saving the environment? I'll submit your name for it."

"You don't have to be such a twat, Eli. We both work too hard for a relationship, and that's it. Besides, we're literally worlds apart. There can't be anything serious between us."

"Bullshit. This isn't the nineteenth century anymore. Class doesn't have to separate people."

To that, I reply nothing. He wouldn't understand, no matter what I'd say. Gen and I have a good dynamic in the sheets, and I enjoy her company out of them as well. But we're severely mismatched and don't have enough free time to sustain a healthy relationship. I know where I stand, even though I'm growing fonder of her every time we meet. There are no delusions in my head that this might lead to some epic love story, to a life together with kids, and all that shit.

Minutes pass, and Eli stays on the couch, looking at me with judgment. "Will you stay here all day?" I groan.

"I don't know. Will you be a stubborn dick all day?"

I glare at him, unimpressed by his attempt at getting a confession out of me. There's nothing to confess, so he's wasting his time.

With dry and angered gestures, I open the cabinet below my desk and take out my iPad. "Enjoy the couch, mate," I tell him, standing up.

"Where are you going?"

"The roof."

I'm already in the hallway when he shouts, "Jake, you're being a fucking coward about this!"

But I'm not. I'm being realistic. Gen's a great woman, but I'm not her type—the opposite, in fact. We're just having fun, and when we're done with it, she'll find someone from her world—hopefully not her fucking ex—and she'll lead a perfect little life.

In no scenario am I the man she chooses for anything other than some naked fun.

I might have clawed my way out of the gutter, but I still reek of it. To people like her, I'm inconceivable.

And it's probably better that way.

CHAPTER
Twenty

Gen

I'M ON A HIGH AS I make my way up to the 63rd floor. Being all pressed up against Jake has got to be the best form of transportation ever. Ultimately, I'm happy he swayed my mind and pushed me to trust him on this. There was something relaxing in the sways of his bike, the air against my limbs, his deep breaths that I felt within me …

And on my leg, I can still feel his fingers softly dancing across my skin every time we were at a stop.

I tried. I really tried to stay professional and just head to the building, but my desire to kiss him won over. And now, I'm struggling to quench my elated grin. *Friday can't come soon enough.*

By the time I arrive at my floor, I'm more composed and my face is a mask of indifference as I step into the open space. A few people greet me on my way to my office, and I reply with a polite smile and a nod. Just as I reach my door, Daisy gets up from her desk.

"Good morning! I was about to text you to make sure you were alright," she explains while we enter my office, holding a clipboard.

Right, shoot. I'm a solid twenty minutes late. "So sorry about that. I've had a rocky morning."

"It's alright. It's just that you're usually here before most of us, so I worried."

"I appreciate that, thank you," I say genuinely, giving her arm a little squeeze. "You have something for me?"

"Oh, yes! Mr. Sinclair came by ten minutes ago. I think he wanted to see you about the merger."

I cringe, glimpsing at my colleagues behind the glass wall. Of course, the one day I'm late, my boss visits me uncharacteristically early.

"Okay, I'll go handle him. Anything else?"

"The reports you asked for should arrive within the next two hours." When she bends closer to me, acting suspiciously secretive, I brace myself for something bad. "Also, Mr. Hoffman came earlier. He wanted your schedule. I think he's planning a surprise for you or something."

My entire body tenses with dread. What is Edward doing? What does he have in mind?

"What did you do?" I ask, hoping my worries aren't too noticeable.

"Well, I know you two aren't together anymore, so I told him I couldn't share personal information with him," she whispers. I can't quite contain the relieved sigh that sinks my shoulders. "Did I do the right thing?"

"You did the perfect thing, Daisy. Thank you so much."

"You're welcome, Miss Kensington. Since you usually already have a coffee with you when I arrive, do you want me to bring you one?"

"Thank you, but I'm alright. I already had a couple," I explain, still surprised by Jake's appreciation of robust coffee.

Daisy nods and brings the clipboard closer to her chest. "Let me know if you need anything."

"I will."

Once alone, I settle my bag by my desk and boot up my computer. I take a few moments to check my emails, and then I go to the other side of the floor to see what my boss wants. When I arrive, his door is wide open, and Ralf Lowell is talking with him. I knock on the panel, attracting their attention.

"Ah, Genevieve, there you are. Had a little pillow incident this morning?"

"My apologies for the mishap, sir. I had to handle an unforeseen circumstance. My assistant told me you were looking for me?"

"Yes, do come in. Ralf and I were talking about the merger. He told me he finished crunching the numbers yesterday."

"Actually, I did that," I correct.

"Anyhow, the odds are looking good for us. They want a detailed report upstairs; we have about a fortnight to produce it. Do you think you two can get your teams to finish it for the ninth?" he asks. Ralf and I nod, confident in our departments' abilities to do it in time. "Perfect. Genevieve, I know you have asked for a day off that Friday. Can you push back whatever plans you have?"

After a few seconds of frantic thoughts mixed with confusion, I shake my head. "I'm afraid I can't, sir."

"Really? This is terribly important, Genevieve."

"I'm sorry, but the request was approved months ago. I can't come in on the ninth."

"What could be more important than this?" Ralf snickers.

My annoyance for the man was somehow contained because he didn't open his mouth, but since he has, I don't hold back the glare I give him. "A personal matter that doesn't concern you."

I turn to my boss again. "Sir, I'm sorry for the terrible timing, but do trust that I will have everything you need ready by the eighth. My absence the day after won't pose an issue."

His lips are pinched in a displeased manner, and I expect him to argue again and force me to come in on the ninth. I didn't complain in the past about Christmas and New Year's, but this, I can't.

Mr. Sinclair eventually sighs and walks around his desk to sit on his big leather chair. "Alright, you two take a seat. We need to organize ourselves."

I nod and move to the closest chair while Ralf approaches the other one. For the next two tedious hours, we listen and take notes. The report needs to be much more detailed than I expected, and it would be a challenge even if I were coming on the ninth. But I've handled worse in the past, so I know I can make it.

By the time I come out of my boss's office, I'm properly drained. The man's ability to talk all the time and get constantly sidetracked is uncanny. And I'm not as good as Ralf at faking interest and licking our boss's ass, so it's torture.

Because I need to recharge, I head toward the break room rather than my office. That coffee Daisy offered earlier doesn't sound like such a bad idea now. My pace slows as I get closer. Every time I approach this room, I'm reminded of the awful words my colleagues spewed about me. Part of me fears it'll happen again, and I'll have to endure more humiliation. That worry gets even more intense when I discern hushed voices in there. More specifically, Isabel's voice.

"I swear it was her. And he had a big motorcycle and tattoos."

"And she kissed him?"

"Girl, she practically swallowed him whole. It was so weird."

No. Not again. They can't be talking about me again—about me and *Jake*.

"So that's why she was late, then?"

"Maybe, yeah."

Because I've had actual nightmares about what happened last time, it takes a second for my brain to process that this is all true. This is really happening. I'm not making this up.

"Was he hot?" someone asks.

"Eh, I didn't see him because of the helmet, but he couldn't have been. Have you met her? The tattoos were sexy, though."

Oh, if that bitch knew just how hot Jake is, she'd have a stroke.

"Unless he was an escort or whatever," Isabel continues.

"A gigolo? And she paid him for the night?"

"Where else is she gonna find someone? All that harpy does is work," Larry snorts.

The fact that they are insulting Jake infuriates me. With a quick, deep breath, I straighten up and walk inside the breakroom. Their attention instantly falls on me, and they try to act as if nothing happened. I do the same for a few seconds, fetching a mug and moving to the coffee pot.

As I pour myself a steaming cup, I boldly meet Isabel's eyes. "So you were late this morning?" I ask.

Surprise flashes on her face. "Uh, I—yeah. But you t—"

"No, don't even go there. I was late for the first time in three years. You were late for the fifth time this month."

I lower the coffee pot down a little harder than needed, startling them all. The nerve of them to spit their venom behind my back and then act like scared little rats as soon as I'm here. I can't let them do this to me, to my authority, and to Jake. It's my personal life, my *private* life.

I take a packet of stevia and a stirrer, gathering the little more courage I need, then turn to them again. They think I'm a harpy? I'll show them what that's like.

The temptation to fire Isabel and Larry is great, but I'll need them if I want the report ready by the eighth.

"I let it slide last time because I believe in character growth and hoped you would abstain from gossiping about me again. I see that was naive of me, so this time, I will file a complaint with HR to let them know there's an issue. And the next time I catch someone gossiping about me—or anyone in the office for that matter—they are getting fired. Is that clear?"

They say nothing, staring at me with their eyes widened and their jaws slacked. I can't believe I felt so intimidated by them. They are nothing, just a bunch of overpaid adults with a high school mentality. They aren't worth all the attention and pain I allow them to get out of me.

"Is that clear?" I repeat louder.

They collectively nod, some mumbling "Yes" along with it.

"Good. Now, go back to work. We have a new assignment, so we'll meet in the conference room right after lunch."

They scatter like the cockroaches they are, and I end up alone in the break room, feeling victorious.

Wherever this came from, I like it. It's empowering.

I'm still not over it when I reenter my office with my coffee. Those threats I made weren't just to scare them. I will actually enact them and reach out to HR with a detailed account of the incidents, as well as names. And if I hear more nasty gossip, I'll ensure NexaCorp throws them to the curb, where they belong.

My phone's waiting by my computer when I sit, so I grab it to check if anything happened during the past couple of hours. Hana sent details about her birthday to the group chat, *The Times* pushed an article in my notifications, and Jake texted. As soon as I see that last one, my heart races, and my lips bend into a broad smile. I open it before everything else and smile even harder when I read it.

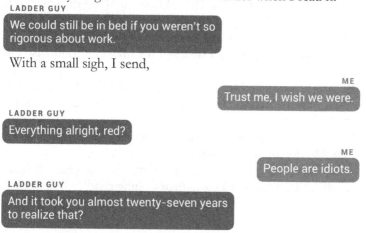

LADDER GUY
We could still be in bed if you weren't so rigorous about work.

With a small sigh, I send,

ME
Trust me, I wish we were.

LADDER GUY
Everything alright, red?

ME
People are idiots.

LADDER GUY
And it took you almost twenty-seven years to realize that?

> **ME**
> I always suspected it, but today is strongly confirming it.

> **LADDER GUY**
> Anyone bothering you? You want me to come and break some jaws?

I giggle again, truly entertained by his attempt at cheering me up. It's definitely working.

> **ME**
> I'll manage. It's just frustrating because the day started so well. I was in such a good mood :(

> **LADDER GUY**
> I know what you mean. Eli is a twat. The fucker killed my vibe three minutes in.

> **ME**
> Do you want me to come and break his jaw?

> **LADDER GUY**
> And deprive me of the pleasure of doing it myself? Never. I appreciate the offer though.

Because I have the feeling we could keep chatting like this for the remainder of the morning, I rip myself from my phone and put it in a drawer so I can get back to work. If I'm not rolling around under the sheets with Jake, I might as well make the best of today. First, I email my team, informing them there'll be a meeting in the conference room after lunch. Then, I begin drafting my email to the head of HR, who I know will take my complaint seriously.

I'm in the middle of it when someone knocks on the glass door. My eyes travel up, expecting Daisy, but the masculine figure isn't her. *Eddie.*

Before I can invite him or recuperate from the shock, he opens the door, taking my acknowledgment of him as an invitation to enter.

"Hey, Gen," he greets me with a small smile.

"Hi. Do-do you need something?"

"No, I just thought I'd come up and have a little chat." When he closes the door, I know it's more than a "little chat".

I notice how riveted people are outside in the open space, and my brain clicks on what's happening. The gossip I heard in the breakroom has spread. I didn't nip it in the bud, catching it too late.

"I've heard rumors," Edward uneasily starts.

"Have you?"

"Yeah. Are they true?"

"I don't know. What are the rumors about?" I ask, feigning cluelessness.

"That you arrived with someone this morning."

"Why is that a problem?"

"A *male* someone, that you kissed."

I'd understand and accept if he was confused or hurt. But more than that, it's judgment that I read in his eyes. And I can't tolerate that.

"Sorry, but I don't understand what's happening here," I say, standing from my chair. I come around the desk, lean onto it, and fold my arms over my chest. "I seem to recall that *you* broke up with me, Eddie. So, why is it a problem if I'm seeing someone?"

"I didn't expect you to move on so fast."

My jaw drops. "Are you slut shaming me?"

"No! Heaven's sake, no! I'm just … surprised. I mean, we barely made time for each other, and now you're seeing some guy."

Now, I feel a little guilty because he's not entirely wrong. But the only thing I can think of to explain it is Jake's novelty. Being with him is exciting, exhilarating, invigorating … I feel like I haven't felt since Victoria died. And that sensation is addictive.

Jake once told me I go to him to feel alive, and it's true.

"I'm sorry, Eddie. I don't know what to tell you. I'm trying to take more risks and be bold, not be boring like you said."

Now, he's the one feeling bad. His mouth opens, but nothing comes out of it. When he tries again, his voice is filled with regret. "Gen, I didn't mean it like that. It was just the—"

"No, you were right. I was boring, and now I'm pushing myself to get out of my comfort zone."

"With some random guy?"

"I had to start somewhere, didn't I?"

He sighs, scratching his perfectly shaved jaw—something he does when uncomfortable. I wish I could cater to his hurt feelings more, but I have too much work for that. And in all truth, I want out of this weird atmosphere. I don't know how to handle it, and right now, I don't have the mental capacity to figure it out.

"Eddie, I'm sorry, but I have a mountain of things to handle today."

He lets out a small, mirthless chuckle. "Some things never change, do they?"

"We can talk about this another time if you want. Just not today."

"Yeah, sure. I'll go back to my things, and you'll do yours."

When he turns around, I notice a collective movement outside. The people in the open space weren't working, but spying on us, aware that we broke up and that I'm moving on.

I dismiss how awkward it makes me feel and walk Eddie to the door. Just as he's about to leave, he turns back to me. "Oh, uh, can you wish Hana a happy birthday for me on Saturday?" he asks.

"Yes, of course. You still have her number too, right?"

"Hasn't she blocked me yet?"

I grimace, aware that it's a possibility. Hana was never a big fan of Eddie, so she might have blocked his number as soon as the breakup was official.

"I'll tell her for you, don't worry," I diplomatically offer.

He thanks me with a smile and a nod before walking away. I don't linger there, giving the space a long scan to ensure people are done with the show and back to work.

The fact that it's still morning is preposterous because when I sit back in my chair, I'm ready to go home and forget this day ever happened. What absolute carnage. Actually, not all of it. The first hour was pretty spectacular.

I can't help but fetch my phone from the drawer. The only good thing today was Jake, and I need more of him to cope.

ME

For real, next time, we stay in bed all day.

LADDER GUY

With pleasure, red.

Yes. Definitely a lot of pleasure. On both our parts.

CHAPTER
Twenty-One

Gen

HANA'S BIRTHDAY IS OUT OF this world. I didn't think I'd be having such a blast, but here I am, dancing and singing my heart out. Everything is so loud and dark that no one can clearly see or hear me. It's liberating.

It wasn't so much fun at first. Not when I realized that all the friends Hana invited are either married, engaged, or having a kid with the love of their life.

But all that stopped being a problem maybe five tequilas ago. Or is it seven? Shoot, I lost count. It is an odd number, at least I'm sure of that.

The club Hana picked is fantastic, with music from when we were younger but remixed into even more danceable tunes. We have a whole VIP booth to ourselves, and the waitstaff has been instructed to keep the champagne coming. And it seems they are very good at following instructions because we've drunk at least one bottle each by now.

We're both vibing to a catchy version of Lady Gaga's "Bloody Mary", facing each other with our sick moves. The others have all migrated back to the VIP lounge, and it's just the two of us left now. My thighs burn every time I lower, I can feel sweat running down my back, and my feet have been killing me for the past hour. But all of this is a sacrifice I'm happy to make.

Although we haven't done this together in a while, Hana and I are still great at it. My hands are above my head, like the song demands, and my hips are swaying along with the beat, my whole body undulating with it. I'm mirroring Hana, or she's mirroring me—I can't remember.

Everything is delayed and altered by the booze, which is why I won't have another glass tonight. I've gone far enough. Needless to say, Hana's objective to get hammered is beyond accomplished. The only thing that could make this moment even more perfect is Jake.

So, when a pair of masculine hands snake their way around me, and a body comes against my back, moving in sync with mine, it takes a couple of seconds for me to register. Jake! He's here!

A smile stretches my lips as I lean harder into his body so that my ass is right on his crotch, wrapping my hands around his wrist. Again, it takes way too long for me to realize that the man behind me is too short and not muscular enough to be Jake. Confused, I look down and see that the hands holding me so intimately aren't covered in tattoos, and the golden wristwatch is way too tacky for Jake.

I pry the arms away from me and turn around, wishing I could set more distance between us. But the club is packed, and there's nowhere else to go but by Hana's side, a mere foot away from the stranger. He says something that gets lost in the loud music, his hands trying to bring me back toward him.

"I'm not interested," I shout, writhing out of his hold.

Hana's eyes are closed, so she doesn't see what's going on and can't come to my aid. The man is stronger than me, so he manages to pull me against him. The intense smell of his cologne assaults my nostrils, and I wonder how I could have believed, even for a second, that he was Jake.

"Come on, Bella," he shouts in my ear. "I know you want this."

"No, I really don't!"

I'm still trying to pry myself away from him when the wet touch of his tongue begins exploring my ear. "I'll fuck you so good, Bella," he says before licking me again. The sensation is invasive and awkward, nowhere near as sensual as the man expects.

All I want is to get out of this, so I do the only thing my brain has the capacity to come up with. "I said no!" I shout just as I send a blind knee kick between his legs.

That makes him let go of me instantly with a grunt, his hands reaching for his crotch rather than me. I swiftly grab Hana, who whips her eyes open, before tugging her behind me and making my way to the VIP section. The man posted there recognizes us and moves to the side so we can climb the steps. We soon arrive at our booth, where the music isn't as intense, and we have a view over the pit.

"Are you okay?" Hana asks as we sit down.

"Yeah, just a creep. We're good now."

"It's the dress," Cindy, a woman we went to Harvard with, says in a matter-of-fact tone. "A redhead with a red dress is like a giant billboard for them."

I look down with a frown. Hana picked it for me earlier when we got ready at my place, and who am I to say no to the birthday girl? The Dolce and Gabbana mini dress isn't the boldest I've seen out there tonight, but it's a lot, with a lingerie-like bustier and a form-fitting skirt. With this heat, wearing so little fabric was a good call, though.

"I'm thirsty," I say, ready to go to the bar.

But one of Hana's friends, whom I didn't know before tonight, hands me a tiny glass. I down it in one go. The unexpected taste of tequila makes me grimace. "I meant water!"

On the table, all we have are partially emptied champagne flutes and more shot glasses. Since I really need fluids that don't contain alcohol, I stand on clumsy legs and slalom my way to the bar.

I finish the water the person behind the counter gives me and then ask for a refill.

"Are you alright, babe?" Hana asks, appearing by my side.

"Yes, my head's just spinning really hard."

"Do you want to head home? I know you had a long week."

She's not wrong. I've been working my ass off since Mr. Sinclair gave us the assignment. I have the feeling that Ralf, that asshole, will cut himself and his team some slack, knowing I'll take the heat if the report isn't completed on time. So, because I refuse to let him win, I'm working even harder than anticipated. I'm not happy with this, but it's only for two weeks—nothing I can't handle.

The most annoying part is that I'm not getting my fill of Jake. Yesterday, I only allowed myself three hours at his place before returning home. And while it's a good start, it's not enough. I regretted not waking up in his embrace this morning, feeling robbed.

"I don't want to go home," I tell Hana.

"You're sure?"

I nod. "I wanna go see Jake."

The worry on her face switches to a massive smile, her eyes luminous. "Really?"

"Yeah. I miss him."

"You do?"

"All the time."

Her smile grows even more prominent. "Let's get you to him, then."

"You can't leave your party."

"I could use some fresh air. I'll come back after."

"Hana, *I* can't leave your party."

"Are you kidding? Who am I to get in the way of young love?"

"It's not love," I say with a frown, drinking more of my water. "I just really like him."

"Well, that sounds like—"

"His dick. I really, *really* like his dick." And the rest of him too, but Hana doesn't need to know that. She's already getting all the wrong ideas. "Having drunk sex is on the list, right?"

"Yeah, I think it is."

"I need to go see him."

"You do. Let's go."

I'm not entirely sure how she manages that, but we're in a cab heading to Brooklyn before I know it. The cool air feels amazing, so we have the windows down the entire ride. Because it's the middle of the night, there isn't any traffic, so we're there in record time.

"Is that his tattoo parlor?" Hana asks, pointing at a storefront a little further ahead.

"Uh, I think the ground floor is the art gallery. Upstairs is the parlor, and then the rest are his apartment units."

I do one final check, ensuring I have my phone, home keys, ID, and credit card still in my tiny clutch. Good, I didn't lose anything. Then I turn to my best friend, who looks entertained by all this. "Hana, I can't leave you on your birthday," I whine, overwhelmed by remorse.

"It's past midnight, so it's not my birthday anymore. Now get out, go see him, and check another item off your list."

"You promise you don't mind?"

"I promise, babe. Shoo!"

So very grateful for her understanding, I twist to hug her hard. She pats my back gently and then urges me again to go. As I make my way to the door, I adjust my dress, lowering it down my thighs. There's a row of buttons to the right of the door, and I look for his name. It's nearly impossible, given that the letters are moving around. How uncooperative of them.

I still haven't found it when the door opens on its own, and someone comes out. Upon seeing me, the guy holds the door open, and I use the opportunity to slip inside. Before it closes again, I give Hana—who's watching over me from the cab—a wave.

Thankfully, I'm familiar enough with the industrial elevator to work it, even in my state. My feet hurt too much to walk up five flights of stairs. Once I'm at his door, I push the doorbell, hearing it chime from out here. His dog barks twice, and I wait. When he doesn't come to open it, I ring again, which prompts more barking.

Shit, I don't even know what time it is. Is he not here? Is he at his bar? Or is he with another woman? Before the hurtful thought can do any damage, I hear the door unlocking.

When it swings open, I'm welcomed by a powerful torso covered in tattoos. I diligently traced those with my tongue yesterday. All Jake is wearing are gray sweatpants, and his hair is a joyful mess like it gets when we fuck.

"Gen?" he asks, still half asleep. His eyes rake up and down my body, which seems to energize him a little.

"Did I wake you up?"

The dog chooses this moment to come and greet me, so I graze her big head. "Hey, Mullsi—Mugru—" I give up with a sigh, "hey, doggo."

"Mulli, bed," Jake orders her. She instantly obeys, and I somehow find his authority really hot. "Gen, it's two and a half in the morning. What are you—"

His question is cut short when I drunkenly clasp his nape and pull him down to press my lips on his. In my eagerness, I compromise our balance, but he secures it by grabbing the door frame while his free arm slides around me. I can feel that the kiss I give him is clumsy, with too much tongue and teeth. And since everything I experience is delayed, I'm not as good at following his movements. But it doesn't matter, because it's still the best feeling in the world.

"I missed you," I moan into his mouth, pushing so we enter his apartment.

He closes the door behind us, holding me close. "You saw me yesterday."

"It wasn't enough."

When I move to kiss him again, he prevents it and looks down at me with indulgence. "How much did you drink tonight?"

"I lost count."

Again, he refuses to let me kiss him. "Did you have water?"

"Two glasses."

"That's not enough. Come, sweetheart."

I'm confused and a little lost when he holds me by the hand to lead me to the open kitchen. Why isn't he ravishing me? I thought the dress would work its magic like it did on men at the club, and he'd be dying to enter me.

"Jake, I'm not here for water," I protest while he fills a tall glass. "I'm here to fuck."

"Drink," he orders, handing it to me.

With a pout, I comply and sip on the cold water. The glass is too big, so I only manage half of it. "There. Now, can we fuck?"

He chuckles, tugs me closer, and lays a kiss on my temple. "I'm not fucking you in this state, red."

"Why?"

"You're completely hammered."

"No, I'm just a bit hammered," I protest.

He laughs again. "Say you what, if you still want to fuck in the morning, I'll oblige."

"Of course I will. I want to fuck you all the time, it's ridiculous."

"Well, ditto, love."

"Then fuck me now," I demand, sending a hand to his crotch. Is it me, or is he wearing nothing under his sweatpants? Also, he's somewhat hard, isn't he?

"Tomorrow," he insists, pulling my hand out of harm's way.

"Jake," I whimper, pouting like a child to look endearing.

"That won't work on me, Genevieve. Come, I'll help you get ready for the night."

He retakes my hand, and this time, he leads me to the bathroom. Like the rest of his loft, it's in the open, with a large bathtub in the middle and a shower in the continuity of the enclosed toilets.

While he searches for something in the cabinets, I seek the little zipper thing high on my back. Once I grab hold of it, I slide it down and slip the black straps of my red dress to the side, tugging it all down. Once I'm left with nothing but my red lace thong and high heels, I wait for him to turn around again, convinced that'll win him over.

I notice the surprise on his face when he spins toward me, and he can't quite hold back from taking me in for a moment. When his green eyes darken, I'm convinced I've won. He doesn't do anything about it though, and his jaw tenses with restraint.

"All I have are these makeup-removing wipes," he says, extending one to me.

"Are you really not going to fuck me?"

"Not right now, sweetheart."

He sounds determined, and the fact that I left Hana's birthday party for nothing is slowly sinking into me. Why does he have to be so reasonable?

"Why do you even have those?" I mumble as I grab a wipe with a scowl.

"I was a manwhore, remember? Nearly replaced my front door with a revolving one to make it easier," he jokes as I pass the wipe over my right eye, then the left one. When it's smudged with makeup, he hands me another one.

"And now you're a whore only for me," I caustically remind him, in case he ever forgets.

He grins like a proud idiot at that, unaffected by the meaning behind my drunken words. "I am, yeah."

"One more wipe," I demand. When he hands it to me, I thoroughly clean my ear, making sure there is nothing left of that creep's saliva.

"What happened to that specific ear?" Jake asks with humor.

"Some guy licked it."

The amusement on his face falls into a dark expression. "What?"

"I kicked him in the balls for it. But maybe I was wrong. I'm sure *he* would have fucked me. Without having to ask as nicely as I did for you."

Jake clearly doesn't like my sound logic, given how he harshly pulls me against him, my bare breasts squished onto his broad torso. "You think I'm not dying to fuck you right now?" he mutters. I blink several times, surprised by the intensity of his tone. "The only reason why I'm not ripping that tiny scrap of lace and burying my cock inside you is because we're not *that* yet, Genevieve."

What does he mean? What else could we be? I'm trying to make sense of his words when he releases me and spins me around. "Now, go shower while I find you a spare toothbrush." He punctuates his words with a dry slap on my ass, which makes me squeal in surprise.

I feel like a scorned child, which is something I'm used to with my parents, but not him.

When I step out of the shower, I have to admit it felt great. The stickiness of the club is gone, washed down the drain, and I feel like a new person. A fresh towel is waiting for me, as well as a neatly folded T-shirt and a pair of boxer briefs. Once I'm dry and dressed for the night, I find a toothbrush ready by the sink with toothpaste already on it.

I'm brushing when Jake returns with another glass full of water and a small white pill. "Take this when you're done," he instructs, setting the tablet on the counter. "And if you can finish this glass before bed, I'll be very proud."

Maybe it's because I've made my peace with the fact that we aren't having sex, but I can now appreciate how sweet he's being with me.

On impulse, I pull the toothbrush out of my mouth and bring Jake down, giving him a quick kiss. "Shoot, sorry," I apologize, wiping away the minty foam I left on him.

Before I can feel like an idiot for it, he grins and gives me another peck, showing me how little he cares about the mess.

"Do you think you'll be sick?" he asks after passing a towel over his mouth.

"As a Kensington, I'm above that."

He laughs, the muscles of his abdomen flexing with it. "Right, sorry, milady. I'm still gonna fetch you a bucket."

Chuckles are still rolling out of him when he disappears from my sight. By the time he's back, I took the pill, emptied the glass—

earning myself some much-deserved praise—and I can't wait to be asleep.

Jake helps me slip under the covers and quickly joins me there. We reach out for one another, and I end up with my front plastered on his side, my head resting on his broad shoulder while his hand gently grazes my wet hair.

Even if we're not having sex as I intended, this is very nice.

"I'm sorry for waking you up in the middle of the night," I whisper.

"It's alright. I'd rather have you here than off with that ear-licking twat."

"You know I wouldn't have asked him to fuck me, right?"

He gives my forehead a kiss. "I know, we signed an exclusivity addendum."

I look up with a frown, not sure if he's being playful or not. "It's not about the addendum." Now, it's his turn to seek my eyes with a confused expression. "I never want anyone else to fuck me. Only you, Jake."

"Then it's a good thing I only want to fuck you, Gen."

My chest fills with pride and affection, and I wriggle closer to him. This man wants me, and *only* me. I don't care what the people at work might think. I'm worthy of such a man's interest, and that's all that matters.

"A woman I work with saw you the other day," I unexpectedly confess as if it needs to come out of me. "She saw us kiss."

"Shit."

"I caught my coworkers gossiping about it. They think you have to be ugly to be with me. Or a gigolo and I pay for your company."

"That doesn't sound right, sweetheart. They shouldn't be saying those things."

"Yeah, I know. You're the hottest guy I've ever seen."

"I didn't mean it like that. I meant—"

"Did you know," I cut him off, "that you're exactly like a wombat?"

"A wombat?"

"Yeah, you're like, so cuddly. And you can be adorable at times. And you come from Australia too."

"Those three very valid points make me *exactly* like a wombat, yes."

I can hear a smile in his voice, and I wonder if he's making fun of me. But I'm already half asleep, lulled by his warmth and deep breaths. "Jake?"

"Hmm?"

"I really like you."

His arm around me tightens, holding me closer. "I really like you too, red."

Shortly after that, I sense myself drifting into slumber, a contented smile bending my lips. This, as it turns out, might be even nicer than sex.

CHAPTER
Twenty-Two

Jake

HAMMERED GEN IS A SNORER. I don't mind it though, because the small raspy sounds that rhythmically come out of her are adorable compared to Mulligrubs's. There's also much less drool going on—albeit there is some.

I woke up nearly an hour ago with her all snuggled up against me, her hair a wild mess. It's the first time I've seen it so wavy, so I reckon she usually does something to have the smooth length I normally see her with. I've been waiting for her to wake up, but nature's calling, so I have to get out of bed.

Careful not to stir her, I maneuver my way out of her sleepy embrace, giving her red hair a gentle caress when she lets out a grunty protest. After a trip to the loo, I fight the urge to return to bed with her. I need to feed Mulli, have a coffee, and send a couple of emails.

As soon as she sees I'm up, Mulligrubs stands from her round mattress and comes to greet me enthusiastically. "Hey, Grubsy girl," I whisper, squatting to take her big smiling head between my hands to scratch her the way she loves. She then follows me to the kitchen and sits by her empty bowl. Today's Sunday, and she knows it means a special meal. The pet catering service ensures she has a nice treat in every weekly delivery, as well as a new chew toy. That one though, she'll get when Gen is awake.

Once Mulls is fed, I take her to the roof so she can do her business—I'm too lazy to do a proper walk, and can't even be bothered to put a shirt on. When that's over, we return to the flat, and I head to the bedroom with my iPad and a steaming cup of dark brew. I settle down on the lush leather armchair that faces the bed and set the cup on the vintage hardwood flooring. Yes, I have to work, but I can do it with a view. And what a sight she is, wrapped in my sheets, wearing my T-shirt, her plump lips pursed together by her cheek pressed onto the pillow, her face a veil of comfort and serenity. As soon as she wakes up, she'll have to handle a nasty hangover, so I'll let her enjoy this state of oblivion for as long as possible.

She's still out by the time the emails are sent and I'm done with my coffee. Mulli is lying by my chair, already back to sleep. I'm unsure what compels me, but I unlatch the stylus and open Procreate. My first two attempts at capturing Gen's likeness are a failure, even though an untrained eye might find them excellent. It's not quite her, something is missing. She switches position in her sleep while I'm halfway through the third one, so I also dismiss it.

For the fourth try, I silently bring the chair closer, careful not to wake her. Then, I take a moment to observe her before drawing even a single line. Her colors are exquisite, as if autumn manifested an entire human being. Her hair is flamboyant, her eyebrows a darker shade of it, and her skin a pale but warm tint. The golden specks of her freckles make her radiant, and the pink of her parted lips adds to how irresistible she is. Her position is one of contentment, with a hand over her stomach while the other is thrown over the pillow next to her. I wish I hadn't taken out the T-shirt for her because with the duvet low like this, her perky breasts would be exposed to my eyes. I'd much rather see their rosy tips than the AC/DC logo.

Well, maybe one day she'll let me draw her in the nude. I really hope she does.

This time, I'm much, much better at this, my gestures more certain. My eyes travel between her and the tablet, the stylus dancing over its smooth surface to capture this moment. I'm just done cleaning up the sketch when I notice the first symptoms of her awakening. The delicate arches of her eyebrows, which were in such a relaxed state moments ago, are now bent in a manner that portrays some amount of discomfort. Then, the hand on her pillow twitches before I'm done setting up my color palette.

The instant her eyes flutter open, I put the stylus back in its place and turn off the screen. She'd feel weird if she knew I was drawing her, wouldn't she?

I notice the confusion on her features as she takes in her surroundings, unmoving, and then she turns to seek me on the other side of the bed. When she doesn't find me there, she rises to her elbows to look around the room.

When her blue gaze finds me, I smile. "Hey."

"Hi," she mumbles, her voice throaty. "Were you watching me sleep?"

Yes, she'd definitely freak out if she knew about the drawings. "I was working—sending out emails," I explain, showing her the iPad. She falls back into the pillow with a dramatic sigh. "There's water on your nightstand. And another tablet of ibuprofen, if you need one."

She sits up with a groan and grabs both of those. While she takes them in, I rise from my chair and leave the tablet on it. As soon as she's done drinking, she returns the glass to the stand and lies back. I don't resist the temptation to join her under the covers and bring her back to my front, settling us in a spooning position.

"Hmm, this is nice," she says with approval.

"I know. I'm very cuddly."

I'm holding myself in a way that allows me to see her frown as fragments from last night come back to her. "Did I compare you to a wombat yesterday?"

"It was this morning, but yes."

She grimaces, lets out an embarrassed whimper, and buries her face in my biceps under her. When she's recomposed herself enough, she twists to meet my eyes apologetically. "I'm so sorry for coming here in the middle of the night. I don't know why I did that."

"Oh, I know exactly why. You were very clear about *why*," I tease. Her cheeks go from pink to red, and I lay a kiss on the apple of one. "I really didn't mind, love. Feel free to come to me anytime you want some dick."

"Just not when I'm hammered."

"Well, I'd fuck you tipsy, but not when you can barely walk straight."

"Really? I was that far gone?"

I nod. "But at least you didn't get sick, so it seems Kensingtons *are* above that."

"Oh, God," she whines, remembering more. "Next time, don't let me in, okay?"

"I'll *always* let you in, red."

My hold on her tightens, and she wriggles closer to me. With her bum against my crotch, I'm hard as hell between us. But neither of us does anything about it, aware that she can't handle it right now.

After several minutes of silence have passed, I begin to think she's asleep again. "Love?" I whisper.

"Yeah?"

"I know Sundays are your special days free of human contact to recharge from the week, but if you want to spend it here, I promise I'll give you all the space you want."

She ponders for a moment, and I tell myself she'll refuse, so I'm ready for the rejection. I fully expect it to go that way when she says, "I have some work to do today. But as long as I have a computer and internet, I'm good to do it here."

"Well, you're in luck because while we're not as advanced as the Upper East Side, we do have Wi-Fi here in Brooklyn." She lets out a small, lazy giggle. "And you can have my laptop. I'll use my tablet."

"Perfect."

After another few beats of silence, I ask, "Do you want me to cook breakfast?"

More thinking on her part and, "Where's my phone?"

"I think your clutch is still on the bathroom floor. Let me get it."

I slip out and return within seconds, handing her the tiny bag. I watch as she extracts her phone from it. "Crap, I'll need a charger, too," she notes.

"Not a problem either."

When she opens a food delivery app, I ask, "What are you doing?"

"Ordering breakfast so you can stay right here while someone else handles it."

"Really?" I chuckle.

"Yes. As much as I love your cooking, right now, I need you to be my emotional support wombat and cuddle with me until my brain stops hurting." She tilts her head sideways to meet my eyes and asks, "You think you can do that?"

"I definitely can, yes."

We move in unison to share a kiss, our lips meeting with eagerness. I let her dictate the mood, willing to take whatever she can give in her state, and when she unlocks her jaw to demand more, I happily indulge. In seconds, we're tongue-fucking each other's mouths, her hand reaching back to hold my neck while mine cups and fondles her breasts under the T-shirt. I can't stop my hips from grinding onto her when she begins writhing, and I feed on the little moans and gasps she lets out, which end in my mouth.

"Do you want this?" I mumble into our kiss. "Do you want me to fuck you like you asked for when you arrived?"

"Yes, but I'm not sure I will enjoy it as much as I should," she whimpers.

That's all I need to force myself to slow down until I release her, still spooning. With the pad of my thumb, I caress the rosy curve of her cheek. "We can wait, red. We're in no hurry, especially if you spend the day here."

"But this seems painful," she argues, pressing her arse harder onto my raging hard-on. It is.

"Don't worry about it, love. It'll go away. For now, I'll be content being a cuddly wombat."

She smiles, and it's so bright and genuine that it makes the blue balls worth it. We return to our position, and she picks up the phone she dropped to continue her search for sustenance. I help her find the best place around here, and we pick whatever looks good. Given the quantity, there will be no cooking today.

And like the whipped wombat I am, I'm perfectly fine with it if the alternative is more cuddling in bed.

As promised, I give Gen the space she needs to do her thing. She settles on the couch, where Mulli joins her, and I sit on a stool at the high counter of the kitchen.

Breakfast, or rather brunch, was stellar. Her idea to get it delivered was great because now, any time we fancy a snack, we have a bunch of options to pick from. I offered to pay for it, but she insisted that it was her way of thanking me for welcoming her into my home in the middle of the night. As if I would have let her fend for herself in the state she was in—oscillating and talking too loud, drunk off her face.

I look up from the article Eli sent earlier and observe Gen from afar. She's sprawled on the couch, her bare feet on the coffee table before her. The laptop is on her lap with her eyes reading whatever's on the screen, one hand scrolling while the other mindlessly pets Mulli's head resting on her stomach. Beelzebub is on the other side of the table Gen's feet are leaning on, glaring at them with judgment, like always.

These three are getting along very well. A lot better than what usually happens when I bring women home. I guess it's because of the consistency. Gen knows Mulli is a gentle giant, and the dog has seen her enough to grow some form of attachment. As for Beelzebub, I don't know what the fuck is happening, but I think he likes Gen even though I've never seen him like anyone before—not even the hand that feeds him.

My gaze seems to compel hers because Gen looks up. She gives me a smile, we stare at each other for a moment, and she returns to the laptop's screen. I haven't heard her make a call, so I figure her colleagues are enjoying their Sunday like normal people. Her lack of complaint tells me she's used to it.

I remember how she joked about losing her weekends as she would climb up the corporate ladder, and I still can't make sense of it. We're supposed to work to live, not live to work. I do long hours, but it's my passion, a craft I take great pride in practicing.

Maybe corporate law is the same for her, but I don't buy it. It can't be anyone's passion. Especially not an adventurous and bold woman like her.

"Stop staring," she demands with a grin, her eyes never leaving the screen.

"How do you know I'm staring?"

"I can feel it. It's distracting."

"You're what's distracting. My shirt on you is fantasy-inducing."

She snorts, shaking her head before glancing at me. "Should I remove it?"

"Fuck yeah."

"Something tells me I won't get any work done if I walk around naked."

The dog reacts before I can, her head springing up at the magic word. Fuck, I'm being a terrible dog dad.

Mulligrubs excitedly jumps on the couch, to Gen's confusion. I slide off the stool and walk up to them. "You activated her with the word 'walk,'" I explain. Repeating it makes Mulli even more frantic. "I'll take her out for a bit. She hates being cooped up in here all day. Do you think you can handle half an hour without me?"

I bend over Gen, leaning on the couch's backrest until my lips are close to hers. "It'll be hard, but I think I'll survive," she gravely replies.

I'm grinning like an idiot when I kiss her. "Alright, Grubsy! Off we go!"

The Rottweiler rushes to the door, and I join her, grabbing her leash and a tennis ball. I'm not really dressed to go out—a hoodie, sweatpants, and slippers—but it's fucking Sunday, so I'm not doing anything about it.

"See you in a bit, red."

"Have a nice walk, *wombat*."

Once outside, I don't waste any time before heading to the nearby dog park. There, I play fetch with Mulli, throwing the ball far to tire her faster. After twenty minutes and a fuming pile of shit that I handle, we're on our way back to the flat. Upon entering the lift, I'm amused by how spent my dog is now. She couldn't wait to get out, but now she'll slump onto one of her mattresses as soon as we're in.

"So, what do we think of Gen?" I ask her when the lift takes off. Mulli looks up at me with her dark brown eyes, tilting her head to the side. "We like her, don't we? Isn't she nice?"

Mulli blinks, reminding me very few thoughts are running through her big skull. "I think she's nice," I decide. "Nowhere near as uptight as I first thought. And I know you have no beauty standards regarding humans, but she's smoking hot too. And funny. I fucking adore her humor. So dry and unexpected."

We reach the fifth floor before I can have a longer conversation with Mulli, and then we're back in the flat. Just like I predicted, Mulligrubs heads to the closest bed on the floor and curls up onto it.

Gen isn't on the couch anymore, and I spot her in the kitchen, searching for something in the fridge. She straightens up with a bottle of orange juice just as I join her there. "Do you have a no-drinking-from-the-bottle policy?" she asks.

At this point, her question is almost silly, isn't it? She's sucked my cock, swallowed my cum, I've licked her pussy, and I fully intend on eating her arse one day. We're way past sharing saliva on a bottle's cap. Instead of answering, I walk up to her and grab her jaw with a firm hand.

When I try to open her up, she looks perplexed, so I hold back a smirk and tell her, "Number thirty-six."

It takes her less than a second to understand, and when she does, her eyes darken with arousal, the void of her pupils eating away the blue of her irises. I fucking adore that my crudeness still surprises her because the way she stares at me with her round eyes while pink creeps up her cheeks is everything.

I don't force her, in case she doesn't want this, and her jaw unlocks on its own, her lips parting with consent. Her submissiveness hardens my cock, and when she slightly brings her tongue out, it aches. My naughty red wants this as much as I do.

So I give it to her.

She almost looks surprised when I spit right into her mouth, as if she didn't believe I'd do it. Or maybe it's even more intense than she expected. As if she knows how sexy this looks, she gives me enough time to gaze down at the dollop of my saliva on her pink tongue before swallowing it down, clearly affected by the rawness of the moment.

"Do you want to ask your question again?" I cockily offer.

She shakes her head, having learned her lesson, and I release her. With trembling hands, she unscrews the cap and drinks straight from the neck. I accept the bottle from her when she's done, still feeling very proud of myself. I'm the one who settles it back in the fridge, and when I turn to her again, she's leaning back onto the counter.

"I'm feeling better," she says.

"That's great, love."

"No, you don't understand. I'm feeling *so much* better."

I swear I'm a fucking moron because it takes her suggestive smile for me to get it. "Oh fuck, right."

I've been wanting to enter her since she appeared on my doorstep with her sexy dress and lewd demands, so I don't need more than that to spring into action.

Within seconds, I've hoisted her up on the counter to stand between her parted knees. My hands avidly explore her under the shirt while my lips claim hers. She's just as eager as I am, her fingers tugging at my T-shirt to peel it off, her tongue bold and demanding against mine. I'm fully naked before she is, and I'm moving on to removing my boxer briefs from her when she pushes my face away with her hands framing it.

I don't know what's going on, nearly panting from how much I want to fuck her, and she surprises me by returning my earlier gesture. Inching closer, she spits in my mouth without a warning, and I swear to God, it's one of the hottest things she's ever done. The timid little lawyer who first waited for me in The Plaza's bar is long gone, isn't she?

I fucking devour her to reward her boldness, avidly sucking in her tongue to share her spit. Then, my mouth drags away from her and lowers, eager for her taste.

"Jake," she moans when I lean forward to capture a perky pink tip between my teeth. Her hand is already in my hair, pulling me closer, and the other one is gripping my shoulder. "Jake, get the whipped cream and the chocolate syrup."

My cock twitches between us, loving the idea. I release her nipple and give her a delighted smirk.

"Oh, you naughty, naughty girl. You want me to devour you, don't you?"

"Yes."

I'm complying and taking some stuff out of the fridge when she adds, "I've wanted to do this one for a while."

Right, food play is also on her list.

I don't like the idea of checking off yet another item, but I'm also looking forward to having myself some chocolate-flavored Gen. And while I won't put any of that on her pussy, I don't mind. Gen-flavored Gen is my favorite.

Her eyes are on my stiff cock as I return with the goods, and she looks impatient to be impaled on it. I share the same desires, but before we get to that, I'm getting my fill of her.

She watches, her eyes hooded with want as I settle the things next to her on the counter, and then yelps with surprise when I pull her off of it. It turns into a giggle as I lower the briefs to finish undressing her, kneeling down as I do.

Her hand is tangled in my hair before I even shove my face between her creamy thighs. "Jake …" she moans as I lick up her slit, entranced by her flavor and smell.

I'd do this for hours if she let me, but we have other plans. So, after one last lap at her cunt and a final kiss on her clit, I rise up and flip her around in one smooth movement. "Jake, what are you—"

My hand pushing to bend her over on the cold counter stops her. She stays there, motionless and slightly panting, as I grab the whipped cream and pop the cap open. My eyes are on the prize, focused on the small hole I intend to feast on.

"What are you doing?" she hesitantly asks while I shake the can.

"I think it's time I eat your arse."

She tenses all over, her hands clenching at her sides. I can't see her face as she looks away, but I see the tip of her ears turn pink.

"Is it too much, red?"

For several seconds, she thinks about it, fighting against her instincts so she can give in. We both know she showered about an hour ago, so she's as clean as it gets. "You enjoy it when I finger your bum, don't you?" I ask, even though we both know it's true—she's begged for it a few times.

She twists around, her amazingly blue eyes hesitantly meeting mine. Without a word, she nods.

"Then you'll love this. And it's like a treat for me."

"Really?"

"Yes, absolutely."

I bend over to give an eager kiss to her butt cheek. "Let me do this for you, love."

It's clear she's not entirely sold, but she gives me a single nod. I'll go slow and let her get used to it. When she faces away again, I give the can another few shakes. She jumps with surprise at the first squirt of cold whipped cream in the valley of her freckled arse, but I have a solid hand on her back, anticipating her reaction. Past the initial shock, she shows no sign of resistance, utterly immobile as I trace down a path of whipped cream.

Once I'm done, I set the can next to her and then kneel again. "Relax, sweetheart," I soothe as I take hold of her hips. She has no idea how much I want this, does she? I guess I'll have to show her.

Holding back a grin, I lean forward, famished.

CHAPTER
Twenty-Three

Gen

JAKE IS THE ONLY REASON I'll survive these intense two weeks of work. I'm not sure how I would get through them without his uncanny ability to help me relax and blow off some steam.

The list is kind of on hold, and I'm okay with that. Instead of putting any pressure on ourselves to tick more items, we do whatever we feel like doing in the moment, which is still pretty spectacular every single time. And because he knows just how busy I am, he goes out of his way to make it work.

On Tuesday, he comes by my place for a couple of hours of naked cardio, then leaves after a goodbye kiss to let me finish what I'm working on. On Thursday, when I'm stressed and considering ripping my hair out in frustration, I send him a text, which makes him come all the way here again and fuck me silly. On Friday evening, I decide I've missed enough after-work drinks with the team, so I force myself to head there rather than meet with Jake at The Devil's Court. As soon as it's over though, I text him to see if he's still up.

Turns out he is, so he hops on his bike. By the time I get home, he's at the foot of my building, eagerly waiting. Really, getting to see him is what makes me get through all this. I hang on, knowing I'll keep getting more of him.

Now, it's Saturday morning, more than halfway through my fortnight of hell. We're in the kitchen to get ourselves some much-needed sustenance, still reeking of sex and looking the part. The sleep last night was scarce, the sex was plentiful, and I have no regrets. I needed that after the long week I had.

"Do you want bacon?" I ask him, looking into my fridge.

"Sure. Do you have more bread? There's only two slices left in this one."

"Let me check the pantry."

I give him the bacon before I make my way to fetch the bread.

It's disappointing that he has to leave right after breakfast, but it's better this way. I have to work, and he has important things to handle. Today, they're welcoming their new guest artist, a woman who comes all the way from South Africa to stay at The Parlour for three weeks to tattoo New Yorkers. According to Jake, Kaya is so famous in the business that half of her time here is already booked, and people are coming from across the country to get inked by her. So, Jake has to pick her up from the airport at eleven and then settle her in the apartment unit he keeps available for guest artists.

When I return from the pantry with more bread, Jake still looks like the only thing I want to eat this morning, wearing nothing but black underwear. By now, he has to know how mad that drives me, and he's doing it on purpose. Just so he can get a taste of his own medicine, I'm wearing only his T-shirt, and I keep finding excuses to stretch up or bend over.

I'm not necessarily saying he'll be late to the airport, but I claim no responsibility if he is. He started it with the underwear thing.

When he asks for the maple syrup, I hold back my grin and position myself in a way that puts my ass right in his field of view. Bending at the hips, I reach the lowest drawer and pull it open. I pretend to look for the syrup, knowing it's not here at all. I'm sure he can see every intimate detail of me from where he stands.

When he lets out a grunt, I bite my lower lip. "Genevieve, I will fuck you up," he threatens.

Mustering my best innocent voice, I ask, "Why?"

"I can't be fucking late."

"Then don't be late."

I close the drawer and fetch the maple syrup, which was in plain sight on the counter the entire time. "You look a little tense, wombat," I tease, handing him the bottle. The wombat joke is still going strong, and I think that every time I use it, it becomes a little more serious. I'm still grinning when I suggest, "Maybe you should try meditation."

"Next time you flash me your cunt, you're getting a spanking. That'll relax me."

"And you think that's a threat?" I chortle.

"A spanking is nothing like the occasional slap on the bum, red. A proper one will remind you how much of a bad girl you've been every time you sit down for the next two days."

He walked right into that one, so I don't have any remorse when I grab his hand and slip it between my legs under his T-shirt I'm wearing. Like he can't help himself, he cups my intimacy. "I already will," I rasp, stretching up to take his lips.

His groan lands on my tongue, and he devours me with ravenous intensity. If the kiss he gives me is any indication, it'll be fast and hard. He'll leave me with weak legs and a pulse beating in my core, and I'll love every brief minute of it.

Two of his thick and tattooed fingers are deeply shoved into me, fucking me, preparing me for his dick, when we both hear the latch of the main door being undone.

What the—

We separate just as I hear the door opening. I scramble to readjust myself, but there isn't much to set right. I'm naked under the shirt, and Jake's in his damn underwear. Footsteps come in, and I try to think past the anxiety. Only three people have the key to my apartment. The concierge, Hana, and—

"Gen?" a masculine voice asks from the entrance.

Edward.

I give Jake a panicked look. This can go wrong in a hundred different ways. Before I can say anything, Eddie comes into view, scanning the room for me. When they land on their goal, his eyes go huge with shock. Understandably, he didn't expect to find me half-naked in my kitchen with an even more naked man who's covered in tattoos and twice my weight in hard-earned muscles.

All three of us say nothing for a few seconds, staring in utter silence. This has got to be the most awkward thing I've ever been through. And I've been through a lot.

Jake's the first one to do something, clearing his throat and leaning back on the counter behind him, crossing his powerful arms over his broad chest. When I look up at him, I swear he's holding back a proud little smirk. Clearly, he doesn't mind Eddie finding us like this.

When I turn to my ex again, none of the shock has dissipated from his face. It's as though he's frozen. "Edward, wha-what are you doing here?" I stammer.

"I need my tuxedo."

"So you just let yourself in?"

"I sent you texts. Like, twenty. And I tried to call." His attention latches back to Jake, who's still silently observing the scene as it unfolds. "You're that Jack guy from the gallery."

It's a statement, not a question. But the half-naked man beside me still feels compelled to say something. "Jake. Glad to see you remembered me this time, Edward the Third," he taunts.

"Are you two …"

Jake barely holds back a snort. "Does it look like I'm her personal chef, mate?"

The confusion on Eddie's features is slowly turning into anger and frustration. "Gen, is that the man from the other day? The one who drove you to work on his bike?"

Before I can answer, Jake replies, "You're smarter than I reckoned. I am that bloke, yes."

Understandably, Jake's patronizing tone doesn't sit well with Eddie, who now looks enraged. But my ex is good at containing strong emotions, so he takes a couple of breaths and forces himself to look away.

"I'll go get my tux and leave," he dryly says.

I consider holding him back, but I can't think of a good reason why. The sooner he leaves, the better. So I watch, disoriented, while he heads to the bedroom we shared for four years.

With evident amusement, Jake says, "Oh, he's going to love what we did to your bed."

Shoot! That would have been a good reason to hold Eddie back.

I haven't opened the window yet, so the room will have the stench of sex still etched into the walls. In the middle of it, the bedding is covered in cum and sweat, and I'm fairly sure there's a substantial stain of my arousal still clearly visible on the fitted sheet, right where Jake pinned me while we had sex upon waking up earlier.

There's no way Eddie will miss any of it as he makes his way to the walk-in closet.

My heart's in my throat while we wait for him to return. The anxiety isn't because I'm still hoping something might be fixable between us, but because I care about him in some capacity. He doesn't deserve to see the remnants of my night with Jake. We dated for five years, and if the roles were reversed, I'd feel nauseated and insulted.

When I finally hear his footsteps return, my whole body tenses, my hands balled into tight fists at my sides. If only I'd taken a moment to check my phone this morning or to switch off the Do Not Disturb setting. When he appears again, Eddie is fuming, his jaw tightly clenched, and his face scrunched into a furious scowl. His tuxedo is in its protective bag, thrown over his arm. Instinctively, I make my way around the kitchen island and walk up to him.

"Eddie, I'm so sorry—"

"Don't," he stops me. "I don't even want to hear it."

I reach out to him, trying to lay a comforting hand on his arm. "Please, I didn't want you to see thi—"

He grabs my wrist firmly, letting his anger get the best of him. "I said I don't want to hear it!" he utters.

"Let go of her," Jake commands, now standing right beside me. When Eddie doesn't comply, Jake's voice becomes even more threatening. "Let go, or I will break your fucking hand, you daft cunt."

That works, and Eddie releases me with a huff. I pass soothing fingers around my wrist, surprised by how hard he squeezed.

"I don't get it, Genevieve. We spent five years together, *five*, and I got nothing, barely scraps. Then you meet this guy—what, two weeks ago at the gallery? And you turn into a shameless whore? What the fuck is wrong with—"

Before the words can even hurt, Eddie is shoved away from me and slammed into the wall behind him, held against it by an enraged Jake. The tuxedo drops to the ground as my ex reaches for the tattooed forearm pressed against his throat. I swiftly join them, laying a hand on Jake's flexed biceps to make him release Edward.

I've never seen him like this, with murder in his eyes. The gentle wombat I know is long gone, replaced by a man who looks like he could kill.

"Did you think I'd let you call her that and let it slide?" Jake snarls. "Is that what you would have done? Like a dickless cunt who lets daddy handle all his problems?"

Eddie tries to talk, but nothing comes out except an indiscernible gurgle. He's barely touching the ground, standing on the tips of his shoes. "Did you ever stop and wonder if maybe you don't know how to fuck?" Jake growls. "That she only gave you scraps because you had nothing to offer in return?"

Now, Edward's face is turning an alarming shade of red, so I gently pull on Jake's arm, using a soothing voice when I say, "Let him go, Jake. Please, stop."

But nothing seems to reach past the pure rage he's experiencing.

"Do you want to hear a little secret, nepo boy?" he asks with a sadistic grin. "We started fucking *before* the gallery's opening. We'd already done it a few times like wild fucking animals—not that you'd know what that's like. And while you were busy networking with the guests like the trust fund little bitch you are, I was making her come all over my tongue and fingers in the restroom. Again, not that you'd know what that's like."

"Jacob!" I protest. Now he's going too far. While I understand why he'd want to protect me, it's clear that he's only trying to hurt Edward. Whatever is in my tone compels him to look at me. "Let go of him. Now!"

He glares at Eddie again, and after one last harsh shove, he releases him. Edward slumps down against the wall, barely managing to stay upright. A fit of coughs shakes him, his hand reaching up to massage his throat.

Jake displays no pity as he looks down at my ex. "Give her back the key that you have," he demands. "And then get the fuck out."

Edward's hands tremble as he pats himself to find his key chain. When he does, he takes it out of his pocket and fumbles to unhook my key. He lets it fall on the tiled floor and then bends to pick up his tux. I'm still in shock when he scurries out of the apartment, slamming the door behind him.

The silence that follows is deafening, and I don't know if we'll ever manage to break it. What the hell just happened? Everything was flipped upside down in five minutes, and instead of getting my way with Jake in the kitchen, I have to deal with a monumental crisis. And my lower half is still bare.

Flustered and confused, I look up at Jake, who's fuming. "Why were you protecting him?" he asks.

"What?"

"After what he said to you, why were you protecting him?"

"I wasn't protecting him, I was protecting *you!*"

"Really? It didn't look like it."

I huff, unimpressed by his lack of trust in me. "People like us sue, Jacob. We don't care about some honor to uphold. When we get assaulted, we hire the best lawyers in town to sue. So, excuse me for not letting you give Eddie the means to do that to you."

His lips pinch in a thin line, jaw ticking as he understands I not only mean it, but I'm also right. "Also," I continue, "Eddie and I work together, we have friends in common, our families frequent the same circles ... I don't need him to know those sorts of intimate details about me—especially not when you've just humiliated him, which might make him vindictive. You had no right to disclose the information you did."

"And he had no right to call you *that.*"

Something in his tone, in how hurt he sounds about Eddie calling me a whore, makes my chest ache. He's right, Eddie shouldn't have said that. But it doesn't mean slamming him against my wall was the proper course of action.

"I'm sorry I lost my temper," Jake says. "I just—I saw red, and I wanted to make him swallow his fucking tongue for saying it."

Again, the vulnerability I discern in him is touching, and I don't know what to make of my torn feelings. Part of me appreciates that he stood up for me like this, but another part hates how he went about it.

Something tells me that Jake wouldn't have reacted so harshly had Eddie only insulted him. Jake has thick skin, and his nonchalant and cocky attitude allows him to brush off a lot more than most. But hearing the insults veered toward me is apparently another thing.

I don't even know what to say anymore, so I walk the space that separates us and wrap my arms around him, pressing my front on his bare torso. After a second of uncertainty, his arms also come around me, and he holds me in a hesitant embrace.

"Thank you for protecting my honor," I whisper, my temple and cheek plastered on his shoulder. "But please, never do that again."

"I don't think he'll give me the opportunity to."

"Yeah, that's unlikely."

I look up, still not quite over everything that just happened. His green eyes meet mine, and his hand comes to my face. With a delicate thumb, he grazes the length of my cheekbone. "You know you're not what he said, right?"

I nod, mesmerized by the softness of his irises and the fondness clearly visible in them.

"Just because a woman enjoys sex doesn't mean she deserves to be shamed for it. No matter how many partners she has, her history, her kinks, her pace, her needs … You understand that, right?"

My head bobs up and down again. I'm touched that he's making sure I'm okay after Edward's hurtful insult.

"Good, because you're fucking perfect, red, and you don't deserve to have any doubt about the kind of person you are."

I cup his cheek, contending with a swarm of feelings too strong to register. "You're the one who's perfect, wombat."

I'm rising to my toes to kiss him when he mumbles, "Hardly."

Because it's too late to counter him with words, I show him just how much I mean it with my actions. My display of affection isn't supposed to turn into anything more, but we get lost in the moment. Adrenaline ran high, and we're both looking for a way to let it out. Maybe that's why my heart seems to have doubled in size. It feels like it might explode at any moment, overwhelmed with emotions and feelings.

I don't protest when Jake lifts me by the back of my legs, settling my bare center right onto his boxer-clad crotch.

"Where do you want me?" he asks into our kiss.

"The bedroom. I think we can make it all even filthier—in case he comes back because he forgot a bowtie or something."

His chuckle echoes everywhere within me, and I beam in return. "I love the way you think, Miss Kensington."

"Thank you. I'm very smart. I even went to Harvard."

"You did?" he sarcastically asks. "I had no idea. You *never* mention it."

"Dick," I mumble. He laughs again, and this time, I'm with him.

When he sets out to bring me to the bedroom, I'm reminded he had plans that didn't involve sex this morning. "Wait, what about the airport?"

"I'll text Eli to pick up Kaya. This is more important."

While he carries me back to the bedroom, I kiss every inch of his face, entranced by all of him. I'm still not sure that I like the way he handled Edward, but in my heart, I can't blame him for it.

I'd have done the same thing for him.

CHAPTER
Twenty-Four

Gen

THAT REPORT DAMN NEAR KILLED me. I can't remember when I last had to work this hard, and I hope I won't have to ever again.

To my dismay, my suspicions were on point, and Ralf and his team didn't take the assignment as seriously as they should have. I'm the one leaving a day earlier, so I'd be the one blamed if it's incomplete. This means my team worked twice as hard as his, and I worked five times harder than anyone else.

But at least it's done, and I can take my Friday off without getting penalized for it or compromising the promotion I'm after. Alas, it means finishing at two in the morning and not getting to see Jake before taking off to the Hamptons for the weekend.

I briefly saw him twice since the Edward incident, which is way too little. He doesn't complain about it, even though I can feel how reluctant he is whenever he has to leave earlier than he normally would. We've agreed that I'll try to return not too late on Sunday and go straight to him. I'll even spend the night at his place, and since I have my car with me, I'll drive to work on Monday morning and keep my weekend things in the trunk.

With everything going on, I almost forgot it was my birthday. But I received a text from Jake a little after midnight, while I was still up in the NexaCorp tower, that read, "Happy birthday, red." That energized me enough to push through and finish everything within the next couple of hours. Then, this morning, I woke up to a text from Hana, also wishing me a happy birthday. Now, I'm not expecting texts or calls from anyone else.

I don't have a Facebook account that'll remind everyone of it, and I don't have any friends close enough to care to set a reminder for it. As for my parents, they tend to forget that today isn't just Victoria's day. Eddie won't message me either, that's for sure.

After his unexpected visit, I hired a moving team to pack up every last thing he left behind and deliver it to the place he shares with his friend. My apartment feels a little empty now, but I'll quickly fill the spaces left by Eddie's complete disappearance from my life. That void is only material though, because mentally and physically, I've never felt more fulfilled. Which is insane, because I want even more of Jake despite him being infinitely more than any man I've had before him.

I'm just done packing my things when my phone buzzes from a text. It's Jake again.

WOMBAT GUY

> Have a safe drive today, love. Text me when you get there.

ME

> I will. And I'll let you know when I have an ETA for Sunday!

WOMBAT GUY

> Perfect. Happy birthday again, sweetheart.

Today doesn't feel as emotional as I expected, and I think it's because of him. He's been distracting me from my gloomy thoughts, even more than the report I've been working on. Every free moment my brain has is devoted to Jake—daydreams that involve him, fantasies of what else we might try together, or reruns of moments and conversations we've had. He has become a solid obsession, and I'm not even trying to fight it. It brings me too much joy for that.

Because I barely ever use my car, it looks brand new despite having it since I moved to New York after Harvard. It's an Audi A5 Cabriolet I gifted to myself for passing the bar. Because I don't feel safe driving with the roof folded down when I'm stuck in traffic, it's still on when I roll out of the building. About an hour later, once the city is in my rearview mirror, I make a quick pit stop to let it open. Then, I'm on my way again to East Hampton.

The drive is smooth but feels longer than it is. Probably because I'm apprehensive about spending the weekend with my parents. It's never a walk in the park, but it gets even worse around this time of the year. And later today, there's the "little" gathering Mother organized in loving memory of Victoria, which I'm also not looking forward to.

I feel guilty enough as it is. I don't want to face everyone who ever loved or cared for her.

I'm making another pit stop when I receive an additional birthday text, which genuinely surprises me and warms me up inside.

ELI

> Jake told me it's your day, so happy birthday, Genny bean. I'll buy you a drink at the DC when you come back (or five, so I can finally beat you at pool). Enjoy your weekend while I'm consoling Jake over here ;)

ME

> You'll never beat me. I'm a pool goddess.

Maybe I have more friends than I thought, after all.

The massive gates of the Kensington Estate feel ominously unwelcoming when I stop in front of them. I count to sixty in my head, building up more courage with each number, and then press on the intercom. A few seconds later, a cold "Yes?" emerges from the speaker.

"It's Genevieve," I say with a clear voice.

No one answers, but the gates slowly part. I drive through the three-hundred-yard lane and stop the car in front of the house. Or maybe I should call it a modern castle, because this can't be called a mere house.

I'm just done taking my Louis Vuitton duffel bag out of the car when someone from the staff comes out to welcome me. "Miss Genevieve, I hope you had a good drive," John greets me.

"I did, thank you."

"Happy birthday from the staff, miss."

"Thank you, John. Are my parents home?"

"Your father is in the city, but your mother is in the ballroom."

When he reaches out for my bag, I let him take it. I know better than to do the job meant for "the help" and get another earful for it. Before I forget, I send Jake a text.

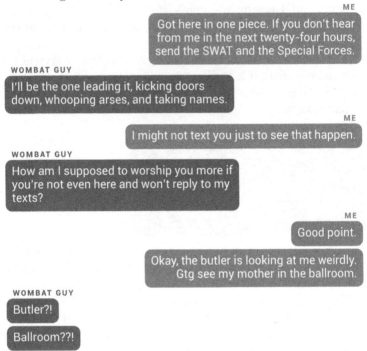

ME

Got here in one piece. If you don't hear from me in the next twenty-four hours, send the SWAT and the Special Forces.

WOMBAT GUY

I'll be the one leading it, kicking doors down, whooping arses, and taking names.

ME

I might not text you just to see that happen.

WOMBAT GUY

How am I supposed to worship you more if you're not even here and won't reply to my texts?

ME

Good point.

Okay, the butler is looking at me weirdly. Gtg see my mother in the ballroom.

WOMBAT GUY

Butler?!

Ballroom??!

I stifle my laughter as I walk into the house with John at my heels. While he heads toward the bedrooms with my things, I venture to the large room we use for receptions. Sure enough, Mother is there with an army of people from whatever event service she hired. As I suspected, this isn't a little get-together. This is an opportunity for the Kensingtons to show off their wealth while networking and getting sympathetic condolences from the guests.

Because I was in a deep state of shock when it happened, I didn't realize back then that Victoria's funeral was meant for my parents more than it was for her. They invited people who never knew Vicky, work relations who couldn't possibly refuse the invitation, clients, partners ... My dissociative state blinded me, but that fact still sits wrong.

"Good morning, Mother," I salute Vivienne when I reach her.

"Genevieve, you've arrived." Since she can't help herself, she scans me from head to toe, her eyes unforgivingly precise. "I see your work situation hasn't improved since I last saw you," she notes with pinched lips.

"It actually got worse, thank you for noticing."

Either she doesn't notice the sarcasm in my voice, or she doesn't care because she continues with, "Good thing I have a hair and makeup team for both of us. You'll look more presentable."

Isn't maternal love the sweetest thing in the world?

I force a smile on my lips and look around the room. Tables have been arranged, enough to host about a hundred people. The caterer's team is setting porcelain plates, crystal glasses, and silver cutlery on the white tablecloths, and the event team is adjusting floral arrangements, setting candelabras, and finding room for various decorative trinkets.

Victoria would have hated all of this. She always felt uncomfortable when our home was turned into a venue for one of our parents' receptions. There's nothing more invasive than dozens of tipsy people venturing into the house after too much French wine and fine food. My twin wasn't a very social person, easily triggered by crowds, so it was a lot worse for her than for me.

"The first guests will arrive at five," Mother tells me. "Maybe you could go lie down and get some rest. I'm not sure makeup will be enough for those bags under your eyes."

I don't even say anything because I actually want to go to my room and never come out of it. So, I smile instead and give her a nod. "Great idea. I will take a quick nap and join you for lunch."

"Oh, we are not having lunch. You know how I get before those receptions. My stomach is in knots."

Well, that's on me for not taking the time to eat before leaving. Maybe I'll sneak to the kitchen once I'm done with my much-needed moment alone.

I walk out of the ballroom, welcoming the stillness that fills the rest of the house. It's as silent as ever while I make my way to the private wing, where my old room is. When I pass the door of Victoria's room, I momentarily stop my course and lay a hand on the golden plate with her name engraved on it.

"I'm sorry," I whisper, hoping that wherever she is now, she knows just how much I mean it.

A few steps later, there's the same plate with my name this time, and I push the door open. The space still bears traces of my younger self, even though it isn't as bad as it used to be. Something switched in me the day Vicky died, and I matured overnight. I still remember how I ripped my One Direction and Twilight posters. Now, all that's left to testify for their existence are small pinholes in the wallpaper. On the shelves though, I still have the books I used to love, CDs, and trinkets.

With a sigh, I lie down on the bed, staring emptily at the white ceiling. Right there, I used to have a Jacob Black poster. A smile tugs at the corner of my lips as I realize I wouldn't say no to a Jacob Clarke one.

I swear we must be connected because my phone vibrates in my back pocket, and I just know it's him.

WOMBAT GUY
Should we set up an hourly check-up or something?

ME
Maybe. I already want to leave :(

WOMBAT GUY
That bad? You haven't even been there for half an hour.

ME
You'd understand if you knew my mother.

WOMBAT GUY
As someone who lost his mum way too young, I tend to remind people to be grateful for having a mother at all.

My heart drops all the way to my guts, and I suddenly feel terrible for even complaining to him. He's had it so much worse than me, and he doesn't deserve my entitled ranting.

ME
Crap, right. I'm so sorry, Jake.

WOMBAT GUY
It's alright. I finished mourning her a long time ago.

ME
Still, it was insensitive of me.

WOMBAT GUY
Are you still with her right now?

No, I'm alone on my old bed. She sent me here to rest because I apparently look like a corpse.

I chew on my bottom lip, hoping he isn't annoyed with me—which he would be entirely entitled to. Instead of a text coming in, it's a call. I pick up and press the phone to my ear.

He opens with, "Alright, maybe I was wrong about your mother."

I giggle, relieved. "She's something, that's for sure."

"Honestly, if corpses looked like you, necrophilia would be a much bigger kink."

This time, I let out a conflicted laugh. "What a weird and twisted compliment."

"I excel at those."

It's so good to hear his voice that I can already sense my anxiety dissipating. But it's also weird to be here and talk to him. The most that ever happened in this bed were a few self-inflicted orgasms with tentative fingers in the middle of the night, and on the other side of this phone is a man who's made me come harder than I ever thought I could, who's licked every part of my body, and who can set me on fire with a mere gaze.

It's like two worlds are colliding together.

Now, I kind of understand why that was on the list—raunchy sex in a childhood bed. It feels taboo, forbidden.

"Did you know," I ask, "that among the things I removed from the list, there was one about having sex in my childhood bed?"

"Really?"

"Yep. 'Have you ever had the nastiest, naughtiest sex in your childhood bed as an adult?'" I quote from the quiz word for word.

"And why did you remove it from the list?"

"Because it's a hundred miles away, and you can't meet my parents."

"Fair."

We say nothing for a moment, and an idea grows and grows in my mind. We could do two birds with one stone since we haven't checked phone sex off the list yet.

Hesitantly, I say, "Do you think we should—"

"Abso-fucking-lutely. Let me lock the door of my office." His eagerness makes me giggle, but then I let out a curse, so he asks, "What?"

"My door doesn't have a lock."

"Really?"

"My parents argued we shouldn't have anything to hide from them, so it was unnecessary."

"That sounds healthy. So, what do we do?"

I think about it for a moment, glaring at the door. I really could use some serotonin right now. And it's my birthday, after all. "We do fast," I decide.

I distinctly hear a lock being secured on his side of the line. A thrilling shiver runs through me, my heart racing under my ribs. My free hand tremblingly flies to my waist, where I undo the button of my jeans. This is insane. The man has the ability to make me do the most unhinged things. But as I tug at the waistband to lower it, even if I know my mother could come in at any point and not even knock, like always, I can't stop myself from wanting to do this.

He must hear me struggle to push my jeans down because he commands, "Put the phone on speaker and set it next to you."

Smart. I do just that and then shove my pants and underwear all the way to my knees. "Is your pussy bare?" he asks.

"Yes. Is your dick out?"

I can hear his smile when he answers, "Yes."

"How—how do we proceed?"

"Well, normally, we take it slow and get ourselves in the mood, but time is pressing. So, I will tell you what to do, and you will obey. Alright?"

Just the thought of it makes something throb inside me. "Yes."

"Good. Since I can't see you, don't hold anything back, red. I want to hear every moan, every whimper, every breath ... You give them all to me. Is that clear?"

"Yes."

"Good girl."

My walls clench again.

"Do you have a sex toy hidden somewhere in your old room?" he asks.

"No." Because Mother used to snoop around our rooms whenever we were away, I only invested in one after I left for Harvard.

"Then fingers it is. What are you wearing, love?"

"Partially jeans and a blouse. Oh, and that green lacy lingerie you like."

"I like all your lingerie. I need you to open the blouse, Gen."

"Completely?"

"Yes. And when you're done, you'll pull your bra up and free your beautiful tits."

My fingers shake as I follow his instruction, tension growing in my core and chest with each button I undo. If someone comes in right now, I'll never be able to set foot in this house ever again. Which, admittedly, wouldn't be such a terrible thing.

"There, done," I say once my breasts are exposed to the open air.

"Are your nipples hard, red? Are they all pebbled and perky, begging for my tongue to play with them?"

"Yes. I can even feel them tugging."

"Hmm ... Touch them. Pinch them with your fingers. Twist them between your thumb and index. You love when I do that, don't you?"

My hands don't even need my brain's command to move into action, my entire being devoted to Jake at this moment. "You know I do," I mumble, surprised by the small electric shivers my fingers trigger.

"Now, pinch them hard enough to hurt, Gen. Imagine I'm biting them." Again, I do what he asks, ripping a small moan out of myself. "Hmm, such an obedient girl. Gently caress them with your thumbs like I would with my tongue, soothe the pain away, sweetheart."

"Jake," I whimper, pressing my knees together to fight the urge growing inside me.

"We'll get there in due time, red. But perfect tits like yours deserve some attention. This morning, I rubbed one out to that pic you sent me back then. You have such beautiful nipples."

"Hmm," I moan, twisting my tips again between my fingers, wishing he was doing it instead.

"Alright, I want you to keep fondling your left breast, but move your right hand between your legs." He gives me enough time to comply. "Are you wet?"

"Yes ..."

"I bet you are." I hear a spitting sound, and I imagine him with a dollop of saliva in his hand that he coats on his erection. "You're always so wet, love, flooding my cock with your cum when you orgasm. It drives me fucking mad, you know that?"

"Jake, please ... What do I do?"

"Your index and middle fingers. Run their tips over your soaked slit. Get them all glistening for me, red."

"God, I'm so wet."

He groans on the other side of the line, and it makes my clit pulse with need. "Circles—draw tight circles around your clit, Gen. But softly at first. Tease yourself. You say you hate it when I do that, but it's a lie, isn't it? Don't you love when I edge you to the brink of insanity just to make you shatter even harder?"

My back arches against the mattress, my fingertips as light as feathers on my needy little bud. "Mmh, yes."

"The way you beg, red, how you plead with me to let you come … It's the sexiest thing in the world. Are you still playing with your nipple?"

"Yes. Jake, I need more."

"How much more?"

"Everything. I need everything."

"That's my greedy girl. Go ahead, press harder. Give yourself those little shivers of pleasure that make you jolt."

How well he knows me should be worrying, but I'm too absorbed by my hand twisting and pulling the rosy tip and the other drawing tight circles between my legs. My breathing is irregular and shallow, and I can hear his too, which comes out in deep, heavy pants.

"Jake, I need—aah, I need more."

"You need my cock, don't you? You need my big fat cock to fill your tight little cunt."

"Yes! Oh God, yes!"

"Then use your fingers. Three of them. Bury them deep inside your pussy, red. Inside your tight, wet, and warm cunt."

I pinch my nipple hard enough to make it hurt again and lower the hand between my legs to align it with my opening. I don't waste any time following his order, shoving my fingers inside me as far as I can. I made a tactical error when I didn't remove my jeans entirely because I can't spread my legs enough to take in every knuckle. Still, it's better than nothing.

"Aah, Jake!"

"Does that feel good, red?"

"Yes!"

"As good as my cock?"

"Not even close. But—Aah. It feels good."

"I wish I could see you right now, writhing and fucking yourself like the horny woman you are, desperate for release."

He sounds so tense, speaking through a clenched jaw as he fucks his fist. I can actually hear it, the rhythmic sound of his hand fisting his magnificent dick and the silver chain that bounces on his wrist. "Thrust them in and out, red. Fuck yourself with them like you wish I was fucking you. I bet you want it hard. And fast. You want to come all over my cock, don't you?"

"Jake, I'm so close! Oh God, I need—"

"Let go of your tit. Suck on the fingers of that hand. Make them all wet and ready for your clit."

While I keep up with the intense pace between my legs, I bring my index and middle finger to my lips and welcome them against my tongue. I suck on them like I would suck on his cock if he were there, bringing them all the way to the back of my throat. I don't even have to force the moans that I make around them, completely entranced and lost in the moment.

"Now bring them between your legs. Touch your clit. No circles this time, but left and right, over and over again. Fast."

His commands are scattered, rough words thrown into the phone as he closes in. He's almost there, just like me.

"Ahh! I'm gonna come!"

"Good. Keep the same pace, red. Keep fucking yourself with your fingers, keep rubbing your clit. God, you're so fucking wet I can hear it."

Just like I can hear the intense pace of his hand as he fucks himself.

With my eyes tightly shut, I keep doing everything he demanded and only think of him. Using his groans and pants, I build a mental image of Jake vigorously fucking his fist in his office, pumping his big, hard, and pierced cock like a possessed man. I can see it perfectly, down to the precum that coats his tip and the letters inked on his knuckles. In my vision, his eyes are closed, and he imagines me in the state of absolute abandon that I am in.

That's what gets me to finally tilt—knowing he's doing precisely the same with me.

With a soft cry, I reach the peak he brought me to, my toes curling and my back arching off the mattress as my muscles flex under the intensity of my orgasm. Around the three fingers that I keep pumping inside me, I can feel my walls clench, wetness gushing out of me and turning my insides all creamy and slick.

"Yes! That's it, red. Keep going, keep fucking yourself. Don't. Fucking. Stop."

His broken sentence ends with a deep and mighty roar that I know all too well because I've heard it uttered right into my ears so many times. He's following me in bliss, his cum spilling in thick, white ropes. I don't stop, pushing my orgasm to the verge of discomfort as I ignore the way my wrist hurts from the repeated motion, my fingers cramping.

"Aah, fuck," he grunts between whimpers, his breathing as erratic as mine.

When I can't take it anymore, I pull my fingers out of my spasming intimacy and lay my drenched hands on each side of me, completely spent. For several long seconds that turn into minutes, we don't say anything, my heaving breaths matching his. I have never, in my entire life, given myself such a phenomenal orgasm. Especially not with just my fingers, which usually turns out so mild and unsatisfactory. But this ... this was almost as good as when he fingers me himself.

"Jesus fucking Christ," he whimpers.

"Happy birthday to me."

"And to me, at this point. Holy fuck, that was ..."

"I know. Heaven's sake, my entire body feels like Jell-O."

"I can't even get up right now. Fucking Christ, the things you do to me, woman."

"Well, ditto."

We fall silent again, still struggling to recuperate. When my phone blips next to me, I expect it's some random notification. I throw a vague look at it though, and I see it's a message. From him. Puzzled, I pick up the iPhone and open the text. He sent me a picture.

No, he sent me the *hottest* picture I have ever seen in my entire life. Sexy enough to make my insides spasm one last time.

I must have made a sound, a moan or something, because he cockily asks through the speaker, "See what you did to me?"

Oh, I do. I really, really do.

In the picture he took, I can see his softening dick with the piercing at the tip catching the light, but the main star is his big and strong hand. His palm and fingers are sticky with semen, white and thick against his calloused skin.

"Did you lose your tongue again, red?"

That brings me back to the present. I kick my feet to get the jeans to lower, so I can spread my legs better. "Yes. It's on its way to New York to lick all of that off you."

He lets out a surprised laugh. Trying to be discreet so he doesn't see it coming, I bring the phone between my legs, struggling to figure out how to take a decent picture of my drenched folds.

"Do you want me to save it for you in a vial or something?" he offers.

"Don't tempt me. I'm so hungry right now."

"Then go eat something."

"I will."

The first picture I snap is out of focus, so I delete it and try again. This one isn't perfect, but at least better, so I hit send.

A second passes. Two. Three. And—

"Fucking hell ... That's not fair, red."

"You started it, and I finished it."

"We clearly both finished."

His wit makes me laugh until I hear a sound outside. Shoot, right. I'm busy pulling my pants up when he asks, "Can I print and frame it? I promise I won't let anyone else see it. But your pussy is a fucking work of art, and after you come, it's a masterpiece."

"This is for your eyes only, wombat. It doesn't leave your phone—*ever*."

"But I need something to start my Genevieve Kensington shrine."

I giggle again. "I'll give you a lock of my hair if you want, but not that."

"Well, now I want both."

Another sound echoes from the hallway outside, and I have to accept that this fun moment is coming to an end. I lower my bra and rebutton my blouse. While I hate being sticky like this, I like the idea of not washing up right away, so I can feel the remnants of what we did for the next hour or so. Until I have to get ready for Victoria's memorial.

"I'm sorry, but I have to go," I reluctantly say. "Thank you for this, Jake. I feel a little more ready to face the day now."

"Oh, trust me, it was my pleasure, red."

"Yes, I heard. I'm not sure when I'll be able to talk to you again because things will be intense over here, but do keep me in your thoughts and prayers."

"Always," he chuckles. "And I'm here if you need to vent."

"Thank you for that."

We linger a little longer, not ready to let go yet, and a knock on his office door forces us to cut the call. I roll to the side with a long and satisfied sigh, observing the room. Being here brings back many painful memories, but Jake and I just worked on making a new one. I'm sure that steamy phone call will be my first thought every time I pass this door now.

That's a lot better than memories of the sister who died because of me.

THE REST OF THE DAY goes exactly as I expected it to—disastrously. Especially since relatives arrived shortly after I did, which means that avoiding people becomes particularly hard. Unless I remain in my room, which doesn't even work because my aunt comes to see me there, as well as three cousins.

When I hear the distant sound of a helicopter landing on the dedicated space at the other end of the estate, I become even more adamant about disappearing and never resurfacing. My father, Gerard Kensington, has returned from his affairs in the city. We don't have a flag to hoist up whenever he's home, but maybe we should—it's always a big deal that rarely occurs. The Queen of England herself was never as busy as Father, which is saying a lot.

The best course of action is to sneak out of the house and head to the beach, where I sit in the sand and watch the lazy waves roll in and out. If it were my choice, I'd stay here the entire weekend. I lose track of time, listening to the seagulls and watching the hypnotic motions of the water. Victoria always loved the beach, whereas I grew jaded since we lived right by it.

At some point, I hear someone making their way onto the sand, approaching me from behind. I don't look because I don't care who it might be. Either way, they'll be an inconvenience. Only when I discern a man's silhouette sitting down beside me do I rip my eyes from the sea to look at him.

It's my brother, whom I haven't seen in months. Because he's twelve years older, Vicky and I were never close to him. He understandably had different interests than spending time with his baby sisters, and then left when we were seven to study business at Columbia in the city. Every time I see him, I'm reminded of how much he looks like our father. He's his spitting image, with light brown hair, angular features, and the blue eyes we all share. And it seems like he'll follow the same prestigious path as our genitor, given how involved he is in the Kensington empire.

"Hey, Gerry," I greet him, somehow glad it's him. Better my broody brother than Aunt Felicia, who never shuts up.

"Hey, bug. Happy birthday."

The nickname brings back a surge of memories I wasn't expecting. Our old nanny used to nickname Victoria and me "ladybug" because of the red of our hair and the spots of our freckles. But as we grew, it became clear I was no lady, so I became "bug" while my twin kept the original pet name.

"Thank you," I tell my brother. "Where are my favorite nieces and sister-in-law?"

"Your *only* nieces and sister-in-law stayed in town."

"How lucky."

He nods pensively, his eyes on the waves. "We found out last week that Camellia has generalized anxiety disorder, so we didn't want to put her through all that stress."

"Oh, I'm so sorry to hear that, Ger." I knew that his second daughter was having some issues, but I never thought it was something this serious. He looks clearly affected, so I wrap an arm around him and lean in closer, laying my head against his shoulder. "I'm sure she'll be fine," I say hopefully. "She's got the best mom in the world and an okay dad."

The teasing earns me a small shove and a look down as he grins and shakes his head. "Yeah, she'll be okay. Her therapist says we caught it early, so she's optimistic about us getting solid results before the year ends."

"That's amazing, Ger."

We exchange smiles, don't say more, and watch the waves together. He doesn't ask how I'm doing, and I prefer it that way. The answer to that is unknown even to me.

"When did you arrive?" I ask after a while.

"With Father. We had a meeting early in the morning."

"I see. Did it go well?"

He nods, eyes still on the ocean. "Our inheritance just got a lot more profitable."

The way he puts it makes me laugh.

About ten minutes into this weird and silent bonding between siblings, he clears his throat and stands. "Mother sent me to fetch you. She wants to make sure you're ready on time."

He extends a hand to help me up, and I take it, sighing. Begrudgingly, I pat my behind before we return inside.

Let the show begin.

CHAPTER
Twenty-Five
Gen

ON MY WAY TO MOTHER'S quarters, all cleaned up and in my Valentino dress, I cross paths with a few family members, only one of whom wishes me a happy birthday. When I enter the master bedroom, I'm surprised to see how many people are there. The clothing racks are also unexpected, and indicate there's a stylist present, with loaned dresses and accessories.

I'm not sure where to start, a little disoriented by the swarming activity. Vivienne comes out of her massive dressing room, wrapped in a silk gown and with her hair already done.

"I'm just done with hair, so you can start with that," she instructs. Then she changes her mind. "Actually, see with the stylist first. Your hair will depend on the dress you pick."

"I already have a dress," I protest, looking down at it.

Mother disapprovingly glares at the Valentino. "That won't do. Ask the stylist."

She doesn't wait for a reply and leaves me with my jaw hanging to sit on the makeup artist's chair. "Hello, Miss Kensington," a woman says to my right. "I'm the stylist. All of this rack has been picked for you," she explains.

It's just a weekend, I tell myself. Forty-something hours, and then I'm back in the city. Back to Jake.

I try on the first dress, and while the zipper closes, it's way too tight. A second dress knows the same fate, and by the third, the stylist is mortified. "I am *so* sorry, Miss Kensington. Your mother told me you were a size six, so I planned accordingly."

I glare at the back of Vivienne's perfectly styled head. "Well, I was a size six in high school ten years ago. Now I'm a size eight."

Vicky was a size six as well. Is this my mother's cruel way of reminding me that the memory of my sister will forever be better than whatever I might become?

"I may have a couple of dresses that will work great with your lovely shape," the stylist explains. "Otherwise, your green dress was gorgeous, and we could accessorize it."

"Let's try on your dresses, then we'll assess."

Eventually, we settle on a beautiful black Alexander McQueen that fits me well, except at the chest, where my breasts are squished together and up. It makes the cleavage a little too intense, which might not be appropriate given the occasion. But two can play my mother's game, so I choose it.

I head to the hair stylist before Vivienne can see the dress, and then come out with perfect waves cascading down and spilling to the front, over my left shoulder, with Swarovski pins that secure the hair above my right ear to reveal the diamond chandelier earring I'm wearing there.

Mother is gone when it's my turn to get my makeup done, so I ask for smokey eyes and red lips—the furthest thing from innocence I can think of. As selfish as it might be, I don't want everyone to look at me tonight and see Victoria. Ever since meeting Jake, I've felt seen and worthy. Tonight, I want to be more than the remaining half of a twin set.

I want to be my own person.

By the time Mother's team is done with me, I feel incredibly sexy. I'm pretty sure I am, so I snap a few pictures and send the best one to Jake, then another one to Hana.

I'm still sad my best friend can't make it tonight because she's the only person I like who was invited. But she's visiting her fiancé's family with their toddler all the way down in Orlando. Honestly, she'll have a better time there than here.

Because I can't have my phone with me, I take a detour to my room and leave it there. Then, I reluctantly make my way to the vast entry hall, where a few guests are already arriving.

Somehow, I managed to avoid Father the whole afternoon, so I'm seeing him for the first time as I join them by the door.

Gerard Kensington has been in a rush his entire life. Or it seems like it, at least. The man barely made any time for Vicky and me when we were growing up under his roof, too absorbed by his work, meetings, and travels. He also never hid that Gerry was his favorite child, the perfect son who can do no wrong. As long as we came home with good grades and didn't make waves, he saw no point in getting involved in our education. And with Vivienne and her hand of steel in charge, we didn't need discipline from anyone else. I've always been fine with it because I don't need another parent meddling in my life.

"Good evening, Father," I tell him with a nod.

"Evening, Genevieve."

Gerry is on the other side of him, wearing a perfectly tailored tuxedo, and we give each other a nod. When I settle next to Vivienne, I can feel her eyes on me, and without even looking at her, I know she's fuming. I'm usually a lot better at complying and doing whatever she needs from me, but today, I can't be bothered to fake it. "What are you wearing?" she asks, barely containing her annoyance.

"McQueen. Isn't it beautiful? I really like it, especially the neckline."

"You need to change."

"I can't. The hair was done for it," I counter, meeting her glare.

Someone new arrives, saving me from whatever she's about to say. After a moment by the main door, all four of us migrate to the ballroom, where the guests have been converging. Most are unknown faces, very few are acquaintances, and none are friends.

The bar offers a variety of overpriced alcohol and fancy cocktails, and before Mother can catch me, I order myself a lemon drop martini. I haven't been to one of these events in almost a year, and I can safely say that I still hate it. Even when it's to save the environment, I despise this exhibition of wealth, the vain conversations, the networking ... But on an evening like today, to celebrate my dead twin?

I abhor it.

At some point, my brain dissociates, and everything goes on autopilot. I sit, eat, drink, talk, and laugh. But I'm not there anymore. I feel empty, devoid of human emotion. This entire "commemoration" is a painful reminder I don't need. Victoria, the best twin, isn't around to do all the good she always planned on doing. And I, the bad twin, can never live up to the promise of her bright future. No matter how hard I try, I never will. This past decade is proof of it.

When Mother tells me to stand, I comply like a puppet. I follow her, Gerry, and Father to the stage, where a microphone awaits. With everyone's eyes on us, I regret choosing this dress because I know what they're all thinking. Victoria would have been a size six and fit it better. She would have picked something less tacky. She would have been the perfect image of the Kensington's legacy.

I really am a stain in this picture-perfect family—a failure among success.

Father talks, his words a blended litany of self-pitying declarations, retellings of moments he remembers wrong, truths that are only his and Mother's—not mine and Vicky's. His sentences mourn the loss of his precious daughter ten years ago, but his throat isn't tight, his hands aren't trembling, and his eyes are dry.

They didn't deserve her. Victoria was precious, yes. She was my other half, the best sister in the world, the sweetest person to have ever lived. But they barely knew her because they couldn't be bothered to care for us, other than analyzing report cards, disciplining us when we weren't perfect, and dressing us up for the family's Holiday pictures.

It's Mother's turn to speak now, and she's a little more affected than Father was. Tears glimmer in her eyes but never spill over. I don't know how she does it, but it's a skill she's mastered with time to make sure her makeup doesn't get ruined. She too retells an account of Vicky that I remember differently, painting the image of this impossibly perfect teenager who never did anything wrong.

But she was right there with me, smoking that joint we found in a guest room after our uncle's visit. We were together when we first snuck out of the house and walked two miles up the beach in the middle of the night to attend a bonfire. It was she who convinced me to leave the hotel undetected in the middle of the night during our sophomore-year trip to Paris. I can still remember how we walked the streets the entire night, watched the Eiffel Tower's twinkling lights, and returned exhausted but fulfilled, just in time for breakfast.

She was perfect, yes, but not for the reasons my parents think.

Gerry didn't spend enough time with us to truly know her either, but he shares a few anecdotes about his sometimes-mischievous baby sisters, and it rings truer than what our parents said. Because I wasn't given notes or asked to prepare a speech, I know I won't be expected to speak as well. It should hurt, but it doesn't. I'm not sure I'd manage to say anything anyway.

When both Vivienne and Gerard share the microphone, I distractedly listen, curious to hear what other false truths they will utter about Vicky.

"This is why," Father says, "to commemorate the ten-year anniversary of our cherished daughter's passing, we are inaugurating the Victoria Kensington Foundation."

My jaw slacks open, my eyebrows knitting together with surprise. Behind them, two people come to pull on the fabric that covers a massive panel. Before I can see what's on it, my attention is grabbed by Mother, who speaks to the assembly.

"This foundation will support individuals affected by car accidents and promote road safety. It will aim to provide financial assistance, emotional support, and rehabilitation services to accident survivors, helping them rebuild their lives and regain independence. Our girl might not have survived her fatal crash, but in her honor, the Victoria Kensington Foundation will be the road to recovery for many."

With all the worthy causes she fought for during her brief life, and knowing all the injustices she wanted to defend once she grew up, they decided to center this around her death? To make the worst day of her life the one thing she would forever be remembered for? How conceited can someone be?!

People applaud, some stand up, and all I can do is try to remember how to breathe. But it's all over when my eyes fall on the panel behind them. I'm going to be sick. The acrid taste of bile gathers in the back of my throat, and the realization that I might vomit in front of those people hits me. This can't be happening.

A deer. They chose a deer to be the foundation's emblem. The very animal that sent Victoria crashing into a telephone pole. Do they not realize how wrong that is?

Since no one's paying attention to me, I stumble down the three steps while my parents announce that the foundation will gladly accept donations tonight. I hastily walk toward the exit, nearly colliding with a waiter and his tray full of champagne flutes.

My feet take me to safety, to the bedrooms, while my brain scrambles to make sense of everything that just happened. When I open the door, shock strikes me.

This isn't my room.

It's Victoria's.

Contrary to mine, my twin's room is the perfect diorama of her on the day we turned seventeen, an untouched time capsule, a still that'll never move again. The curtains are open, and the moon's glow gives it an ethereal appearance, like all this might disappear if I switch on the lights. But I can see it all: the Taylor Swift poster over her bed, the fairy lights she put around her vanity table, and the Polaroid board she'll never fill out. On the bed, there's even Sir Spotty, the plush ladybug she got when we turned five. Her clever little brain decided that since not all ladybugs were ladies, hers would be a gentleman.

My chest hurts like there's a bag of sand that weighs a ton settled on it. This tight dress is smothering me and not leaving enough room for all the emotions wrecking me. Ten years have passed, but I still would give anything to hold her again, to hear her pearly laugh, to inhale her scent.

Feeling like I might crumble if I don't, I close the door behind me and wobble to the bed to lie on it. Sir Spotty ends up in my embrace as I pull myself into a fetal position, fighting against my uncooperative lungs to breathe, forcing them to fill. Ten years of guilt are crushing me, and I don't know how to stop it.

"I miss you, Vicky," I whisper. "I'm so sorry. It should have been me."

I'm still not breathing correctly when the door cracks open, the warm light of the hallway spilling in. Because I cannot let Mother find me like this, I let go of the plush and sit up.

"Genny?" The feminine voice isn't Vivienne's, and the silhouette is too tall. Also, no one's called me that in years. "I couldn't find you in your room, so I figured you were here. Are you alright?"

The newcomer flicks the light on, and I can see her face now. It only takes me half a second to recognize her, even though we haven't seen each other since she finished high school a year before me. To me, she was an acquaintance, a familiar face in the hallways, but to Vicky, she was more.

"Penelope?"

She confirms it with a smile. "Hi."

Vicky had the biggest crush on her. I still remember how she used to rush to my room to tell me about all the little things that happened between them. Our parents were never open-minded, so Victoria kept it a secret. She lived in fear that they might figure out that she preferred women because they would have made her life hell for it.

"Hey, hi," I say, standing from the bed and walking up to her. "It's so good to see a friendly face."

"Sorry I didn't come and talk to you down there."

"It's alright. I was so out of it I didn't even see you." I give her a quick hug, genuinely happy to see her.

When we release each other, she says, "I think your mom invited everyone who was at the funeral. And then some."

"Looks like it, yeah. You're probably the only person Vicky would have wanted here."

"Your sister would have hated it," Penelope says with a wince. "Even that foundation. She always preferred animals to humans."

I'm surprised to see how well she knew my twin. They were both on the cheerleading squad and had a couple of school projects together, but I never realized they were close enough to know such details about one another.

"How have you been?" I ask.

"Good. Great, actually. The small business I started is booming. I'm married," she proudly explains, showing me her wedding and engagement rings. "And my wife and I are looking to adopt, so it's all perfect."

"I'm so glad to hear that."

"And you," Penelope asks, "how have you been doing?"

"Uh, good. Surviving."

"Aren't we all?" she laughs.

"I actually got dumped a few months ago," I confess. "But that's okay because I've been having the time of my life since."

"Have you met someone new?"

Just like that, I feel like a gossipy teenager again. "Actually, I have. It's been fantastic, even if we're not anything serious."

"My wife and I weren't anything serious either," she explains with a wink.

"Oh no, it's not like that, I promise. I'm too busy for that, and Jake isn't the kind to settle down."

"Well, flings can also be fun in their own way. But with the way you're blushing just talking about him, I'd say you have a solid crush on that man."

"I have a cursed complexion, don't I? Vicky was the same, so she must have blushed all the time around you." My blunt admission, which stems from God-knows-where, surprises her as much as it does me. "Oh God, I'm so sorry. That is not something I should have said."

"No, it's fine. I knew she had a crush on me. And I had one on her."

"I noticed." The following moment is a little awkward, so I look around to find another topic. When my eyes land on the nightstand, something clicks. "Would you—I'm so sorry, but would you help me elucidate a mystery that's been in the back of my head for a decade?"

"Uh, yes, sure."

A little shaky, I go to the nightstand and take Vicky's diary out of its drawer. It's her very last one, and the unfinished words inked in it have been driving me mad with curiosity ever since I read them. I return to Penelope with it, seeking the last written page.

"So, Victoria had this diary, and the night she … the night it happened, she was writing an entry. It's unfinished, but I thought you might know something about it because she mentioned you."

"She did?" Pen asks, both troubled and sentimental.

"Yes. But under a code name because our mother used to sneak in and read our journals. I stopped writing in mine because of it, but Vicky used a different approach." I finally find the page, so I show it to her. "You were Odysseus."

Pen smiles at that, and then her eyes scan the delicate cursive letters my sister wrote on the pinkish page ten long years ago. I don't even need to read it to know exactly what's written on it.

Dear diary,

Today is my birthday, and it has been the best one of my life. I haven't written in a few days, but it's because so much has been happening. First of all, Mother and Father agreed to let Genny and I choose the destination for our next family vacation as one of our birthday gifts. I really want to go to Japan in the spring, to see the cherry blossoms. I'm sure I can convince my sister to agree to it. But that isn't the best gift I received this year. On Friday, Odysseus asked me to meet under the football field's bleachers before 6th period. I really didn't know what to expect, but—

And the words stop there, the continuation of Vicky's story forever lost. I'm full of hope when I look up at Penelope. Her eyes are glassy, her trembling hand covering her mouth.

"What happened under the bleachers?" I ask softly. Penny's gaze meets mine, and just like Victoria that day, I don't know what to expect. "Our parents barely did anything for us that year, so I know they weren't the reason why it was the best birthday of her life," I explain.

Penelope shakes her head, which gives me hope that she knows exactly what Vicky was talking about. "I knew it was her birthday that weekend. And I was way into those string bracelets I used to make. So I made one just for her and gave it to her. She asked if it was a friendship bracelet," she recalls, smiling. "I told her it could be if she wanted, but it could also be a relationship bracelet. I finally confessed that I wished to be more than her friend if she was okay with that. Then I kissed her, and she kissed me back."

My heart skips a beat and relocates to the back of my throat. Ever since her death, I've been convinced that Vicky never got to kiss someone she genuinely liked—a girl rather than a boy because it was expected of her. I remember those long conversations we had all the time, where I pushed her to embrace her nature and stop trying to conform to a norm she would never be happy with. Knowing she and Pen actually shared this moment changes everything.

"It was just supposed to be a peck," Penelope continues. "But I think we liked each other more than we ever realized because we spent the entire period making out. We agreed to keep it a secret at first, but we were officially a couple. Your sister was my first real girlfriend," Pen discloses with fondness. "Then, the next day, Saturday, we spent the entire afternoon together, doing it again."

"I remember. She left because she had to meet with her study group at the library," I say, surprised.

"Well, I was the study group, and the library was my bedroom."

"Did you two …?"

Pen shakes her head. "It didn't go that far. We did say 'I love you' to one another, though. Which sounds so silly now because it was so early, but we were teenagers with our own understanding of love."

Penelope looks around the room, and I can see in her eyes that she was genuinely fond of my twin. When she spots something on the desk, I look in that direction while she approaches it. There's a cardboard box that looks out of place, which contains Vicky's belongings from the day of the accident. Pen picks up something small and colorful that's sitting on top.

"This is the bracelet I made for her," she explains, looking at it like she's seeing a ghost.

"Really? I remember seeing her with it, but since she only had it for a couple of days, Mother figured it wasn't sentimental, so she wasn't buried with it. I'm so sorry, Penny. Had we known—"

"No, it's fine. It was a secret, no one could have guessed."

I reach for her to gently touch her shoulder. "Do you want to have it?" I offer.

"Could I?"

"Yeah, of course. It holds more value for you than it does for any of us, Pen. You deserve to have it."

Her eyes are watery when she nods. "Even though we barely dated, your sister's death really shook me, you know? It took me two years to finally take the leap and ask her out and then two days to lose her. I think we all have this idea that we'll live forever when we're that age, so that wrecked me."

"I know, yes. I became non-verbal for an entire week, and then it took months for me to return to a semblance of normalcy."

"I can't imagine what it's like losing a twin."

"Like losing half of yourself."

Pen offers me a small, compassionate smile and then looks at the bracelet again. "Do you really not mind?"

"Not at all. She would have wanted you to have it."

Penelope nods, wipes away a stray tear from her cheek, and then moves to take me in a warm embrace. "Thank you, Genny."

We hug for another few moments, and then she pulls away. "I should go back to my wife," she says. "Thank you so much for the bracelet."

"And thank you for the answers. Knowing she was loved and in love when she died changes everything."

She gives me a small nod. "Let's not wait another decade to meet again, okay?"

"Yes, I would love that, Pen."

Penelope hugs me one last time and salutes me with a smile before heading out into the hallway. After a few seconds of confused uncertainty, I set the diary back in its place and walk up to the Polaroid board. For the first time since she died, this room feels different. I learned something new, even though I was sure there wasn't anything I didn't know about my sister.

In the middle of the photos, I see the one we took in Paris during our illegal outing. I unpin it from there to look at it closer. Despite being identical copies, we were so different in some aspects. She was much more reasonable and prudent—the quiet one. But she was always ready to go on an adventure if it was with me, which I pushed her to do quite a few times.

The one time that mattered the most though, she didn't. And I'll forever regret not listening to her words of caution.

With the picture still in my hand, I go out into the corridor. One last look at the room, one last smile at Sir Spotty, and I turn off the light and close the door. I'm in my own bedroom soon after.

I don't want to be here anymore. I never wanted to be here in the first place. But now that my parents did what they did, I can't possibly spend the weekend here, in a house of lies where I'm the only one who really knew Victoria. I don't think I can last two days of smiling and biting back the truth or letting my parents treat me however they want because I robbed them of their favorite daughter.

Although I grew up here, it hasn't been my home since the moment Vicky stopped living in it. Following Penny's revelations, I need to be somewhere I feel cared for and valued.

A couple of knocks on the door pull me out of my thoughts. Before I can invite in whoever is outside, it opens, and Gerry enters. He looks uneasy, and I expect him to reprimand me for my hasty exit. But I realize I'm wrong when he gives me a compassionate look.

"I tried telling them it wasn't a good idea," he explains with a grimace.

"We shouldn't even have to, Ger. They should have realized that on their own."

"You know how they are. Mother has been working on it for months with her team of advisors. They did polls and everything, and they decided to go with this."

"So they can give themselves this flattering image of mourning parents who survive their child and look adversity in the eye to turn it into something for the greater good?"

"Exactly."

"Then this is about them, not about Vicky. There's a hundred things they could have done for her. Like opening shelters for dogs. With how much she begged and begged them to let us have one, it would have been fair."

"I don't know what to tell you, Genny. They are doing it, and there's nothing we can do to stop it from happening now."

I press my lips together in discontentment. He's right. It's too late now. "Well then, if that's the route they want to take, I won't stay here and act all supportive of their decision. It's above my strength."

"You want to leave?"

"I can't stay, Ger. I'll go insane."

He looks around for a moment while pondering. "I'll tell them you had a work emergency, then. I'm sure they'll understand."

"Really?"

"Yeah. I know you and Vicky had something very special. I loved our sister, but for you two, it was beyond that. So I understand if you can't stomach this mess."

In three steps, I'm hugging his tux-clad frame. "Thanks, Gerry."

"Consider this my birthday present, bug. Oh, and Malory and I also got you this. I didn't get to hand it to you earlier," he says, pulling away to take a small velvet box out of his pocket.

When I open it, the two beautiful and huge diamond studs inside catch the light, glimmering on the black velvet. "Wow, Ger, it's— They are beautiful."

"You can thank my wonderful wife for them."

"Let's have dinner together soon so I can do it properly, then."

"Great idea. Now, the fireworks are going off in ten minutes, so you should use the distraction to sneak out when everyone's on the beach."

"Fireworks?" I echo, a little stunned.

He shrugs, aware as much as I am that this is ridiculous. I hug him once more, we exchange a few more words, and then he's out. As soon as I'm alone, my hands fly to the zipper hidden under my armpit, and I pull it down my side to remove the McQueen. Time to pack everything again and leave. If Mother or Father has something to say about it, they can come say it in person, in the city.

I'm done with this farce.

CHAPTER Twenty-Six

Gen

THE STREET IS DARK, AND rain pours lightly over the car's windows and windshield. On the other side of the asphalt, the familiar door feels like a beacon of hope, a ray of sunshine in this somber abyss.

Part of me wonders if I would have chosen to come here if Hana was in town. Would I be in Tribeca, where her townhouse is? It would be a more logical choice since I've known her for years, and we've always been there for one another. She's my ride-or-die, infinitely more than Edward ever was.

But deep down, I know that I would still be here, not at Hana's. My long drive from the Hamptons, which was punctuated with remorse, fears, and questions, would have led me to this very door, no matter what. *He* is the only person I want to see right now.

The thought is somehow scary, and it brings another surge of emotions and questions I'm not ready to handle. Six weeks. I've known Jake for six weeks, and he's supposed to be just a sex thing, not my comfort person. But here I am, hoping he's home because I need his strength. I need him to hold me and tell me everything will be alright.

Although I should switch the engine on and drive home because it would be the proper thing to do, I ignore my doubts and reach for my phone on the dashboard.

ME

Are you still at The Devil's Court?

I try to look up, but between the rain and the angle, I can't see the windows of his loft, so I can't tell if any lights are on.

This weight on my chest never really went away. My breathing still doesn't feel right, and my mind might burst into a thousand broken pieces at any moment. I need Jake because he always makes me feel so strong. As soon as I'm with him, all of this will go away, and I'll be able to contain it and not feel like this anymore.

The idea of heading to the bar to see if he's there crosses my mind, but before it can mature into a decision, his answer comes.

WOMBAT GUY

> I got home half an hour ago. Why?

With my phone and my handbag, I exit the car. I can barely feel the rain as I cross the street and look for his name on the intercom. The button makes no sound when I push it, making me wonder if this system works. But it does because the speaker crackles, and then his voice pours out of it.

"Yes?"

"It's me."

"Gen?" He doesn't need my confirmation, immediately buzzing me in.

As the elevator takes me up to the fifth floor, I question again if I should be here. It's weird, isn't it? Who in their right mind goes to their booty call for comfort? But I'm not in my right mind, and I'm so alone in this world that he's the only person who can help.

When I arrive at his floor, he's standing in front of his apartment's door, hands shoved in his jeans pockets while he waits for me with a frown.

"Is everything alright?" he worriedly asks.

The instant relief I expected from seeing him doesn't happen. In fact, with every step my feet take toward him, this acute pressure on my chest intensifies. I can barely breathe by the time I'm with him, and my vision is blurred with tears. He notices, and before I can do anything, he takes my face into his warm hands and forces me to meet his green gaze.

"What happened?"

I shatter in a way I haven't in ten years.

Air comes in and out of me in frantic sobs, tears uncontrollably spilling onto my cheeks, my entire body shaking with sorrow. In an instant, I'm wrapped in his solid embrace. Without it, I would have crumbled to the floor like a boneless pile of limbs.

Jake talks, his voice is soothing and full of concern, but I can barely hear it. My mind is being torn apart, and I can't contain all those emotions.

"Gen, sweetheart, talk to me. Did something happen? Did someone hurt you?"

"Sh-she ki-kissed her," I struggle to say between hiccups.

"Who?"

"Victoria. She had a-a girlfriend."

This probably makes no sense to him, but he keeps me in his tattooed arms, right against his broad chest. The intensity of my sobs becomes ridiculous, and embarrassment begins to settle in me.

"Come here, love," Jake murmurs before passing an arm to the back of my knees and lifting me.

I'm curled up in his hold, my face shoved into his neck as he carries me inside the apartment and kicks the door closed behind us. He brings me to the couch, where he sits down with me on his lap, still holding me close. My bag is removed from my shoulder and dropped beside us on the cushion. Mulligrubs comes to greet me with her wet nose and enthusiastic licks, but I can't even react to it.

Jake sends her to her bed and then focuses on me again. His hands are soothing, one gently grazing up and down my back while the other caresses my hair.

"Shh," he murmurs into my ear. "I'm right here, sweetheart. Everything will be alright."

I was wrong. He doesn't give me the strength that I need to keep it all in. He gives me the safe space that I crave to let it all out.

In the aftermath of my twin's death, I cried so much that I believed I reached my quota of tears for the rest of my life. I poured every single one I was allowed in this life, and there wouldn't be more. But it seems I was wrong, they were merely recharging. And now, they all want out at the same time. Under me, Jake's shirt is damp with them, my hand clutched at his neck while I keep him close.

Eventually, his gentle ministrations and whispers dissipate the ache. The tears slowly decrease, and I'm able to breathe rather than take in short and broken hiccups of air. I sniff rather inelegantly, which makes me realize it's not only tears wetting his shirt. God, I'm such a mess.

At least I got rid of my over-the-top makeup before leaving my parents' place, so it's not as bad as it could have been.

Jake senses that I'm feeling better, and he softly rearranges us so he can look at me. His eyes are full of compassion as he wipes away the wetness from my cheeks and chin, his touch delicate and caring.

"Tell me what happened, love," he softly asks.

"It's my sister."

"The one who had a car accident?"

I nod, sniffing again, and pass the back of my hand under my nose. "I thought she died never having even kissed a girl because she was so scared our parents would find out she was gay. And today, I learned she had a girlfriend, and they were in love."

The thought of Victoria and young Penelope, who were so full of hope for their future, so full of love to give to one another, rips another small piece of my shredded heart. When a resurgence of tears comes, Jake is quick to react.

"Hey, it's alright, sweetheart," he murmurs, wiping them away before they can get anywhere. "Isn't it a good thing?"

"I don't know. I thought it would be because at least she knew love. But she only got two days of it. I keep thinking of all the things she had yet to experience, of how she finally got over her fears about our parents, how she had so many great firsts coming her way ... And because of me—"

A sob shakes me, preventing me from uttering the rest, and Jake pulls me in again, embracing me with patience.

"I'm so-so sorry," I stammer. "I haven't cried in ten years, and I'm unleashing all this on you."

"Ten years?" he echoes, surprised. I nod, passing a hand on my cheek to dry it. "I cry quite often."

"Really?"

"Oh, yeah. I watched The Green Mile the other day. I *wept*."

Somehow, the image of Jake crying is so unexpected that it triggers a small giggle. "Losing my twin was such a traumatic experience that everything else became inconsequential. Edward sometimes called me a heartless robot."

"Fuck that cunt. You're not heartless, and you're not a robot. He's just a dickhead."

"Still, I'm sorry. You shouldn't have to handle this mess. It's probably because I barely slept this past week. I'm at the end of my tether."

"Let's put you to bed, then. We can talk more in the morning, but you need some rest, sweetheart."

I nod, but neither of us moves. It feels good to be in his arms like this, snuggling on his lap, his hands grazing my hair and back, and the soft kisses he sometimes presses on my forehead.

My chest begins to hurt again, but it's a different kind of ache. Instead of it feeling compressed, it's like it's pushing from the inside, swelling past its capacity. I've felt this several times before around him, and I can't keep pretending like I don't know what it means.

I bring a hand to his torso and push against it to look at him. He's so impossibly handsome. I'll never get over how beautiful he is, with his sharp jawline, lush lips, perfectly imperfect nose, amazing eyes … But the best thing about his dashing face is the expression on it right now. His affection for me goes beyond what we agreed on, and so does mine for him.

I can't help myself, so I take his face between my trembling hands and press a kiss on his lips. When I move back, his eyes harbor even more tenderness.

"This is more than just a sex thing, isn't it?" I whisper.

Jake's gaze scans mine, and he brushes a strand away to tuck it behind my ear before carefully cupping the side of my face. "I think it is, yes."

My heart races in my chest at his confirmation. This isn't casual and simple anymore. Strings have attached themselves without us realizing it, and they already seem so hard to untie.

"How do you feel about it?" he cautiously asks.

It's my turn to gently graze his cheek, thinking of my answer while I admire his stunning face. "It's scary. I didn't—This wasn't the plan, not so soon."

"You have regrets, then?"

I shake my head. "No. Maybe I should, but it's … *you.*"

His soft smile sends butterflies loose in my stomach, and their number doubles when he leans in to kiss me.

"What about you?" I ask before our lips meet. "You were so adamant about wanting something casual."

He adjusts under me, and I realize my weight might be uncomfortable. When I try to move though, he keeps me right there.

"I've changed my mind. *You* have changed my mind, red. I fall asleep thinking of you, and before my eyes are even open in the morning, you're already in my thoughts. My days feel incomplete if I don't have my dose of you, even if it's just a few texts. I've lost all interest in other women. There's only you."

"Really?"

"Yeah, I don't even see them anymore. Eli and Kill have been giving me shit about it. But I don't care because whatever way I put it, this is a win."

I don't even have to ask if he means it because the genuineness on his face is unmistakable. Although I probably look like a wreck, he welcomes me when I endeavor to kiss him. I'm the one demanding more and more, overwhelmed by everything I'm feeling. It's alleviating, empowering, and infinitely better than the guilt and anguish I've been experiencing for the past few hours.

When I start writhing on top of him, tiredness be damned, he lets out a groan. "Love, you need to rest." I nod but don't stop, which makes him chuckle. "Alright, let's put you to bed."

Holding onto me tightly, he rises from the couch, dislodging us. Since I can't access his lips anymore, I kiss the exposed skin of his throat instead. I'm not ready to let go when he puts me down, so he gives me one last peck. Leisurely, he undresses me, peeling the clothes off me piece by piece until I'm left in my panties. Then he leaves me there, almost naked, and comes back with a T-shirt. I lift my arms to help him put it on me, and when my head comes through, he gives me a tender kiss as a reward for cooperating.

"Your toothbrush from last time is in the cup with mine," he explains, tugging at his shirt on the back of his neck to remove it.

Seeing our toothbrushes together brings me an obscene sense of happiness. It feels right. And I can't believe I never offered for him to have one at my place too, given how many times he's spent the night. Now, it's all that I want—to see his toothbrush with mine at home so that even when he isn't there, he kind of is. I'll even get rid of the second cup that Edward used just to make the vision as complete as this one.

"I want you to have a toothbrush at my place," I impulsively say, turning around.

The jeans are gone now, and all that's left on him are black socks and underwear. Seriously, only this man could wear socks like this and still look impossibly sexy with his muscles, tattoos, and the small piercing at his nipple.

His smile as he bends to remove a sock is luminous. "Alright, I will. And if you have hair, skin, or whatever products you need daily, feel free to leave some here as well."

The second sock is gone now, and he makes his way toward me, effortlessly alluring. When he's right in front of me, his hands mold to my hips. "Are we really doing this, red?"

"Only if you want to, wombat. And we can take it slow, see how it feels."

"I reckon it's been feeling fantastic so far."

"It has, hasn't it?"

"Yeah. I really want to date you, Jessica from the dating app." The nickname throws me back in time, making me chuckle at the absurdity of our first encounter.

Quenching it, I ask, "Even if I'm a mess who arrives unannounced in the middle of the night either to get laid completely drunk or to cry like a maniac and leave tears, drool, and snot on you?"

"*Especially* for those two reasons. Anyone else would be so boring in comparison."

Our smiles join with intensity, and we're greedily kissing again. He slips his hands under the shirt and onto my back to hold me in his big, strong arms, and I melt. There's something different in our embrace now, in the way we demand and give. It's like this odd sense of ownership, like he's mine to kiss and claim—and mine only.

A few moments later, our teeth are brushed and we're in his bed. He flicks off the light on his side and comes to cuddle with me under the comfy duvet. The faint red glow of the clock on his nightstand commands my eyes.

"It's my birthday for another minute," I note, amused by the timing.

"Then happy birthday for the last time, red. Until next year, that is."

I know I'm supposed to blow out candles to make a birthday wish, but I close my eyes and make one, anyway. And I wish that in a year, when it's mine and Victoria's day again, he'll still be right there with me, sharing a bed and holding me like all the space we have is a twin bed instead of a king size.

While he enfolds me in his warmth, I bask in the knowledge that we both accepted this relationship is more than what we bargained for, and we're okay with that. In the back of my mind, I'm aware of how phenomenally lucky I got, because this man … This man is everything a woman should ever want.

And I'm the only woman he wants.

What are the odds of that?

CHAPTER
Twenty-Seven

Jake

EVEN THOUGH IT BROKE MY heart to see Gen in such a state of utter despair, I feel gratified that she came to me. The fact that she felt safe enough to seek me in her moment of vulnerability fills me with pride. We haven't known each other for long, but clearly long enough for her to see me as a reliable bloke who'll welcome her with open arms when she needs it the most, and that has to be one of my greatest accomplishments.

She wasn't joking when she said she was exhausted. It's almost one in the afternoon and she's still out. On my side, I walked Mulli, exercised, showered, watered the plants, and lunch slowly simmers on the stove. I'm now in the armchair by the bed, trying once again to catch her likeness on my tablet. I'm getting better at it, and the attempts honor her beauty more than when I first tried. This time, as soon as I notice the early signs of her sleep coming to an end, I drop everything. I tug down my sweatpants, slip off my T-shirt, and very carefully return under the covers.

Even though she's still asleep, she naturally comes to settle in my arms when I gently pull her in, her back plastered on my front. It takes another few minutes for her to fully emerge, and when she does, I'm hard as a rock between us. This isn't exactly the mood I planned on for this moment, but my body can't help itself around her. It seems she doesn't really mind though, because before she even opens her eyes, her perfect bum inches back, pressing itself harder onto my cock.

"Hmm," she mumbles. "Did you take a gun to bed, or are you happy to see me?"

"I'm not Americanized enough to have a gun in bed, red. And I'm *always* happy to see you."

Her lazy smile fills me with contentment, and she tugs on my arm to tighten our embrace, her eyes still closed. "Something smells divine," she notes.

I dip my nose in the curve of her throat, inhaling her cherry scent. "I think it's you."

She giggles, arching against me as she stretches her sleepy limbs. "Did you cook?"

"I prepared lunch, yes. Thought you might wake up hungry."

Her eyes whip open, her auburn eyebrows frowning. "Lunch? What time is it?"

"Around one in the afternoon."

"Oh no, shoot."

"What?"

"I was looking forward to morning sex."

It's my turn to laugh, which comes in the way of the small kisses I'm laying on her shoulder. "Might mid-day sex be a good enough alternative?"

Her hand takes hold of mine just under her chest, and she slowly brings it between her legs. "I'm sure we can make it work if we try really hard."

My fingers trace a tentative path over the lace of her underwear as she parts her knees to grant me access. I thrust against her arse, letting her feel all of me. "Is that hard enough for you, red?"

"Yes," she breathes out.

I tease her over the garment for a moment and find her clit to give it a few firmer rolls. When she begins to undulate against me, I slip my hand under the lace and resume, grazing her folds with deft fingertips, entering her only to retreat, and playing with the small nub.

I wake her body slowly, tenderly, like we have all the time in the world. Because we do now, don't we? It's not just about getting through her list and moving on. It's about exploring this thing between us, this connection, the chemistry ... and seeing just how far it'll take us. I've never been an optimistic guy, but I'll venture this could go pretty fucking far.

"Gen?" I murmur in her ear.

"Yes?"

"Yesterday we talked about this, about us. But you were in a difficult place emotionally, so I want to make sure." I dip two thick fingers inside her, pressing on her clit with the pad at the base of my thumb. She moans again, and I resume my question. "Do you still want to do this? To take this to the next stage?"

The nod she gives me lifts a weight that I didn't know was on my heart. "Yes, I do." Her hand presses mine harder, her hips writhing to get more.

"Then will you go out on a date with me?"

Her movements pause, even though my fingers are still slowly fucking her, and she twists her head to meet my eyes with her big blue ones. Her cheeks are rosy just as I love them, her lips parted with slight surprise.

"Friday. Go on a date with me, red. A real one, not just a couple of drinks at The Devil's Court."

Her head bobs up and down in agreement, and her hand leaves mine between her legs to clutch my nape and bring me to her. We share a deep, profound, and unbreakable kiss. The undulations of her hips resume, and I help her climb higher and higher. She's sopping wet now, and my fingers make this moist sound every time I thrust them in, which drives me mad with want. My cock will be there soon, crammed in all that softness, stretching her warm walls with its girth.

I feel the first spasm of her orgasm, squeezing my fingers inside her, and I tighten my hold on her, dipping my tongue in her mouth to feel her moan around it. Her whole body tenses, her small scream of ecstasy vibrating against my lips as she tilts. My needs become secondary to her bliss, so I push her further, still pumping inside her as she jolts and shivers, overtaken by pleasure. I'm merciless, granting her no break to recuperate from her climax, already adamant about bringing on a second one. One day, I'll have to see how many times I can make her come like this, her orgasms a long and endless string of wrecking pleasure.

When I can feel that she's close again, I use my hand under her head to reach for her breast, finding a nipple over the fabric and pinching it, twisting it.

"Jake," she whimpers, her eyes glassy with need.

"I know, you're so close. Do you want to come around my fingers again or around my—"

"Your cock. I want your cock. Please …" There's really nothing I could refuse her when she begs like this.

I let go of her and suck on my fingers while I kneel, feasting on her taste. With trembling hands, she removes the Led Zeppelin T-shirt to free her glorious breasts. She hastily lifts her bum when I slip my fingers in the sides of her thong and then raises her legs for me to tug it off. My underwear is quickly discarded, thrown in the mess of the sheets around us, and I give the head of my cock a relieving pinch. We're not entering her quite yet.

Before she can see it coming, I bury my face between her legs and lick up her pink and drenched folds. Her taste coats my tongue, and her soft pleas fill my ears. I swear to God, I'm in fucking heaven when her fingers come to clutch my hair, her hips writhing and lifting under my mouth. She's so fucking receptive, always eager to get more pleasure, and never above begging for it.

I work her up to another climax, palming both her tits with my hands while my tongue, lips, and teeth work their magic on her cunt. Her clit is swollen, looking like it's about to burst, and I feel the involuntary spasms that shake her.

"Jake!" she cries out, trembling from head to toe. "Oh God, Jake!" If her hold on my hair is any indication, she's close. Very fucking close. So I let go of her again, leaving her high and disoriented. "What are you—"

"You said you wanted to come around my cock," I remind her, taking my position in the cradle of her parted thighs, pressing my erection onto her drenched slit.

She looks completely appalled, so I have to hold back a smirk when I bend down to kiss her. My teasing is quickly dismissed in the intensity of our embrace, especially when I align myself with her entrance and start pushing in.

I'm slow, the slowest I've ever been, taking my time so I can enjoy the blissful sensation of sinking into her drenched cunt. For every inch I give her, she tries to get another one, thrusting up and arching, but I counter her every time, holding my own desire on a tight leash. By the time I bottom out, a veil of sweat already coats my back.

She feels so fucking good. All wet and tight, so warm I feel like I could live there and never want out. When she tries to move, to initiate a momentum between us, I lower to trap her between my hips and the mattress.

"Jake, what are you doing?" she frustratedly whimpers.

"I want to go slow, red. I want to worship you and show you how much I adore you."

"I would appreciate it if you worshiped faster."

Only she can make me chuckle in such an intense moment. I adjust myself to lean on my elbows, and with my hands on each side of her face, I graze her freckled cheekbones with my thumbs. "Let me be slow. And tender. And intense. I promise you'll like it."

I'm not saying the words, but I'm sure she can hear them because something clicks in her mind, and she understands what I want. What I *need*.

Let me make love to you.

Visibly emotional, she nods, adjusting her thighs higher on my sides and resting delicate hands on my back. I leisurely follow the outline of her plump lips with the tip of my tongue. She patiently waits for me to finish, her pussy spasming around me until I conclude it with a deep and passionate kiss.

When I begin to thrust in and out of her—so slowly that she can probably feel every piercing dragging on her walls—she lets me lead. Her hands follow my pace as she pulls me in every time, her hips arching in rhythm with mine. We're plastered together, her tits squeezed between us as I take her, their pebbled tips poking against my chest.

I take her like this, with all the tenderness I hold despite the electric intensity that sparks every time I'm balls deep inside her. Between her moans and her body's reaction, I feel her get closer and closer. I won't need to send a hand between us and tease her clit—not at this angle. The base of me drags along it every time I slide inside her.

After long minutes of this have passed, she finally gets that second orgasm I've been taunting her with. I still while she shatters underneath me with her face pressed against my throat. She shivers and twitches, her gushing pussy clenching around my cock. Surely, I'm spilling precum in her because the pleasure it brings is unbelievable.

Her soft cries, the way her nails dig into my back, the arching of her hips … Everything works against my resolve. She unknowingly tests my stamina with this one, but again, when doesn't she? I ride through her climax with clenched teeth. No matter how much she tries to milk it out of me, I hold back from spilling my seed.

Her body gradually relaxes, and her hands stop clawing at my back while her cries turn into breathless whimpers. Even after she comes down, I give myself some more time, aware that I'll need it to last all the way to her next orgasm.

"Slow is good," she breathes out. "I like it. It's different, but I really like it."

"You've seen nothing yet, red."

Her little giggle is unexpected, but it makes sense when she says, "You're so damn cocky."

"You like my cockiness."

"Yes, I love your cockiness."

I move back enough to stare down at her flushed face with a lopsided grin, which she answers with a crooked smile.

When she lifts to demand a kiss, I refuse her and pull out all the way to the tip so I can unhurriedly sink back inside her. I witness how her pupils dilate, her mouth opening with a sigh.

This time, I watch every little detail of her as I make love to her, maintaining the same measured intensity. Now that I'm higher up, we can both gaze down and watch as my cock pumps in and out of her. It's coated with her cum, and so swollen and stiff that it looks angry. The glistening skin catches the light, the veins bulging as if it might blow up soon. Which it really fucking might.

"You feel so good," I groan.

"You too. I feel so stretched, so full."

"You're about to feel even fuller, red. Do you want my cum? Do you want me to fill you up with it?"

"Oh God, yes!"

"You have to come once more for that, sweetheart."

"Then make me, please."

The slow pace I started with has been progressively speeding up, and while it's still not as intense as when we usually fuck, the momentum isn't as tender as earlier. My hips slap against the inside of her thighs with each punch into her overworked pussy, and we're both glistening with sweat now. My arms burn with the effort it takes to keep myself upward, so I know we've been doing this for long enough.

I lean onto my left elbow and send my right hand between us to tease her clit. She mewls my name, her knees tightening on my sides, and I take it as an encouragement. While my cock keeps pumping inside her, my fingertips roll and pinch, giving her the little extra stimulation she needs to follow me into heaven. My balls are tightening; I'm so fucking close.

"Jake! Aah! I'm—" A hiccup of pleasure steals the rest, and her walls clamp around my rigid girth.

Perfect fucking timing.

Five more thrusts and she shatters, screaming my name and pulling me to her with her nails fucking up my back. The pain of it, the way her pussy strangles my cock, her helpless moans, cries, whimpers ... bring me right there with her. A first rope of cum jets out of me, splashing right against the door of her womb—which I feel against my tip as I ram harder into her. My groans join her whimpers. I come so damn hard that I lose all notion of space and time, my eyes locked on her ecstatic face until I can't take more of it and shut them. This is one of the best orgasms of my life.

It's not just my balls that I empty into her, it's my heart, mind, and entire person. This woman fucking owns me already, and I think she has no idea.

By the time I'm done shuddering over her, I feel fucking empty, but in the best possible way. I'm plastered all over her, my temple resting on her breast as I pant like I ran a hundred miles. Under my ear, I can hear the hectic tempo of her heart beating as wildly as mine. Who knew lovemaking could be as remarkably satisfying as the intense fucking we're used to? We'll have to do this again in the future. Repeatedly.

When I try to move away from her, she stops me, squeezing her thighs around me and restraining me with her arms. "No, stay," she whispers.

"Can you breathe?"

"Barely, but I don't care."

I chuckle softly and readjust myself so I don't weigh so much on her. My eyes wander to the pink nipple in my field of view, and we stay like this for several minutes, immobile and silent. Between us, I can feel my cum seep out of her from around my softening cock.

This is so fucking nice.

"I know it isn't my birthday anymore, but can this be my gift from you?" she asks with humor.

"The sex?"

"The *spectacular* sex."

"I'll return the actual gift I got you, then."

"You got me a gift?" She sounds so surprised and happy that I have to look up and see the big smile on her face.

"Of course I did."

"Can I see it?"

"It depends. Am I allowed to move again?"

Her energetic nod makes me laugh.

My limbs are still weak as fuck when I push myself up, pulling out of her sloppy cunt in the process. I can't believe my legs are actually wobbling as I walk to the closet. There, I take out a medium-sized package and return to the bed. She's sitting in the middle of it, her creamy skin still flushed, her cheeks pink, and her eyes sparkly.

"There you go, sweetheart," I say, handing her the gift.

She looks like a child on Christmas morning as she tears the paper open, and I find her excitement terribly endearing. Her eyebrows twitch as she discovers the red leather, and then she takes it out to unfold it and hold it before her. I went out of my way to find something up to her standards, and the clerk at Bloomingdale's insisted I couldn't go wrong with such quality Italian leather.

"I've been driving you around on my bike a few times, so I reckoned it's better if you have some protective gear. I snooped around your closet one evening while you were showering to get your size. But I noticed you don't have a leather jacket, so we can return it if—"

She interrupts me with a quick and eager kiss and then grins at me broadly. "Are you kidding! It's so beautiful, oh my God."

I watch, reassured, as she opens the zipper and slips it on. It fits her perfectly, and I don't think I've ever seen her looking so hot. The red leather compliments her hair and skin, and her nakedness below beckons fantasies I didn't know I had. Especially since she looks thoroughly fucked at the moment. And she very much is. I want her to ride me wearing it, with the swell of her tits half hidden and her nipples peeking through as she bounces on my cock.

Maybe we'll do that for *my* birthday.

She jumps out of bed, rushing her little bum to the tall mirror on the wardrobe's door. Wholly entranced, I admire her while she examines her reflection, twisting around to see it all, her luminous smile never fading. She closes it, reopens it, poses …

Does she know how fucking sexy she is right now? The jacket reaches a little below her belly button, so the triangle of curls at the apex of her legs is in full view. For fuck's sake, I can even see my cum coating the inside of her thighs.

"It's so perfect, Jake," she squeals as she returns to the bed before attacking me with a series of kisses. "I love it so much."

Before I can return any of her enthusiasm, she's off again to the mirror.

Greatly entertained by all this, I lie back on the headboard with a forearm behind my head. I never thought I had much boyfriend material in me, if any, but if small things like this are all it takes to send her over the moon with joy, I might nail it.

She looks very proud when she turns to me again, and the mischievous glimmer on her face tells me I'm not ready for what's coming next. "I don't even need to get my bag from the car anymore. This is how I'll spend the entire weekend," she declares.

Well, fuck me. It's like God heard prayers I haven't made yet.

"If you don't have any objection, of course," she cautiously adds.

"Do you object to getting fucked hourly?"

Her face, which only now started to return to its normal state, flushes again as she gnaws on her lower lip. She shakes her head, and I give her a carnivorous smile. "Then I have no objection, red."

If we end up strolling around naked like this all weekend long, then I'm beyond confident that this thing between us will take us pretty fucking far.

CHAPTER
Twenty-Eight

Gen

WHO KNEW THAT CRYING LIKE a lunatic in Jake's arms would get us to where we are now? I don't know if it was always bound to happen or if my pathetic display triggered his protective instinct, but I'm thankful for the turn of events.

Although it was a joke, we did spend the weekend naked, aside from a few outings at the dog park or to eat out on Saturday evening. It was strangely liberating to stay bare, as if we had nothing to hide from one another. I did find it a little exhausting, though. Jake truly is a sex machine. He spent the weekend eyeing me with hunger, looking like he could pounce on me at any moment. Which he did quite a few times.

But between sex sessions, we delved into deep conversations that fulfilled my soul even more than the naked intimacy. He listened to me talk about Victoria and asked many questions, desirous to learn more about my lost sibling. Some part of him must have sensed that I needed to let it all out because he was sweet and patient the whole time.

Even though I had to catch up on a couple of things at work, I got to see Jake a few evenings throughout the week. He officially has a toothbrush at my place, and I relocated the spare cup to the back of a drawer. The joy I feel every time I see our toothbrushes hanging out together is ridiculous. My obsession with the man seems to come from a bottomless well, and no matter how much I give into it, I still come up with more.

Tonight is date night, and I know that whatever he has planned will feed that insane infatuation. That is, if I can decide on what to wear.

I got off work early just to get ready for it, and I've tried eight different outfits so far, none of which were good enough. The only thing I have figured out is the lingerie—a strapless balconette bra with a coordinated cheeky, as well as thigh high stockings. I need help with this because I'm clearly unable to handle it alone. So now, I'm sitting in my underwear in my dressing room, anxiously waiting for Hana to pick up the phone. It's been ringing for over thirty seconds now, so I'm about to hang up when something finally happens.

My friend appears on the screen, and I let out a sigh of relief. "Hey, babe," she greets me with a smile.

"Hi! Oh my God, I'm so glad you picked up."

"Is everything alright?"

"No. Yes. I don't know. I need your help. Do you have a moment?"

"Sure! I just fed this little milk addict, so we're good to go," she explains, angling the phone away so I can see Lucas thrown over her hip as she holds him there with her free arm.

He looks adorable with his chubby cheeks and big smile. Hana and Tyrone really created the most perfect baby, with his warm brown skin, beautiful eyes, and a head full of tight curls.

"Hey, baby boy!" I cheer. "You're growing so fast!"

Although he's far from speaking, Hana excitedly tells her infant son, "Say 'hi' to Auntie Genny. Can you say that for me, my sweet prince?" When he replies with nothing but gurgling, she sighs and gives him a kiss on his tiny dark-haired head. "One day. And remember that if you say 'Dada' before 'Mama' I will drop you at the nearest orphanage." I laugh incredulously at her savage joke, which brings her attention back to the phone. "So tell me, darling. How can I help?"

I scan the extensive wardrobe surrounding me, feeling stupid for not finding one good thing despite my plethora of choices. "I'm meeting with Jake," I explain, "and I can't figure out what to wear."

"Does it really matter? You'll end up naked in five seconds, won't you?"

I wince. I've been waiting for the perfect opportunity to tell her, and this is it. "Tonight is actually a date."

She freezes so hard that I think it's a connection issue at first. But then she echoes, "A date?"

"Yes."

"A date-date?"

"Yes-yes."

Her shock is almost comical, but I hold back from chuckling. Her gaping mouth turns into a huge grin, and she shakes her head incredulously. "You're a terrible godmother; I almost dropped my child. Are you and Jake seriously dating?!"

When a broad smile tugs at my lips, I feel like an infatuated teenager—especially when I sense my cheeks warming. "We are. I told you I left my parents' gala and went to his place, but I didn't tell you everything."

"You sneaky, sneaky hoe. What happened?"

"Well, I cried—probably enough to fill a bucket."

"You did?"

"Yeah. And he was so … Hana, I swear, he's so perfect. He was gentle, and patient, and tender … He comforted me while I confided in him and then held me the entire night. And in the morning, he made love to me in a way I've never experienced before. It was like we were one being, like we began and ended with one another."

"Oh my God, Gen. I can't believe you didn't tell me!"

"I know, I'm sorry. You've been such a vocal advocate of Jake, I suppose I wasn't ready to share yet. I needed to sort out my feelings by myself, you know?"

"I get it, babe. I can be very pushy at times, especially since you can be so stubborn. Have you figured out how you're feeling?"

"Oh, I'm falling for him. *Hard.*"

"Of course you are," she says, nearly squealing with excitement.

I sigh, overwhelmed by the mere thought of Jake and tonight. "He's so perfect, you know? And he makes me feel like myself. I don't think I've felt that way since Victoria died, and I'm like, alive, and free, and so damn happy every time we're together." My eyes scan the room around me and the clothes hanging on their racks, and frustration overwhelms me. "And now we're having our first real date, but it won't be perfect because I can't find anything to wear."

"Oh come on, that's impossible. Show me what you've tried so far."

For the next five minutes, I settle the phone against a console and show her the outfits I've tried and dismissed. She agrees some don't work but calls me irrational for a few others.

"But I really want to wear the leather jacket he got me," I insist, showing it to her again. "And those colors don't match."

"Hmm, I kind of see what you mean, yes. You know what would be perfect with it?"

"Obviously not, or we wouldn't be having this conversation," I mumble cynically.

"Remember that black dress you had at Harvard? The one with the lace?" It doesn't take long for my brain to picture exactly what she means. Oh, she's good. She's *really* good.

Leaving the phone where it is, I sprint to a closet on the other end of the dressing room. There, I hoard the clothes I probably won't ever wear again but refuse to give away. It takes a full minute for me to find the black lace dress—settled on a hanger inside protective plastic wrap. I'm pulling the zipper down as I return to the phone. Thanks to a freshening sheet in there, the dress smells flowery and clean when I take it out.

"Oh my, it'll be so perfect," Hana excitedly says from the other end of our call.

"I hope it still fits."

"Bitch please, you look as good as when I met you eight years ago."

I grimace, thinking of how my mother would disagree with that one. My hands are slightly trembling with anticipation as I hold the first part of the dress down and step into it. It comes up easily, and the zipper barely resists.

"God, you look so sexy," Hana supportively approves.

The silk under-dress is way too bold and, yes, definitely sexy. The strapless bodycon barely covers anything, with a sweetheart neckline that hugs my breasts together tightly and a skirt that ends high on my thighs. It's tighter than I remember, but it isn't too constricting.

I pick up the lacy second half of the dress and slip it on from the top, then slide my arms into the sheer long sleeves as it comes down.

This time, the zipper that goes from my lower back to my nape resists a little more. I adjust everything and step to the side to observe myself in the floor-to-ceiling mirror. I was right to think my best friend would solve everything.

The lacy part of the dress is more reasonable, with a round collar tight around my neck, sleeves that reach my wrists, and a skirt that goes just below my knees. The design of the lace is beautifully intricate, delicate, and very, very sheer, exposing the skimpy under-dress in an elegant manner. The whole thing is skintight, and I know without a doubt that Jake will love it. His tongue might even roll out like that Tex Avery wolf.

"Try it with the jacket!" Hana demands. I don't need to be told twice.

I grab the beautiful leather garment and put it on, making sure none of the rivets or zippers get hooked into the lace. Once it's settled on my shoulders, I admire the perfect result.

"Forget Jake, I'm the one taking you out on a date," Hana jokes.

I smile at the phone, adjusting my wavy hair to perfect the look. Whatever Jake has planned for us tonight might end up being shorter than intended.

Lucas begins to stir at Hana's side, so while she's busy soothing him, I walk up to my wall of shoes and grab a pair of shiny black Louboutins. "I hope he's not picking you up on his bike," she points out.

"I'm meeting him at his place. He offered to pick me up, but since he planned something in Brooklyn, I thought it would be simpler to go to him."

"Smart. Then you guys can take an Uber to wherever."

"Exactly."

The dainty gold watch on my wrist informs me that I have less than ten minutes left before the ride I scheduled arrives. "Can you think of anything I can improve?" I ask Hana, twisting around to inspect my back in the mirror.

"No, I really like it. You can't wear a necklace with this dress, and those studs are perfect."

"Thanks," I say with a smile, reaching up for the earrings my brother got me last week.

She must notice how my hands slightly tremble because she asks, "Are you stressed, hun?"

"A little. I really, *really* want this to work out. But I'm also aware that I'm putting a lot on the line. My parents will never approve of him, and it'll make everything with them so much more complicated."

She sighs, momentarily looking away as she tries to figure out what to say. "My parents really didn't like Tyrone at first, remember?"

I nod, aware of that. It was hard on Hana, and she was a mess for months. Her parents wanted a nice Korean man for her, with a well-paying job and prospects. Seeing their daughter end up with a struggling artist wasn't in their plans. They began warming up to him when he had his breakthrough, thanks to Constance, who recognized his immense talent and exhibited his photographs in her gallery. Now, they know that their daughter is the happiest she's ever been, with the love of her life by her side and their baby boy.

"He grew on them eventually," she reminds me. "And he isn't as charming and social as Jake. No, my awkward introvert of a man still won my parents over. I'm not worried that Jake won't do the same."

With all my heart, I want to believe her. My parents, while strict and prejudiced, can be reasoned with, I think. And the ease with which Jake made his way into my heart proves how good he is at winning people over.

While it would be easier, I'd never wish for him to be more like me or the people in my world. There isn't a single thing I want to change about this man, no matter how complicated it makes everything.

Little Lucas fusses again, and Hana offers me an apologetic wince. "Sorry, I think the little prince needs to be changed."

"It's alright, Hana. I need to do some makeup touch-ups, anyway. Thank you *so* much for helping me out. I was really desperate."

"Girl, that was purely selfish. I need Jake to knock you up fast so our kids can be best friends."

An incredulous laugh rips out of my chest. "Jesus Christ, don't say things like that. This is literally our first date."

"You two have had plenty of evenings together before. Even spent a whole weekend cooped up," she retorts with a roll of her eyes.

She's not entirely wrong, but still. Tonight is meaningful and feels more official than anything we've ever done.

Hana and I stay on the phone for a few more minutes, then we mutually decide it's time to hang up. I'm reapplying a layer of red lipstick when I receive a notification. I expect it to be my ride, but it's a message from Jake instead.

WOMBAT GUY
When's the driver picking you up?

ME
In five minutes. Why?

WOMBAT GUY
Just making sure :)

I make my way to my bedroom to throw the last of my toiletries into my overnight bag. After one last look in the mirror and an approving nod for myself, I exit my apartment, heels clicking on the marble floor.

The notification that the car has arrived comes when I'm in the elevator, so I seek a sleek black sedan once I exit the building. It's easily located, as well as the driver standing beside it, his hands professionally folded together in front of him. But my attention is swiftly drawn to what's parked right in front of it. The deep green vintage sports car is undoubtedly a beautiful sight, but it's nothing compared to the man leaning against it. In my stupor, I stare at a very handsome, very mine, Jacob Clarke, grinning with pride like a cat that got the cream.

He's wearing all black, and the crisp shirt that hugs his broad torso has a few buttons undone at the collar, and the sleeves are rolled up, which exposes some of his tattoos. I thought I did a good job getting ready for tonight, but dear Lord ... he absolutely nailed it.

I'm still processing what's happening when the driver of the sedan steps to the side and opens the door for me. My heart flutters, my eyes stuck on Jake's handsome face.

"Miss Kensington," the driver says, gesturing for me to enter.

"Sorry, but I won't—I won't be needing your services," I say to the driver, finally ripping my gaze from the mesmerizing sight.

"Miss?"

"I'll pay the fees and whatever. Sorry again."

Without another word, the driver offers me a nod and returns to his car to drive off. I return my attention to Jake, whose cocky smirk never wavered.

"You were 'just making sure?'" I say, failing to contain my cheerfulness at seeing him. Pleased isn't adequate to express how his unexpected presence makes me feel. I'm elated.

"What kind of man would I be if I let another bloke service my woman on our first date?"

I'm so entranced by his gorgeousness that I almost miss the fact that he called me *his* woman. Already, I know that I'll want tonight to last forever.

As I stare into Jake's jade eyes, I feel like the luckiest woman in the world.

"Is it cheesy if I admit I came because I couldn't wait to see you?" he asks, half joking, half embarrassed.

I laugh at his blunt admission. "Definitely. But you're in luck because I love cheese."

We grin at one another like two enamored buffoons, and I step closer to him. His eyes take me in, raking up and down my body with nothing but appreciation. "Fuck, red, you look stunning," he praises once I'm by his side. "But how am I supposed to kiss you with those lips?"

The evident frustration in his voice makes me giggle, and I twist my face to the side and present my cheek to him. He mumbles, "That won't be enough," but still bends down to kiss me there, wrapping an arm around me to hold me close. I should have expected it, but it still surprises me when his lips slowly travel from my cheek to that tender spot behind my ear, then down my neck, dropping eager and amorous kisses on my shivering skin.

Ripping himself away from me, he gives me one last longing look before saying, "Alright, let's go before I start undressing you in the middle of the street to kiss your other set of lips."

Like a proper gentleman, he opens the passenger door for me and takes my overnight bag. "This is quite the car," I say, admiring the beautiful design of the vehicle.

"I know. Ever heard of an old show called Stingray?"

"Never," I admit as I lower into the car, helped by his steady hand.

Once I'm safely tucked in, he closes the door and walks around the car. He sits down on his side and twists around to set my bag behind us. "When I was a kid, I became obsessed with this obscure TV show from the eighties. This guy called Ray was some kind of shady but good guy," he explains before turning the engine on. The sound of it is just as vintage as the look. "He was a badass who drove a 1965 Corvette Sting Ray."

"Same as this one?"

"Yeah, but black."

I chuckle, amused by how sentimental he is sometimes. He easily drives out of the parking spot and puts us on our way to whatever he planned for tonight. "You used to watch a lot of weird stuff as a child, didn't you? I checked out what Mulligrubs is, and dear God ..."

His lopsided smirk isn't lost on me. "I'd blame it on Australia's TV network, but I think I actively looked for that shit. Mum worked a lot, and TV was an easy and cheap babysitter. I don't blame her for it though. Those weird shows made me who I am, in a way."

"I definitely appreciate them for that."

The not-so-subtle compliment and evident appreciation of his mind earn me a quick look, as well as one of his signature smirks. His hand comes over to my thigh, resting on the lace of my dress, and his thumb mindlessly grazes back and forth.

"Did you have a good day at work?"

"Eh, things have been tense on my floor since I demanded that the gossip stop. And I think my boss is annoyed that I keep skipping the Friday after-work drinks."

"Shit. Maybe we should start relocating our time together to Saturdays or Thursdays."

"No way. I want you on Thursday evenings, Friday evenings, *and* Saturday evenings."

"Greedy, are we?" he says with a chuckle.

"With you? Always."

Because I really don't want to talk about my work and bring the mood down, I ask him about his day instead. Some über-famous soccer player—whose name doesn't ring a bell because I know next to nothing about sports—wants a tattoo from him, so Jake has been sketching a lot all week, trying to find the perfect idea. I'm so distracted by the conversation, entranced by the passion I can hear in his voice, that I pay barely any attention to the streets outside. It's only when he stops in front of the wide door of an underground garage that I look around.

"Wait," I start, confused, "isn't this your building?"

"It is." The door is now open, so he drives in.

"Are we having a date at your place?" I genuinely don't mind if that's the plan, but he told me it would be something special, so I didn't expect this.

"Not exactly."

The garage has a few more cars, and I spot his bike, as well as a couple others. He parks the car in a wide and free spot and then cuts the engine. I'm still a little confused when he makes his way out with my bag and comes around to open my door. His hand helps me out, and he guides me toward a flight of stairs. It leads to the hallway of his building, which I'm familiar with by now. I'm still not sure what he has in mind when we step into the old elevator and ride it up to his floor.

"Let me just put your bag in the flat, and we'll be back on track," he explains.

I wait, standing by the elevator as he does so, taking slightly longer than I expected.

"Alright, sweetheart," he says once he's back, taking my hand in his warm one, "stairs again, and then our evening can start."

It's only when he leads me to the staircase and up that I understand. I know the roof has some accommodations because he's mentioned it in the past. I've never been up there though, so I have no idea what to expect. There's a heavy metal door at the end of the stairs, and he lets go of my hand to open it. We step outside, and I take in the space he has created there while he uses a latch on the wall to secure the door open.

A sense of wonder washes over me, and my eyes widen at the beautiful setting. The early evening sun casts a warm, golden glow across the horizon, painting the sky with hues of orange and pink. There's just one building higher than Jake's, giving me an unobstructed and splendid view of Brooklyn's beauty.

What truly captivates me is the lush, verdant paradise that surrounds us. Dozens of plants of various sizes and species create a miniature forest that fills the rooftop with life and vibrancy. It's like a hidden oasis in the heart of the city. Garden furniture is arranged—a lounge area, sunbathing chairs, and a sumptuous round bed that looks like something from a dream. A hot tub is nestled in a cozy corner, and on our left, a small outdoor kitchen area. In the middle of this haven, a table is set for two beneath a pergola adorned with fairy lights. This must have taken hours, and I can't help but be filled with excitement and gratitude for his efforts.

"Do you like it?" he asks, slipping a tender hand around my waist as he returns to my side.

"I absolutely love it. Are you telling me there's been this lush oasis up here the whole time, and you never showed me?"

"We were usually busy doing other things," he reminds me with amusement.

"Still, Jake, this is beyond beautiful."

"I'm glad you like it." He lowers to kiss my temple and silently encourages me to take the three steps down to the exotic wood decking.

As we walk up to the table and closer to the kitchen, a mouth-watering smell reaches my nostrils. That's when I see white smoke twirling out of a large smoker's chimney. The kitchen is more equipped than I first thought, and I notice an oven, a small fridge, and a griddle.

"Do you use this space often?"

"As much as we can every summer. We've been a little busy this year, but ever since I bought this place, we usually spend our evenings here as soon as the weather is mild enough until far into autumn. Eli likes to climb up the emergency stairs to sunbathe. I've caught the fucker as naked as a worm more than once."

I smile at that, continuing my exploration of the magnificent space while he follows a few paces behind. "Who handles the plants?"

"I used to, but I don't have enough free time anymore. I only do the ones in my flat. I set timers to water everything, and a guy comes once a month to clean up and take care of the plants."

"I see." My hands graze the green leaves of what looks like a Juniper.

When I reach the hot tub, I dip my fingers in the clear water. It's cold, which I suppose is expected as they probably only heat it before use.

"Want me to turn it on?" he offers, as if reading my thoughts.

"Not tonight, but we're definitely doing this soon." As I say that, I send him a very suggestive side glance. He catches it, of course, and something naughty appears on his dashing features.

"I don't recall sex in a spa being on your list, red."

"We'll say it's on my personal list, then."

Appreciation flickers in his gaze as he pulls me closer, plastering my front to his muscular body. "And how long is that one?"

"Oh, way too long to write down and ever-growing."

"Music to my fucking ears."

He apparently doesn't care about the lipstick any longer because he claims my mouth earnestly. I, too, forget about it and answer with matching intensity, allowing our tongues to mingle the way they crave to. His hands are all over me, pulling me into his embrace like he wishes we could be just one being.

When he pulls away, I'm panting and heated, aware that my face must be flushed with smudged lipstick all over—just like him. "Oh no, we made a mess," he lets out, his tone suspiciously unbothered. Holding back a proud grin, he pulls out something from his back pocket. "Good thing I snatched the makeup wipes when I dropped your bag."

So that's why he took longer than expected. Torn between amusement and surprise at his cunningness, I take the wipe he offers before he pulls one out for himself. We clean up and then do damage control on one another. I can't shake my entertained grin the entire time.

Something rings in the kitchen, and Jake reacts to it. "Ah, that's the scalloped potatoes," he says before taking off.

I follow him to the kitchen and watch as he deactivates the alarm on his iPad on the counter. With expert motions, he takes out a dish filled with perfectly golden potatoes, which are thinly sliced and bathed in a creamy sauce.

"That looks delicious," I appreciatively note.

"This is my signature dish, so get used to it, love."

Once the potatoes are returned to the turned-off oven, he moves on to the smoker and opens it to check the meat. The smell when he lifts the lid makes me salivate, and I find myself wondering if I really deserve such a man. An artist who cooks, has a heart of gold, and fucks like a god? It's like I'm cashing in all of my karma points at once.

As soon as his inspection is over, he returns all of his attention to me. "Alright, love. I have champagne, or I have a fruity red from the Napa Valley. The red's for the meat, but if you want a glass now, it's been decanting for over an hour, so it should be perfect."

"The wine sounds great. No need to open two bottles, wombat." The nickname really grew on him because his face lights up when I use it, and he can't help but give me a kiss, like a little reward.

"I truly don't mind opening the champagne."

"Red's perfect."

"Heck yeah, she is," he cleverly retorts. "Great to see you're catching up, sweetheart."

I think my ovaries react to his words because I feel something swell and pulse deep inside me. Maybe Hana wasn't wrong, and I should get pregnant. Baby trapping this man sounds like the greatest idea I've ever had.

He sends me to the lounge area with our glasses of wine and then joins me with a beautiful board full of various finger foods. "You must have spent the whole day cooking," I say, overwhelmed.

"Just the afternoon. I started on the meat yesterday, though, and it's been slow cooking all day."

"I need to make sure this evening is all worth it, then."

"Oh, I have the feeling it will be, red."

I hand him his glass, and before we drink, he raises it, his gaze locked on mine. "To our first date," he toasts.

I tap my glass with his and repeat, "To our first date."

And to many, many more to come.

CHAPTER
Twenty-Nine

Jake

I GENUINELY CANNOT BELIEVE THAT this gorgeous, clever, and witty creature sitting by my side is mine. Life doesn't get any better than this, does it? All the struggles I've been through to get to this moment have been worth it. A million fucking times over. Especially when her pearly laugh fills my ears like it does now. I bagged Genevieve Kensington, and no accomplishment will ever be that rewarding.

"I swear," she struggles to say between laughs. "My mother grabbed my arm and dragged me out so fast. 'Genevieve, this man is a former president of the United States!'" she adds, mimicking what must be her mother's shrill voice. "But how was I supposed to know?"

"How old were you?"

"Six!"

"Yeah, I reckon that's fair," I reply, amused. "What happened after?"

"Well, I was forbidden from attending galas, which I really didn't mind. But then Victoria refused to go if I couldn't come, so my parents decided to debrief me a lot more instead."

"Did you obey?"

She doesn't say right away, mischievously biting her lower lip. I know the answer right then, even before she shakes her head. "Within a month, I got us out of gala duty for good."

"So, you've been a determined little thing your whole life. Consider me warned."

A small giggle spills out of her pink lips, her eyes lifting from her nearly empty glass. "Your turn. Tell me something about your childhood," she softly asks.

There are two different versions of me as a kid, one of which is always hard to talk about. Before my mother's death, I was like any child with a single parent struggling to make ends meet. What came after though, was devoid of innocence and joy, a dark era that nearly ruined all of her hard work.

"I told you my mum was a nurse, right?" I ask, to which Gen nods. "Well, when I was too young to take care of myself and she couldn't find a sitter, she sometimes smuggled me into the hospital's break room, gave me a pile of blank paper sheets from the copier, a cup full to the brim with pencils that she nicked from the pediatric wing, and she left me there while she worked. She came back to check on me as often as she could, and she sang me lullabies when I was ready to fall asleep on the beat-up couch. I think that's where my passion for drawing stems from."

"She sounds like a great mom. She really tried her best to care for you despite her little means."

"She was, and she did. Life wasn't easy, but she shielded me from all her money struggles. She used to tell me I was the best thing she'd ever done, her perfect boy with the face of an angel. After her death, I spiraled into some bad stuff until I realized I was ruining everything she had worked so hard for, destroying her legacy by being a stupid twat. So, I picked myself up, stopped the self-pitying, and decided to become a man she'd be proud of, her perfect boy. I work hard, make honest money, respect women, give to charities … She's also the reason why I never had piercings or tattoos on my face."

"Really?"

"Yeah, I reckon that if we're to meet again in the afterlife, I want her to see me with the angel face she always thought I had."

Gen gives me a small smile, and her soft hand comes to rest on the side of my jaw, giving me a tender caress. "She would be so proud to see how far you've come, wombat."

I twist my face enough to kiss the inside of her palm. We've been sitting here for half an hour, eating, drinking, and chatting like it's the most natural thing in the world. I didn't expect it to last that long, but we never run out of things to talk about, which is a great sign.

Still, the potatoes won't remain hot for much longer, so either I excuse myself to turn on the oven, or we move on to the next stage.

"Should we eat?" I suggest.

"Yes, please. The meat smells so good I'm practically drooling."

We stand up together, and I motion for her to go ahead. As she walks her perky little arse up to the dinner table, I admire her silhouette, as mesmerized as when I saw her exit her building. She removed her leather jacket earlier, and I think this might be my favorite dress she's ever worn. I don't know if it's a single thing or two pieces, but I'm going to need her to wear those two things separately—the lacey one and the tiny one, with nothing but those shoes.

Fuck, this woman is beyond gorgeous.

She offers to help me set up the plates, but I refuse and refill her glass with more wine instead, pulling out her chair for her to sit.

I sense her eyes on me as I work with efficient moves, cutting thin slices into the meat, which is juicy and tender, and using a cookie cutter to create perfectly round servings of potatoes. I add a precise pour of rosemary-infused gravy and some fresh rosemary for decoration and get rid of the apron.

"Do you realize how sexy that just was?" she asks when I approach with the plates.

"What was?"

"You, cooking."

"Well, you should see me cook naked," I tease with a half grin.

"I have seen you cook naked. Jumped you before you were finished, remember?"

"Oh, I remember *everything*, red."

She blushes from delight rather than embarrassment, and I settle our plates on the table. As I sit, she leans forward to smell the result of my hard work. Once I'm seated, she allows herself to take a first bite with some of everything on her fork. That causes her to moan and roll her eyes.

"I hope you know you're ridiculous," she says after swallowing.

"I am?"

"Yeah, I know you're faking it. There's no way you're *this* perfect, Jake."

"I assure you I have my fair share of flaws, red."

"Name one."

"I'm possessive."

Something flickers in her eyes, but it's more like approval than judgment. "I don't mind that. I'm ashamed to say it, but I quite like it, actually. Next."

For the next few minutes, we play this fun little game where I list my flaws and she argues in their favor or diminishes their impact. I'm a workaholic—welcome to the club. I'm stubborn—she's probably worse. I'm impulsive—she reminds me she joined a dating app to get dicked by a guy with piercings. I'm competitive—she's willing to crush her colleagues to get to the top. It goes on and on until I run out of things to list.

"See?" she insists with pride. "Not a single flaw on you."

"What about you? Any you'd like to share?"

Under the table, her foot has been grazing up and down my calf for a few minutes now, and it comes to a full stop as she frowns, acting deeply offended. "How dare you? I'm obviously flawless." Her graveness breaks quickly, though, and her perfectly plump lips stretch in one of her immaculate smiles.

I absolutely adore this Gen. So confident and carefree. The anxious and uptight woman I first met at The Plaza has entirely vanished, replaced by this foxy, playful, and blooming creature. I hope, maybe arrogantly, it was my influence that broke her out of her shell.

"Believe it or not, but I realized that very quickly, red," I confess. "I was wondering if you had anything you wished you could change about yourself—which I reckon would be a shame."

She thinks about it more seriously this time, the perfect arches of her auburn eyebrows knitting together. "I wish I were better at balancing my work life with my private life, but I think I'm slowly getting there. I'd be bored to death with my colleagues in some bar otherwise. Also, I wish I could be better at handling my parents because it would make everything so much easier. And lastly, I wish I was strong enough to say no to the amazing sex and go to Pilates instead."

That last one rips a genuine and frank laugh out of me. "I'm using my veto to demand you never fix the third one."

"The studio actually emailed me, Jake! They wanted to make sure I was still alive."

"What did you tell them? That you switched to a more pleasurable sport?"

"Ah, I should have," she realizes with a small pout.

We finish our plates, and when I offer her another serving, she shakes her head. "I'll have some again later—when we're in need of sustenance to keep going."

That is actually a great plan, so I dismiss my own desire for more. I'll perform better if I feel lighter. I take out the individual pavlovas I ordered for the occasion, passion fruit and mango, and set them on their own plates before I return to the table. The sun is now low under the horizon, and the fairy lights I worked on earlier give the place an enchanting aura.

"Jesus Christ, Jake. Did you bake this as well?" she asks when I put the dessert before her.

"I didn't, but I can bake a mean pavlova. Just didn't have time for it today."

"Of course you can. I'll eventually find out whatever flaw you're hiding from me, you know."

We dig right in, and the fact that she doesn't downright moan at the first bite kind of makes me proud. That's only for *my* food.

"You know you never showed me your work?" she points out halfway into it.

"Really?"

"I saw some of your sketches lying around, and I went on The Parlour's Instagram and found a couple of tattoos done by you. But you never actually showed me your drawings."

"That's an omission on my part, then. I have my tablet here, so we can settle somewhere, and I'll show you some of my latest stuff."

"I would love that, wombat."

The way my heart melts every time she uses that fucking pet name is ridiculous. I dread the day she lets it slip in front of Eli or Kill because they'll have a field day with it. But I enjoy it too much to ask her to stop.

We finish the desserts—I finish hers too—and while I clean up in the kitchen, she returns to the lounge area with our glasses and the rest of the wine. I do the bare minimum, just enough to avoid spoiling food, and join her there with my tablet. She's settled on the round day bed, looking at the few stars we vaguely see from here.

"Alright, time to woo you with my artistry," I say as I join her.

We arrange ourselves in a cuddling position, with our backs to the many cushions, and I unlock the screen to open my drawing app. Since I was using it earlier as I cooked, it's already opened on a full back piece, my latest artwork.

"Oh, is this for the soccer guy?"

"Yeah, he wants something with a Coleoptera native to Brazil."

"What kind of bug is that?"

"A beetle. I've been working on something that would work with what he has and the style he wants," I explain, opening a first draft.

We go through a few of those, and her little exclamations of surprise and admiration nearly do me in. Part of me wants to end this now and carry her downstairs like a caveman, but another part feeds on her approval with pride.

"You told me you did insects, but there's so much more than that, Jake. There's a whole masterpiece around it."

"Yeah, this is a big one, and I can't cover all of him in beetles. I reckon I can tattoo pretty much anything—I'm shit at the watercolor stuff, though."

"This is amazing. I'm so sorry I didn't ask to see it sooner."

"It's alright, we were busy with other things."

As if my teasing reminds her of those other things, she wriggles closer to me, her warmth seeping through our clothes. Now that it's dark out here, the temperature is dropping, so I ask, "Are you cold, red?"

"No, you're like a furnace. Keep going; I want to see more. What's your favorite one you've ever tattooed?"

For that, I have to go back to the other folders. I do that, scroll down, and realize I've made a terrible mistake when she tenses and says, "Wait, what was that?"

Shit.

"What?" I ask, still scrolling.

"There was a folder named 'Gen.' What's in it, Jacob?"

Fuck, fuck, fuck. Not the government name.

As tempting as it is, I'm not gaslighting her into thinking she saw wrong, so I reluctantly scroll back up. She takes the tablet from my hands as she sits up and clicks on the folder herself. Feeling like a fucking moron, I keep my eyes on her face as she opens a first drawing. Then another. And another.

"You've been drawing me?" she asks, her tone so unreadable it's utter torture.

"I started the morning after Hana's birthday. I was bored and watching you sleep. Then it became an obsession because I could never capture the real you, and it drove me mad."

When she opens a new drawing that has her naked from the navel up, I wince and consider removing the tablet from her hands. This isn't how I expected the evening to go.

She's conflicted as she takes in the art, and I look down at it too. She looks like a Greek nymph, with her pink lips parted as if she were sighing, the lushness of her red hair that surrounds her porcelain skin, the delicate column of her throat, and the full breasts and their perky, rosy tips below.

"It's not a sex thing, Gen, I promise. Those are for my eyes only; I never took pictures, never shared these …"

"I'm too beautiful," she says out of the blue, still frowning.

"What?"

"You said you couldn't capture the real me. It's because I'm too beautiful in those drawings."

It's my turn to frown as my gaze repeatedly travels from her to the tablet. "You're exactly right in those drawings, red. It's your aura that I never manage to replicate."

She doesn't believe me, clearly unconvinced. So I reach for the screen and zoom in on her sleeping face. "Those drawings are exactly as you are, love. You've seen the beetles, you know I'm good at catching likeness. This is you. All of you, minus the most intricate details of your soul, which I'm still working on."

She blinks several times, her hold on the tablet becoming slack enough for me to pick it up and set it aside. "You really see me like this?" she asks, still puzzled.

"This and more. I see all of you, Gen. The beauty within and without. And I can safely say that I have never in my lifetime encountered a more gorgeous creature than you."

Several seconds pass without an answer, and I'm fairly certain I've managed to ruin the evening. Anguish gnaws at my insides, a heavy lump stuck in my throat. She's still hesitant when she finally replies.

"Coming from an insect guy, this isn't the compliment you think it is, Jacob." The shy ghost of a smile makes the corner of her lips twitch, and there's an unmistakably humorous glimmer in her eyes.

Maybe it's because I was so stressed, but I burst into laughter, both amused by her response and relieved that everything isn't lost.

Once it recedes enough, I grab her nape and pull her in for a kiss, tilting my head to the side and enjoying the fruity taste of her. When I pull back, I lay my forehead on hers.

"I'm sorry for the sketches, red," I say with truthfulness. "I realize we never agreed on this, and I abused your trust when you were at your most vulnerable. It won't happen ag—"

"As long as they are only for you, I don't mind," she cuts me off. "I was surprised, yes. But ultimately, those drawings might be the most genuine compliment I've ever received."

Yet again, I'm thankful for how she's handling this, and anxiety slowly leaves my body. She's the one who initiates the next kiss, and we end up sprawled on the day bed, pulling and groping one another, lost in a lascivious embrace.

"Thank you for tonight, Jake," she says after several minutes of fervor, looking at me with wonderment. "It was even better than anything I expected."

"It was my pleasure, red. And you're not quite done with the surprises. I have another one for you."

"Really?"

"Yeah. It's in my trousers."

Her first reflex is to pat my front pockets, and when she finds nothing there, she tries to slip her hands toward my bum to check the back ones. "Oh, my sweet, innocent red." I can't help but say with a chuckle. "I said in my trousers, not my pocket."

Those big blue eyes meet mine, just in time for me to witness the way they widen when she realizes what I mean. The surrounding light is weak, but still enough for me to catch her blown-out pupils, black eating away the ocean of her irises. I lean back when she reaches for my belt and watch with amusement as she opens the zipper and button of my trousers. I'm not ready for her boldness when she shoves a keen hand in there, slithering it into my underwear to reach for my cock.

I'm hard as fuck, and she doesn't hesitate to wrap her slim fingers around me. Instantly, she understands what I meant, and her eyes become huge. When she tentatively grazes my rigid length, I clench my jaw, fighting back the pleasure she can bring with such a simple touch.

"You removed them all," she breathes.

I did. All seven piercings are in a sterilized box in the bathroom, waiting to be worn again after I've had her like this a few times. "I thought it would be all me tonight. Is that okay with you?"

"Of course it's okay," she assures me, stealing another hungry kiss.

We get caught up in it again, but this time, she's wanking me with her soft, delicate hand. I groan into our kiss, worried I'll come in my briefs like a fucking teenager.

"Can people see us from here?" she wonders, ripping herself away before kissing a heated path down my throat.

"No one ever called the cops on Eli for indecent exposure, so I don't think so—especially not at night like this. Why?"

"Who's innocent now?" she retorts with amusement.

I watch, entranced by her splendor, as she lowers herself on the bed and tugs my trousers down. "Oh, my naughty red. You want to have sex up here?"

She shakes her head, smirking mischievously. My cock's out now, *au naturel*, and she lowers to give it a kiss right on the underside of the head. It doesn't fail to do a little jump, a jolt of pleasure traveling down the length and into my balls.

"This is going to be so easy," she murmurs to herself, licking it from base to tip.

Fucking hell, of course this is what she wants. She's gotten even better at sucking me off with the piercings in, but like she said, this will be a walk in the park in comparison. Impatient to try, she doesn't tease me and wraps her warm mouth around the head of my dick. Then she lowers, her tongue sticking out underneath.

"Jesus fucking Christ," I groan, sending a hand on the back of her head.

I resist the urge to press her down when she lifts up, popping my glistening cock out of her mouth. Her hand that's holding the base starts wanking me, and I genuinely worry about how fast I'll be coming.

"Tell me," she starts, eyeing the tip with curiosity. "When you come without the apadravya in, does it—"

"Yes, it comes out of the piercing holes, too."

I don't even take a moment to think it might gross her out. But that would be a wrong assumption. Gen is adventurous and curious, first and foremost. My answer seems to delight her, and her hold on me tightens as if she's impatient to make me climax and witness the explosive result for herself.

All other thoughts I might have are relocated to the back of my mind when she takes me in her mouth again, her deft little tongue licking the sensitive underside.

Fucking hell, how could this woman ever think she was boring?

THIS LITTLE EXPERIMENT IS GOING great, and I almost regret not removing the piercings sooner. First, Gen has a much easier time sucking my cock, nearly deepthroating it with her usual eagerness.

Then, it helps with my stamina since I don't have the sensation of the piercings adding to the pleasure of her tight little cunt. I was a goner in three minutes on the roof, but then I lasted a solid fifteen minutes in bed before I came like a maniac. Now, we're going twenty minutes, and I'm confident I can hold back another ten.

Last but not least, the lack of piercings doesn't get in the way of Gen enjoying my cock. No, she still comes with remarkable ease, even without them dragging on her walls.

If I had any doubts about that, the way she's riding me right now would have dismissed them. Her back is to me, and her arse jumps up and down as I let her do the work.

Leaving the dog with Eli was a good idea because my innocent Grubsy can't catch us being this wild and uninhibited. She'd lose her spot in dog heaven, for fucking sure.

My wild cowgirl has gone full reverse, and while I regret not seeing her flushed face twisted by pure bliss, I sure as hell don't mind the view. Her freckled bum is right there for the taking—which I do, kneading the mounds with my fingers and palms. At least I get to enjoy her moans and soft cries as they echo in the loft.

I'm confident I can withstand another one of her orgasms when she apparently decides to prove me wrong. She leans forward, abandoning her upright position, and that exposes everything between her legs, from the puckered hole above where she's impaled on me to the swollen and drenched lips of her pussy stretched wide around my cock. She has a hand down her front, rubbing her clit to finish herself.

Fuck, that's it for me. Men are visual creatures, and this immaculate spectacle will have me nutting in under a minute.

Because it's my only option if I don't want to finish before her, I move my thumb to the tight hole above where I'm slipping in and out of her and push it in. I don't wait for her approval because we both know she loves it when I finger her arsehole.

"Aah, Jake!" she cries out when I fuck her with it.

"You want more, red?" I taunt.

"Yes!"

Instead of my thumb, I shove my index and middle finger inside her, pumping them in and out as she keeps riding my cock. I can feel her spasms around me and even *see* them, her whole pelvic floor pulsing from her pending climax. Because I know it'll make her topple over the edge, I add my ring finger and use all three digits to wreck her.

She cries out my name and tenses, and then everything spasmodically clamps down as she experiences her biggest orgasm of the night. I squeeze my eyes shut as she rides it.

One more. I need to stay strong one more time, and then we come together. After that, we can get ourselves some leftovers from dinner and have a short nap before we start again.

My jaw is locked and every muscle is flexed while I fight the urge to join her in bliss. I can't believe I came twice tonight and already find myself fighting for my life. But her gushing pussy feels so good, and her cries of bliss are so enticing. The power this woman has over me is un-fucking-believable.

The hectic ups and downs of her hips eventually slow, and so does the clenching of her pussy and arse. I don't know who I owe my success to, but I didn't come, and I'm really fucking proud of that.

As she recuperates, I slip my fingers out of her and reach for the wet wipes we settled on the nightstand earlier. I give each of my fingers a thorough clean and then start over with a fresh one. No cross-contamination in this house.

With one last sigh of abandoned bliss, she removes herself from my lap, my hard and angry-looking dick slipping out of her to fall back on my stomach, covered in her cum. She's a messy girl, always flooding my cock when she comes, and I love it.

She turns around, exposing her reddened face to my gaze, and I gorge on the view of her spent body, her limbs weak and shaky as she makes her way up to me. She presses herself on my side, as sweaty as I am, and grants me a long and lazy kiss. Her delicate hand reaches for my erection, which she tentatively strokes with a feathery and unhurried touch.

"I take it you like my cock even without the piercings?" I cockily ask.

"Definitely. It feels more manageable, like we can fuck all night and I won't have a limp in the morning."

It's a little insulting how she underestimates me like that. Time for another lesson. "How about we test out that theory?"

She thinks about my offer for a few seconds, her eyes locked on my length as she keeps running her fingertips over it. "Jake, I think I—I think I want to try."

"To fuck all night?"

"No, that one's a given. But it looks a lot less intimidating, and I think I want to try to have it in my ... other part?"

That, right there, is another very valid reason to regret not removing the piercings sooner.

"You want me to fuck you in the arse?" I ask just to make sure.

"I want to *try*. You used three fingers on me just now, right?"

I nod, grazing the soft curve of her hip.

"And there was nothing but pleasure from it. I think if we take our time, you could fit inside me."

Clearly, I want to do it. I've been dying to do it since I first saw that screenshot Eli sent me. But I don't want her to rush into it or feel obligated to on my account. I've made a few jokes about it in the past, but they were in no way passive-aggressive attempts at making her yield.

"You're sure you want this, red?"

She nods, looking beyond edible with her pink cheekbones, messy hair, swollen lips, and glimmering eyes. "We'll stop if it hurts or I don't like it, okay?"

"Of course. You'll set the pace, love. I will only enjoy it if you do, so let's make it pleasurable for both of us, yeah?"

She nods, almost shyly, and we exchange another one of those longing kisses. Because I know how to make it good for her, I decide to take charge. I grab another wipe off the nightstand and use it on her, cleaning her up.

Her body harbors some tension but is pliant as I reorganize her toward the edge of the bed, with her front lying on it and her knees on the floor. I throw the lube from my nightstand on the mattress next to her. Then, I spread her cheeks with eager hands and take a moment to admire the pink and drenched folds of her cunt, as well as the tight hole above. When I bend down to lick the taut spot she wants me in, she's a lot more relaxed than when we did it with the whipped cream.

I lick her, sometimes lowering to plunge my tongue into her slit, and she arches and moans on the bed, pushing her delectable bum harder against me to demand more. When she begins mewling my name like a plea, hands fisting the covers and body writhing, I decide that's enough, and I drag my tongue all the way from the crack of her arse to the back of her neck.

With a hand between us, I gather some wetness from her pussy and spread it higher.

"So, you want me in there, red?" I tease right into her ear, pushing three fingers in but only a knuckle deep.

"Yes," she whimpers.

"You want me to fuck this?" Another set of knuckles sinks into her, and I gently fuck her with them.

"I do. Please, Jake."

"My cock's a lot bigger than these. You realize that, love?" The fingers disappear inside her fully, which makes her cry out softly.

"I'll take it. I promise I'll take it."

"What a good girl you are. Relax for me, love," I whisper, stretching her wider by spreading my fingers apart. "That's it. You really want my cock in there, red. You're working so hard for it."

She moans, arching against my hand to get more.

"You think you're ready for it?"

"Yes."

"I think you are, too."

I let go of her, and after a quick cleanup with a wipe, I take the lube and spread a generous dose of it on the relaxed ring. Then I squeeze a line on my cock, and spread it all over the length.

She complies when I pull her up on the bed. I sit down with my back against the headboard and bring her on top of me, straddling me again but with her front to mine this time.

"We'll do it like this, love. You're in charge, you take your time, and you don't force it, alright?"

She nods, visibly nervous, and I do the only thing I can think of to distract her. We kiss in a manner that is both tender and lustful until she's writhing on top of me, her fingers clutching the short hair on the back of my head.

While she's distracted, I reach for my cock between us and align it with the tautness of her arse. I don't have to give her any more encouragement or reassuring words, it seems, because she immediately pushes back against the tip. "That's it, red. Open up, take my big cock."

I'm almost taken by surprise when the head fully slips past the recalcitrant muscle. "Fuck, you feel so good, love. So snug and hot."

A shy roll of her hips makes her sink lower, and we both let out a small moan. "Does it feel good for you too, red?"

"Yes, I feel so full."

"There's a lot more of me left, baby."

"I know, just ..."

Up and down she goes, and another inch of me disappears in her. Fuck, she's doing great. I'm closely monitoring her focused expression, making sure she's not hurting herself on me. There's some discomfort on her heated features, but pleasure seems to drown out everything else.

"Stay relaxed, love, and everything will be fine."

My hands graze a languorous path down her back as she writhes her hips slowly, taking barely more of me every time she lowers. With my palms full of her bum, I bring her closer to me so the wet expanse of her pussy is pressed on my lower abdomen.

"Do it like this," I softly suggest, using my hold on her to bring her up and down. Her slick center drags against me, stimulating her clit on my lower abs.

I let her lead, like I promised, regardless of how much I want to push inside her tautness. The ring of her arsehole is choking my cock, and since she can't take much yet, it's the sensitive head that's enduring most of it. But I'm so focused on her that I don't even think of how fucking good she feels.

When she takes my lips, I eagerly comply, distracting her the best I can with our kiss. She's rubbing herself on me to seek pleasure, bouncing up and down and swaying her hips from front to back. We kiss, and we fuck, or rather she fucks me, and I get lost in time enjoying her, completely entranced by her scent, the softness of her skin, the greed of her tongue, the raspiness of her moans ... She's a goddess, and a mere mortal like me doesn't deserve her perfection.

She's the one ripping herself away from me first, moaning my name in a way that makes my cock throb.

"You're doing so good, red. So *fucking* good."

My words seem to trigger a need to please me even more, and she takes a whole other inch inside her. She whimpers helplessly, and her forehead comes to my shoulder. "No, look at me," I demand, craving the connection.

When she does, still keeping up with her careful momentum, I notice that her eyebrows are twisted with what resembles pain. "Does it hurt?"

She adamantly shakes her head. "There's a stretch, but I like it."

"Of course you do, my naughty, naughty girl."

I let go of her bum and palm one of her tits instead. Her nails dig into the skin of my shoulder when I take its rosy tip in my mouth. I play with it the way she likes it, sucking, licking, biting … Her momentum gains in assurance, and she's soon riding me as if I were in her pussy, still grinding her clit on me with every thrust.

That's when I start losing my concentration because I'm not as worried about her comfort and can focus on how fantastic she feels around me. Nearly all of me has disappeared inside her now, and I'm so proud of her for this.

I can feel my tipping point nearing, but that's okay because she's getting close too. Those small cries are familiar, and she'll explode with pleasure soon.

"You feel so good in my ass," she moans, unprompted.

Just like that, I'm a goner. The climax that strikes takes me by surprise, and I barely have time to grab her hips to hold her down as my cock throbs inside her. Cum shoots out of my tip, coating the warm walls of her arse. Jolts shake me as I find relief, and I keep her close, emptying my balls inside her. I curse when I realize she isn't quite there yet, but I can't do anything about it right now, too lost in bliss.

As soon as the last spurt is out, I force my muscles to relax and bring a hand between us. I'm not subtle or gentle as I deftly handle her clit in a way I know will make her finish. In seconds, she's letting out a scream with my name on it and tipping into bliss. Her insides pulse and compel a few more drops of my cum to seep out.

Once her climax is over, she turns boneless, her sweaty and satiated body sprawled against me. She shows no haste in pulling me out of her, so I take it she doesn't mind the sensation. We slowly come down together, panting in unison.

"Anal on the first date," I groan as soon as I remember how to form sentences. "I can't believe you ever thought you were boring."

She lets out a breathy, exhausted giggle. "You're an idiot."

"And you're fucking perfect, red."

Her head is against my shoulder, and her febrile finger follows the intricate designs inked on my chest. I rake my hands over her back, forever in awe of how soft she is everywhere. These post-nut moments with her are a delight. Before her, my goal was to make whoever I brought home leave as soon as my balls were empty. But Gen made me discover what comes after, and these moments are just as much a part of it as foreplay. We're always so relaxed and blissful, satisfied beyond words, and in complete communion.

I've never felt this close to anyone before her, and I doubt I ever will. My soul and hers are entwined, and no matter our outcome, part of her will forever stay with me. Proper little Miss Kensington has carved herself a spot in my heart. A big one.

"You know how I removed some other stuff from my list, not just anal?" she asks, her voice almost a whisper.

"Yeah, I remember."

"Well, I was obviously wrong about this one, so I'm probably wrong about those, too. I think I want to try them as well."

"With pleasure. There's one we're never doing, though."

She frowns and looks up, meeting my gaze with her blue eyes. "Which one?"

"The threesome. We'll do me and a toy, but no one else gets to fuck you, red."

She thinks about it briefly and then wonders, "Even if it's with another woman?"

"Sharing you isn't an option. I told you I was possessive."

Her understanding smile shows she doesn't mind, and she kisses the underside of my jaw. "Then we'll do you and a toy. Not that you need it, you're a damn powerhouse."

I'm smiling like an imbecile when I kiss the top of her head and pull her closer.

"Wombat, can I return the favor and take you on a date next Friday?"

"I'd love that, but ..." I hesitate. I want us to bask in this moment a little longer, but I've been delaying this news for long enough.

She senses that something's off and pushes herself away enough to face me. "What?"

"I didn't want to tell you sooner because it wasn't a sure thing, but it was confirmed earlier today. I'm flying to LA for six days next week, from Thursday to Wednesday."

"Really?" The disappointment in her voice is hard to bear.

"Trust me, I'd rather stay here with you instead. It was supposed to be ten days, but I wanted to be here on the 21st, so I postponed my departure."

"What's on the 21st?"

I raise a brow at her, poorly hiding my pride. "You don't know?"

She ponders, eyebrows knitted together as she does. Then it clicks, and her face lights up. "Two months. It's our two-month anniversary."

I kiss her, endeared by her elation. "It is. I first found you perched on that stool at The Plaza on April 21st."

"So, we're celebrating before you leave for LA?"

"We absolutely are."

She grins and returns to her previous position, plastered all over me while she outlines my tattoos with her fingertips. "I'm going to miss you," she mumbles.

"Me too, red. Looking forward to the phone sex, though."

She giggles, and I welcome the sound. It's less than a week, and I'm sure we'll manage to keep things interesting despite being twenty-five hundred miles apart.

Then when I come back, we're on for a proper fuck fest.

CHAPTER
Thirty

Gen

I SHOULDN'T BE SURPRISED THAT Jake managed to make anal such a pleasurable and binding experience. I feel tied to him more than ever, as if the moment propelled us into even higher spheres.

His concern for me, how sweet and soft he was throughout, will be forever embedded in my mind. That man puts me first—my needs, my comfort, my pleasure—and it's a novelty for me. No one ever cared for me this much, aside from Vicky, and it makes me feel worthy and alive.

Because Jake will be away for nearly a week, we spend as much time as we can together. The weekend following our incredible date is spent in his apartment with Mulli. Then, he comes to spend the night at my place on Monday and Tuesday. I temporarily give him Eddie's old key so that he can let himself in on Wednesday to prepare things for our celebrations. I leave work earlier than I usually would to make the most of it.

When I arrive, the whole place smells divine, and he welcomes me with a flute of champagne. Later that night, after a delicious *Boeuf Bourguignon*, the rest of the bottle goes down in a less traditional way. He has fun pouring cold streams that make goosebumps erupt on my skin, the prickly bubbles igniting shivers before he has time to lick up the wet paths. I find my own way to drive him mad, blowing him with champagne in my mouth, giving him a go at his own teasing.

On Thursday morning, he's gone before I wake up, which saddens me. But the note he left on the kitchen island cheers me up a little.

> I'll be back before you know it, red.
> It's too small to match, but think of me
> every time you use the purple vibrator
> in your nightstand, yeah?
> PS: I stole that sexy black thong you
> wore yesterday. A token to remember
> home while I'm away.
>   Your wombat

I'm grinning so hard that my cheeks ache. This man is so corny sometimes, but I wouldn't have him any other way. I walk up to the fridge and pin his note with a magnet. Then I grab my phone, edit his name, and send him a text.

ME
Maybe I should invest in a bigger vibrator. This one will leave me wanting more.

MY WOMBAT
It's perfect this way. I'm the only 'more' you need, love.

ME
Are you at the airport already?

MY WOMBAT
Just arrived. I'll call you as soon as I'm through the TSA.

I excitedly fetch my AirPods and set them up. I'm making scrambled eggs when his call arrives. While I get ready, we talk about nothing and everything. Even if our interests don't always match, there's a genuine desire from both parties to listen and learn.

When I casually mention that I'm undressing for my shower, he brazenly asks for a picture. I make him work for it a little and then send him a shot of my reflection in the mirror, tastefully angled so he can see part of my behind and the side of my breast. Maybe I should be more cautious of such things, but I know he would never share my body with strangers. He's too greedy and possessive for that. The approving grunt he lets out as he receives the photo makes the risk worth it.

He waits while I quickly clean off the remnants of our night together, and he's still on the call when I come out. I'm done with my makeup and am getting dressed when he sighs heavily.

"Alright, sweetheart, they are doing the last calls. I have to go."

"Oh, they started boarding?"

"Twenty minutes ago. I wanted to wait until the last moment to get on, and this is it."

"Ah, I see. Have a safe flight, wombat. And let me know when you land."

"I will. Thanks for the picture, red. I'll put it to good use."

He's all the way to the boarding desk when we hang up after some quick goodbyes.

IN THE DAYS THAT FOLLOW, those little phone calls become our norm. Whenever we're both free, we spend it together like this, using video when our surroundings allow it. It's not easy, given our busy schedules and the three-hour time difference, but we make it work. In the end, I miss our physical proximity, but I don't miss *him* as much as I thought I would. We actually spend even more time together than we normally do because I often have a Bluetooth earbud nested in my ear—even at work, hidden by my hair.

Neither of us cares if it's ridiculous. We're needy like that, and we embrace it. I wasn't even this clingy as a teenager, but there's nothing rational about the effect this man has on me, so I stopped questioning it.

His trip to LA, as I understand it, is focused on an international tattoo convention that invited him as a speaker. Adding to that, he is supposed to stay in town as a guest artist in one of the parlors that sponsors the convention. This means he works a lot, mainly in the afternoons and evenings. Jake makes sure to be available around my bedtime, and I fall asleep while on a call more than once.

To our shared surprise, we're not having as much phone sex as we expected. It's hard to find the right moment for it when I'm at work by the time he wakes up, and his day ends when I'm already asleep. During the weekend, though, we indulge when he finds a moment to isolate himself.

On Monday morning, I'm all giddy and happy. Jake's coming back the day after tomorrow, and I can't wait to hold him in my arms again and feel the softness of his lips on mine, his weight on me, the stubble of his jaw on the smooth skin of my inner thighs … Ah, how I miss my wombat.

I'm grinning like a lunatic, alone in my office, thinking of our reunion on Wednesday. I have planned a fun date for us, which will end in my bed. I'm even getting off work early again to get him at the airport myself.

An enamored smile is still on my face when someone knocks on my door. My assistant is on the other side of the glass, and I invite her in.

"Miss Kensington," she starts, coming in to set a pile of documents on the corner of my desk. "You have a meeting in ten minutes in the blue conference room."

Ah, right. This will be another one of those time-wasting meetings where all the executives on this floor and the one below have to listen to Mr. Sinclair talk for an hour to say something that could very well fit in an email. I'm too busy for this, but if I start skipping my boss's vanity gatherings, I can kiss my promotion goodbye.

In a few minutes, I finish up and rise from my chair. Just as I'm about to head out, my phone dings on my desk. Given the hour, I know exactly who it is, which is why I eagerly pick it up.

MY WOMBAT

> Are you free?

Jake just woke up on the other side of the country, and, as usual, he texts me right away.

ME

> I'm about to head into a boring meeting, so I won't be able to talk.

MY WOMBAT

> I can do the talking if you want. I'll make it less boring.

This actually sounds like a great idea, so I take my AirPods from the drawer and head off to the conference room. I'm just done setting up our call when I reach my destination, people still filtering in. As discreetly as I can, I slip the earbud in and adjust my hair in an inconspicuous way.

"Good morning, red," his voice pours in, all sleepy and low. I'm about to answer when a colleague greets me as she enters the room. "Don't talk," Jake commands.

It's safer this way, so I don't say a thing and join the others around the massive oval table. Ralf is already in there, talking to Mr. Sinclair with his usual ass-licking tone.

"Ah, there's Genevieve," my boss says, gesturing toward me. "Everyone's in, so we can start."

"Genevieve … how formal," Jake murmurs, audibly smiling. "Does he also call you that when you've been a bad girl?" Heat spreads on my cheeks as I find an empty chair between two people from the overseas division. "No, I bet you've been such a good girl while I was away. Except yesterday, when we had our little fun."

Images of what we did flash before my eyes. We had a video call, and he coaxed me into getting my vibrator out and using it while he pleasured himself. He demanded no less than three orgasms out of me, and I fell asleep soon after to the lulling sound of his voice recounting his day.

"I was dreaming of you when I woke up, and my cock is still fucking hard. There's a family-sized tent over here."

My cheeks are officially hot, and I consider hanging up. This might be a bad idea, after all. Mr. Sinclair makes it impossible, though. "Alright, let's get on with it. This one's important, so I better not see a single phone out," he demands with authority.

I'm doing my best to focus on the presentation when Jake lets out a falsely discontented mumble. "This one won't go away. I'm afraid I have to take care of it."

My eyes widen with shock, and I can't help but look around at my colleagues. What if some of them guess what's happening? But I can barely believe it myself, so I doubt it.

The low, raspy moan Jake releases has me pressing my knees together under the table. "I can't wait to be back with you, red," he says, his voice altered by lust. I can already hear the metal of his thick bracelet as he pumps his erection. "I miss the soft touch of your hands, the deft grazes of your tongue, and the tightness of your pussy. You have the best cunt I've ever had, you know?"

Yes, I know. He's been very vocal about it in the past and never fails to remind me.

Mr. Sinclair keeps blabbering about whatever expansion he has in the works, but I can't register any of it for the life of me. Not when I have Jake in my ear, letting out small grunts and moans, his breath heavy and his voice tense as he pours lustful promises into my ear. "We'll be doing that sexathon when I get back, red. I'll fuck you for—What was it? Twenty-six hours and some minutes?"

I nod, even though he can't see me.

"Your pussy can't take that much of me, though, can it? I'll have to give it some breaks and fuck your throat instead. And your arse, too. Best fucking arse I've ever had as well, by the way. Jesus fuck, I can't wait to ram into that tight hole again and make you scream my name. I'll pull your hair the way you like it and make you take my whole cock. Maybe we could try it with the piercings too. I bet you'd like them rippling in and out of that little pink hole of yours."

I know he's using those words to fuel his own fantasies as he masturbates, but they work on me too well. I'm wet and aching, my clit throbbing at the prospect of him doing all those things to me.

This is insane. I'm stuck with two dozen of my colleagues and my rambling boss, and in my ear, Jake is spewing the lewdest, dirtiest promises I've ever heard. If anyone looks my way, they'll notice how flushed I am and how I can't stop rubbing my knees together.

"Fuck, baby," he groans, the clinking of his bracelet speeding up as he jerks off faster. I can even hear the fleshy sound of his urgent tugging. "I wish I could put this load inside you. Nothing's more beautiful than your cunt when it's been fucked raw. It looks so pretty, drenched in your juices while my thick cum seeps out of you. And I know you fucking love it when I pump you full of it. You clench around me like a proper little cum whore, and it drives me fucking insane."

My insides clench as if following his directions, and I realize I'm breathing too hard. I'm trying to focus on it, to contain myself, when he adds, "It's all yours, red. All of it is for you. Will you take it? Will you swallow it every time I come down your throat, keep it inside you when I nut in your arse, and stuff it back in your pussy when it overflows?"

"Yes," I breathe out, my voice so quiet only the man to my left hears it, turning around with a questioning glance. I dismiss him with a brief shake of my hand, too absorbed by Jake to come up with an excuse.

"Here it is," Jake grunts in a way that I know all too well. "Here's my cum for you, red. It's all for—Ah, fuck!" he roars.

I sit there, the most aroused I've ever been at work—if not ever—while Jake comes all over his hand on the other side of the continent. My clit pulses in unison with his moans and grunts. If I could sneak a hand between my legs, it would only take a few rolls of my fingers to follow him in bliss.

The rare brain cells that aren't devoted to this auditory masterpiece are used to keep my composure, sitting perfectly immobile when all I want to do is find the nearest bathroom stall to seek my own release.

"Jesus fuck, red," he whimpers. "Just knowing you're there makes wanking phenomenal." I can hear the relief and fulfillment in his voice, which was so rough moments prior. Contrary to him, everything in me is still tense and needy. "Fucking hell, I ruined the sheets with this one."

There's nothing but his heavy breath for a moment. "I bet you're so fucking wet right now," he says with pride, "sitting with all these arseholes, wearing your perfectly tailored suit like you're one of them. But I know you're so damn horny you wish I could be there to fuck you. We'd show those cunts how it's done, wouldn't we? I'd hoist you up on whatever table is there and eat you out like you're my whole lunch, red. I'd make you shatter on my tongue, maybe fucking your pussy with a finger or two as I do. Then I'd probably turn you around so you can see them watch you as you get fucked from behind. I'd make it so good, love ... I'd make it so damn good you can't help yourself but come hard all over my cock. And every single guy in the room would wish they were me, getting to fuck you this good. But they could never, could they? Only I could make you come so hard you see stars."

His dirty words and raspy voice have me nearly toppling over the edge. I can see so clearly how shocked they would all be, realizing I'm not, after all, a block of ice with a hole in it.

As if I'm getting punished for the scandalous thought, the woman on my right taps my shoulder, pulling me out of my fantasies and ripping me from Jake's invisible hold. I jolt back into the present at once, and the scene before me might as well be right out of a nightmare.

Everyone's focus is on me.

Did I accidentally moan or something?

It becomes clear that Mr. Sinclair, on the other side of the table, is waiting for me to say something.

"Ex-Excuse me?" I ask, my voice a trembling mess.

"Oh no, I hope I didn't get you in trouble," Jake says in my ear.

"I was asking if you could share the advances we've made regarding the merger," my boss repeats.

Shoot, I'm so not ready for this. As I push back to rise from my chair, I accidentally knock down my neighbor's pen, which falls to the floor. Seeing this as a perfect opportunity, I lower myself halfway under the table and remove the earbud. I discreetly place it in my jacket pocket and grab the pen to hand it to my colleague.

"Are you alright, Genevieve?" Mr. Sinclair asks. "You look unwell."

"Sorry, I'm feeling a little hot, is all."

"A bit early for menopause, isn't it?" A few people laugh at his joke, all men, and he waves his hand in a dismissive way. "Ralf will handle it. Don't worry, dear."

Part of me is relieved that I won't have to talk right now, but another is seething. The condescending tone and the patronizing attitude rub me the wrong way, and they instantly make my arousal fade away. The rest of the meeting unfolds without incident while my phone vibrates in my jacket now and then.

As soon as it's done, I rush out of the room and fish it out.

MY WOMBAT

> Sorry, I didn't realize it was the sort of meeting where you're expected to participate.

> Damn, your boss is a cunt. I'll menopause his arse. How do you put up with him?

> This is the Ralf guy? He sounds like a twat.

> I'm sorry again, red. It wasn't supposed to cause you any trouble.

It looks like Jake is still on the call, but I can't handle this right now. Not without cooling down first. I hang up, return the loose AirPod to its box, and head to the closest restroom, needing some alone time. I find a stall and lock it behind me before pressing my back against the door.

The phone vibrates in my hand, and when I check, it's Jake again.

MY WOMBAT

> Gen, talk to me. I'm sorry.

As embarrassed as I am, it's not his fault. I could have removed the AirPod, discreetly passing a hand in my hair and shoving it in my pocket. I was the one who kept it in because it was too hot to miss. This might have been one of the most erotic experiences of my life, and the only thing that tarnished it was my misogynistic boss.

> **ME**
> It's okay, I'm just a little shaken up. But it's not you, wombat. That was so fucking hot.

MY WOMBAT
> You can get revenge tonight if you want and call me while I'm tattooing some poor bloke. I'll work bricked up and mess his shit up, but oh, well.

I giggle, which didn't feel possible moments ago.

> **ME**
> Maybe I'll do that. I'm getting used to the vibrator, and I might keep using it after you come back.

MY WOMBAT
> No. Your pussy's mine when I'm around to take care of it.

> **ME**
> We'll see.

MY WOMBAT
> Don't "we'll see" me, Genevieve. The purple usurper returns to the drawer when I get back.

I bite down my lower lip in a failed attempt to contain my smile as I type the next text.

> **ME**
> We'll see.

I hastily return the phone to my pocket, planning on letting him simmer for a while, and exit the stall. I'm still grinning when I come out of the restrooms, my mood greatly improved.

I'M RESTLESS ON WEDNESDAY BECAUSE I'm hours from seeing Jake again. His plane lands at JFK a little after six, and I'll be there to collect him like a much-awaited gift. I have a hard time focusing, constantly checking my phone for a message from him or something. We're nearing noon, meaning he should be at LAX. But so far, I haven't received a single text from him.

A few more minutes pass until I give in and send him one.

ME

> Everything alright?

MY WOMBAT

> Brilliant.

I'm confused when his reply comes right away. Why didn't he text me sooner if he was already up?

ME

> Are you at the airport?

MY WOMBAT

> No.

Now, I'm beyond confused. I'm worried. The one-word replies aren't like him at all. Maybe he's in a rush and doesn't have time to talk. That would make sense, given how LA is a nightmare when it comes to traffic.

I still haven't accomplished anything around twenty minutes later because of the anxiousness twisting my insides. I need to know what's up before he gets on a five-and-a-half-hour flight, or the rest of my day will be ruined.

My unsteady fingers are typing when I get a text from him.

MY WOMBAT

> That color looks incredible on you.

The first reflex I have is to look down at my peacock-blue dress, frowning. Then my brain clicks and my head whips up to scan what's beyond the glass of my office.

My heart skips a beat, then a few others, when I spot a tall, charming, and dashing man smirking at me from the middle of the open floor. He looks very smug and proud, his T-shirt stretched over his chest, his muscular and tattooed arms crossed over it.

He looks so out of place among those assiduous and somber-looking people that I wonder if he is a hallucination. Have I gone mad from the withdrawal?

But if he's a figment of my imagination, then why is everyone else peering and glancing at him?

It's him. It's really him. That sneaky man got a much earlier flight to surprise me.

The pure elation I feel upon understanding turns into something sour when I notice Isabel whisper something in her colleague's ear. Larry is out there too, looking as shocked as the rest of them.

Oh, no ... More gossip is the last thing I need right now.

CHAPTER
Thirty-One

Gen

ANXIOUSNESS MAKES MY THROAT SWELL as if something is lodged in it. I roll my chair back and stand to walk up to the door. In the pit, people's gazes drift from Jake to me, and it doesn't help my nervous state.

He takes a few steps toward me on the other side of the glass, and we meet right at the threshold of my door, which I open with a trembling hand.

"What are you doing here?" I ask, my attention anxiously darting left and right as I take in the stares of my colleagues.

"Thought I'd surprise you and take you out for lunch, red."

"How did you even—I was supposed to pick you up this evening."

"This guy I was tattooing yesterday had a private jet leaving for New York in the middle of the night, and he let me come along."

I can hear the surrounding whispers, and my chest tightens with unease. Unsure of what to do, I grab his muscular arm to pull him into my office and close the door. People can still see but can't hear if we keep our voices down.

"Jake, you should have texted me," I say in a shaky voice.

Something turns somber in his green eyes as if I've offended him somehow. He turns around and looks at the crowd outside. They're still staring like we are some circus attraction.

"This isn't the kind of workplace where romantic partners and friends get to swoop in," I try to explain.

As if God himself wants to make me pay for the half-lie, a blonde woman with a stroller walks into the lobby, accompanied by two young children. I wince when I recognize her as Chamberlain's wife. The latter arrives in a tan suit with a broad smile to hug her and their children before they all head off to the elevator for lunch.

Jake didn't miss the scene either, and he turns to me with a cocked-up brow, challenging my statement. "I meant it very rarely happens," I try to justify, speaking the truth.

Something else catches my eye out there, and dread fills me. Mr. Sinclair is making his way through the open floor, and he glances our way. That only aggravates the stress clogging my throat. Before things can get worse, I close the privacy curtains of my office to isolate us for good.

I have no idea how to handle this, and I hate that the messed-up situation spoils our reunion. When I look up at him again, he seems to be experiencing his own crisis.

"Are you ashamed of me, Gen?" he asks. The hurt that lingers in his tone breaks my heart.

"No! I'm not. It's—"

"You are. You're ashamed that your colleagues know you're with a man like me."

"Don't be like that."

"Like what? Expecting to be treated with the same decency I treat you? I know who you are, Gen, and I want you exactly that way," he answers with contained frustration. "I would never try to hide you because we're an atypical match."

"I'm not trying to hide you. They just—they wouldn't understand."

"Why do you give a fuck about that?

"Because I've been working toward this for a decade! I've sacrificed too much for this job, this position, this career ..."

Silence follows my words, and I'm torn at the idea that I might have ruined his much-awaited return by being so cautious. Maybe he's right, and I shouldn't care about what they think of him. He matters infinitely more than they do. But it's hard to overcome my insecurities. I can't jeopardize everything I've worked so hard for. Not when we can be discreet about it.

"I'll go," he ends up deciding. "You're right, I should have texted you instead of trying to surprise you."

"Jake, please. You have to understand—"

"I don't *have* to understand anything, Genevieve."

Before I can stop him, he opens the door and leaves my office. Everyone outside hastily returns to their work, pretending they weren't listening through the poorly insulated glass.

Completely lost, I stand there for a couple of seconds, unsure what to do. I don't want him to leave like this, but I also can't cause a scene. My eyes are glued to his broad back, watching him walk away with frustrated and determined steps.

I genuinely can't believe he's doing this to me—having a temper tantrum at my place of work. Anger mixes in with my confusion, and that fuels my body into action. With hurried strides, I go after him, ignoring the looks my coworkers give me.

"Jake!" I whisper-shout after him. When he doesn't stop despite surely hearing me, I try again. "Jacob! Stop walking away from me."

This is ridiculous. I'm making a spectacle of myself. I catch up with him as he reaches the elevators, and to my dismay, one opens just in time for him to step inside. I don't have a choice, so I get on the ride with him. His expression as I join him in the back is closed off, and he barely grants me a glance, looking ahead to the doors that soon close, imprisoning us with ten people from my floor—including my boss. Today isn't going anywhere near as planned.

I'm unable to voice my frustration, so it builds up within me, ready to explode. I glare up at Jake, letting him know just how much I hate this ridiculous fit he's throwing.

The elevator slows down only a few floors below, so I grab his arm and pull him toward the parting doors. To my surprise and reassurance, he doesn't resist, allowing me to lead him out and then to the nearby stairwell.

"I can't believe you did this to me!" I explode once we're isolated, barely containing my voice.

He's just as annoyed as I am when he answers, "Did what? Surprise you for lunch?"

"You know those people are a bunch of gossiping snakes, and you still humiliated me in front of my entire floor! I don't need them to think that Edward dumping me has me spiraling into madness."

Although it wasn't my intention, the rational explanation that I fail to formulate offends him even more, the crease between his brows deepening. "Right, because you'd have to be completely mad to date me," he sarcastically replies, clearly hurt.

"That's not what I meant."

"Then what did you mean, Genevieve?" His words echo in the staircase, so much so that I worry they might have heard him three floors up and down.

"You know exactly what I meant. Stop being so damn stubborn!" I shout back.

When he grabs the handle of the door, a different kind of emotion sets in. Panic. I'm not letting him leave when we're in the middle of this mess. "Don't you dare open that door, Jacob!" I warn.

His hand freezes, and I let out a relieved breath. Gathering my thoughts for a couple of seconds, I try to express what I'm feeling.

"I understand that you find my attitude problematic, and I'm so sorry for offending you. But you know I have issues that I'm working on, Jake. I've made so much progress in the past few weeks, and I'm getting there, but I can't dismiss a decade of not feeling good enough with a snap of my fingers. Yes, I care what people think. I'm trying not to, but it's hard."

My eyes are teary, and I feel like I'm losing it. I'm so scared that he'll resent me even though I can't help it. His face conveys some remorse and a pinch of shock as he finally sympathizes with what I'm going through.

"But I wasn't ready for you to stumble into my workplace and expose our relationship to everyone like this. Maybe you didn't realize the kind of office this is, and how those assholes think we are better than the rest of the world. But it's so stupid because you're the best man I have ever encountered, and not a single one of them is a quarter as wonderful as you. I love you exactly the way you are, so it's not fair to say I'm ashamed of you just because I would rather they didn't end up spreading nasty gossip about us."

When I dare to look up again, he isn't as grave as he was moments before. Instead, he's grinning like an idiot, his gaze all soft as he stares down at me. Is he not taking me seriously? Does he think I'm joking or being too much? That brings back my anger at once.

"What?!" I snap, vexed.

"You just said you love me."

My eyes go round with bewilderment as I try to think back on what I said. *Oh, right.*

This is something I've barely admitted to myself yet, but now that I have, it's like the most obvious of truths. I'm madly in love with Jake, even though I refused to acknowledge those feelings because everything has been happening so fast. But even our calls have fed this warm sensation that glows from within whenever I hear his voice or think of him.

I am inarguably in love with Jacob Daniel Clarke.

Still in the heat of our fight, I defensively say, "Well, you don't deserve it, so I take it back."

"You can't take it back. It's already out there." It's irritating how joyful he looks.

"Watch me do it anyway, you stubborn assho—"

My words are cut short by his insistent lips. I'm stunned and a little whiplashed as he kisses me. My hands are still up in surprise by my sides when he pulls away. The earlier mood has changed, replaced with something longing and sensual. I don't want to fight anymore. Not when he looks at me with so much tenderness.

"It's been true for a while, you know?" I softly confess. "But the moment should have been romantic instead of right after I made you feel lesser than you deserve—like I'm trying to buy your forgiveness with it."

And I'm upset again, a solitary tear rolling down my cheek. This serves as a sour reminder that despite how well we work together, we're not compatible in so many ways. His world and mine are too different.

His gentle and tattooed hands, which I've missed so much, rise between us and grasp the sides of my face with all the tenderness in the world. His thumb wipes away the salty drop as he makes me look up into his green eyes.

"I love you, red," he professes with intensity. My heart flutters hectically, swelling against my ribs. "And it's been true for me for a while too."

The tension vanishes until all that's left is him and me, wrapped in a cocoon of want, need, and love. Jake loves me, and I'm officially the luckiest person in the world.

We move in unison to kiss, eager and impatient. Shivers travel throughout my whole body when our lips meet, half from the long separation and half from the love declarations.

Who would have ever thought this would be our outcome?

I can still remember with perfect precision the moment I first saw him entering the bar of The Plaza—so dashing and uniquely him. He's the one who convinced me to stick around and find out what could become of us. I owe it all to him. Everything.

"I love you," I repeat into our kiss, flooded by a wave of elation, gratitude, and raw adoration. "I love you so much."

"And I love you, red. Every fucking part of you, from your witty mind and clever tongue to the last freckle on your skin."

We get a little lost in it, overwhelmed by a desire to manifest all those feelings physically, but also eagerly getting reacquainted after nearly a week apart. His hands are fondling my behind and pulling me into his erection, and mine are locked in his hair to keep him close.

When a few chatting people pass right outside the door, I'm reminded that anyone could come in. And as much as I want to keep devouring him, I can't let someone find us like this. That could lead to repercussions.

Mustering all the strength I have in me, I rip myself away from Jake. He's not done with me though, so he hungrily lowers to my throat, kissing and nibbling the skin there.

"Jake, let's get out of here," I croak, resting a soothing hand in the middle of his broad chest. He nods, hungrily giving my collarbone more pecks, and eventually lets me go.

I adjust my hair, aware that I can't do anything about the rosiness of my cheeks, and take a deep breath as I reach for the handle. Right before I open it, Jake takes my free hand and gives it a gentle squeeze.

"I'm sorry, red," he whispers when I gaze up at him.

"For what?"

"I couldn't think past the excitement of seeing you again, so I didn't realize that coming here might be too much, too fast. It wasn't fair of me to force you into this, and you had every right to want to take your time. Especially since your ex works in the same building."

His apology is very welcomed, but I understand where he's coming from. I, too, might have done something foolish like this if the roles had been reversed. But his field of work would be chill and unbothered by my intrusion, whereas mine is full of stuck-up vultures.

"I hate that the people out there never bother to think past the tattoos and attitude," I say, emotions tightening my throat.

"They can think whatever the fuck they want. It doesn't matter. Not as long as the proper little Miss Kensington knows who I really am."

"She does. And she loves you to no end for it."

"Then fuck those snobs out there. I have everything I need."

We share one last kiss, intense and poignant, and as we pull away, we both utter at the same time, "I love you."

I'm grinning like a fool in love when we come out into the hallway, back to civilization. My hand is still in his, and I don't attempt to remove it. In fact, my hold tightens when I notice a familiar silhouette. Oh, crap. We're on *his* floor.

Eddie's on his way out for lunch, in the middle of a conversation with some colleagues, when he notices us. He freezes where he stands, his words dying in his throat. The moment is awkward, especially when he looks down at our joined hands. But I still don't rip it away. This is how I make up for my reaction earlier. This is how I accept Jake, proudly displaying that he's mine and I'm his.

Jake noticed him as well, and the two are in the midst of a staring contest. What am I supposed to do? How do I diffuse this?

Unsurprisingly, Edward is the first one to break, looking away to give his colleagues a vague gesture. "Go ahead, I forgot my wallet in my office," he tells them, visibly shaken up. The two men nod, but Eddie doesn't wait for that to turn around and walk away.

"Fucking wuss," Jake mutters under his breath before pulling me back on our way to the elevators.

The ride up is as silent as our way down, but it's charged with something else entirely. Our hands remain entwined the whole time, as if we both need this link. We're forced to let go when we walk out onto my floor though, but I can still feel his warmth all over my palm.

When we reach my office, Daisy springs out of her chair with an armful of printed sheets and a pen. "Good, you're back!"

"Yes?" I ask.

"You wanted to sign the new revised contracts before lunch so I could send them right away. We can do it this afternoon if you'd prefer."

"No, it's fine," I say with a smile.

She hands me everything as I walk up to my desk. I set the papers there and find the few pages where my signature is needed. Once I'm done, I return to her and hand back the contracts.

Jake's standing there a little awkwardly, and I decide it's another great way to show that I'm genuinely committed to this relationship.

"Daisy, this is Jake, my boyfriend," I explain as I intertwine our fingers again. "Jake, this is Daisy, my assistant."

"Ah, Gen told me she had a killer assistant," he greets with a nod, extending his free hand to shake hers.

"I'm doing whatever I can to make her work easy."

"You're succeeding," I kindly concede. "That's why I keep giving you raises. Can't afford to lose you."

She smiles, delighted by the compliment, and glances back at Jake, visibly affected by his allure. Then she shakes herself out of it and says, "I suppose I'll see you around, sir."

"Just Jake, dear. Only this one gets to call me sir in the right setting," he explains with a mischievous wink and a tilt of his head toward me.

I elbow his side, sensing my cheeks warming up, and Daisy lets out a small giggle before she leaves us and closes the door behind her.

"You're lucky she isn't part of the gossiping squad," I scold Jake with a frown.

"You told me before that she wasn't, red. I wouldn't have made the joke otherwise. If it were that bitch Isabel, or that other knobhead, though … Which one's Larry, by the way?" he wonders, glancing at the people in the open space who haven't left for lunch yet.

"The balding one with the dark blue suit and the yellow tie."

"Of course he's fucking balding." Jake easily finds him, eyes murderous, and then turns to me to wrap his arms around my waist. "So, what were you saying about getting out of here?"

"Did you come on your bike?"

"Yeah, I stopped by the flat to drop my things and hopped right on it."

"Then we can be at my place in under five minutes—ten if we stop by that Peruvian restaurant you liked last time."

"And what would we do there besides eat?"

I can't hold back the grin that takes over. "Maybe you can let me show you how much I've missed you? And maybe I can do the same in return?"

"Your break won't be long enough for that, red. But we can call it a warm-up for tonight."

"Sounds like a solid plan, yes."

We kiss once more, and this time, he's the one who puts an end to it, even when I whimper because I'm not ready to let go. "Your place," he asserts. "I've missed the taste of your pussy. And that thong I brought stopped smelling like you days ago."

"Used it too much, did you?"

"Been wanking with it from day one, red. But even that quality of satin and lace isn't as soft as your cunt wrapped around my cock."

Jesus Christ. Maybe we won't stop by the Peruvian restaurant after all, and I'll eat something in my office when I get back.

Impatient to get to my place, I abandon him to fetch my things from my desk, as well as my jacket on the coat rack by the door. With nervous hands, I arrange my hair, hoping I don't look as horny as I feel.

"Everything will be alright, sweetheart," Jake promises as he adjusts a loose strand behind my ear.

His reassuring words are enough to build back my inner strength, and I open the door.

I expect us to walk side by side to the elevator lobby and face the discreet looks and bold stares together, but he surprises me by taking an unexpected detour into the open space.

As soon as I realize what he's doing, my earlier nervousness resurfaces. No, no, no. He can't talk to Larry.

I catch up with him just as he's reaching out to my unsuspecting colleague. "Hi there, Larry," he calls out, making him turn around, surprised. Jake grabs his hand as if to shake it and inches closer, his imposing frame domineering compared to Lawrence's.

Instead of making it worse by panicking, I decide to trust Jake's judgment and stand there in silence, my hands clenched tightly around my things.

There's no one nearby, so only the three of us are privy to what Jake threateningly mutters right into Larry's ear. "Next time you use the words 'block of ice,' under any fucking circumstance, I'll break every last bone in your fingers. Is that clear?"

Larry hastily nods, his face oddly red. That's when I realize that between them, Jake is squeezing his hand in a death grip. I should do something to stop him, but this honestly feels good to watch.

"Good," Jake continues in a condescending tone. "My woman's off-limits to you, Larry, so keep her out of your fucking mouth."

My coworker nods again, and Jake releases him. Jake doesn't even grant him another look, grabbing my hand again and getting us back on our way to the elevators.

"That wasn't necessary," I feel compelled to say.

"Oh, it was very necessary, red. Made me feel fucking splendid."

How could I not love this man with every fiber of my being?

Taking him by surprise, I pull on his shoulder to make him lower and then claim his lips for a poignant kiss—right in front of everyone. They can think whatever they want. I don't care anymore.

When I pull away, he looks down at me with something that resembles gratitude. This was me accepting him, embracing him no matter what, and we're both aware of it.

"I love you, wombat," I whisper, still not over the fact that this is really out.

"And I love you, Miss Kensington."

While I didn't expect to take this step so soon, I'm glad it's done. Now, whatever happens, happens, but at least I was true to myself.

The next big step, and the most arduous of all, will be my parents. I can—worst case scenario—find a new job, but I can't get myself a new family, can I?

We'll get one shot at this, and I hope to God things will be fine. I can't lose this man. Not ever.

CHAPTER
Thirty-Two

Jake

"WHAT AN HONOR TO BE graced by your presence on a Saturday," Kill sarcastically muses.

"Did Gen finally come to her senses and decide she's had enough of you?" Eli adds.

We're in the back room of The Devil's Court, eating greasy burritos I got from the Mexican place at the end of the street. A mediocre bribe, but I hope they help earn my best mates' forgiveness. I've been remarkably single-minded lately, still trying to balance my obsession with Gen with my work and social life. Eli and Kill have been the ones I've neglected because they'll still be there by the time I figure it out.

"Sorry, mates. It's been a little chaotic lately."

"Oh, I know," Eli starts. "I live right below you, and those floors are *not* thick. I can hear just how chaotic your life has been."

The glare I send him doesn't stop him from smirking, proud of his joke. I don't like the fact that he can hear Gen in my bed, but it's not like we have a choice. "Care to move out?"

"Nah, I like the free rent."

"Dickhead."

Since he just took a mouthful of burrito, he can't insult me back but raises a finger for me to wait instead, signaling it's coming as soon as he's done chewing.

"Are things getting serious between you two?" Killian wonders.

I hide my wince by biting the fattest chunk off my lunch. It's been three weeks since we decided this was more than a sex thing. And one of those weeks was spent all the way in LA, working my arse off to spread my brand and network for The Parlour. And since I've not seen the guys as much as I used to, I haven't told them about the new developments.

Just to delay the inevitable, I take my time chewing and swallowing. Then, I straighten up slightly and meet their inquisitive eyes. "Gen and I are dating, and the first one who makes a joke about it will eat my fist."

Despite the threat, I fully expect one of them to say something. Instead, Eli gives me a shit-eating grin, clearly not surprised, and Kill lets out a discontented groan. Then, the former extends a hand over to Kill, who begrudgingly puts down his burrito to get his wallet from his back pocket. He produces a twenty-dollar bill and smacks it into Eli's awaiting hand.

"You fuckers bet on this?"

"And I won," Eli confirms, smirking like a twat. Maybe I should evict him. That'd feel good for a couple of days. But he's a great dog sitter, and I'd miss the idiot.

"Well, you were right. We've stopped pretending this was just a sex thing about three weeks ago."

"Three weeks?!" Eli echoes with shock. "Why the fuck did you not share this fact sooner?"

I raise a brow at him. "You two bellends bet on the success or failure of this relationship, and you wonder why I didn't tell you?"

"Yeah, that's fair."

There's nothing but the sounds of our chewing for a moment. The bar opens at eleven, but there's barely anyone until the middle of the afternoon. It still turns a profit though, especially since Kill is usually the one handling it—unlike today, with Wendy behind the counter.

"I still can't believe it," I spontaneously let out. "She's the finest woman I've ever fucking met, you know? And she wants *me*."

"Yeah, she's pretty hot," Eli concurs.

Kill shrugs, staring at the next spot he'll bite into. "Too skinny for me."

"I'm not talking on a physical level, you wankers. I mean *everything*. She's genuinely the best woman I've ever met."

"Careful there, Jakey. You sound like a man in love," Eli taunts.

I'm not good at hiding the grimace that twists my lips, and they both catch it. "Wait, are you—"

The question stops as they see me take another chunk of my burrito. Fuck, this shit won't be big enough to delay much longer. They patiently wait as I chew. Again, I'm in no hurry to swallow. As soon as I'm done, I take another bite.

"Ah, you're such a knobhead," Killian grunts, falling back into the old leather couch.

I usually don't mind sharing information with them, but this is all new, so I'm still figuring things out. I've had flings in the past with different levels of commitment, but this thing I'm building with Gen is miles from that. I've never considered spending the rest of my life with one person until her, and I'm slowly coming to terms with what it means. It's not like I miss my old ways—I wouldn't ever take it back—but I need to be sure that I'm the right person for her and will be able to satisfy her for years to come.

This time, when my mouth is free again, I feel more ready to clear things up. "I surprised her at work when I came back on Wednesday, and she wasn't ready for it. That place is way more stuck up than I expected, and those people nearly had a stroke seeing me. I thought I messed it up, you know? It was too much, too fast. And in the middle of the argument, when I'm feeling like a proper cunt for putting her through this, she tells me she loves me."

The guys are absorbed by my words, so taken they aren't even eating anymore. "What did you do?" Eli wonders.

"I said it back."

"Was it a mercy thing?" Kill asks.

"No, it was genuine because I'm madly in fucking love with the woman."

There's a silent moment, and Eli grins. "Aw, that's so cute. Don't they grow up so fast?" he jokes to Kill.

The latter ignores him to ask, "Isn't it quick?"

"I have no fucking clue. Maybe? I can't help how I feel."

"Maybe you should have waited a bit longer, then."

"I wasn't letting her be the only one saying it when I felt the same way, mate. She's got enough insecurities as it is."

"Yeah, Kill, be a gentleman. It's almost like you're not even British."

"Because I'm not, *eejit*. And if you think the Brits are gents, I have some bad fucking news coming your way."

I'm done with my burrito, so I squish the wrapper into a tight ball and throw it on the table. I'm wiping my mouth with a paper towel when Eli says, "I call dibs for when you two are looking for a godfather."

I know it's a joke, but fuck, the idea of putting a baby in Gen doesn't sound so bad. It's way too early for that, but I can imagine her stomach round with a child I'd put in there, and it makes my heart flip.

"Calm your tits, mate," I mumble, reeling back my premature thoughts. "We're not there yet. Far from it."

"Still, remember that I put you two in contact, unlike some compulsive liars who pretend they aren't British."

"Elijah, you really need to stop stirring shit before I make you eat it," Kill threatens.

It's good to spend time with these two cunts again. I missed their banter and the complete lack of judgment. All three of us have been making our way through life and success together, and those struggles really made us close like brothers.

"So, if everything's going so well, why aren't you spending your Saturday with Gen?" Eli asks.

"She's got a spa day with her best friend."

"Ah, the poor girl needs some rest from you. Makes sense."

"Go choke on a dick. They're dropping by The Parlour a bit later so I can give them a tour."

"Ah, nice! Hana struck me as a great person."

"She's taken. She's got a soon-to-be husband and a kid with him."

"I didn't mean it like that," Eli protests. "I'm not *always* trying to get laid, you know."

Kill and I exchange a knowing look. It's not that he's obsessed with finding a lasting bed partner, but we think he's got peculiar needs in the sack, and he can't find the right match for it.

"Anyhow, I should probably head back there and make sure everything's in order. Wouldn't want to disappoint the mother of Eli's potential godchild," I joke.

He smugly peers at Kill. "I got the job, bitch."

"Call me a bitch again, and I'll make you mine."

Yeah, this sounds like a good moment to leave before they start making out on the couch. As they launch themselves into another pissing contest, I gather the shit from our lunch and go throw it in the bin behind the bar. I give Wendy a wink and walk out into the gray day. Summer's not quite here yet, despite it being the first of July. It doesn't look like it's going to rain, though.

I arrive at The Parlour and enter via the main entrance. A few visitors are in The Gallery, admiring the detailed work of a street artist we're currently hosting. Tina, whose turn it is to handle The Gallery, is among them, chatting about the art with potential clients. She notices me when I step in, and we exchange a quick wave before I make my way up the stairs on the left. They lead to the waiting area of the tattoo and piercing parlor, with deep green lounge furniture, gold touches scattered in the space, and rich, vibrant tropical wallpaper. Three people are on the couches, skimming magazines we put there or our artists' portfolios and options for flash tattoos. No one's at the front desk, though, but a detector on top of the stairs makes a bell chime, and someone quickly comes out of the employees' private room.

"Hey, Zack," I greet him, coming up to the desk. "I have two people coming later today—Gen and Hana. Can you let me know as soon as they get here?"

"Yeah, sure. I'll buzz you. Do you want me to offer them a drink while they wait for you?"

"They won't have to wait, but thanks, mate." I'm about to leave when I remember something else. "Oh, and I went through those sketches you sent. I really like the pointillism thing you've been working on. Think you could expand on that one?"

"Yeah, sure! I've been trying to develop a technique for it, actually."

"That's great. It looks unique, and I know you've been trying to find your own style, which isn't easy when there are so many tattoo artists out there. But you're close, mate. I can feel it."

"Thanks, boss. That means a lot."

Before I settle in my office to work until my woman and her friend arrive, I peek inside the different booths to make sure everything's in order. Saturdays are our busiest day, so nearly everyone's in, working on some project with their clients.

Thinking I could do the same and be productive might have been naive of me. My mind is absorbed by the prospect of presenting my life's work to Gen.

Eli returns from The Devil's Court and stops by to taunt me some more. "We're really happy for you, bro," he ends up saying with a genuine smile and a pat on my shoulder. "Kill is still a bit on the fence, but he'll come around."

"Nat really did a number on him, didn't she?"

"Eh, he'll find someone with a touch soft enough to domesticate him, I'm sure of it."

"Can you imagine, though? Kill grinning like a lovesick fool," I point out, amused.

"Well, I couldn't imagine you doing those things, but here we are." I smile at his teasing, aware that I've probably been going around looking like an enamored twat. In a more serious manner, he adds, "I know I was joking and being a dick earlier, but I'm genuinely happy that I got to be a part of it, Jake. If you and Gen turn out to be the real thing, I'll have accomplished something great in my life, even if it's out of chance."

It's my turn to rest a hand on his shoulder. "You've done so much already, Eli. This whole place was possible thanks to you. The bar too. We give you shit, but we love you, mate."

A glimmer of mischief sparkles in his eyes. "Like you love Gen?"

"Shithead," I say with a chuckle. "Don't you have work to do? Earn your keep, will you? I'm tired of housing your lazy arse."

We might be back to insulting each other, but even then, the truths I uttered linger in the air while he makes his way out. We owe him everything we have, and I'll give him a roof over his head until the day I die.

Even just for introducing me to Gen. The fucker really had an epiphany with this one, and if I'm lucky, I'll thank him with my firstborn as a godchild.

As it turns out, I don't even need Zack to ring me because Gen sends me a text when their cab pulls up in front of The Parlour. I'm quick to save my work and head downstairs. I find them with Tina, who's just welcoming them.

Their backs are to me, and Gen's wearing a white dress that hugs her silhouette to perfection, and Hana has on jeans and a teal silk top.

"Ah, here's Jake," Tina says enthusiastically as I approach.

When they turn around, I'm close enough to slip an arm around Gen's waist. She's pliant in my hold as I pull her closer, and we share a small peck that lasts a little longer than it should.

"Hi, red," I greet her when I pull away, gazing down at her magnificent eyes and beautiful face.

"Hi, wombat," she murmurs in return.

"Do I get the same greeting?" Hana cheekily asks next to us. "Because I'm not opposed to it."

Gen and I chuckle as we separate, and I give her friend a brief but tight hug. "I'm so glad you two could make it. A tour of the place is long overdue, isn't it?"

"I guess you two were too busy testing the limits of the human body," Hana replies.

"I'll go back to the other clients," Tina tactfully offers. "Let me know if you need anything from me, Jake."

"Thanks, Tina." I turn to Gen and her friend. "So, this is The Gallery by The Parlour. We host artists of all backgrounds, and the exhibit changes every month or two. This one's a German street artist who isn't mainstream yet, but we're confident he'll blow up soon. Most of his pieces have already sold, and the exhibit opened last week."

"How do you select your artists?" Gen asks as we move closer to a painting.

"We work on submissions, where an artist sends us their portfolio. Tina has an art degree and a keen eye for it. Jude's the other one who handles The Gallery, and he's just as good."

"I'm better," Tina chimes in from the other side of the room. "I'm the one who came to you with this guy," she reminds me, gesturing at the art surrounding us.

"She's better," I admit with a whisper. "Don't tell Jude I said that though. Anyhow, we find our artists that way, and all three of us have to agree on the ones we select. When we're not entirely sure, we involve Eli because he usually knows what's trendy and what has the most likelihood of success."

Gen and Hana nod, absorbed by the fine details of a painting. Greifster—the artist's pseudonym—paints major cities in a way I've never seen before, with vibrant colors and organic shapes. From up close, it looks like a barely organized mess, but with a few steps back, it transforms into Paris, London, Berlin, Milan, New York …

Since they don't stay as long on the pieces, the two women end up separating. I come closer and rest a hand on Gen's hip as I bend to whisper in her ear, "Did you enjoy your day of relaxation, my love?"

I can hear her smile when she replies, "The masseuse told me I needed more rest because I kept dozing off."

"Did you explain your boyfriend's a greedy simp who can't get enough of you?"

"Told her I'd rather keep getting dicked down all night, but thank you for the advice."

I chuckle, knowing she didn't say that but liking the idea. She takes my hand in hers as she moves on to the next painting, and we intertwine our fingers together. We go around the whole space, and it doesn't matter if I already know all these pieces. I watch her as she discovers them.

Once they're done, we move on to the level above. "This is our lobby and waiting room," I explain when we get there. "I worked closely with an architect to create a space that makes sense, optimizing the natural sunlight on this floor. The wide and tall windows in the red brick are why the parlor is here and not downstairs. Each tattooing booth has its own window. The piercing ones are a little more sterilized and don't have any."

"Do you have a lot of clients?" Hana asks as she looks around at the few people there. Four on the couches and three at the reception desk, talking with Zack.

"We're on a fast climb to becoming one of the city's most reputable parlors," I explain. "It's great for us because we're very young, so it means a lot that we got people to trust us so quickly. We offer a safe space for all and a judgment-free experience. We do have some ground rules we're not willing to break, though."

"Like what?" Gen wonders.

I think about them for a second; I'm a little rusty regarding that topic. "No slurs or hate symbols, no face tattoos that haven't been thought of for at least six months, no tattoos on drunk people, no tattoos about or for someone you've known for less than a year—unless it's a direct family member. We have a few more, but overall, they're all common sense that we have to enforce because not everyone has it."

Hana is distractedly listening, looking at the flash tattoos in an album on the low table. My sexy redhead is still avidly paying attention right by me, though. "That makes sense. Did The Parlour ever get sued over a tattoo?"

"Never, no. We've also been experimenting with temporary ink, which fades off in around a year. And I'm in the process of acquiring the proper tools and license, as well as a new employee, so we can open a laser station for tattoo removal. We take the permanency of tattoos seriously, but we're also aware that people can change their minds with time."

Gen pulls me in by the hip. "Don't you dare remove a single tattoo off your skin, Jacob Clarke. Not even Eli's."

"That one's secretly your favorite, isn't it?"

"Yes, because you trusted an idiot to leave a permanent mark on you, fully aware that he'd make a mess. And it says a lot about the kind of person you are."

"Then I promise I won't remove it," I concede, lowering for a kiss.

As if we've summoned him, Eli's voice resonates in the hall. "Someone get a crowbar to separate those two."

"Speak of the devil," Gen humors, pulling away from me.

Eli comes to greet her with a hug, and Hana gets the same treatment. "Nice to see you again, ladies. Welcome to our humble abode. Do you like it?"

"It's amazing," Gen and Hana say in unison.

"Since you're so popular, is the waiting list very long?" Hana randomly asks.

"Why? Would you like to get one?"

"I've always wanted one but never took the leap. And I saw a few things in there that were amazing."

She points at the portfolio she was skimming through. "Ah, yes. Zack has a lot of success with women," I explain. "Very delicate and unique designs. He's here today, but he's on reception desk duties. Let me get him for you."

In three minutes, I have negotiated a consultation between Zack and Hana, for which they head to the private booths down the hall. Eli is in charge of the front desk instead, a task he accepts without much bargaining—probably sensing this is my chance to have Gen all to myself.

"Let me show you my office, an essential attraction of this tour," I explain, taking her hand in mine and leading her to a hallway.

"Is it now?"

As we pass various doors, I tell her what's in them, still trying to be a good host. "Tattoos, tattoos, piercings, this one too, tattoos again. That's Eli, and this one right here," I say, opening the door, "is my office."

I shove her in there, and before the door is even closed, I wrap her in my embrace and dive to claim her lips. She's as eager as I am, her hands clutching my hair as we devour one another. It feels like we've been apart for weeks rather than a day.

"Hmm, you smell good," I appreciatively mumble, licking the outline of her upper lip. "What is that? Lilac?"

"I think so."

"It suits you. But I prefer the smell of cherries. Makes me want to eat you whole, red."

She demands more kisses until we're both out of breath and need to recuperate. "You snuck out on me this morning," I groan right before I lower to press my lips on the vein pulsing at the base of her neck. "You have to stop doing that, Gen."

"I'll stop when you stop coaxing me into having sex every time I wake you up," she giggles.

I fill my hands with her bum and pull her closer, so tightly that I bet she can feel the piercings of my cock pressing through our clothes. "Don't act like you don't love it when I wake you with my tongue or fingers. One day, I'll be so very gentle that you'll wake up with my cock buried inside your wet cunt."

She shivers against me, her delectable moan resonating in my ear. "Would you like that, red? Would you like to wake up to me fucking you?"

"I would, yes. I *really* would."

We kiss again, unable to hold back, and it's dirty and sloppy this time, with our tongues wet and needy while our bodies grind where we crave to be united.

"I need you," she whimpers, reaching between us to open my jeans.

"You do? You want me to slam you into a wall and fuck you like I'm trying to make you go through it?"

"Oh God, yes!"

It takes everything I have in me, but I let go of the soft mounds of her arse and rip myself away from her lips. "Then next time, wake me up before you leave."

Once I'm sure she's stable enough on her feet, I release her, quenching my amusement at her appalled expression.

"So, this is my office. This is my desk. This is my computer. And this is my chair."

"Jake, I will find a more amenable boyfriend, I swear."

"Stop leaving me without a good morning kiss, and I'll be more amenable."

"It's not my fault if you're asleep when I do it."

Something warm lights up in me. "You do it?"

She rolls her eyes. "Of course, I kiss you before I leave. I don't sneak out because I want to annoy you but because you work too hard and deserve the rest after our nocturnal activities. Don't you think I'd rather wake you up and banter with you while we're having breakfast?"

I never thought of it that way, but it makes sense. My schedule isn't as tightly monitored as hers, so I usually decide on my own hours. As long as I get the job done, it doesn't matter when—except when I have a tattoo session. But if the roles were reversed, I might let her sleep as well.

"I forgive you, then," I say as I return her into my arms. "Do wake me up, though. I'd rather have the bantery breakfast than the beauty sleep."

"Alright."

When I lower to kiss her again, she avoids it and slithers out of my hold. "No, that ship has sailed. I'm the one withholding the sex now," she says with faked authority.

I stand there as she walks around the place, analyzing my stuff scattered around. Something catches her eye on the desk, and she reaches into the cup holding a few pens there. She smiles as she pulls out a hair stick—the one I stole during our first night together.

"I know this," she says with amusement.

"You never asked to have it back, so I reckoned you weren't missing it."

"Has it been here for long?"

"I found it in my jacket the morning after, and I dropped it in there."

Somehow, I expect her to reclaim it, but she surprises me when she drops it back into the cup. She likes the idea of it being there as much as I do. Still smiling, she continues her inspection.

"I love that you get to have Mulli in here," she notes, gesturing at the round bed on the floor.

"She was being lazy this morning, so I left her upstairs. I'll have to walk her before we head to The Devil's Court. Or maybe I'll take her with us."

"Yes, take her! I love spending time with Grubsy girl, but her selfish dad takes up all of my free time."

"She'll get more of you when I've had my fill."

Gen has gone full circle, and she's back with me. She looks up to meet my eyes, plastering her front to mine in a seductive way. "Which I hope will be never."

"You can bet your sweet arse on that."

I'm about to kiss her again when she escapes me once more and opens the door to the corridor. "I need to make sure Hana is planning something good. See you in a minute, wombat."

I can't even be mad about the blue balls. Not when I lean on the door frame and watch her walk that perfect bum back to her best friend. Thank fuck Eli and Kill aren't here to witness the idiotic smile tugging at the corners of my mouth.

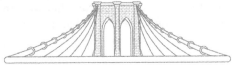

THE DEVIL'S COURT IS MUCH more lively at this hour. We're all settled in the main room around a barrel table with high chairs.

Gen, Hana, Eli, and I are here. Mulli is quietly lying down at my feet, and Kill sometimes pays us a visit when he gets a break at the bar.

Hana ended up deciding on a tattoo to honor her son. In half an hour, Zack drew a beautiful piece based on the birthmark Hana's baby has on his back—a brilliant idea she had. The delicate outline of the mark will become the background for a bouquet of lilies, which are Hana's favorite flowers.

"This place is incredible," she shouts over the table to be heard despite the band, Blood Red Shoes, on the stage. Kill did a great job finding them.

"Isn't it?" Gen adds. "We often have a few drinks here before we head off to Jake's. I love handing them their asses whenever we play pool in the back room."

"They keep playing with you? Don't they know you won state championships at Harvard?"

"They didn't until now, no."

Eli's jaw drops as his eyes dart to Gen. "Hey, not disclosing that is basically cheating! You owe me, like, a hundred bucks!" he shouts, apparently remembering those times they played for money and he lost.

"It was your idea to bet on it *five* times, sweet summer child," Gen taunts.

"You don't want to mess with a lawyer on this one, mate," I tell my friend before turning to Gen. "I, however, need to have a word with you, Miss Kensington."

She grins, not even trying to look apologetic. "A girl's gotta do what a girl's gotta do."

"You mischievous little minx," I grunt, pulling her closer as if she's not nearly on my lap already. "You're full of surprises."

"Gotta keep the mystery alive somehow, you know?"

Eli and Hana launch themselves into a random discussion I can't hear, and Gen and I watch the stage for a moment.

"I have something I want to ask you," she says right in my ear after a while.

"Yes, I'll still play pool with you, even though I know you're a state champion."

She giggles. "That's not it, but thank you, wombat. My brother is hosting a dinner for Independence Day, and he's invited me. I don't know if you have plans already, but he knows I'm seeing someone, so he suggested I bring you along. Would you like that?"

I'm a little shocked and honored that she's making such a considerable leap like this. Her family has always been a worry where I'm concerned.

"Will your parents be there?"

"God, no. They always celebrate it in DC, using their network to get invited to the most exclusive parties. It would be just my brother's family and us. His daughter was recently diagnosed with generalized anxiety disorder, and they don't want to overwhelm her while they're working on it with a therapist."

She told me her brother isn't as uptight as her parents, so it should be okay. "The guys and I planned a barbecue on the roof with a few friends. But they'll understand if I tell them why I'm dropping out."

"To be fair, it'll probably be over by nine. Then we can attend your rooftop party, which, knowing you guys, will last well into the night."

"Probably will, yes," I concede with a smile. "I'll still have to smoke the meat for them and prepare the sides because these two twats can't cook for the life of them. They'll handle the drinks and grilling, though."

"You're so sexy when you take charge like that," she amorously says, grabbing my jaw to pull me in for a kiss.

I know Kill will probably give me shit about it and say it's going too fast, but I don't care. This doesn't feel fast to me because I know what I want.

This woman.

For as long as she'll have me.

CHAPTER
Thirty-Three

Gen

ONE THING I'VE LEARNED ABOUT Jake is that he isn't an anxious person. He breezes through life with ease and doesn't bother with emotions as useless as stress or nervousness. As we make our way out of his car to enter my brother's building in South Central Park though, the confident and easygoing Jake I've come to know and love is entirely gone. The man walking by my side is a jittery mess who can't stop adjusting his necktie.

"I told you the tie wasn't a good idea," I point out as we reach the entrance.

He opens the door for me, holding a massive bouquet over a big cake box while I have a bag thrown over my shoulder holding a few things. We came bearing gifts, hoping it would help our odds.

"I should have listened," he agrees, tugging at the tie yet again. "I feel like I'm being choked."

"You prefer it when I do it, don't you?" I tease.

Even though I'm the one bringing it up, heat spreads across my cheeks while he smirks. We got a little carried away this weekend, and I asked to take the lead and try a few things. Choking him while I passionately straddled him was among them, and he guided me through it until we both orgasmed together.

The concierge in the luxurious hallway knows me enough to require nothing more than a nod, so we head to the elevator lobby.

When Jake checks his reflection in the tall mirror to our right and adjusts his clothes, I bite back a smile. "Relax. My brother isn't as intimidating as my parents."

He's wearing a dark suit, which looks fantastic on him, and a blood-red tie. It works well with the reddish tattoos creeping up his neck. I know that he decided to wear a tie in an attempt to hide those as much as possible. He even suggested borrowing my foundation to hide it. I pointed out that not only do our skin tones not match, but it would also be pointless. My brother will eventually learn the truth.

"Everything will be fine, wombat," I promise, offering him an encouraging smile. When he bends down for a kiss, I gladly give it to him. He needs strength and courage.

I'm not as confident as I look, but I pretend for his sake. After tonight, my parents will eventually hear about Jake, since Gerry might mention him in passing. He works in tandem with our father, after all, so it's a high probability.

But it's alright because I'm serious about this man. This isn't a fling or a quarter-life crisis. If I can't have him, I'll be miserable for the rest of my life.

We enter the elevator together when it arrives and face the doors once inside.

"Do you think they'll like the pavlova? Maybe I should have baked something more American, like a red velvet or—"

"It'll be perfect, Jake. I'm still mad you didn't make a tiny one for me to try beforehand."

"I'll remember for next time."

I force him to meet my gaze and utter, "I love you, Jake, and everything will be okay."

"I love you, red. And at the very worst, we'll relocate to Australia. I haven't been since I left, but I'm sure we can be happy there."

I giggle. "We can be happy anywhere as long as we're together."

"Exactly."

"Oh, by the way. Gerry is Gerard Kensington the Fourth, and if this pops up in the conversation somehow, *please* do not make fun of him for it. He hates it more than you can imagine."

"The fourth? Does it give him social superiority compared to your ex, who was only a third?" he jokingly asks.

"I'm serious, Jake. It's a sour topic for him."

"Alright, alright. I'll behave."

He takes my hand, squeezing it a little too tightly, but I don't complain. I'm touched that he's so nervous because it shows how much he cares about me. His usual nonchalance is nowhere to be seen because he realizes how much this matters to me.

When the doors part again, he clenches my hand harder, and I lead him into the single-door hallway. I ring the bell, apparently too fast. "Wait no—Shit, I needed a second, Gen."

"Take it now, I can hear someone coming."

Sure enough, Malory opens the door, elegantly dressed in a peach cocktail dress. Her smile barely flinches when she goes from me to Jake, and I know her shock is due to the stark contrast between him and Eddie rather than any kind of judgment. She's too good for that and way above that kind of prejudice.

"Hi, you two," she greets after a brief second. "Come in!"

She moves to the side to let us in, and I say, "Hi, Mal. This is Jake. Jake, this is Malory." When she extends a hand, Jake shakes it on autopilot. Then he stands there, tense and unsure of what to do. "The flowers are for you," I say in his stead, picking them up and handing them to her, "and Jake baked the dessert, as discussed. It needs to go straight into the fridge."

Gerry arrives in the small lobby at this precise moment, and just like Mal, he glitches when he sees Jake. Like his wife, he masks it swiftly and comes to us. "You must be Jake," he greets.

"And you must be Gerard."

I think I know this man too well because I can tell he actually restrains himself from adding "Kensington the Fourth." He thankfully does, and the two men cordially shake hands.

"Call me Gerry, please. Come in! The girls have been waiting for their favorite aunt all day long."

"I'm their only aunt," I slip to Jake as we follow them further in. "And they only like me because I buy their love with gifts every time I'm here."

The girls, ages nine, seven, and four, rush to us as soon as we come into view. We reach the kitchen area despite their enthusiastic greetings, and I set the bag on the counter while Mal helps Jake find some room in the fridge for his pavlova.

"Aunt Genny! Did you bring gifts?" The eldest, Marigold, asks.

"I'm afraid I didn't, sorry girls. But my boyfriend Jake did!"

"You have a boyfriend named Jake? What about Uncle Eddie?"

I send Gerry a conflicting glance, not sure what to say. He offers no assistance, shrugging instead. What do children this age understand? "Eddie and I aren't in love anymore, so we've separated."

"Oh, like Anna and Hans! Now, she loves Kristoff!"

Confused, I gaze at my brother again. "It's from *Frozen*," he explains. *Oh.*

"Are you Jake?" the youngest one, Poppy, asks when he joins us along with their mom.

"I am."

Poppy has the broadest grin as she says, "Aunt Genny said you have gifts."

"I do."

When she notices Jake's hands, all thoughts of gifts are gone. Curious, the little girl takes one to look at his knuckles up close. We watch, amused, as she rubs the ink there, trying to remove it.

"Is it Sharpie?" she asks.

"No, it's a tattoo. It's ink in the dermis layer of the skin."

She doesn't seem to understand what that means, but she tries to lift the buttoned wrist of his sleeve. "That's enough, pumpkin," Mal tells her.

"It's fine," Jake counters. "I can show her if that's alright with you."

"Of course."

Jake crouches down and undoes the button at his wrist to start methodically rolling it up over his muscular forearm. Marigold joins us, curious as well, and Camellia observes from afar. Once more of his forearm is revealed, the girls analyze the drawings inked there. Then, Poppy shows interest in the other side, and he indulges. When the little girl tugs on his necktie, I can guess the relief within him as he tugs it off and opens a couple of buttons at his neck to move the collar around and show the girls.

The softness with which he handles them is endearing, and I can swear I hear my ovaries chanting praises for him.

"Are you our new uncle?" Marigold asks.

Jake's a little taken aback by the question while I wince. "I can be if you want, sweetheart. And do you want to hear a secret?" The girl nods energetically. "I'm a lot more fun than Edward."

My nieces look up at me, awaiting confirmation, and I give them a nod. "He's a lot of fun, yes."

"Can I draw on you, too?" Poppy asks as a result.

"Maybe another time, sweetheart."

My niece pouts, so I take out the bottle of wine and hand the bag to Jake, who's still crouched to be level with the girls. The gifts should distract them away from the tattoos.

"So, I talk a bit funny because I'm from Australia. Do you know where that is?" Jake asks. The two youngest shake their heads while the oldest nods. "It's all the way on the other side of the world. We walk upside down there, and we have very special animals." He reaches into the bag and takes out a plush koala. "Ever heard of koalas?" he asks. This time, they all nod. "Well, koalas come from Australia, just like me. And they only eat eucalyptus leaves. This one's for you, sweetheart," he adds, handing it to the youngest. She takes the koala with keen excitement and examines it all over before hugging it. "Then we also have what's called a platypus, which is an animal that lactates like a cow and lays eggs like a duck."

The plush platypus goes to the eldest. The girls are entirely entranced by Jake, and I'm not surprised that his aura also works on kids. There's something about this man that pulls people in, some irresistible magnetism. It's good to see him relaxing already, his worries slowly fading.

"And I'm sure you've heard of kangaroos, Camellia," he continues, addressing the middle one by her name. He asked me many questions about her generalized anxiety disorder to make sure he'd quickly put her at ease. I explained that her selective mutism is getting better, but she tends to be shy around strangers and closes off. Which is why he took extra care of her with this gift. Camellia nods in response, and he pulls out a plush kangaroo from the bag. She takes it without too much hesitation, which is a great sign. "There you go, sweetheart. Did you know that mama 'roos have a pouch on their belly where they keep their babies?"

She nods again, so Jake continues, "I wonder if this one has anything in her pouch?"

Excitedly, Camellia looks into the pouch. When she finds the chocolate and candies Jake hid in there—with Malory's prior approval—her eyes light up. Jake gives her one of his charming winks, and she darts off with her sisters, who have already disappeared somewhere with their new toys.

"Thank you for your patience with them," Gerry says. "They don't have anyone with tattoos in their lives, so that was new to them."

"It's alright. I'm used to being the room's circus freak." Although his words are meant with humor, I'm compelled to lay a supportive hand on his forearm.

"Don't we get plush toys as well?" Malory jokes to lighten the mood.

"The wine and flowers will have to do. I got this one a wombat, so she has something to cuddle when I'm not there," he replies with amusement, gesturing toward me.

He did get me a wombat plush, which I'm only allowed to have in the bed when my living one isn't available. But while I love the gesture and laughed so much when I unwrapped it, I'm not sure I want my brother to think I'm regressing back to childhood.

"Drinks?" I suggest to change the topic.

"Great idea," Mal approves.

They offer to serve a kind of spritz they discovered during their trip to Saint-Tropez earlier this year, and we both agree to try it out. As he gets started, Gerry explains it's made with elderflower liqueur, and Jake, who's definitely feeling more at ease, offers to help him. I nervously eavesdrop while trying to appear inconspicuous. The girls are out of sight, probably in their playroom.

"Oh, you own a bar?" Gerry asks after Jake reveals that fact.

"With two of my mates, yeah. I used to help out behind the counter for a bit, but I'm shi—bad at not breaking bottles. Also, getting pissed with the patrons wasn't encouraged."

"Gen, can you help me with the appetizers?" Mal asks, forcing me to trust the process and leave the men alone.

Things go pretty smoothly though, and we all settle in the lounge area. "Jake was telling me he owns a gallery," Gerry explains to his wife as we get seated.

"Oh, really?"

"Yeah, it's been quite the success so far."

I watch with nothing but pride as Jake talks to them about his life's journey, and I can tell they're both impressed by everything he's accomplished. He's just getting to the ethical values of his parlor when Poppy reappears and snakes her way in front of him. Very proudly, she shows him her arm and the colorful doodles drawn there with a felt-tip pen.

"Poppy, what did you do?" I ask with widened eyes.

"Cami and Goldie helped me!" she reveals with a proud grin. Her sisters choose that moment to join us, their arms also filled with drawings. They look very happy with themselves in their nice evening dresses. Jake is as tense as I am, waiting for their parents' reaction.

"Girls, what did we say about using pens?" Mal asks with a slightly reprimanding tone.

Marigold looks down, putting her hands behind her to hide her arms. "We can only use them on paper."

"At least this will be easier to clean off than the walls," Gerry points out with unmasked amusement. "Is that a dolphin I see?" he then asks Camellia.

"Yes, I did it myself!"

That's enough to dissipate the tension, and the girls return to their jovial little selves as they show us the reason they've been so quiet for the past twenty minutes. When Mal suggests that their nanny help them remove the drawings, my nieces beg to keep them on for the evening. Although reluctantly, their parents agree—as long as they stay away from the white couch.

"You were telling us about your parlor?" Malory tells Jake once the girls are off again, playing with their new toys this time.

Jake returns to the recounting of his many accomplishments, and I'm touched by how genuinely charmed and interested my brother and his wife seem. It's not just me. This man is something else. Seeing him in this setting only proves it. My brother isn't as demanding as my parents, but he remains hard to impress. He has been surrounded by successful and influential people since childhood, after all. Despite that, I can tell that Jake is slowly but surely earning Gerry's seal of approval.

"Refill?" I offer, noticing our glasses are empty.

"I'll help you," my brother insists, picking up two glasses.

We walk together to the kitchen, and as we work on the next round of cocktails, I watch Jake and Mal have a few laughs.

When Poppy comes to demand some attention, Mal's quick to pick her up and set her on her lap, her love for the girl dripping from every pore. This is something our mother never did for us, and it's good to see that the generational trauma ends with Gerry and me. I still can't believe he defied all odds and ended up marrying a woman so different from our world. Maybe there's hope for Jake and me after all.

"She's too good for you," I remind Gerry with a smile.

His eyes are on Jake when he replies, "And *he* is too good for you."

I laugh and admire from afar the dashing Aussie who stole my heart. "I know, right? Isn't he amazing?"

"I'll be honest and say I was a little worried when I heard you and Eddie separated and that you were already seeing someone new. Then, when I saw him in the hallway earlier, I thought you'd lost your mind or wanted to give our parents a stroke. But now I get it, bug. He's vividly interesting and remarkably charismatic."

"He is. And I swear, he's such a great man. His values are amazing, and the respect he has for me is beyond anything I ever imagined. He's had a great influence on me."

"I can tell. I don't think I've seen you this alive and glowing since Vicky's accident."

The reminder of my twin, which always causes so much turmoil, only unleashes a slight twinge in my heart this time. "I haven't been this happy since that day, no. I actually can't tell if I was ever happy those past ten years or only convincing myself of it."

Gerry sighs, gazing at our respective partners, still having their laughs together.

A notification dings, and he pulls out his phone from his pocket right beside me. Without a thought, I casually glimpse at the screen when he checks it. Since I notice the sender is our mother, I feel comfortable enough to check on the message as well. The words written on the screen chill me to the bone, blood draining from my face.

VIVIENNE

> Traffic was horrendous, but we're nearly there.

He doesn't bother to reply and returns the phone to his pocket.

"What was that?" I ask, fearing I already know the answer.

"The parents canceled their trip to DC and are coming here instead."

"What?! Ger, tell me this is a joke."

"Didn't you know? Mal was supposed to text you."

"I think I'd remember if I'd been warned. I'm not ready to introduce Jake to them!"

"Shit, maybe I was supposed to text you. I'm sorry, Gen. I didn't know he was covered in tattoos, so I didn't realize it would be tricky."

"Tattoos or not, this is bad, Gerry. So bad."

I try to assess the situation, wondering if we can make a break for it and be gone before my parents arrive. To make sure we don't cross their path, we can take the stairs down the forty-seven floors. I'd rather do that in these shoes than face my parents meeting Jake.

"Do they know we're here?" I question.

"I told them, yeah." Gerry then looks like something clicks in his mind, and his eyebrows twitch. "Come to think of it, they canceled their DC plans shortly after I told them you were coming with someone."

Crap, so they're coming to meet Jake. An escape would only delay the inevitable. They will eventually meet him, one way or another.

"Do you think maybe they won't mind?" I try, not even believing it myself.

"Of course they'll mind. But he is your choice, Gen. You have to stick to it. If I'd listened to them, I would never have married the small-town nurse. But here I am."

"It's not the same, Ger. We all owe Malory for saving your life. But Jake, he's …"

"It doesn't matter. He's the person you're choosing."

He is, and I have no doubt about it. But there's no way they'll ever accept him, and the strained relationship I have with them will only worsen. Things are hard enough as they are, and I don't think I can handle more resentment and disappointment on their part.

What am I supposed to do when they insist Jake is a mistake and demand that I fix it?

My hands tremble as I set the two cocktails on the coffee table. "Excuse us for a second," I tell Mal, grabbing Jake and tugging to force him up.

He's understandably confused as I drag him to my brother's home office, but he complies without protest. When the door closes behind us, he smoothly wraps an arm around my waist and pulls me in.

"No, this isn't that kind of private moment," I correct him, pushing against his chest.

It takes me a few seconds to gather the courage to break it to him. He'll be as torn as I am and return to his earlier state of anxiousness. "I-I'm so sorry," I stammer at first. "I didn't realize this would be happening, but my parents are coming."

"Your parents?" he echoes. I nod. "Here?" Another silent confirmation. "Fucking hell."

"We can leave," I suggest. "We can take our stuff and go wait it out in the stairwell until Gerry texts me that the coast is clear. But they know we're here, so it might look bad."

"I was already stressed about meeting your brother, red, but this …"

"I know, I'm so sorry, wombat. That's why you get to decide. Either we leave before they arrive, or we come to terms with the fact that it'll happen either way, so we rip it off like a Band-Aid."

He intently thinks about it for several seconds, and I gnaw at my lower lip, my turmoil matching his. "What do you want?" he ends up asking.

"What I really want is to go back to five minutes ago, when everything was going so well, and you were being so perfect with my nieces that I was considering having you put a baby inside me when we get back to your place."

Although it's a joke, the words have a lot more weight than I intended, especially since we haven't talked about children yet. Jake's a little troubled too, and I internally scold myself for piling on more complications to this already tense moment.

"Well," he says after a while, "now I want to go home and pretend we're doing that. We'll call it training before the real thing."

I release a breathy and reassured giggle. We're on the same wavelength, as always, and no matter what happens, things will be fine between us.

"I love you, Jacob Clarke," I assert, framing his dashing face between my hands. "And I know in my heart that as long as we stick together, things will be fine."

"I love you, Genevieve Kensington. And again, Australia is a great alternative if tonight goes to shit."

"I'd face the venomous snakes, human-eating sharks, and crawling bugs for you."

"And I'd face your parents. A much harder task, if you ask me."

I laugh again before pulling him in for a kiss, recharging our courage and strength.

As we head back to the others, I see Jake rolling down his sleeves. "That's useless, wombat. Unless you can wear gloves and a turtleneck."

"Shit, why didn't I think of that?"

I take his hand, interlocking our fingers together. "Don't hide who you are. Be exactly as I love you."

"Your parents won't appreciate it."

"Then they'll miss out on someone fantastic."

When we enter the living area, Malory comes to us with an apologetic look on her face. "Gen, I'm *so* sorry. I thought Ger texted you, and he thought I did. We've been so busy with work, the girls, and Camellia's therapy that it completely slipped our minds."

"We're good, I think. Jake will be his charming, lovable self, and my parents might act like sensible human beings for once in their lives."

"Okay, great. Because they are coming up right now," she says with a wince.

My heart drops down to my stomach, a dreadful shiver crawling up my back under the dress. My skin there is probably covered with a rush of cold sweat, and I hate the ghastly feeling twisting my guts. Why must things be so complicated?

Gerry is out of sight, probably waiting for our parents in the entryway, and we sit back on the couch with Mal. Jake's hand is still in mine. His iron hold is unrelenting, but he doesn't squeeze or hurt me.

"How did you two meet, by the way?" Mal asks, probably trying to jump-start a conversation as we wait.

Jake and I exchange a slightly panicked look, both realizing our mistake. Why didn't we think of that? Why didn't we come up with some elaborate lie to explain how two people as different as we are ended up in a relationship?

Weirdly enough, the front door opening saves us from this uncomfortable moment. The relief instantly dies when I hear Vivienne's voice. "Can you believe this traffic? Next time, we'll take the helicopter," she pesters from the hall.

"Maybe it's a good thing we didn't fly out to DC after all," Father adds.

I only realize that I'm clamping Jake's hand when his thumb gives me a soft caress, so I loosen my grip. As soon as they come into view, preceded by Gerry, I nervously spring to my feet, ripping my hand away. My heart's hammering in my chest as I watch them come further in, and it suddenly stops when their attention narrows on Jake. He stands once they're near, and I guess he has clammy palms as well when he wipes them down the front of his pants.

Mal's the first one to greet them, and then it's my turn to offer a single kiss to my mother and father.

"This is—" My voice breaks, cut off by my nerves. "This is Jacob Clarke. I'm—We've been seeing each other for a couple of months."

I don't even think I'm breathing as they take him in, their haughty looks assessing him from head to toe. Mother's eyebrow quirks up with judgment, and my father's lips stiffen into a thin line.

Jake's the one courageously breaking the silence. "It's an honor to meet you, Mr. and Mrs. Kensington. You've raised a wonderful woman," he diplomatically says, pressing a hand in the middle of my back and extending the other one to shake theirs.

My father takes in the tattooed forearm and knuckles for a few seconds and eventually shakes Jake's hand. Then my mother does the same, and I'm amazed that they aren't already voicing their discontent.

The girls compliantly come when their mother calls for them, and horror appears on Mother's face.

"What happened to your arms, girls?"

"We have tattoos, like Uncle Jake!"

Vivienne freezes, and I'm convinced this will be it. This is when she'll blow up and curse me out for bringing a man like him into this family.

To my surprise, she says nothing, recomposes herself, and gives each girl a dry peck on the forehead. Father does the same, and we all migrate toward the living room.

When Mal asks what drinks she can get for them, Mother waves an unbothered hand. "Stay with us, dear, and ask the help to handle the drinks."

"We've dismissed them for the day," Gerry explains. "The nanny is the only one still on duty."

"She can pour wine, can't she?"

There's a long, awkward silence, and I can *feel* Jake's uneasiness at Mother's appalling behavior. "I'll do it," Malory insists. "Gen and Jake came with a bottle of Bordeaux that looks delectable."

Mother doesn't even try to hide her discontent, but she gives a vague nod and sits down. The tension lingers as we all settle on the couches. When Mal returns with glasses for my parents, she manages to spark up a conversation.

"So, what happened to the senator's Independence Day party in DC?"

"I thought we would shake things up this year," Vivienne explains. "And you know, with those eco-terrorists everywhere, taking the jet for an evening is just asking for trouble."

"Taking the chopper to avoid traffic is fine though," Jake can't help but point out.

My eyes go huge with shock, and I send him a panicked glance. My parents aren't receptive to humor, especially not at their expense.

Mother ignores his apt but unwelcomed remark and continues, explaining how those political events are filled with phony guests anyhow, and she'd much rather spend the Fourth with family. That's a first.

Jake and I are silent participants as Gerry and Mal lead the conversation, and it might be better this way. Especially if Jake can't stop himself from stirring shit. Mal, who's decidedly a great hostess, loops us now and then in the discussion, and the tension slowly dissipates.

Nothing bad has happened by the time we move on to the dinner table. Mother complains again about the lack of staff, arguing it was silly to let them have their day with their family. Jake is seated beside me, and I see the way he clenches his hand on the table. I mindlessly take it and lower it on my lap, giving him a gentle graze. He relaxes, molding it on my thigh and focusing on that instead.

Vivienne and Gerard Kensington aren't the most palatable people out there, but they are the only parents I have. And really, one can get used to this level of entitlement.

It happens over half an hour after they arrived, but Father finally acknowledges Jake directly and asks, "So, what do you do for a living, Mr. Clarke?"

Jake goes over his accomplishments for the second time tonight, using terminology that sounds a lot more serious this time around. Honestly, I'm amazed that my parents aren't having a stroke or throwing a fit. I expected anything but this somewhat indifferent reaction.

Was I wrong in thinking they would disapprove of him?

CHAPTER
Thirty-Four
Gen

RIGHT BEFORE WE MOVE ON to the pavlova, I excuse myself from the table and head off to the bathroom. I do my business quickly, so Jake isn't alone for too long. When I open the door, finding someone standing right behind it makes me jump back with a small gasp.

Vivienne is right there, with nothing but annoyance plastered on her botoxed features.

"Alright, you've had your fun. Now you can stop," she utters, her tone ice cold.

"What do you mean?"

"Whoever that is you came with, he needs to leave without making a scene."

"Jake? He's my boyfriend, I told you."

"No, he's not," she maintains, shaking her pristine head.

"I assure you he is."

"He's someone you're using to get back at me for some reason. I told you to return with Edward, so now you're acting up. This is late teenage angst, your puerile way to rebel. And frankly, I find it ridiculous. God knows you've had a solid serve of it already. But it was expected when you were a teenager. It isn't acceptable anymore."

I'm so lost and confused that I don't know what to say. I always knew Jake might be a problem for my parents, but the past couple of hours gave me hope that I was wrong. Turns out I was just terribly naive.

"I thought—I thought things were going great. You and Father didn't—"

"The only reason we didn't cause a scene was to not ruin these celebrations—even though you took care of that yourself by bringing that man into it."

"He's a great person, talented, and sweet, and funny, and clever. I've never met anyone who treats me like he does, like a queen, like—"

"Oh, please. Of the many problematic things you are, Genevieve, stupid isn't one of them. You can't possibly believe that you and that man can have any kind of future together."

She could have slapped me and it would have hurt less than this awful stabbing sensation in my chest.

"Edward told me, you know," she adds, filled with disappointment. "He told me you were seeing someone new and that I'd be ashamed of the kind of person he is. But even the warning wasn't enough to prepare me for the creature you chose to burden us with."

She knew about Jake already? Edward, that tattling asshole, told her?

"Is this why you canceled DC and came here tonight? You wanted to see him since Gerry told you I'd be accompanied?"

"Can you blame a mother for wanting to protect her child? I'm only looking after you, darling. You might think you know it all at your age, but that's clearly a misconception."

"I'm mature enough to decide for myself, Mother. Jake is a fantastic man, no matter what you think."

"A fantastic man? Have you no shame? To think you've exposed your own nieces to him! Have you seen the influence he's had on them already? They look ridiculous with those drawings all over. What comes next? Alcohol? Drugs?"

"The girls like him! More than they ever did Edward. Camellia even spoke to him a few times. I promise, Mother, he's not what you think."

"He is a man of nothing but sins, Genevieve. Piercings, tattoos, alcohol … That man lives off people's desperation and mental imbalance. And you want me to believe he's a good person? That you're not using him to punish your father and me?"

"He is an artist, and just because you can't understand his craft doesn't mean it's—"

"Why do you insist on being a perpetual disappointment?" she cuts me off, her tone so cold it freezes my blood. "Have you not done enough as it is? Must you plague this family with another tragedy by bringing that vile, lowly freak into it? I will not tolerate—"

"I beg your fucking pardon?"

Jake's threatening mutter sends everything flying in my mind, shattering the confusion into utter panic.

My heart is in my throat, taking so much space that I can't fill my lungs. When I see the pure rage plastered on Jake's features, a sensation of nausea spreads within me and persists no matter how much I try to swallow it back. This can't be happening. Jake having a hot-headed reaction to Edward is nothing like him going off on my mother. In my heart, I didn't care about Eddie, but this is something else entirely.

Which is why I need to stop it before it even happens.

Vivienne looks unfazed, glaring at Jake like he's nothing but a pest. "This is a family matter. You're not concerned by this conversation."

"I'm *directly* concerned. The fuck is your problem?"

"Jake!" I intervene, refusing to let this blow out of proportion. "I'm handling this."

My interjection might have worked had Mother not added to it. "My daughter is too good for you, and if you don't realize that, you're a fool."

"Oh, I realize that. Your daughter is phenomenal, and I'm blessed to be deserving of her affection. But do *you* even know how amazing of a person she is?"

He points at the other end of the hallway, toward the others still seated at the dinner table. "I saw your eyes roll when she talked about that promotion she's after. I saw your lips pinch whenever she laughed as if it made you physically uncomfortable to witness her happiness. So, again, what the fuck is your problem? Why do you loathe your own daughter?"

"Jacob, that's enough!" I intervene.

"Is it? Are you content with this situation? She berates you, and you present the other cheek again and again."

"The complex relationship I have with my daughter is none of your concern, Mr. Clarke," Mother interjects.

"That's where you're wrong. I'm making your daughter's happiness my concern and priority. And you seem hell-bent on destroying it."

I can't even talk, at a loss for words, trying to figure out how to defuse the situation. This is a nightmare, and I'm paralyzed with fear.

"I don't need lessons in parenting from someone like you," Vivienne venomously hisses. "I have no doubt that you have little bastards roaming this city, but I will deal with Genevieve the way I see fit."

"Do you think she'll bear it for much longer? You're going to lose a second daughter, and you'll have only yourself to blame for it."

I don't know what comes over me, but I aggressively shove my hands into Jake's chest, overtaken by a mix of panic, guilt, and fright. "I said that's enough, Jacob!" I shout.

He looks dumbfounded, as if I'm wrong for trying to stop him from ruining everything. Can he not see all the irreparable damage he's causing? It will take months, *years,* to make up for this.

I've worked so hard to maintain a cordial relationship with my parents, bitten my tongue hundreds of times, swallowed back my pride, endured the underhanded remarks ... And he's destroying all of it because he can't contain himself for a single evening.

"This is the man who treats you like a queen?" Mother asks with acidic irony. "Maybe you two deserve each other after all."

I stand there as if my stilettos are glued to the hardwood floor while she makes her way out, returning to the others.

"What a heinous bitch," Jake mutters under his breath as soon as we're alone.

"She's my *mother*, Jake!" I vehemently say.

"That woman doesn't deserve an ounce of the respect and affection you have for her."

"Weren't you the one saying people should cherish their mothers? This is my life, and I will decide what I can and can't have in it!"

"So because she gave life to you, she gets to treat you horribly for the rest of it?"

"I endure it because of Victoria, okay?!"

For a couple of beats, he tries and fails to make sense of my words, his eyebrows twitching as he thinks. "Your sister? Would she want this for you? Would she want to see you endure a miserable life of victimhood?"

"Don't act like you know what my sister would have wanted, Jake. You didn't know her."

"I don't need that to know she'd want better for you! You deserve better."

"No, I deserve exactly this!"

"No one does, Gen. And your sister would—"

"I killed her!" I blurt out, cracking under the immense stress of this situation. Jake's angered features transform into confusion, like my confession isn't clear enough. So, I continue. "She died because of *me*, Jacob. I killed that woman's daughter, and I deserve her punishment."

"I thought it was an accident? That her car hit a deer?"

"She was out there because of me. If my parents want to blame me for it for the rest of my life, I will let them give me every bit of their hatred."

He still looks so lost, and I have no idea how I could lay it out for him any clearer.

"I was perfectly fine with paying for what happened to Vicky. I was fine with it all, but then you came in and ruined everything."

He looks dumbfounded. "*I* ruined everything?"

"You make me want a lot more than I deserve. And I've been so distracted by you that I barely even thought about my sister for weeks. But if I'm not there to remember and love her, who will?"

"It's called healing, and there's nothing wrong with it. Whatever you did, whatever involvement you had in her death, you don't deserve to pay for it for the rest of your life."

I shove his chest again, irritated by his clueless insistence. "Stop acting like you know what this is about! Vicky died all alone on the side of the road because I snuck out for a dumb party. I deserve this life for being so stupid and selfish!"

He thinks about it for a moment, eyes set on mine, and the silence that falls around us is laced with tension. I vaguely notice that we can hear the others talking, meaning they might hear our argument. But I can't be bothered to care.

"So, you think every teenager that sneaks out to party deserves a lifelong punishment like you? Or is it just your self-sabotaging ways trying to find some reason to justify all this shit?" he eventually asks.

"You can't reduce it to just that, Jake. Someone died—my sister, my twin, my other half. And I was doing fine, but you just set everything back *years* with my mother. Couldn't you just hold your tongue for a single evening? Couldn't you set your pride aside and bear it, like I've been doing for an entire decade?"

"It isn't about pride, Genevieve. I learned a long time ago that my appearance means a lot of people will have a bad opinion about me from the start. What's unbearable and what I couldn't let slide was the way she treats you. And how you let her, like a fucking doormat. This isn't how a parent should treat their child."

"And how the fuck would you know about that?"

I realize I let my anger go too far when he looks like I've physically hurt him. His expression turns sad, and I want to hug him and take it all back.

"It took me two hours," he carefully starts after a moment, "to understand that the woman out there, your 'mother,' will never forgive you. You stick around like her willing punching bag, hoping she'll eventually get tired and forget her grievances. But it hasn't happened in ten years, and it never will. She lost two daughters that night, whether you accept it or not."

I want to deny and argue, but nothing comes. My mouth opens and closes a few times, my mind coming back blank.

This has lasted long enough. We have to return to the others and finish this dinner before heading to the guys' rooftop party. Things will be easier then.

"We need to go back, have dessert, and leave," I say.

"I'm not going back."

"What?"

"I'm leaving, Gen. No fucking way I'm staying and sitting in front of your mother like she didn't just call me a vile and lowly freak."

"Jake, please. You can't—"

"I can, and I am."

"Are you serious?"

"Yeah. But I'd hate to ruin that amazing thing you two have going on, so do stay. I'll see myself out."

I'm speechless, stuck in place, while he gives me one last look before he turns around and makes his way back to the others. Only when he disappears do I gather enough brain cells to command my feet to follow him.

Just as I reach the living space, I hear Malory ask, "Oh, you're already leaving?"

"Yeah, sorry," Jake explains, picking up his jacket from the couch we sat on earlier. "I've imposed my presence on you and your family for long enough."

"Nonsense," Gerry counters. "We're about to try your dessert. Stay."

"Let him leave," Mother interjects.

She and Jake exchange a nasty glare, and I stand there, helpless.

"I've got other plans for the evening," Jake explains. "But it was a pleasure meeting you. Thank you for dinner, everything was delicious."

Camellia slides down from her chair and walks up to Jake with hurried steps. "Will you come back?" she asks.

"With more gifts," Poppy adds.

"Uh, I don't know, girls. I'm really not sure."

"Please," the girls beg.

Jake looks around, uncertain. "We'll see, yeah? Right now, I really gotta go, girls."

He pats the girls' heads, shakes Mal and Ger's hands, then spares me a glance after ignoring my parents. Mal goes to open the door for him, and my feet set themselves into motion as soon as he passes it.

"Jake, wait," I call out as I rush through the corridor.

I have to call a second time for him to stop and turn around with a sigh. "You might have no dignity and tolerate your mother's offenses, Genevieve, but I do."

This one feels like a punch in the stomach, knocking the air out of my lungs. "It's not that simple."

"It is. All you have to do is open your eyes and see her for what she is: a malicious bitch who'll make you pay for your sister's accident until the day she dies. And the only reason she can do that, the reason she *will*, is because you not only allow it, you also welcome it. This makes a martyr out of you, and you prefer that to healing and living the life you deserve."

When his eyes dart to something behind me, I instinctively turn around to notice Mother standing in the doorway with her arms crossed.

"Enjoy the rest of your evening, Gen," he mutters. I watch, torn, as he walks away and pushes the elevator button.

Everything in me wants to follow him. But if I do, a decade of sacrifices and hard work to improve my relationship with my mother goes down the drain. Ten years of eating shit and enduring her cruelty, gone in the snap of a finger because I'm being emotional and impulsive.

Jake enters the elevator when it arrives, not sparing me even a glance. Tears begin to roll down my cheeks as soon as the doors close behind him.

What am I doing? He's my Ladder Guy, my wombat, my everything. I need to go to him.

The instant I'm about to step in the elevator's direction, a hand comes to my arm, clasping it firmly. "Don't deprive us of another daughter, Genevieve," Mother demands. "It would be too cruel of you."

"I'm not—that's not what I'm doing."

I can't talk or formulate a coherent sentence. When I attempt to take a step toward the elevator, her hand tightens around my arm and prevents it. "Stay."

"I need to go to him," I say between sobs. I'm so upset I can barely breathe.

"No, you need to stay right here with your family." Her cold hands grab my face to wipe the tears streaming down my cheeks. "There, there, my darling," she consoles.

Her motherly gestures are so unexpected that I'm taken aback. I don't expect it either when she pulls me into a hug, wrapping her arms around me.

It's stiff and unfamiliar, but I've waited ten years for any form of affection from her, so it doesn't even matter. I break down into more sobs. Where's the relief I expected? Why doesn't my mother's embrace alleviate any of this pain?

We stay in this awkward and rigid embrace until she pulls away and rearranges my hair with efficiency. "Come, darling. Let's return to the others and enjoy some family time together."

I'm not fully there as I follow her. Everything inside me is being ripped in half between what I want to do and what I must do. My body passes the door with her, but my mind is with Jake, thinking back on all those precious moments we've shared.

Couldn't he hold his tongue for a single evening? Despite knowing how important my parents' approval was, he didn't even try to make it work. He made himself the victim, but I'm the one suffering the most.

Mother leads me back to the table and makes me sit in my chair. My attention travels to Jake's seat, which is now empty of his beautiful presence.

I feel so numb and hollow, so lost, that I can't even hear the conversation. My brother sets a plate with a serving of strawberry pavlova in front of me, and he gives my shoulder a supportive squeeze.

Jake chose strawberries because I told him it was my favorite fruit. His entire apartment smelled sweet and fruity yesterday from the homemade jam.

Another tear rolls down my cheek while I stare down at the carefully constructed dessert. I craved to taste this all day long, but if I take even a bite, I'll break down into pieces.

Why couldn't things go smoothly? Why did it have to turn into a bloodbath?

And what the hell am I supposed to do now?

CHAPTER
Thirty-five

Jake

THE STING RAY MAKES A worrying sound when I slam the door shut. That's enough to make me realize I need to calm the fuck down before I drive away. With my hands on the steering wheel, I force myself to take long and deep breaths, in through the nose, out through the mouth. It doesn't help that Gen's fancy perfume still lingers in the confined space.

What the fuck just happened? Did Gen really expect me to stay and sit like a well-trained dog? The only way that was happening was if her bitch of a mother left, which wasn't something I could demand.

Sitting through dinner and watching Gen's fucked up dynamic with her parents had been hard enough, but seeing the way she allowed them to treat her ... Her father didn't care for what she had to say, something I'd easily noticed because any time she spoke, he either cut her off or began another conversation with his son. But while his indifference was insulting, it was her mother's behavior that I despised the most. Vivienne never missed an opportunity to bring Gen down, often under the pretense of being a caring mother. But there's nothing motherly or caring about that woman.

My hands tighten around the leather, my knuckles turning white. Gen is an intelligent woman, probably the smartest I've ever met, so how can she be so clueless about this? About them? How can she not see that this fucked up relationship is beyond toxic?

I suppose she does see it, but she accepts it, thinking she deserves to be guilt-tripped for the rest of her life.

I'm still angry as my eyes travel to the building's entrance. This was supposed to be a simple, easy dinner with her brother and his family. Maybe I should have bitten my tongue and stayed like she wanted. Maybe I shouldn't have left her alone with them, without anyone to support and defend her. But she made her choice, didn't she? She chose them.

Something moves in the lit-up entry hall of the building, and my heart jumps in my chest. Could it be her? Is she coming after me?

A couple comes through the large glass door, dressed up for whatever party they are attending. My hopes turn into bitter disappointment. She's still up there with them, sticking to her decision.

Five minutes. I'll give her five minutes and then leave. She deserves at least that.

I count to three hundred, using that time to calm down. And then I count for another three hundred seconds. When I finish this time, I accept that she's not coming down. She's choosing her mother. Not me.

The drive back to Brooklyn is a blur. I replay the evening in my head, feeling hollow inside. How the fuck can Gen descend from those people? It makes no sense that she became the incredible person she is despite growing up under their thumb. But then, she was an entirely different person when I first met her, wasn't she?

She was a haughty snob, so shocked by my appearance that she tried to weasel out of it. It was through time and dedication that I unearthed the woman I've come to know and love. So, maybe I should have guessed the kind of people her parents would be.

When I reach the floor of my loft, I can hear the commotion on the roof. The guys left the staircase door open, and music as well as voices reach me. Fuck, I forgot about this.

I don't feel like joining Eli and Kill up there, so I pull out my keys and unlock my door. I need some time alone with my dog, gathering my thoughts and figuring out what the fuck I'll do now.

"Mull?" I call out as I enter the dark flat. The glow of the streetlights through the large windows is enough for me to notice the stillness of the space. Mulligrubs isn't here, meaning Eli probably took her up there.

I kick the door closed behind me, not flicking the lights on. Once my jacket is thrown on a chair by the entrance, I walk up to the liquor cabinet. I pick up the first bottle and wince when I discern the label. It's the whiskey Gen and I enjoyed when we sampled a few bottles for The Devil's Court.

I don't bother grabbing a glass and go to the couch, where I slump down. Once the cap's off, I drink up a few mouthfuls, the amber liquor burning my throat. It'll soon do its magic, and the pain that won't leave my chest, right under my left ribs, will eventually be numbed by it. And those reruns of our fight will stop playing in my mind over and over again.

The dark stillness that surrounds me is punctuated by the noises that come through the ceiling. It sounds like they're having fun up there, but I don't feel like joining them. Pretending all is fine around friends and colleagues is above my strength.

There's no one I can talk to about this. The guys wouldn't understand, and I'm pretty sure whatever advice they'd come up with would be shit. It's rare for me to miss my mum, but at that moment, I wish she were still around. She'd know exactly what to say, how to make me feel better, and what I should do with this mess. Mum was always patient and soft, and she used to give the best advice.

A question I've been asking myself a few times resurfaces. Would she have liked Gen? The two are very different, and while Mum would have been happy that I found my one person in this world, I can't decide if she would have genuinely liked her. In return, I know that Gen would have loved Mum. She would have seen what a true mother should be like, and she would have understood that Vivienne Kensington isn't worth all the ache she puts herself through.

It's like my whole body jump-starts when my phone vibrates, about twenty minutes and fifteen gulps of whiskey later. Is it her?

I quickly take my phone out of my back pocket to look at the caller ID. Disappointment strikes yet again when I see the words "Aunt Maggie" instead of "My Favorite Redhead." With a sigh, I throw the phone to the side and take another couple of sips.

Gen will come around. She's too clever to let her mother break us up.

The call goes to voicemail, but it starts ringing again moments later. A look to the side informs me it's still my aunt. She rarely insists like this, so I pick up the phone with a frown. I do some quick math as I take the call. It's around noon in Brisbane, so it's not a middle-of-the-night kind of emergency.

"Hey, Mags," I greet her, bringing the phone to my ear.

"Hi, Jakey! I hope I'm not interrupting your celebrations."

"No, it's good. I just got home."

"Isn't it a little early for you?"

The hint of judgment in her tone makes me chuckle. "Things didn't go as planned, so I cut my evening short."

"Oh, I'm sorry to hear that, love. Do you want to talk about it?"

"Not really. What about you? Everything fine down under?"

"Yeah, all good. I just wanted to let you know that the first check will be a little delayed. We had some water damage, so we spent more than we intended in June."

Well, at least I know that stubbornness runs in my genes. I hold back a groan, sitting up straight. "Mags, I already told you there was no need to pay me back."

"We want to."

"And I don't want you to. That money was a gift, my way of repaying you and Uncle Keith. You welcomed me into your home when I had nobody else, and you stuck by me even when I was being a little shithead."

"We said we would reimburse you," she insists.

"Seriously, Maggie. You've got enough going on with the new house and all the repairs. Don't make me call my bank to ask them to bounce your checks."

There's nothing for a moment, and then I vaguely hear her talk to someone in the room with her. But it's muffled by her hand on the phone, so I can't tell who answers. This continues for a few seconds, and then she returns her attention to me. "Keith suggested we finish the remodeling, and once we're financially stable, we'll start the payments."

I roll my eyes, holding back another sigh. "Fine, let's do that," I concede. This will be a problem for future me, who hopefully won't have had as much whiskey.

"In the meantime, do you want us to make you another care box?" she offers.

That brings an unexpected smile to my lips. We've done this a handful of times in the past thirteen years since I left Australia. She fills a box with all sorts of lollies and snacks from my motherland, the kind of stuff I grew up with, and sends it to me all the way in New York. The last one was a couple of years ago, and I have since found a specialized grocery store that sells all those things right here in the States.

But I know how much she enjoys sending me those boxes, so I say, "I'd love that, Mags. Can you put some extra Strawberry Clouds in there? And strawberry-flavored Dairy Milk Snacks, too. I know someone who'd love them."

"Really? Is it your friend who ate all the Sour Ears last time? Killian, was it?"

"No, it's—" I hesitate, wondering if now's the right time to let her know about Gen. I haven't done it yet, and tonight doesn't feel appropriate. "Her name's Genevieve," I end up saying, anyway. Margaret is the closest thing I have to a mother, and I need maternal advice.

"Is she your girlfriend?"

"Yeah. We met about three months ago."

"Jakey, that's incredible! Keith and I were wondering if you'd ever settle down."

"Well, I didn't plan on it until she came along."

"Sometimes it just hits you in the face. You can't help it. But that means she's a great one," Maggie confidently says.

I nod. "She is. She's fucking phenomenal. But she's also extremely complicated."

"How so?"

"She's got this fucked up relationship with her parents. Drives me nuts that she can't see it."

Maggie says nothing, so silent that I check my phone to see if we were cut off. "You know, your mum and I were in that kind of situation growing up," she carefully reminds me. "Our dad would beat us for the damndest things, and Mum … Well, let's just say we had the imprint of her hands on us more than a few times. When you're in that situation, you rationalize, thinking you deserve the slap for burning Dad's toast or to be locked in a closet for spilling Mum's expensive perfume. But it was easy for us to recognize the abuse because we were the only ones in school with bruises. So, as soon as I turned eighteen, I decided to move out and take my baby sister with me. There was no way I'd leave her alone with them."

"I know she was thankful for that," I tell Maggie. "She used to tell me how she would forever owe you."

"Leaving her behind was never even an option. But she didn't want to go at first. She was only twelve, and she thought our parents loved us in their own twisted way, so she refused to leave. I stuck around for a little longer because that was all I could do for her—be there for her, support her, protect her. Then, one day, Dad went too far and broke your mum's arm in two places. I called the Department of Child Safety that afternoon and got custody of her. After that, we left Sydney for Brisbane and never looked back."

We rarely talk about Mum because the topic is a sour one. I vaguely knew about her and my aunt's rough childhood, but I never knew all that. It's painful to know that my mum, that sweet angel, went through so much. And when she was finally out, she got pregnant young from a cunt who didn't want the responsibility of raising me. And then it all stopped because of a pulmonary embolism in the back of a bus on her way home from a long shift at the hospital.

Not being able to give her the life she deserved will forever be my biggest regret.

"I don't know what the situation is with Genevieve and her parents," Maggie continues, her voice laced with care, "but I know how hard it can be to rip yourself out of an abusive situation. Don't judge her too harshly, and be there for her. She needs you, just like your mum needed me back then. I don't know what they would have done to her if I'd left her with them. But I will never regret staying until she was ready to take that leap with me."

"I'm thankful you did, Mags."

"Of course you are. You wouldn't exist otherwise," she says with humor.

I chuckle. "I guess I wouldn't, no."

I hear Keith calling her in the background, and after a brief conversation between them, Maggie refocuses on me. "I'm sorry, Jakey, I have to go help your uncle. We're having a barbie with the kids and a few mates who've been helping us out."

"Yeah, of course. Let me know how much the parcel costs for the lollies. And do not send me a check. I'll send it back. But let me know if you need more money for the repairs. I'd be happy to help."

"Thank you, my boy. I think we'll be good. Feel free to come and visit us to see what your money bought, yeah?"

She always tries to get me to fly down there, and I'm surprised it took her this long to bring it up. "Sure thing, Mags. Say hi to Keith for me. And to the cousins."

"Will do. Bye, Jakey."

We hang up, and I throw my phone to the side again. When I look around, the dark loft seems desperately empty. I'm feeling slightly better, but not enough to join all the ruckus up there. My head falls back onto the couch's backrest as I slouch on it, and I stare at the beams on the ceiling. My aunt's words run through my head, over and over again.

Be there for her. Support her. Protect her.

That's what I need to do, isn't it? Be there for Gen, no matter how much I hate her relationship with her parents. She needs me, because if I'm not there to love her unconditionally, who will?

I'm slowly coming to terms with what it means—that I'll have to bite my tongue every time we meet with her parents or bear seeing her be put down by her mother—when the door opens. The music from the staircase fills the room, and a masculine silhouette comes in.

From where I sit, I don't have to move to recognize Eli. He navigates the darkness with ease and follows the same path I did when I arrived, all the way to the liquor cabinet. He opens both doors and crouches down to take out some random bottles. For some, he takes a vague look at the label, either putting it with the others or returning it to the cabinet.

When he gets up and starts stacking the bottles between his arm and chest, I decide that's enough.

"Are you fuckers already out of booze?" I ask from my armchair.

He jumps with surprise but doesn't drop the bottles. "Jake, you asshole ... You scared me half to death," he says, turning around to find me in the dark. "What are you doing here? Where's Gen?"

"I left her at her brother's."

"Is everything alright?" he wonders, stepping closer.

"Yeah," I lie.

"Then why are you sitting in the dark like some James Bond villain? Is Gen joining us later?"

"I don't know. What are you doing with my liquor?"

"Well, there might be a couple hundred people up there instead of twenty."

"What?"

"Yeah, someone posted a story on Instagram, and things got out of hand."

"Was that someone you?" I caustically ask, raising a brow at him.

"Might have been, yeah. Anyhow, I already used all my booze, and I thought I'd come get yours."

"You do know we have a bar filled with liquor two blocks away, right?"

"That is way too far for me, my brother."

"Lazy twat. Put my shit back, and I'll go get a couple of crates at the Court."

He smiles, looking way too victorious for my liking. "Great. Can you buy snacks as well? Chips, pretzels, Doritos, crackers, pizza rolls … Anything, really. I'm fucking starving."

"I literally prepared everything for tonight, and you two wankers still managed to botch it?" I ask, a little more irritated than I should be.

"Like I said, it blew out of proportion. Plus, someone came with edibles, and Kill and I are completely out of it."

"You're high?"

"Like fucking kites. We hid a few gummy bears in his pocket for you. Which I guess was inspired, because you look like you need to relax."

That actually doesn't sound like a bad idea. With a grunt, I push myself out of the armchair and take a few bottles from Eli to help him put them back in the cabinet. Then, I send him back to the party and go change into something more comfortable than this fucking suit.

Even though I don't like it, I know what I need to do about Gen. I'll stick around, like Maggie did with Mum. I'll be there for her for as long as I can. It might drive me to an early grave, but she's worth it. Given her growth since we met, I'm confident she will soon open her eyes and do something about the situation. My sexy redhead isn't the type to take shit from anyone.

And I fucking love her for it.

CHAPTER
Thirty-Six
Gen

THE SENSATION OF NUMB HOLLOWNESS in my chest only gets worse. What happened leaves me in a limbo that I can't seem to break out of.

It's Thursday now, and I waited all of yesterday for a text from Jake, a call, a visit ... anything. But that didn't come. It's been nearly forty hours since that mess started, and there's been nothing.

We're not broken up. I don't think so. We're stronger than that, and the disastrous evening is only a hiccup. Maybe he needs a moment to cool down before we can discuss this with clear heads. I hated arguing with him and hope it will never happen again.

We haven't gone this long without any contact in ... ever, and I don't know what to do. Should I be the one texting him, even if he's the one who messed up? It's not like I didn't warn him about my parents. He knew about their rigid manners and how strict they are with me.

His temper nearly ruined a decade of arduous efforts, and I'm not okay with that.

Maybe I should be the bigger person and text him. After work, I can stop by my place to get things for tomorrow and then head down to Brooklyn. We'll have a long talk to clear the air, and he'll make love to me for a good portion of the night until there's no tension left between us.

Yes, that's perfect. As soon as I'm done reading these dreadfully dull contract revisions, I'll text him and ask if I can come over tonight. I'm sure he misses me as much as I do him.

I'm not even halfway through the file when two knocks come at the glass door. Daisy's there when I look up, and she opens when I give her a signal.

"Miss Kensington, I'm sorry to interrupt, but Mr. Sinclair's assistant wants to know if you have an opening today for a one-on-one."

This is highly irregular. The man usually summons me without bothering to make sure I'm available or not. It seems Daisy also feels the same because she looks excited about it.

This is about the promotion, isn't it? All my hard work these past weeks, months, years … It'll finally pay off, and I'll be in a position that allows me to steer this department in a much more efficient way. No more vanity conference meetings, no more last-minute change of plans, and no more procrastinating until the whole floor has a week to handle a month-long task. Everyone in this department will have a much better work environment.

"Is it okay if I go now?" I ask Daisy. My voice is uneven from the nervousness.

"That would be perfect. His secretary told me he's free until lunch. So, it's either now or tomorrow."

"Now it is, then."

I swiftly abandon everything I'm doing and adjust my skirt down my thighs. My outfit today is perfect for this, with a dark mauve skirt and jacket, a white silk shirt underneath, and my pearly Jimmy Choos. I took particular care when I picked my clothes this morning because I'm meeting Mother for lunch.

As if she can sense my distress, Vivienne has been showing me a level of gentleness and affection I haven't been graced with since Vicky's accident. In fact, I'm not even sure she ever was the loving and caring type, but at least she's trying.

The fact that I'll get to tell her about my promotion brings a smile to my lips as I exit my office. She'll be the second one to know, right after Jake. The news will serve as a great icebreaker when I text him once I'm done with Sinclair.

My boss's assistant gives me a small smile when I arrive and invites me to step in—Mr. Sinclair is expecting me. Definitely nervous, I take a long and deep breath with my fingers wrapped around the handle. I've been waiting for this for five years, and all the overtime and the insane workload I've put on myself led to this moment.

I feel at peace when I open the door, a smile plastered on my face.

"Ah, Genevieve," he greets when I enter. He doesn't get up from his chair but gestures to the one on the other side of his desk. "Please, sit."

I comply, holding back my grin the best I can. "How have you been doing, dear?" he asks, leaning back into his leather seat.

"Good, thank you. The team's been sailing smoothly, we're ahead of all our assignments, and we're getting ready for the merger to be finalized."

"That's great to hear. If I'm being perfectly honest, I was a little worried when we first hired you. In my experience, people who come from a background as wealthy as yours usually get a job out of boredom or to fit expectations, and they never get properly involved in it. But you have been a great addition to this department."

"I'm glad I exceeded your expectations, then. Working here has been an enriching experience, and I can't wait for more of it to come."

"Good, good." He's pensive for a few moments, probably trying to find the words to break the good news to me. "As you know, I'm retiring in the fall," he starts. "I've been tasked by the people upstairs to find the most competent replacement to fill my position once I'm gone."

"Yes, we have discussed this in the past."

"Well, it wasn't an easy choice because so much has to be considered for the sake of the company. It has to be an informed decision, you see. So, I have been weighing everything for weeks, trying to find the perfect department head. And I finally reached a conclusion, which is why I asked you here."

I'm practically vibrating with excitement. My life's truly turning around, between Jake, my relationship with my mother getting better, and now this.

"I've decided," Mr. Sinclair continues, "that the best person to take over after I'm gone in October will be Ralf Lowell. He's had a lot of great initiatives lately, and he's such a fun guy to be around."

My boss keeps talking, but I can't hear any of it. Ralf Lowell? *Ralf?!* Lazy ass, rapey jokes Ralf is getting the job? Over me? How? In what world is that an informed decision?

"Excuse me, but *Ralf?*" I ask, so baffled I barely realize I'm interrupting his rambling.

"Yes, Mr. Lowell will step into my shoes once I'm gone. Like I was saying, he's—"

"I've been here longer than he has," I remind him. "I have better diplomas than him. I work harder *and* better."

"Genevieve, you are an exemplary employee—no one's denying that. But Ralf is better suited to take over."

"Why? I'm more qualified for the job in every single aspect. Unless the position requires male genitalia, in which case, I suppose I'm lacking indeed."

"Please, let's not make this a gender thing, Genevieve. We both know why I'm choosing him over you."

I stare at him, puzzled and offended. "I have no idea, no."

"Oh, please. There's no denying that you have been scattered lately."

"Scattered?"

"You skip Friday drinks. You're unfocused during major meetings. You come in late, leave the office early … You also filed an HR complaint regarding several of your colleagues and subordinates. And when we had a fundamentally important file to compile with a strict deadline, you took a day off to celebrate your birthday."

"The file was done in time. I made sure of that."

"Ralf's team was the one working hard on Friday to get it done, Genevieve. He told me how much of an inconvenience it was that you would dump it all on his team in favor of your birthday."

"No, that isn't what happened. My team worked hard to get it done by Thursday, and I did so much overtime I nearly passed out from exhaustion. Lowell's team only had the proofreading and formatting to handle."

"And yet, they were the ones working late on that Friday evening. I'm sorry, dear, but you don't deserve the job. You might have, two or three months ago, but I cannot in good conscience give you the position. Ralf will take over, and who knows? Maybe you'll get his position when he moves another step up."

Oh God.

The reality of what it means slowly sinks in. Ralf will become my boss in October. If I thought working under Sinclair was bad, what will it be like with Ralf? The man has been scamming his way up since he started—two years after me. And now he's taking over the job I was owed? How much harder will I have to work to make up for Ralf's incompetence?

I can barely breathe at the thought of it, my lungs uncooperative, and my intakes shallow. This is a nightmare. Ralf fucking Lowell is my future boss.

"I understand that you might be going through some things, Genevieve," Mr. Sinclair kindly says. "Rumors have been circulating that you've separated from your boyfriend. Edward from accounting, was it? If you want my advice, get your act together and focus on what's important. Like I said, you're an exemplary worker, but you've let yourself go. I've seen the kind of relationship you've entertained lately."

"I know my personal life has been complicated, but even with all that, I still work harder and better than Ralf. It's not fair to use my current situation to judge my performance."

"Ralf offers consistency, which is something I value. I wish I could have given you the position, but I cannot trust that you will not spiral any lower than you already have. This department cannot be in the hands of someone unstable."

I can barely think past the indignation. The utter unfairness of his decision hits hard. The promotion I've been working my ass off for the past five years, the logical outcome of my studies and time at NexaCorp, just slipped from my fingers. All because I met Jake and started living my life for myself rather than for work.

As if I need a reminder that this moment can get even more humiliating, the door opens behind me, and a grating voice says, "Celebratory drinks tonight?"

Furious, I twist around in the chair to glare at Ralf and the cocky expression on his stupid face. "Oh, I didn't realize it was you, Genevieve."

Right, so many redheads work in this department.

"I take it Mr. Sinclair broke the news to you," he continues, looking so smug that I want to choke him with his ugly tie.

"He did. Congratulations on the position, Ralf. God knows how hard you worked for it," I say with acerbic sarcasm.

"Better luck next time, eh? So, Victor, are we on for drinks tonight?" Of course, first-name basis now.

"Sure. We have to celebrate. Genevieve, will you be joining us?"

I would rather eat a bucket of nails. "I'm afraid not. I have plans."

"It's alright. We'll organize an office party soon to announce the news to the rest of the floor."

Great.

I sit there, feeling like a failure, while they talk and joke like old friends. Where did all of this go wrong? When I didn't do rails of coke with Sinclair in club bathrooms like Ralf did? When I naively thought this professional ladder could be climbed with impeccable ethics and hard work rather than politics and ass-licking?

Or was it when I began prioritizing my love life?

My phone buzzing in my pocket rescues me from this torturous moment. "I have to take this," I pretend without even checking the caller.

Because it would make me actually vomit, I don't congratulate Ralf again before I leave. I pull out my phone and see it's my mother. As always, a surge of panic chills my blood. But we're past that now. She's been so kind to me since Gerry's dinner that I feel ashamed for the guttural reaction.

"Hi," I say as I pick up.

"Genevieve, good morning. I just booked a hair appointment early in the afternoon. Would you mind if we met for a coffee instead of lunch?"

Some things will never change. I'm so used to coming second to the rest of her life that I barely feel insulted. "Sure, I'll see if I can free myself soon."

"I'm actually here now. Doesn't the lobby where you work have a coffee shop?"

"It does, but—"

"Perfect. We'll have coffee, then I'll have lunch with Lilian."

"You said it was a hair appointment."

"After Lilian, yes. But I'm here now to spend time with you, darling. So, are you coming down, or did I come all this way for nothing?"

"I-I'm coming down."

She hangs up before I've even removed the phone from my ear, and I stand there, a little dumbfounded. This feels an awful lot like her old pattern, but I can't believe she'd fall back into it so quickly. Maybe I was too naive thinking she could change.

As naive as when I thought I'd get Mr. Sinclair's job. Oh, God. I hope Mother doesn't ask about the promotion now. If she does, I'll have to tell her someone else got it, and she'll launch herself into another tirade about coming to work for Father.

Everything was going so well two days ago that I can't understand how I'm in this position. Looks like I used all of my luck on getting a man as incredible as Jake, and now I'm running out of it.

And the worst part is, I'm not even sure Jake is still mine.

The coffee shop Mother spoke of is a sleek space nested in the NexaCorp building. It's nothing stellar, but it's better than what we brew in the break room.

I enter it with my handbag tucked under my arm, seeking my mother's perfectly styled head. She's easy to spot, with her blue-gray ensemble and a row of pearls around her neck. The sight of her, sitting rigidly there with her back straight and facing away from me, triggers the same kind of reaction her phone call did. Something cold crawls up my back, and my chest tightens anxiously.

Will this ever go away? If we stay on this path toward bettering our relationship, will I ever be able to see her as something other than a tyrant?

Before I head there, I switch my phone to silent mode, knowing how much she hates it when it rings during these moments together.

When I sit in the empty chair opposite her, she offers me a small and brief smile. "I can't stay for long," she explains first. "So I already ordered something for me and a green tea with a slice of lemon for you. Did you know green tea is a great ally for weight loss?"

How could I not know that, growing up with an almond mom? "I know, but I don't really like the taste."

"You'll get used to it. I have a cup every day after breakfast and lunch. It works wonders."

Her obsession with my weight seems to be at an all-time high, and I can't help but wonder if she isn't projecting her insecurities on me. Now that father has a young and pretty mistress, I'm sure Vivienne is scared the woman might get pregnant and steal her lifestyle away.

What a pathetic way to live.

"We didn't have time to discuss it during Gerry's dinner, but the gala to commemorate your sister was a resounding success," she discloses with pride. "Your absence for the second half was barely noticed, so no need to feel guilty about abandoning us for God knows what."

"I was feeling ill," I lie.

"That always seems to happen to you at the most inconvenient times. But that's alright. Like I said, you didn't ruin anything."

Our drinks arrive before she can say more, and as soon as the waitress is gone, she offers me a content look. "We raised a lot more than we expected for your sister's foundation."

"It isn't hers," I mumble behind my steaming cup of tea.

"What was that?"

"It's *your* foundation, not Victoria's."

"It's in her name, so there's barely any nuance there."

Before I can stop myself, my eyes roll up to the ceiling in an exasperated way. Mother notices and sets her coffee down with a miffed expression. Nothing good ever happens when she pinches her lips like this.

"What is it?" she demands.

I wince, focused on the slice of lemon floating in my cup. "Nothing, I'm just ..."

When my words die off, unsure what to say, she sighs exasperatedly and says, "Please, don't tell me it's about that barbarian of a man. You did well to breakup with him."

I frown, confused as to why Jake is suddenly the subject of our conversation. "We're not broken up. Things are a little tense, but that's it."

"You're not? Genevieve, I thought I was being very clear."

"And I thought I was twenty-seven and in charge of my own decisions."

"Of course you are. But if you want to be part of this family, you cannot bring that man into it. I won't tolerate it, and neither will your father."

"So, it's either the man I love or my family?" I ask, stunned.

It's her turn to roll her eyes. "You do not love him."

"Don't tell me how I feel, Vivienne."

"You barely know the man."

"I know him a lot better than you knew Father before marrying him. And the more I learn about Jake, the harder I love him."

Contrary to you and Father, who hate each other a little more with every day that passes in your stale marriage.

"Those feelings will fade with time. But family is forever, Genevieve."

"Obviously not, since you're giving me an ultimatum."

"Don't put it like that, dear. It's a question of morals. You can't expect us to welcome him into the family, so being with him will ultimately cut you off from us."

"No, *you* will make the conscious decision to cut me off if I stay with him. Jake has never tried to control my life or force me to do things I didn't want to."

Her irritation is growing more apparent with every word I utter, and the mere fact that she doesn't blow up at me betrays her ploy.

"Is this why you've been so involved with me since it all happened?" I ask, feeling dumb for not realizing it sooner. "That's your plan to solve this 'problem?' Blinding me with fake affection so you can manipulate me into ending things with Jake?"

"'Manipulate' is such a strong word. I'm only looking out for you, Genevieve."

No, she's not. She hasn't been looking out for me in a decade, and she isn't now. Why would she suddenly care about me like that?

It's as though everything snaps into place. All the bullshit, all the brainwashing, all the gaslighting … It all becomes so obvious that I can't keep denying it. I always knew my mother's actions were wrong, but deep down, I convinced myself I deserved it. It didn't matter if Hana disagreed or if my therapist called it toxic. Mother had every reason to treat me this way.

But Jake was right. I was a teenager who made a mistake. Yes, it had terrible consequences, but millions of kids have done the same and lived perfectly normal lives. My sister's death was an accident, and while my involvement played a part in it, it wasn't my fault.

And more importantly, Victoria would have wanted so much better for me. She was a caring and loving person who would have wanted me to live on and not let her death define the rest of my life.

Also, she would have adored Jake with his fantastic humor, great values, and uniqueness. Vicky would have pushed me into his arms as much as Hana did. She would have wanted the best for me, just like I did for her.

And the best for me is Jake. A hundred times over.

"Oh my God," I breathe out, staring at my mother in shock. "I can't believe it. He was right. You'll never forgive me, will you? I'm just a puppet in your cruel hands. You want me to be miserable for the rest of my life because of what happened to Vicky."

She blinks a few times as if caught red-handed. Her stupor doesn't last though, and she says, "See? He's already putting these ludicrous ideas in your mind, poisoning it. This is manipulation, Genevieve."

"You'd know that, wouldn't you? You've been toying with me since the night it happened, keeping me on the edge of guilt and remorse and convincing me I deserve to pay for what happened to Vicky. I can't believe it took me ten years to see it."

"Genevieve, stop this. You're making a spectacle of yourself," she mutters, embarrassedly looking around at the surrounding people. My voice was loud enough to attract the attention of a few of them, but I couldn't care less.

Her concern only makes me angrier. "Oh, shut up," I utter. "Always so worried about what others will think that you barely allow yourself to live. And you've imposed that on everyone around you. But I'm so done bending and contorting myself to squeeze into this perfect little box you expect all of us to fit in. I am *done*, Mother."

Maybe it's because of what happened with Jake, or upstairs with Ralf, or more likely the ten years of tyranny I've endured, but there's something in me that wants out. The freedom I've deprived myself of is breaking out of its cage.

"You're a pathetic trophy wife with nothing but regrets for your own choices. So, you decided that if you're going to be miserable, then you might as well take everyone down with you. But I'm done being the person you get to berate and ruin just to feel better about yourself. I'm your daughter, Vivienne. The only one you have left."

"Contain yourself, Genevieve!"

"No. Fuck you. You have been mentally abusing me for a *decade*. And I let you because you convinced me I deserved it. But I lost someone too, you know? My sister, my half, the one person I loved the most in this world. I couldn't even grieve her the way I needed because you never failed to remind me I did this to the family, that I had myself to blame for the ache tearing me apart."

"Because you *are* responsible! You disobeyed, and she died!"

"I was seventeen! I was a teenager who wanted to celebrate her birthday with her friends! And you refused because it was too much work for the staff. What was it to you? You had an evening at the opera anyway—Swan Lake, Vicky's favorite. Ever thought that if you'd been a less self-centered bitch, you would have taken us along with you and Father? She would still be alive if you genuinely cared about us."

She looks so appalled that it's almost comical. "How dare you put the blame on me!"

"And how dare you put it on me all this time?!"

Vivienne can't seem to find anything to reply, and even if she did, I already know it would be bullshit. I finally opened my eyes and grew a backbone.

Fuming, she picks up her bag and rises from her chair with dry and angry gestures. "Your father will hear of this, you ungrateful little brat."

"I'm not as afraid of him as you are, you know? What's he going to do? Stop giving me an allowance? I'm making my own money and even paid back what I owed for Harvard."

"I cannot believe you're doing this, Genevieve. Rejecting your entire family for a man with horrible manners and tattoos."

"And piercings," I can't help but add. "In unexpected places, but God, do they feel good."

The redness on her face intensifies, and I can hardly believe I ever feared this woman. She looks ridiculous with that vein about to pop on her forehead. Why did I let her dictate my life for so long?

"You will regret this, you know," she venomously spits out. "And when you come crawling because he's found someone more interesting than you, don't expect us to take you back."

"Perfect. Don't wait on me."

Now that she's tried everything and failed, she gives up with a frustrated huff and turns her heels around. I watch her disappear, feeling infinitely lighter than I did upon entering the coffee shop. I pick up my tea and take a sip, grimacing at the taste. No, this isn't for me at all.

CHAPTER
Thirty-Seven
Gen

STILL REELING FROM WHAT HAPPENED, my eyes mindlessly stare beyond the glass wall that separates the coffee place from NexaCorp's hall. When I catch a glimpse of three familiar figures, my attention latches on them.

What happens next might be because of the adrenaline still pumping in my veins, or because I'm done being a pushover. I'm barely aware that I stand up from my chair, but before I know it, I'm out of the coffee shop. Even as I rush through the vast hallway, I'm not sure of what I'm about to do.

"Mr. Sinclair!" I call out once I'm only a few steps away. Ralf, our boss, and his boss all stop and turn around at once.

"Genevieve, you disappeared so abruptly earlier, and we—"

"I quit," I bluntly cut him off. All three men stare at me in shock for several seconds. "And because my contract doesn't require any sort of notice, my resignation starts right now."

"But we—You can't do that. We need you with the merger and the—"

"Yes, you do. You need me a lot more than you need him," I confirm, pointing at Ralf, "because we both know I work harder than him, and I'm better at this job than he'll ever be. Which is why I'm quitting. I refuse to work under an incompetent clown whose sole achievements in this company have been the ones he stole from me and my team."

"She's lying," Ralf interjects. "I never stole anything from her."

"Really? Do you want the list? It's as long as my arm, you pathetic buffoon."

"Miss Kensington, no need for hysterics," Sinclair begins.

"That's misogynistic, but you wouldn't realize that even if it slapped you in the face, would you? Let's just blame my erratic behavior on 'that time of the month' or early menopause," I sarcastically offer. "But even with that, I mean every word. Good luck finding a replacement for me. It'll probably take three hires to manage all the work I've been handling since I started here. Then, maybe you'll realize how big of a mistake you made by disregarding me as a good candidate just because I dared have a life outside of my work."

"You're simply not good at balancing your work life and your private life," Ralf snickers.

"Oh, fuck off. You have a wife, a girlfriend, and a mistress. I'm not taking any sort of advice from you."

I could stay here and call them out on their bullshit all day, but another familiar face is making her way out of the building.

"Anyhow, I quit, and I mean it," I quickly tell them before turning to my boss's superior. "Good luck keeping this department afloat with Ralf in command and without me to make up for it."

Their answer doesn't matter, just like I don't care if they think I'm being a lunatic, so I leave them there. I'm done putting so much importance on other peoples' perception of me. Not when they don't matter, at least.

"Daisy!" I call my assistant as I hurriedly come down the flight of stairs in front of the building. She twists around, looking up from her phone.

"Yes, Miss Kensington?"

"Please, I can't believe I never asked this before, but call me Gen. It comes a little late though, because I just quit."

"Oh, no. Is it because you didn't get Mr. Sinclair's position?"

"That, and … I think I just hate this job. It's so greedy, and dull, and corporate. I can't do this for the rest of my life, or I'll turn into one of them, you know?"

She nods, obviously confused by my hectic behavior. "This is very short notice for you, I'm so sorry. I'm sure they'll find someone to replace me in no time. And if you want to reinvent your life too, I'll write you a stellar recommendation letter. Anything you want to thank you for all your hard work."

"That's very kind of you, Miss Ke—Gen."

"Great. I need to go see my boyfriend to tell him I've been an idiot and hope he takes me back. Would you put all my things in a box and have a carrier take it to my place?"

"Of course. Should I, uh, let everyone know you're quitting?"

"Yeah, sure. Whatever. Oh, and if you want the plant, you can have it. You've been the one watering it. Also, that paperweight you always loved? Yours."

"You don't have to," she politely protests.

"Have it, I don't mind."

Another thing pops into my mind, and I utter it, too hyped up to hold back. "Would you be interested in coming to work for me if I start my own firm?" I offer. Her eyebrows shoot up, her eyes going round. "As a paralegal, not an assistant," I add.

"Uh, yeah, I'd love that."

"Amazing. We'll keep in touch. And if you're okay with it, let's grab drinks one of these days to catch up."

"I would love that, yes."

Grateful for her, the only good thing during my years at NexaCorp, I give her a quick and tight hug. "Thank you again, Daisy. You made it all a little more bearable."

"I'm glad I could help, Gen. Now, go find that handsome man of yours and reinvent your life."

I laugh from the relief, the stress, and the hundred other things rushing through my head at the moment. It feels as though my life starts today, and I'm scared I won't have the one thing I genuinely want in it.

But I have to try, so I rush to the sidewalk and hail a cab. One stops soon after my first attempt, and I hurriedly open the door and lower inside.

"To Brooklyn," I demand before murmuring to myself, "To Ladder Guy."

THE FAMILIAR FRONT OF THE Parlour doesn't feel as welcoming as it used to. Within these walls lies the answer I desperately seek and need.

Will Jake forgive me for being as blind and obtuse as I have been? I abandoned him in favor of my horrible mother two days ago, and he has every right to reject me for it. Even if every cell in me knew it was a mistake, my mind was too far gone to realize it.

I'll never do something that stupid ever again. Vivienne and Gerard Kensington are out of my life. I won't let them ruin my future like they did my past.

Standing in the middle of the sidewalk, I stare at The Gallery's window, trying to muster the courage to enter. The taxi dropped me off a few minutes ago, and I've been right here ever since. "Come on, Gen," I mumble to myself. "If you can't fight for us, then you don't deserve him."

I can still picture the hurt in his eyes, the betrayal on his face … I messed up, and I'm so scared it's irreparable.

Someone enters The Gallery, and as they hold the door open for me, I'm compelled to step inside. While the person remains on the ground floor, I slowly make my way up to The Parlour's waiting room. There's someone I don't know behind the counter, and when I pass the detector that makes a bell chime, the woman turns to me and offers a smile. She looks very welcoming, with her pink hair, light brown skin, and round cheeks.

"Welcome to The Parlour," she says when I reach the high desk. "Are you here for information, or do you have a booking with us?"

"I'm, uh, is Jake here?"

"Yes, I think he's in his office."

"I need to talk to him."

"Are you a friend? Who should I announce?"

"I'm his girlfriend." God, I hope I still am.

"You're Gen? It's so nice to meet you! We've heard so much about you."

"Oh, thanks. I haven't been around here much, so I didn't get to meet all of you guys."

"I'm Cass, Cassidy. I was one of Jake's first hires. He came to get me all the way in Atlanta when he opened this place."

"That's amazing! The few people I talked to last time told me how great of a workplace this is."

"Your boyfriend is one hell of a man."

"He really is, yes."

The small talk helps soothe my nerves a little, but the reminder of Jake's incredible personality only makes me feel stupider.

"Gen?" a friendly voice calls out. I turn and find Eli coming out of the hallway that leads to the offices. "Hi! What are you doing here?" he asks.

"She's here to see Jake," Cassidy explains in my stead.

"Oh, you're in luck. He hasn't left for his lunch yet. Aren't you supposed to be at work?"

I shake my head.

He takes my arm and leads me toward the hallway. "Did something happen? He's been all moody since that dinner you had the other day. But he won't tell us what it is."

"I messed up, but I'm here to fix it. Can you go get him, please? But don't tell him it's me."

"Why?"

"Because I don't think I can handle it if he refuses to see me," I confess, swallowing back tears.

Eli's usually merry eyes turn sad. "I'm sure he wouldn't, Gen. Before I go, do you need a hug? You look like you're about to break."

"It can't hurt," I say with a small shrug.

His kind smile warms me up. He doesn't hesitate to enfold me in his arms and give me a supportive hug. *Please, God, let Jake take me back.*

As if I've conjured him with my thoughts, his voice echoes next to us. "Anyone care to explain what's going on?"

We rip away from one another as if we were doing something wrong. Jake looks so good in his dark green shirt with a tartan pattern that my chest hurts at the thought that I might have lost him. The sleeves are rolled up his muscular forearms, and a few buttons are undone at his chest, which allows me a glimpse at the inked drawings I now know by heart.

"I-I came here to see you," I explain, swallowing the knot in my throat.

"I'll leave you two alone," Eli offers before heading off to his office.

With him gone, it's just Jake, me, and the awkward tension. I'm not sure how to start this because my earlier rush of adrenaline and courage wore off during the ride. It would be so much easier if I had the same bravado as when I quit my job.

But this needs to be handled with a clear head and not high on some empowering spell.

"I read somewhere," I carefully start, "that some people use tattoos as a form of therapy. Is it true?"

"It is. For some people, marking their skin helps with trauma, as it can give meaning or closure. And while we're not licensed professionals, a lot feel the need to talk while it happens. Also, the pain can be grounding, in a way."

"Then would you tattoo me, Jake?"

His eyebrows twitch with surprise and confusion. "You want a tattoo?"

"Only if you do it. And I know you're a very famous artist with a busy schedule, but it won't take long, I promise."

He swallows back a smile as if I just said something utterly ridiculous, and I can't help but see it as a good sign. "No way I'd let anyone else tattoo you anyway. Come, my station is in room three."

Jake guides me toward the room with a "3" painted on it, and after a quick knock to make sure no one's in there, he opens the door and invites me in. The space is clean, with an exposed brick wall and a wide window. On each side of it, there's a cushioned chair that looks like it can be adjusted in every possible way, as well as a movable cart and a rolling stool.

Jake takes my bag and hangs it on a hook by the door before he adjusts the volume of the music. Then he returns to me, locks the door, and goes to sit on the stool before rolling closer.

"What do you want, and where?" he asks.

"Since it's my first time, maybe somewhere discreet?"

"The most discreet spots for women are around the bra area or the hips and lower back. That can be hidden even under a swimsuit."

"Hmm … I think I would like somewhere on my ribs," I explain, showing him a spot on the left side.

"It's a painful area."

"I can bear it."

"We might have numbing cream somewhere if you—"

"No, that's okay," I decide, removing my jacket.

"And do you know what you want?"

"I want a small ladder."

"That corporate ladder you're so eager to climb?"

I shake my head with a wince. "No, I want it to have six steps and be yours. It's Jake's ladder."

His eyes darken with possessiveness, and again, I feel like everything isn't lost yet. "I'm afraid I can't do that, Gen."

"Why?"

"It's one of our rules, remember? No tattoos about someone you've known for less than a year."

"Oh, right. Sometimes, I forget we met so little ago. Then I suppose I could get …"

I think about it, but nothing comes to mind. I really want him to do this because it would be a grand gesture and give us some time to talk.

"Do you trust me?" he asks out of the blue. I don't even hesitate before I nod. "Then let me decide for you."

Anything. I'll give him anything he wants. "I trust you, Jake."

"You can remove your blouse and get comfortable while I prepare everything," he offers.

I nod and start with the tiny buttons holding my shirt closed. By the time I'm done with them, he has assembled a few things on a steel tray and is adjusting a lamp. Once the blouse is hanging next to my bag, I unclasp my bra as well and leave it with them.

My chest is bare when he looks at me again, and his eyes zero on my breasts with hunger.

"Cheap shot, red," he mumbles.

"You said bra area, so I thought it would be in the way. And it's not like you never saw them before."

"It never gets old. Come, take a seat."

I diligently follow his instructions and take my place in the weird chair before him. His eyes are locked on my nipples, and I bite back my amusement. Men are such simple creatures. He's done slipping on a pair of black latex gloves when I lean back into the seat.

"First things first," he professionally says before ripping a lengthy piece of paper towel. I'm intrigued at first, but when he lays it on my chest, I giggle. "There, now I'll be able to focus."

"You're so suggestible."

"You have amazing tits, is all. Now, lean over to your right a little. I'll need access to this bit right here," he explains, gently grazing the area he means—on the side of my ribcage, right next to my heart, like I showed him. I ignore the small shivers his touch ignites and comply.

He looks very focused and professional, and I love seeing this side of him. First, he uses a disposable razor to remove the invisible hairs that must be there, and then he wipes the skin with a piece of gauze doused in rubbing alcohol to disinfect it. His expression turns even more serious when he picks up a marker from his tray. At the first touch, I jolt away with a giggle.

"Sorry, sorry," I say, fighting against my smile.

I'm prepared for the second time, so I contain the tiny electric jolts he triggers.

"You were right," I decide to say to distract myself.

"About what?"

"The way my parents treat me. It took you one evening with my mother to understand something I couldn't see for a decade."

"Sometimes, it's hard to see clearly when you're too close to the situation," he justifies with a shrug.

"But I should have seen it. The day my sister died, I died along with her, in their eyes. They stopped treating me like a daughter—I became a nuisance, a disgrace. No matter what I do, it'll never be enough to overcome that."

It seems he's done with his sketch on my skin because he puts the cap back on and tosses the marker on the tray. When I try to lift my head and look at what he did, he stops me. "I thought you trusted me?"

"I do. I'm just curious."

"You'll see it in an hour, an hour and a half. Depends on how often this slips," he says with a nod at the paper towel hiding my breasts.

I'm tempted to take it away to tease him, but I resist the urge.

Without a word, he picks up a tattoo gun from his tray and proceeds to set a sterile needle on it.

"When did you do your first tattoo?"

"In juvie. With a needle someone stole from the infirmary and ink from a pen. Then, I worked at a parlor for a bit when I came out. And after my brief stay in prison, I moved to Japan, where I learned with a true master of the craft."

"The one who tattooed the geisha on you?"

He nods. "I stayed ten months with him then came to the US. I found a few parlors to work with and saved up as much as I could to start my own thing. When Kill came up with the idea to buy back The Devil's Court, Eli and I quickly followed him into it. From then on, money came faster, and I was able to invest in this building."

"A true rise to success."

"I'm doing what I can with what I have. Alright, red. I'm going to make the first line. I'll go slow, but try to stay perfectly still, okay?"

I nod and stare at the ceiling, praying the pain isn't as bad as my expectations. His tattoo gun is a lot smaller than I thought and battery-powered, so it might be a good sign.

The noise of it turning on startles me, but I don't move. And because he warns me just before he sets the needle on my skin, I'm not surprised by the contact. The sensation isn't too uncomfortable and more like heat than actual pain. My skin warms up around the area he's poking, but the breaching itself doesn't hurt for long.

"Was that okay?" he asks, lifting up the tattoo gun and turning it off.

"Yeah, it really doesn't hurt that much."

"It can get overwhelming after a while, so let me know if you feel sick or need a break, alright?"

"I will."

"Perfect. Let's get on with it, red. You have a therapy session pending."

Something tells me that I could stay silent the whole time, and we'd still be good. His attitude toward me, despite how terribly I handled the situation with Vivienne, is proof of it. Jake doesn't resent me, even though he has every right to.

But I need to apologize and empty my heart to him because he deserves it. I need him to understand and believe that I'll never treat him like that ever again. I'm growing out of my insecurities and problematic patterns. From this day forward, I will always put him first.

He's my wombat, and I will never take him for granted ever again.

CHAPTER
Thirty-Eight

Jake

I DIDN'T EXPECT GEN TO show up like this, asking for a tattoo. She should be at work, and yet she's here, sitting on a tattooing chair with nothing but a flimsy piece of paper to hide her perfect tits. This looks like a grand gesture if I've ever seen one, trusting me to ink her skin forever.

No way I'll be a dick about it, though. So, as tempting as it is to mark her with "Property of Jacob Daniel Clarke", I'll do something she'll love, something she needs. This is the closure she's craved all this time.

The shitshow at her brother's really threw us off, didn't it? Even now, with the trust she's putting in me, an uncomfortable tension lingers between us.

"I saw my mother earlier," she explains. Her voice is uneven, either from the nerves, her emotions, or the slight pain of the needle.

"How was she doing? Still her charming self?"

"She tried to bullshit me into leaving you. Making it sound like she was looking out for me. I don't know how it happened, but I … snapped."

"You did?"

"Yes. I called her out on all her bullshit and the trauma she caused me. Even called her a self-centered bitch."

A low chuckle rumbles in my chest. "I would have loved to see that."

"The place has cameras, so that might be negotiable."

"You did it in public?" I wonder, impressed. Her cheeks get rosy with embarrassment.

"I did. People gave me side looks, but I didn't care. It felt so good, Jake. Liberating. Like I had a rock in my shoe for ten years and finally got rid of it."

I have a hand on her ribcage, and with my thumb, I give her a gentle caress.

"I'm proud of you, Gen. I'm sure she'll think about it twice next time she tries to use her tricks on you."

"She was very clear about what would happen if I chose you, so I won't see her again. Anyhow, I refuse to spend time with someone who loathes the man I love. There are too many things I'd rather do."

I pause for a second, turning off the wireless gun. "I don't expect you to cut all ties with your family for me. I refuse to see your parents again, but it's your choice if you want to."

"I don't," she insists, shaking her head. "I'm done with them. Family is important, but I'd much rather start over than stick with the one I have. Gerry is basically Switzerland, so I'll still have him. And I also have you, Hana, Eli, Mulli, Belzeebub ... It's a solid support system."

"It is. Kill's a great bloke, too," I say before returning to the tattoo.

"I don't know him enough to form my own opinion, but I'm sure he is, yes."

The room is silent for a moment, with only the buzzing of the gun and the music.

As much as I hate what happened, I can't blame her for it. Not entirely, at least. There's always been two of her—the adventurous and free Gen that comes out when I'm around, and the Gen her parents forced her to become. As time went by, I saw less and less of the latter, but she lay dormant within her. I guess being with her parents the other night dragged that rigid and brainwashed Gen out of the deep confines of her mind.

It's not her fault—my aunt helped me understand that. A lifetime of indoctrination ought to fuck up someone's mind, and I can't expect her to break out of it in barely three months together. What matters is that she's here now, trying to mend things and fix us.

"Can you tell me exactly what happened to your sister?" I ask, focused on a delicate part of the tattoo. A few more minutes with this color, and I'll give it a wipe to move on to another ink.

She tenses, her eyes lost on the window to her right. When she speaks after gathering herself for a moment, her voice is unsteady but determined. "It was our seventeenth birthday. Vicky and I tried for weeks to get to celebrate with our friends. We were good with anything as long as we could have a little gathering. But our parents refused, over and over again. They argued seventeen wasn't an important number, but we'd have a party for eighteen. So, on the day of, all we had was a cupcake each from the cook and the promise of a trip we'd get to choose."

When she pauses, I use the break to ask, "Is everything still alright? Do you need a moment?"

She shakes her head. "No, I think I get what you meant when you said the pain could be grounding. It helps."

After a soft graze of my thumb on her ribs, I resume tattooing, and she continues her story. "Our parents were off for an evening in the city, and my boyfriend at the time called me. He had organized a bonfire with our friends and wanted to help us break out so we could attend. I was elated, even though we'd have to be back before our parents' return at midnight. I tried to get Vicky on board. I did everything I could to convince her to come, but she refused, arguing we'd get in trouble and have our rights revoked, as well as the birthday trip."

Gen's voice wavers with contained sobs as she continues. "I called her a coward. I told her she was pathetic for always trying so hard to please our parents and be the good twin. I was so angry at her for it, Jake. I wanted to celebrate with our friends like we'd tried this whole time, but it meant nothing if she couldn't be there."

I stop the tattooing and focus on her broken expression instead. "All she wanted was to stay home and watch The Parent Trap, like every year, but I left and snuck out through the beach."

"Is that the movie with the twins?"

"Yes, it was our favorite. But I decided my friends were cooler than a kids' movie, so I broke our tradition. The bonfire was nice, but it felt so empty without Vicky that I didn't even enjoy it. When it was time to leave, my boyfriend was too drunk to drive, and I couldn't find anyone willing to take me home. Midnight was coming, so I panicked and called my sister. I begged her to come and get me so I could be back in time and our parents would never know I misbehaved again and snuck out."

Gen observes as I place a needle on a new gun, taking a much-deserved break from her recounting of that night. "That's when she had the accident," I say once I'm done.

She nods, wiping a tear from her cheek. "I waited, and waited, and waited. But she wasn't there. Midnight came and went, and she didn't pick up when I called. I really thought ... I thought she wasn't coming on purpose to teach me a lesson. We were close, but like any siblings, we had our petty moments. But, of course, Vicky immediately got in a car to get me.

"I still remember when the police pulled up at the bonfire. Everyone scattered around, and I knew. The moment I saw them, I knew this dreadful feeling in my gut wasn't just the fear of repercussions. I knew something terrible had happened. They took me home without telling me anything. When we arrived, Mother and Father were on the front porch in their fancy opera clothes, talking with more police officers and looking devastated. I clung to the hope that Vicky was just injured. But they broke it to me that she died in the car. I didn't know the specifics back then, but a few years later, Mother cruelly told me she died drowning in her own blood over several minutes."

This time, Gen's emotions become uncontainable, so I set everything down and rise from my stool. "Sweetheart, look at me," I softly demand, framing her face between my gloved hands. "It was an accident. You were a kid who went to a party. The rest was out of your hands."

"But what if—"

"No. It's useless to dwell on the past, red. It happened, and there's nothing you can ever do about it. *Nothing*. The best course of action now is to live a life your sister would be proud of."

"I thought I didn't deserve that."

"If the roles were reversed, what would you want for her? If you were the one getting her at that bonfire, the one who hit that deer. What would you want her to do?"

Gen thinks about it for several seconds, her watery blue eyes avoiding my gaze as she ponders. "I'd want her to move on. I'd want her to be with Penelope and be happy. I'd want her to keep me in her heart, always, but never let the memory of me hold her back."

"There you go, sweetheart. She wouldn't want what you've been forcing on yourself for a decade."

When her eyes meet mine again, I see the gratitude in them, as if she's waited her entire life to hear this. Because I can't resist the urge, I give her forehead a long and tender kiss. Then, I wipe away the tears from her cheeks, and after one last look at her reddened face, I sit back on the stool. Following a change of gloves and a wipe to clean the blood and ink from her skin, I pick up the gun again to resume.

"Vicky was destined to become a great person," she continues, "so I tried to become more like her and have a great career, exemplary life, immaculate image ... I owed a perfect person to the world, so I had to become one."

"I find you perfect without those expectations you set for yourself," I point out, never tearing my eyes from my work.

"Which is what made me realize my mistake. Myself, the person I am deep down, has every right to exist—as much as Vicky had every right to live. By acting the way I did, I didn't replace her. She can never be replaced. I only stopped myself from existing. So now, I need to find out who I am outside of my parents' expectations."

Gen's hand comes to cup my cheek tenderly, so I look up from the tattoo to meet her eyes. "That person might as well be a stranger to me, but you've tugged and tugged at her, and now she's out with a desire to live and be heard. You've changed me in the deepest, most incredible way. No one else but you could have done it, wombat. No one else could have pushed me to find my true self the way you did."

"I wanted the real you. That's who I fell in love with, red. You're bold, daring, and not afraid to take what you want. Your strength is the sexiest thing about you, and getting to witness it and see you grow out of your shell has been an incredible experience."

"Well, maybe I got a little too bold," she says with a grimace. "I quit my job before heading here."

My eyebrows shoot up. "You did?"

"I was so done with that shit. My boss gave the promotion to Ralf Lowell, and I couldn't bear the idea of working under him."

"I'm sorry to hear that. You deserved that position."

"It doesn't matter. I'll do something more significant with my life than keep working for a tech conglomerate that only cares about money. I don't know what I want to do with myself or what I'll become, but I know, with absolute certainty, that I want to do it with you. I want your face to be the first I see every day, your voice to be the first I hear … I want your arms to become my home because I've never felt more like myself than when I am in them. You're the only thing I'm sure of, Jake, the only one that matters."

Her declaration halts for a brief moment, and her eyes fill with tears again. "I know I messed up, and I know I should have realized that sooner. But I promise, wombat, I promise I'll never take you for granted again. I'll never put you second. You're my everything, and it's something I'll never forget. So please, forgive me for what I did the other night. I should have run after you and left everyone else behind."

The smile tugging at the corners of my lips is unstoppable as I bend forward to set my face close to hers. "I forgave you before you even arrived, red. I sent you a text."

She frowns, confused. "When?"

"Half an hour before you barged in. I thought you were here about it, but it became clear you didn't read it. Did you block me or something?"

"No, I set my phone on DND before I met Vivienne, and then …"

Before I can even stop her, she rushes out of the chair, making the paper towel fall to the floor. With trembling hands, she pulls her phone out of her bag and unlocks the screen. I watch as she reads the long text I worked on yesterday and this morning. I needed time and space to gather my thoughts and lay them all out for her to see.

Also, when I woke up with a hangover on the 5th, the lack of messages from her triggered a plethora of doubts. Part of me thought it meant she was moving on, and we were over. That's why I only reached out earlier today when the pressure became unbearable.

Her eyes go left and right while her hand rests over her mouth, and I do my best to remember what I wrote.

> I realize that you have a complicated relationship with your parents, something that affects who you are at your very core. I don't blame you for what happened because I know you've been conditioned to accept their behavior. And while I might never truly

understand it because I've been robbed of a parental figure for too long, you would rather have them in your life than not.

And I'm here for you, even if it hurts me to watch them treat you the way they do. I'll stand by you, ready to build you up when they tear you down and to remind you of your worth when they make you doubt it.

You're an incredible person with an amazing heart, and nothing they say or do will ever change that. You're strong, fascinating, beautiful, and deserving of all the love and respect in the world. If I have to be the only person out there giving you that, then so be it.

I miss you and your freckles.

Your wombat.

A silent tear rolls down her cheek, and she wipes it away with a hurried gesture. "You really sent me this?" she wonders as if the proof right before her eyes isn't enough. I nod with a low chuckle. "And then you let me sit there in agony for forty-five minutes?!"

Her indignation brings another chuckle out of me. "I wanted to hear what you had to say."

"You're a dick, Jacob Clarke," she protests. I keep my eyes on her determined expression as she makes her way back to me. I'm shorter than her from the stool, so when she grabs my face, I'm looking up. "But you're *my* dick."

"I am."

Her mouth falls on mine, like heaven and bliss wrapped in a tender graze of her lips. It's sweet, soft, and more meaningful than any other kiss we've ever shared. This is a seal, an unbreakable promise.

When her warm tongue lasciviously touches the opened seam of my mouth, I put an end to it with a groan. "Let me finish your tattoo first, then I'll drag you upstairs and let you continue."

"Great idea."

She returns to her chair with haste, and I do another glove change before resuming. It takes thirty more minutes, during which she tells me more about her meeting with her mother earlier, as well as her work rival getting the job.

Once I'm done with the finishing touches, I use a fresh wipe to clean up the last of the ink and blood on her tender skin. Before I've put on the ointment, I tell her, "All done, red. You can go see it."

She doesn't look entirely confident as she gets out of the chair and walks up to the floor-to-ceiling mirror in the corner of the room. I can't blame her. I just marked her skin for life, and she has no idea what I did. But as soon as she twists and lifts her arm to see the detailed drawing, her face lights up with what looks like pure joy.

"Oh my God, Jake," she whispers. I'm right behind her now, and we look at it together.

It's a small piece, barely longer than my thumb, but I worked hard on the finer details. The bright red ladybug is on a small cherry blossom branch—Victoria's favorite flower. The artwork is delicate and feminine, matching Gen's aura.

"Do you like it?" I ask, slipping a hand around her waist on the other side.

Her eyes are bright and teary as she looks up at me with excitement. "It's amazing. It's—it's *her.*"

"She's forever with you now, even if you have days you don't think of her, even if you move on with your life and live it the way you want to. Victoria will always be a part of you, in your heart and right here," I explain, grazing the skin under the ladybug.

"It's perfect. It's so perfect."

Her elation pushes her to turn in my hold and bring my face down to kiss me. This time, things go a little further than before, and our tongues lick and invade, hungry and determined. It's hard to resist the temptation of her, especially when I can feel her erect nipples poking through the thick fabric of my shirt.

"I love you," she says into our kiss. "I love you so much, Jake."

"And I love all of you, red—down to the last freckle."

I'm so proud that her inner strength, the reason why I love her so much, finally grew enough for her to demand the things she's owed. Fuck her parents and that job. They don't deserve her. She's destined for so much more, and I'll be right there every step of the way, lifting her up and encouraging her.

"I need to take care of your tattoo first," I mumble into our kiss when her delicate hands reach between us to start working on the buttons of my shirt.

"Will it take long?"

"A couple of minutes. Just the ointment and a non-stick bandage."

"Let's do this. And after, maybe I can pay for it with my body?" she suggestively offers.

"I'm a very expensive tattoo artist, Miss Kensington."

"And I'm recently unemployed, Mr. Clarke, so I have all the time in the world to compensate you fairly. Also, I've been told I give amazing head."

I can barely stay in character as I stifle a laugh. "Who told you that?"

Her arm is thrown over my neck, keeping me close as if she refuses to let me go. It's not like I'd move even an inch away from her, anyway. "Some guy I met through a kinky dating app."

"He probably knows what he's talking about, then."

"Oh, he does. Best sex I've ever had. Best man I've ever met. And the best ladder I've ever climbed."

I'm still laughing when we kiss again. As we get lost in one another, I show her she's my best everything, too. My sexy redhead, my proper little Miss Kensington, my naughty Gen ...

God, how I love this fucking woman.

EPILOGUE
Epilogue
Gen

"Get naked," I giggle with excitement.

Jake chuckles low as we both hurriedly tug and pull at our clothes. "I'm already halfway there."

"Get nakeder, then."

The air is warm even though the night has fallen, and the sand under our feet still bears the lingering heat of the sun. We navigate solely from the blue glow of the moon, which shines above the ocean, its distorted reflection stretched on the lazy surface. It seems there's no one around for miles, and aside from a few nocturnal animals singing the song of their people and the waves rolling onto the beach, it's perfectly silent.

We parked our rental about a hundred yards away and then rushed to where we are now, impatient to get this over with. We made sure this beach wasn't popular enough to still have visitors so late in the day.

I kick my flip-flops off while I lower my shorts, and as I come back up perfectly naked, he pulls me into his solid embrace. When I sense that he's going to lay me on the sand, I protest. "Jake, no! The comforter."

He groans in disapproval but doesn't complain, taking the thick blanket we prepared for this out of the bag. I help him, and in no time, we have created a little nest for us to carry on.

Jake doesn't wait to lift me into his arms and lower me onto it, his haste making me squeal with a mix of enthusiasm and panic. I still haven't recovered from being literally swept off my feet when he lowers onto me to press his lips at the base of my throat.

We're still obsessed with one another, still loving sex together as much as when we first started.

Delighted sighs pour out of me as he lays pecks all over my skin, nipping the perky tips of my breasts when he encounters them, steadfast toward his destination. When, finally, his mouth settles over my intimacy, I entwine my fingers in his soft, dark hair and brace myself for what's coming. Somehow, he's gotten even better than he already was, and I'll never get over how good it is to have his tongue flicking on my clit.

"Hmm, baby ... Yes," I moan, already sensing the shivers spreading under my skin. I arch my back and spread my knees wider.

We usually enjoy taking our time, but this is a special occasion. Since we're both impatient to get it over with, there will be no delayed gratification or teasing. We're going to fuck hard and fast— we'll reconvene later for a softer round.

Still, I don't expect it when he shoves two fingers inside me to assist the perfect pace and pressure of his tongue. The wet noises of them pumping in and out join the other ones, and I look down at his dashing face between my legs. His eyes are already on me as he eats me out, and despite the darkness, I can guess at their intensity. The pleasure steadily builds in my core, and even though the moment is nothing but carnal, a surge of tenderness takes over me.

I graze the side of his face and moan, "I love you so much. Oh, God!"

My head falls back when he curls his fingers, hitting my front wall right where it feels so damn good. The entirety of my body is as tense as a bow. I'm about to explode.

Until his tongue and fingers retreat at once.

The unexpected change leaves me disoriented and frustrated. "I was so close," I whine with discontentment.

"I know. You started spasming."

He doesn't look sorry for me as he arranges his broad body on top of me. My legs spread wider to allow for his hips to meet mine, and with a hand between us, he aligns himself with my greedy entrance. I get no warning before he plunges into me, stretching me with his imposing girth and piercings.

"Ah, fuck," he groans. "Best fucking cunt ever. I swear to God."

Like a man on a mission, he doesn't allow me any time to get used to it. He pulls back, the piercings dragging along my insides, and then rams into me. I'm as eager as he is, my hands gripping his round ass to invite him deeper, silently begging him to go harder. Even if the pace is rough, he remains loving in his own way.

"You feel so good," I moan, seeking his lips.

We kiss in a messy way, with too much tongue and teeth to call it perfect, but neither of us cares. I don't want him to slow the intense ramming of his dick inside me, so this will do.

He knows exactly what to do, and with every shove, the base of him slaps onto my clit. I won't even need to send a hand between us to make myself come. He, however, might need a little help to get there as quickly as I will. Never breaking our kiss, I squeeze my intimate muscles around him and reach for his pierced nipple at the same time. When I twist it just as he likes, he lets out a rough, "Ah, fuck!"

My proud smile comes in the way of our kiss, so I pull away and admire the perfection of him instead. He looks so good in the moon's glow, with his tattoos darkening his skin, the defined muscles of his arms protruding from the effort, his powerful shoulders bathed in dim blue light … This man is mine, for now and forever, and I'll never get over my luck.

Out of all the women he could have had, he chose *me*. This gentle soul with the body of an inked Greek god, the mouth of a sailor, and the patience of a saint, chose me. And despite our differences, despite how far apart our worlds were when we met, we're beyond perfect together.

"I love you," I whimper, framing his face with my hands and pulling him down.

Because I'm getting dangerously close, I squeeze around him again, desirous to reach the finish line together. Which we do.

The merciless pace he settled on brings us to our climax in under three minutes. We shatter together with a roar and a helpless cry, trembling and arching in the dead of the night. His hips slam into mine in small but adamant punches, and I feel his pleasure shoot deep inside me. There's so much of it that it starts pouring out from around the base of him before he's even done.

I don't understand why I love it so much when he comes inside me like this. Maybe it's because I know that one day, he'll put a child in me, and while it's a little early for that, I look forward to it. It's amusing that, eventually, something as dirty as the raw fuck we just had will lead to the most precious little being.

The bliss of my orgasm and the thought of our future together make me smile like an idiot. But it's fine because he can't see me with his face tucked in the curve of my neck. Only the stars and the moon witness my euphoria.

His weight on me slowly increases, but I don't mind. That's something I love too, sucking the life out of him. My worries that I might be boring in bed are long gone, and I have absolutely no doubt that I'm the best lay he'll ever have.

"Fucking hell, that was fast," he groans, pulling himself up.

He observes me for a few seconds, scanning my relaxed features in the darkness of the night, and then he gives me one last enamored kiss. I want to keep him on top of me, but we have one more thing to do before our mission is over. So, I let him pull out and roll to the side.

"Get my phone," I demand, patting his chest lightly.

"Aye, aye."

Jake fumbles in the bag for several seconds and then retrieves my phone from it. We settle together, plastered so close there isn't a lick of space between our sweaty bodies, and he unlocks the screen himself.

"Can you believe it took us almost a year to get through your list?" he asks as he opens the browser.

"We took our time. And we did a *lot* more than what was on the list. Also, I was not having sex on a beach back home."

"Could have done it right in front of your parents' place in the Hamptons. Give them a private representation to show them why you chose me over them," he jokes.

"Jacob, that is foul, even for you," I retort with a laugh. I can feel my cheeks warming up at the mere thought of it, and for once, I'm glad he cannot see the blush. He'd think I secretly like the idea, which I do not.

Or at least, I don't think I do.

"Okay, first question," he very seriously starts. "Have you ever had the nastiest, naughtiest sex in your childhood bed as an adult?"

"We did the best we could on this one, so it counts as a 'Yes,'" I say. He taps on the green checkmark, and we move on to the next question.

"Have you ever gone down on someone while pleasuring yourself?"

"Of course."

"Have you ever had sex in a public place?"

"I don't even want to count how many times because I might walk into a police station to surrender with a confession."

We go over more questions, and to each one of them, I answer a resounding "Yes." We allow ourselves one joker, which is when the threesome question comes. A few times now, I've taken both Jake and my vibrator simultaneously, so we decide it counts.

Then, the most important question arrives, and Jake beams as he reads it. "Have you ever tried a Jacob's ladder or other genital piercings?"

"Hundreds of times."

"Fuck yeah, you have." Without even looking up at him, I know he's smirking with pride.

I'm giddy with joy as we go over the rest, so incredibly proud of my progress in the eleven months I've known Jake. When he reads, "Have you ever had sex on a beach?" we high-five and check the "Yes" option again.

"Okay, are you ready for the result?" he asks once we're done, barely containing his excitement.

I nod energetically, adjusting my position so we can read it together. He clicks on the last "Yes" and the result screen appears.

"Wow, you're a 'Yes' person through and through, aren't you?" Jake reads out loud. "You're the ultimate go-with-the-flow master. You've got that can-do attitude that could conquer anything, even the quirkiest bedroom adventures. Your enthusiasm is unparalleled. You embrace every opportunity, and spontaneity is your middle name. You've probably turned mundane occasions into scandalously naughty moments. When it comes to life's sexiest adventures, you're the undisputed champion! There's a lot you can teach to the rest of the world, so keep shining like a radiant 'Yes' beacon. We bow down to thee, you sex goddess!"

I'm smiling so hard that my cheeks hurt. "I'm a sex goddess," I proudly say.

"You are. And I didn't need a test to know that."

"You're biased because you love me."

"Fair point, but I already felt that way before I fell in love with you."

"What a clever man you are, wombat," I amorously offer as a compromise before I lean in to kiss him.

He turns the phone's screen off and tosses it somewhere on the blanket, and it's just us and the stars again. I feel deliciously satiated, sensing our mixed pleasures between my legs as his hand grazes random swirls on my back. The sound of the waves mixes in with his heartbeat, and it lulls me into a state of pure contentment.

Ever since that day I went to him and asked for a tattoo, we've been basking in perfect harmony. The only arguments we've had were easily resolved with an open-hearted talk, some minor compromises, and makeup sex.

I've been true to my promise to him and haven't spoken to Mother again, even when she tried to reach me a couple of times. Therapy has helped me tremendously since that day in NexaCorp's café, and although I'm feeling more liberated than I ever have, I still insist on going every two weeks. It took a few tries, but I found my perfect match, and I owe a lot to my therapist. Going no-contact with Vivienne and Gerard has only been beneficial. I don't miss them, unlike what I thought, and my life has been a lot smoother. It was like cutting off a cancerous limb, and the rest of me is now stronger and healthier.

"I'm so happy we got to take this trip, red," Jake murmurs.

"Me too. And that we detoured to Japan to see the cherry blossoms. I can't believe it's your first time in Australia since you left."

"I wasn't ready yet."

"I know, wombat, and I'm so proud of you for this. Your aunt is such a sweet woman and was so happy to welcome us into her home for a few nights. And your uncle has the best stories about your teenage years."

"They did the best they could raising me despite having their own three kids. And even if I got out of line a few times, I'd say they've done a good job."

"They did an excellent job. You're a fantastic person, Jake. And Maggie's pavlova? Gosh, I thought yours was good, but hers is … Ugh, we need to come back soon."

"We will."

"For your birthday in September."

"Anything you want, sweetheart."

For some seconds, there's only the waves and his heart again, and I softly ask, "Are you ready for tomorrow?"

"Yes. I look forward to it."

"Me too. I need to pay my respects and thank her for creating you. You said her favorite flowers were peonies, right?"

"Yes. She bought a bouquet whenever she could afford one, and the fragrance filled the house for days."

"We'll find a flower shop before we head to the cemetery, then. And if you're okay with it, I'd love it if we could have a bouquet at home now and then—as an homage to her."

He nods, smiling softly, and I snuggle closer to him. Part of me wishes this trip would last forever, but another is eager to return to New York. I'm in charge of our anniversary date, a week after we get home, and what I've planned is stellar.

First, we'll have drinks at The Plaza Hotel's bar, to pay tribute to the night we met. Then, I've booked the exact room we went up to that night, and I'll have a little surprise there for him: a tattoo gun, as well as everything he might need to finally ink that six-step ladder I asked for all those months ago. I already know it'll be amazing, so it'll make up for having to leave this paradise in favor of the bustling city.

Also, since I finally managed to sell my apartment, I now have the funds to launch my own law firm, which is another thing I'm excited about. Since leaving NexaCorp, I've joined a small firm based in Brooklyn that primarily takes on pro bono cases. It's been great to help out people in need of a good lawyer and get them justice. Instead of serving a big corporation, I now work for the people they abuse. I've gone from darkness to light, and my soul feels grander for it.

My life took an unexpected turn the day I drunkenly created that dating app profile, and I still struggle to realize how far I've come. The Gen I was a year ago wouldn't recognize the one I've become. And sadly, she'd probably think this new version is the worse one of the two.

"Do you ever think of what would have happened if Eli didn't find my profile on that app?" I wonder out of the blue.

"I do sometimes, yeah."

"It makes me so sad that we almost never met. Can you imagine? A tiny difference in the algorithm and none of this would have happened. What a sad life it would have been."

"No, you're wrong there."

My brows come together as I lift myself up to look him in the eye. "What do you mean?"

"We were destined to meet. This, right now, was always going to happen, regardless of whether Eli found you or not."

"Like destiny? That's very cheesy," I say, doubtful.

"The evening at The Gallery on Fifth," he explains with a coy smile.

"What about it?"

"You were going. So was I. We would have met there, with or without Eli."

It takes several seconds for me to register what he's saying, and when I do, I'm still not as confident as he is. "There were a hundred people there, Jake. You probably wouldn't have given me a second look."

He shifts until we're facing each other, lying on our sides. It's insane that we're buck naked on a random beach in Australia, but it figures. This man really can make me do anything.

With a tender hand, he rearranges a few strands of hair on the side of my face. "I would have noticed you because you're the most stunning woman I've ever seen. I would have come to you to flirt in the way that gets your cheeks and the tips of your ears all rosy. You would have pretended to hate it because you're a proper lady, and you would have rejected me, probably bruising my ego. But that, the very moment where you became unattainable, would have sealed the deal for me, red. I love a challenge, and I would have dedicated the rest of my evening to winning you over."

I adore that he thought about this. Maybe our fortunate encounter wasn't as random as I thought. Perhaps we were always meant to meet and become exactly who we are now. Together.

"Do you think I would have managed?" he asks, swallowing back a smirk because he already knows the answer.

"It probably would have taken you longer than it actually did, but yes. And even if I refused to give you my number, you would have asked Constance for it, right?"

"You know me too well, red."

Our shared laugh comes to an end when we move in unison to kiss.

Of course, this was meant to be. This moment, on this very beach, about to make love with all the adoration and tenderness we hold, was bound to happen. Deep down, I believe him. We were always going to end up together because this is the life I'm meant to have. Without him, there would be no point in all this.

This man opened the world to me, all thanks to a surprising feature.

My favorite ladder ever.

The End

THANK YOUS

Publishing Up the Ladder independently has been a tremendous amount of work, and without the right people supporting and surrounding me, I never would have gotten to this point. So, I would like to thank some of the many people who've been there to help me through some, most, or all of it.

First of all, thank you, reader. Thank you for purchasing (hopefully) and reading Up the Ladder. This story will forever have a special place in my heart, and I hope Gen and Jake have carved themselves a small spot in yours. If they did, join me for the next installment of the When in Brooklyn Series, which will revolve around Killian and his perfect match (not Elijah, but that would have been fun to write).

Maman, Papa, thank you for believing in me and allowing me to pursue my dream. Even though you have never been—and will never be—allowed to read my work (for all our sakes, really), you've been my number one supporters from the start. Be assured that I'll never take that for granted. There will be no crappy nursing home for you, my darling parents. Je vous aime très, très, très fort.

Claire, my platonic love, you're the one who showed me what writing can really be, and I'll forever owe you for jumpstarting my passion for contemporary romances. Thank you for being there to listen when I need to bounce ideas off of someone (often late into the night). It's amazing to know we'll always be there to help each other navigate the insanity that is the publishing world.

Maddie, Dai, Trini, Gülşah, and Aaru, thank you, my lovely betas, for keeping up with my ever-changing ideas and supporting me from all around the world. Knowing you guys have my back makes this whole thing a little less scary. I love you, my dudes, and here's to more wild plot twists I'll be throwing into the group chat ;)

Katie, oh, Katie. Thank you for making the process of hiring an editor so remarkably delightful. I couldn't have found someone better to help me polish Gen and Jake's love story. Thank you for rooting for them as hard as I do! If anyone's looking for an amazing editor, you can find her at betweenthecoverseditorial.com

Jessika, Daisy, Amal, Nattie, Toni, Snehal, Pamela, Marie, Zara, Bev, Casiana, Izzy, and literally so many others ... I don't have enough space to mention everyone that's been there from the start, but thank you, guys. You know who you are, and you know how much I value your support!

To my street team, thank you, girlies. You've made this whole process a lot more enjoyable than it would have been without you in my corner. Thank you for believing in this story before you even read it!

Thank you all, from the depths of my heart, for your unwavering support, encouragement, and belief in me and my work. I am endlessly grateful for each and every one of you who has played a part in bringing this book to life. Your kindness, dedication, and friendship mean the world to me.

With sincere appreciation and love,

Ana

ABOUT THE AUTHOR

Ana D'Arcy crafts romances bursting with heart, humor, and a generous dose of steam—in which the hero often falls first but they both fall hard. On most days, you can find Ana working with a cup of tea by her side while her three cats are curled up nearby. When she's not typing or daydreaming about her imaginary characters, she enjoys recharging her creative fire with a good TV show or a movie.

If you enjoyed this book, Ana invites you to connect with her on social media. You can find her on various platforms like Instagram, TikTok, and Facebook under the username @authoranadarcy. By following her, you'll stay updated on Ana's upcoming books and behind-the-scenes insights into her writing process.

As a debut author, Ana greatly values your feedback and support. If you have a moment, she would be incredibly grateful if you could leave a review of Up the Ladder on your preferred book retailer or platforms like Goodreads and Storygraph. Your reviews help other readers discover Gen and Jake's story and mean the world to Ana.

Thank you once again for choosing to embark on this journey with Ana. She hopes you'll join her for the next installments of the When in Brooklyn Series. In the upcoming book, you'll delve into Killian's story, where you can expect plenty of heart, humor, and steam—just like in Up the Ladder.